*Douglas Reeman writes:*

'As someone whose books are published in sixteen languages, I am always being asked to account for the perennial appeal of the sea story, and its enduring interest for people of so many nationalities and cultures.

'I have thought about it a great deal, both when I served at sea, and later when I became a professional writer. It would seem that the eternal and sometimes elusive triangle of man, ship and ocean, particularly under the stress of war, produces the best qualities of courage and compassion, irrespective of the rights and wrongs of the conflict. In war it is inevitable that only one side can triumph but honour and self-sacrifice are not the attributes of the victors alone.

'The sea has no understanding of righteous or unjust causes, and cares nothing for the flags of battle. It is the common enemy, respected by all who serve on it, ignored only at their peril.'

Also by Douglas Reeman in Pan
**The Iron Pirate**

# Douglas Reeman

# In Danger's Hour

**Pan Books**
in association with Heinemann

First published 1988 by William Heinemann Ltd
This edition published 1989 by Pan Books Ltd,
Cavaye Place, London, SW10 9PG in association with
William Heinemann Ltd
9 8 7 6 5 4 3 2
© Highseas Authors Ltd 1988
ISBN 0 330 30575 1
Printed and bound in Great Britain by
Richard Clay Ltd, Bungay, Suffolk

For my Kim,
for all the help
and all the love
you freely give.

Life to be sure is nothing much to lose,
But young men think it is, and we were young.

*Engraved on a memorial in the Old Naval Cemetery
at Vis in the Adriatic, in 1944.*

*A different battleground: the same sacrifice.*

# Contents

# Author's Note

Minesweeping . . . a war without glory, where death lurked beneath the sea or floated from the air. A war without mercy or discrimination. The mine was impartial and gave no warning.

The men who fought this lonely battle did so knowing it was an essential one. Every day each channel had to be swept, otherwise the country's lifelines were clogged and the vital cargoes could not move.

They were a mixture of young men and old sailors; many of the latter had spent much of their lives trawling for fish, most of the others had been schoolboys before the war.

To keep the sealanes open, four hundred minesweepers, 'the little ships', paid the price, and nearly five thousand officers and men died doing it.

D.R.

# 1

## *Officers*

The sky above Dover harbour was a clear washed-out blue, so that the afternoon sunshine gave an illusion of warmth and peace. Just an occasional fleecy cloud drifting on a fresh south-easterly breeze, but none of the too-familiar vapour trails which betrayed the silent air battles, the pinpoints of flame as friend or enemy fell into the Channel.

It was April 1943, only a few days old, and the harbour, like the weather, appeared to be resting. There were not many warships of any size moored to the jetties; most of them went to safer harbours, *round the corner* as the sailors termed it, in the Thames or Medway, or in the East Coast base of Harwich.

Here there was little peace for long. Sneak raids by fighter-bombers, or the deafening arrival of the great shells fired from Cap Gris-Nez to land in the town or amongst some coastal convoy as it scuttled through the Channel.

Lying side by side at one wall were two fleet minesweepers, their ensigns and Jacks lifting and rippling in the breeze to make bright patches of colour against the drab grey and camouflage dazzle paint. They were twins, and to a landsman might appear to be small, foreshortened frigates.

Straight-stemmed, with a spartan superstructure of bridge and solitary funnel making them look businesslike, only the clutter of minesweeping gear and derricks right aft on the cut-down quarterdeck marked them apart from any of the escort vessels.

There was no visible sign of life on board. Sunday afternoon, and make-and-mend for the duty watch, a chance to snatch some rest after weeks of sweeping the deadly mines, often within sight of the French coast.

Dover Castle with its bombproof headquarters beneath stood guard over the harbour and its approaches. For at this point the enemy were just twenty miles distant — a jarring thought, if anyone still needed reminding.

In his cabin in the outboard fleet minesweeper, Lieutenant Commander Ian Ransome unclipped a scuttle and opened it to let the weak sunshine play across his face. It was good to be leaving the long nights behind, even if the risks might be extended accordingly. He narrowed his eyes to study that part of the town which was visible from his cabin. A defiant, battered place on the very elbow of Hellfire Corner, as the newspapers named it. His mouth moved slightly in a smile. *Shit Street* was the sailors' nickname. The smile made him look younger, like a shadow passing away.

He saw his reflection in the scuttle's polished glass and ran his fingers through his hair. It was dark, and although not originally curly it had somehow become so. Too many days and nights up there on an open bridge, in salt spray and in all weathers. He turned and looked at his cabin. Small, and yet spacious compared with his tiny hutch behind the bridge, where he could snatch an hour and still be ready instantly when the alarm bells tore a man's heart apart.

He saw the calendar propped on his little desk and it all came crowding back again. The fourth of April 1943. He had been in command of this ship, his ship, for one year exactly.

He stared round, his ears seeking some familiar sound to distract him. But the ship was quiet, with only the far-off murmur of one of the Chief's generators to give a hint of life.

Ransome sat down at the desk and stared at the clip of signals which had awaited their return to Dover. He had known they would be in harbour for this day. They would have shared a solemn drink in the wardroom, perhaps invited some of the old hands to enliven the occasion.

His reefer hung carelessly from the only other chair, the two-

and-a-half wavy lines of gold lace on its sleeves. The Royal Naval Volunteer Reserve. A wartime navy; the amateurs who were now the true professionals. On the jacket's breast above the pocket was a single blue and white ribbon. The Distinguished Service Cross. For gallantry, they had said. He smiled again, but it was sadder than before. For surviving, was nearer the truth. He pulled up the sleeve of his grey fisherman's jersey and studied his watch. Nearly time. It made him feel sick. Uneasy. Perhaps a year was too long in any ship. Or was it the job? He had gone into minesweepers almost immediately after entering the navy at the outbreak of war.

He reached out and opened a small cupboard, so that the untouched bottle of Scotch seemed to wink at him in the reflected sunlight. He had been hoarding it for today.

He toyed with the idea of pouring a glass right now, and to hell with everything. Later perhaps. He might even invite the skipper from their sister ship *Ranger* aboard to join him. Even as he considered it he knew he would not.

He began to fill one of his pipes with fierce, jabbing thrusts from an old jar he had found in a junk shop at Plymouth.

Nobody had been to blame. It had happened before. Others would die because of that momentary distraction. Lack of vigilance? Who could tell?

It was often said that the danger from sudden air-attack was at its greatest when a ship was making for harbour.

They had been doing just that after weeks of sweeping, with let-ups only to refuel and take on extra ammunition. No matter how skilled his men had become there were some who had been thinking of a run ashore, a brassy pub behind the blackout curtains where just for a few hours they could dream or make-believe.

David Rule had been an excellent first lieutenant in every sense. He had never tried to gain popularity by being soft, but even at the defaulters' table he had usually managed to end the day without malice.

Ransome knew he had not always been easy to work with; he had been at it a long time. In war even six months could be an eternity, and Ransome had been sweeping mines for three years.

That was when he had not been needed for escort work, for picking up convoy survivors and anything else a senior officer might dream up. But Rule's cheerful disposition, impudence when he thought it was needed, had made them into an unbreakable team.

Ransome looked at the ship's crest on the white bulkhead. HMS *Rob Roy*, built by John Brown's on Clydebank just two years before the Germans had slammed into Poland, built when men cared about their craft, before ships were flung together, almost overnight it seemed, to try and balance the horrific toll in vessels and men alike. He nodded, as if David was here with him, as they had intended it would be.

Together they had made the little *Rob Roy* the best sweeper in the group.

It had been an early dawn when the sweep had put up a mine. Ransome had peered aft from the open bridge as Rule's sweeping party had slowed the winch, and a boatswain's mate had passed the word that the drifting mine had snared a wreck, or part of one. God knew there were enough wrecks littering the seabed on the approaches to every harbour.

Just a minute or so with every eye on the mine's bobbing, obscene shape, a signal lamp stabbing from the ship which now lay resting alongside, so that the shattering roar of a diving aircraft had made several believe that the mine had exploded. Out of the clouds, perhaps returning from a sortie over the mainland; they would never know. The rattle of machine-guns and cannon fire, then another roar of power as the plane had climbed away to the clouds, heading for home.

They had not even time to track it with the Oerlikons, let alone the main armament. It was over in seconds and David lay dying, his blood thinning in the spray boiling over the stern as they increased speed away from the mine, which was dispatched by marksmen on the trawler that always followed astern when they were sweeping.

Mercifully he had died before the ship had berthed alongside. The cannon shell which had cut him down had blasted off his shoulder and half of his face. Nobody else had received so much as a scratch.

The telephone jangled sharply on the desk, and Ransome had to pull his thoughts together, to accept that the ship was connected to the shore switchboard.

It was a woman's voice, a Wren from the S.D.O.

'Lieutenant Hargrave will be joining *Rob Roy* as expected, sir.'

Ransome stared at the ship's crest. He must get over it. A new first lieutenant? So what?

The voice said, 'Are you there, sir?'

Ransome pushed back his unruly hair again.

'Yes. Sorry.' What was she like, he wondered? 'Too good a lunch, I expect.'

She laughed. 'All right for some, sir.' The line went dead.

Ransome tried again. He stared at himself in the small mirror beside his bunk. Shadows beneath his eyes, lines of strain which seemed to tighten his mouth. He leaned closer and touched his sideburns. White hairs. He straightened his back and tried to grin at himself. He noticed that the grey eyes did not smile back at him.

He sighed. Aloud, he spoke to the small cabin. 'Not surprised. I feel bloody ancient!'

Ian Ransome was twenty-eight years old.

Lieutenant Trevor Hargrave returned the salutes of two passing seamen and swore silently under his breath. He carried a heavy suitcase in one hand and had his respirator haversack and steel helmet slung from the opposite shoulder. Even sailors who normally went to great lengths to avoid saluting anybody seemed to take a delight in doing it when an officer had his hands full.

Hargrave was tall and had even features and blue eyes which had made several of the Wrens at the base watch him as he passed. He shivered slightly as he looked at the moored vessels, and an idling Air Sea Rescue launch about to get under way from one of the jetties. His deeply tanned face told its own story. He had been back in England for six months, but even now in April it seemed bitterly cold after the glistening expanse of the Indian Ocean and South Atlantic.

He thought of the powerful cruiser which had been his home for over a year. She had been employed as a main escort for long-haul convoys, most of which carried troops and all the equipment and vehicles they might need when they were finally delivered to their theatre of war. Simonstown, across the ocean to Ceylon or down to Australia and New Zealand. They were there just in case a commerce raider, or some death-or-glory German cruiser, broke out to savage the convoy routes before she was run to earth. Just one major enemy unit could tie down convoys for weeks; even the rumour of one was bad enough.

But all in all they had seen little of the real war. Lines of deep-laden merchantmen, sometimes with an escort to provide air cover for the dicey parts where ocean-going submarines, German and Japanese, might be at large.

It was as if the war had been held at arm's length. The cruiser reacted accordingly, and there was little difference in her ordered world from the days of peace. Mess dinners, banyan parties on the islands, even some regattas when they had been down-under with the Aussies.

He thought of his dismay when he had gone to London to protest about his new appointment. *A minesweeping course.* He could still see the contained amusement on the commander's face in the dusty Admiralty office.

He had tried to discover his father's whereabouts but had met with a stone wall. The Western Desert, Scotland – nobody knew or would tell him. At the back of his mind he nursed the suspicion that his father was behind it somehow.

Hargrave stopped and looked along the old stone wall. The course was over. It was not next month. It was now.

He felt the breeze flapping at his blue raincoat. Everything looked tired and run-down. Like the town with its bombed houses and boarded-up shops. And London with its wailing sirens and shabby people, ration queues and uniforms everywhere. He had never seen so many foreign servicemen. Free-French, Norwegians, Polish, Dutch – the list was endless, as if to record the enemy's total oppression of Scandinavia and Europe.

His eyes narrowed as he saw the two fleet minesweepers. At this angle they were almost bows-on to him. As if they were resting, leaning against each other for support.

His gaze rested on the outboard one and he felt his heart sink still further. He had read all he could about HMS *Rob Roy* but seeing her in the frail sunshine was still a shock.

He saw the scars on her paintwork. Coming alongside in the dark, or manoeuvring against another vessel to take off survivors probably. Hargrave knew quite a lot about *Rob Roy*'s history. She had even been at Dunkirk where she had made several trips, returning home each time loaded with exhausted soldiers.

He saw her pendant number, J.21, painted on her side, the thin line around her single funnel which marked her as the senior ship in the flotilla. It gave him no comfort at all.

He went through the details once again in his mind. It had not taken him long to gen up on the ship; after all, she was not exactly a cruiser. Two hundred and thirty feet from stem to low stern, 815 tons with an armament of two four-inch guns, two Oerlikon twenty-millimetre cannon and a few heavy machine-guns. He began to walk along the edge of the wall towards her; the nearer he drew the smaller she seemed to get. And yet crammed into her neat hull she carried a total complement of eighty officers and men. It did not seem possible.

He reached the steep brow which led down to the inboard ship. He saw her name was *Ranger*, built in 1937, the same as *Rob Roy*. The year made him start. How would he have felt about the navy had he known this would happen?

He had applied for the submarine service when the time had come to leave the big cruiser. Apart from his other qualifications he was a good navigator, and on the long hauls and across those far-off oceans he had had plenty of opportunity to extend his knowledge and make full use of the ship's chartroom.

After a brief interview his request had been turned down. His own captain had merely informed him that he had been considered unsuitable for submarines. What the hell did that mean? As soon as he had this appointment sorted out he would apply again and make certain he saw the right people. He was being childish and he knew it. Destroyers then? He stared down at the minesweeper's deck and saw the sentry watching him with mild curiosity. He did not move to help him with the suitcase, however.

As Hargrave clambered down the steep brow and saluted, the

sentry tossed up a careless acknowledgement. For some reason it irritated him.

Hargrave snapped, 'I'm going across to *Rob Roy*.' He looked meaningfully at the slack webbing belt and heavy pistol holster. 'Aren't you going to ask for my identity card?'

The sarcasm was lost on the gangway sentry. 'You're *Rob Roy*'s new first lieutenant.' He hesitated and added as slowly as he dared, '*Sir*.'

By the time Hargrave had crossed the deck to the other side his arrival had been noted. Both the quartermaster and gangway sentry were ready and waiting for him.

Again the salutes, then the quartermaster said, 'I'll 'ave yer case put into yer cabin, sir.'

Hargrave looked around. She seemed crammed with equipment and loose gear. But the two boats, one a whaler, looked smart enough, and the ship's bell was freshly polished.

The quartermaster's words made him turn. 'I'd better hold on until the first lieutenant has cleared out his own stuff,' he replied.

The man eyed him curiously. 'All done, sir.'

'Well, thank you.'

The seaman gestured towards a steel door. 'Wardroom's through there, sir. Time fer tea.'

I could use something stronger, Hargrave thought bitterly.

As soon as he had stepped over the lobby coaming the quartermaster said to his companion, 'Bit stuck-up, eh?'

The seaman grinned. 'The skipper'll 'ave 'im fer breakfast.'

The quartermaster rubbed his chin worriedly. 'I 'ope so.' He added, 'Never thought I'd ever miss an officer, but the old Jimmy was a good bloke.'

They lapsed into silence and waited for the watch to change.

Hargrave climbed down a steep ladder and found a white-coated petty officer checking a list against some tins of biscuits.

He gave a lop-sided grin. 'Arternoon, sir. I'm Kellett, P.O. steward. I looks after the captain an' the wardroom.' Again the grin. 'In that order, so to speak. Care for some char, sir?'

Hargrave nodded and pushed the heavy green curtain aside before stepping into the wardroom.

Like most small ships it was divided in half, if necessary by

8

another long curtain. To starboard was the dining space with a bulkhead sideboard and pantry hatch beyond. A faded photograph of the King was hung above it. Hargrave noticed that the glass was cracked. On the opposite side the place looked snug, but again it was a cupboard after a cruiser's wardroom. Bench seats and some padded chairs, their red leather worn but well polished, enjoying being without the canvas covers normally used at sea.

A letter rack, a glass-fronted case of revolvers and a tiny fireplace with a club fender completed the fittings.

Hargrave looked at the officer who was sitting propped against the side, his jacket unbuttoned to reveal a none-too-clean sweater. He was an RNVR lieutenant but his appearance made Hargrave stare longer than he normally would. He was very fair, and his lashes looked almost white against his deepset brown eyes. A lean, high-cheekboned face, like one in an old portrait.

The lieutenant put down a dog-eared copy of *Men Only* and returned his gaze. It was almost physical. Even insolent.

'I'm Philip Sherwood, Render Mines Safe Officer, a new addition to the senior ship.' It seemed to amuse him. 'They feel safer with me aboard.' He nodded casually to another figure slumped in an armchair whom Hargrave had noticed. The officer was relaxed in a deep sleep, his mouth wide open like a hole, and Hargrave saw with disgust that his false teeth were in a glass beside one which still held some gin. The man was old and unhealthy-looking, with a heavy belly poking over his belt. He was quite bald, and appeared to have no neck at all.

The lieutenant explained in the same soft voice, 'Yonder is Mr Alfred Bone, our Gunner (T).' He smiled gently. 'Aptly named, don't you think?' When Hargrave remained silent, he said, 'He and the Chief are the ancient mariners – the rest of us just *feel* that way.' He smiled as the sleeping warrant officer groaned noisily. 'Means well, but as ignorant as shit.'

'Do you always discuss your fellow officers in this vein?'

Sherwood replied abruptly, 'Usually.'

The petty officer entered with a tray of tea cups and the Gunner (T) jerked into life as if responding to some silent signal. In two deft movements he downed the flat gin and replaced his dentures.

9

He saw Hargrave and muttered thickly, 'Welcome aboard.' He looked even older awake.

The curtain moved aside and a figure in a white overall peered in at them. 'I'm John Campbell, the Chief.' He made to offer his hand but saw it was smudged with grease so withdrew it. 'You'll be the new first lieutenant?'

Hargrave moved to the club fender and studied the ship's crest above the empty grate. It was very suitable for a ship of her name. A lion's head wearing an antique crown with the MacGregor's motto, *'Royal is my race'*, beneath.

Hargrave knew he had made a bad start without understanding why. He recalled something he had read as a boy, how the Campbells had seized the lands of the MacGregors and driven them out.

He faced the others and said, 'You must feel out of place here, Chief?'

Campbell sipped his tea. 'I manage.'

The petty officer fussed around as if he sensed the coolness amongst his charges.

'I'll take your coat, sir.'

Hargrave slipped off the raincoat and reached out for a cup. The others stared at the straight stripes on his sleeve.

Sherwood gave a soft whistle. 'God, a bloody regular!'

Hargrave swung round and noticed for the first time that Sherwood wore a medal ribbon he did not recognise. He recalled how he had described himself, the R.M.S.O. They were the ones who defused mines when they fell ashore or in harbours.

He decided to ignore Sherwood's comment. 'Weren't you ever scared doing that job?'

Sherwood picked up his book. 'You only feel fear when there's an alternative.' The pale lashes closed off his eyes.

The Chief, a commissioned engineer with a lifetime's experience and skill symbolised by a solitary gold stripe, said awkwardly, 'There are two subbies in the mess, er, Number One.' He seemed to falter over the title, and Hargrave felt that Sherwood was watching him again.

The Chief continued, 'Bob, or should I say *Bunny* Fallows is the gunnery officer, and Tudor Morgan assists with navigation.

There is of course our Mid, Allan Davenport.' He gave a tired smile. 'Green as grass.'

Sherwood spoke from behind his book. 'And all bloody hostilities-only, except for the two ancient mariners here. I don't know *what* the Andrew's coming to.'

Seven officers who would eat, write their letters, laugh or weep in this small confined space. There could not be many secrets here.

The petty officer named Kellett said, 'Beg pardon, sir, but the Captain would like to see you right away.'

Hargrave picked up his cap and smoothed his hair, still bleached by the sun.

As he left the wardroom he heard Campbell exclaim, 'One of these days, Philip, you'll say something you'll be made to regret.'

'Until that day –' Hargrave did not hear the rest.

The petty officer steward said, 'This way, sir. Don't worry about your cabin. I'll get anything extra you need.'

He pointed to a door labelled *Captain*, a few yards from the wardroom. Further along past a watertight door Hargrave heard the clatter of crockery. Petty Officers' Mess most likely. Little steel boxes welded together into one hull.

Kellett brushed a crumb off his white jacket and said quietly, 'This ship's been through a lot just lately, sir. Some of 'em 'ave got a bit on edge.' He dropped his eyes as Hargrave looked at him. He repeated, 'Been through a lot, all of us.'

The tannoy squeaked and then a boatswain's call shattered the stillness.

'D'you hear there? Duty part of the watch to muster! Men under punishment fall in! Fire parties to exercise action in fifteen minutes!'

Hargrave nodded to Kellett. At least that was the same everywhere. He rapped on the door. Perhaps when he had done a tour of the ship he might feel differently.

But try as he might he could not dispel the picture of the cruiser's impressive wake as she ploughed beneath the stars of the Indian Ocean.

'Enter!'

Now for the next step. He thrust open the door.

11

After his first meeting with Ransome on that sunny April afternoon, Hargrave often asked himself what he had expected. Perhaps all, or maybe none of the things he saw as he stepped into the small cabin with his cap jammed beneath one arm.

Hargrave did, of course, know something about his new captain and had told himself that he did not care about serving under an officer whom Sherwood might sarcastically describe as *hostilities-only*.

Ransome had spent most of his war sweeping mines and had won a D.S.C. somewhere along the way. The vessel he had commanded prior to *Rob Roy*, a veteran of the Great War, had hit a mine one night in the North Sea. She had lost most of her forecastle and should have gone to the bottom there and then. But with a last bulkhead shored up and weeping at every rivet, Ransome had somehow got her back to port. In six months that ship had been repaired and with a new company had carried on with her sweeping. Three months ago she had hit another mine and had blown up with a terrible loss of life. Bad luck? Or was it that Ransome no longer stood on her bridge?

As Ransome cleared some files from the spare chair Hargrave studied him guardedly, and took time to glance around the cabin to glean any extra information about the man upon whom he might depend for his next step to a better appointment.

Ransome was younger than he had expected – an alive, interesting face, tired perhaps, but it did not conceal the man's alertness, a sudden warmth as he smiled and gestured to the chair.

'Take a pew. Sorry about the mess. All a bit of a rush.' He looked at the deckhead as feet thudded somewhere. The fire parties getting ready for another night in harbour with a good chance of an air-raid or two. There would be a moon tonight. The bombers' favourite. Ransome continued, 'You've been thrown in at the deep end, I'm afraid. I've seen your report from the minesweeping course – you did well, I think. Bit of a change after a cruiser, I suppose.' He did not anticipate an answer. 'You'll soon settle down. I think you may have met some of the wardroom?' His eyes came up, level and unmoving, like a marksman adjusting his sights. 'Good bunch for the most part.'

'The RNVR lieutenant, Sherwood —' Hargrave tried not to blink as the eyes studied him without emotion. 'I just wondered —?'

'Not what you've been used to, I expect.' The eyes dipped and Ransome began to refill the pipe he had been holding as Hargrave had entered. 'Sherwood is extra to complement, but he's an experiment of sorts. The Germans are using more delicate ways of making our job nasty. We need an expert who can strip down a mine or a fuse and perhaps save time as well as lives.' He watched Hargrave through the smoke as he held a match over the bowl. 'He's a brave man, but there are limits to what anyone can stand. He needed to get back to sea, and for that I'm grateful.'

'That medal, sir.'

'George Cross.' Ransome sat back and watched the smoke drift towards the open scuttle. 'Sat on a bloody great magnetic mine and defused it.'

Hargrave remembered Sherwood's hostility. 'I suppose a lot of his sort —'

'His sort?' The grey eyes levelled again. 'I should have mentioned. The mine was alongside some fuel tanks.' He leaned forward suddenly. 'And if you're bothered about serving with temporary officers you'd better tell me right now. I need a first lieutenant badly.' His eyes hardened, like the sea's colour before a storm. 'But not that badly. This is a crack flotilla, and I intend to keep it that way!'

Hargrave looked away. 'I only meant —'

Ransome pushed his fingers through his unruly hair. 'Forget it. It must be harder for you. Rank hath its privileges. Using it on you is not my style.' He grinned. 'Normally, that is —'

He turned sharply as someone tapped at the door. Hargrave could not see who it was but Ransome stood up and said, 'Excuse me. One of the hands. I'm packing him off home.' He stared at his pipe, which had gone out. 'His family was killed last night in a raid on London. I had the job of telling the poor kid this morning.' He walked past the chair and as he opened the door, Hargrave caught a glimpse of a very young seaman, dressed in his best uniform with a gunnery badge in gold wire on his arm. He was very pale, like a frightened child.

He heard Ransome say, 'Well, off you go, Tinker, the coxswain's fixed it up for you.'

Hargrave heard the youth give a sob, and then Ransome went out and closed the door behind him.

Hargrave looked around the cabin, and tried to picture the cruiser's captain dealing with a situation like this. He could not. Instead he examined the cabin piece by piece, while his ears recorded sounds and directions beyond the steel plating which would soon be familiar to him.

There were several pipes on the desk, and a handwritten letter from somebody. His glance moved to the bulkhead where a smaller version of the ship's crest was displayed. In a frame nearby was a pencilled drawing. An oilskin bag of the kind sailors used for money and documents in case their ship was sunk lay beneath it, and Hargrave somehow knew it was for the picture.

He studied it more closely. It portrayed a young man in sweater and slacks sitting with his back to a partly built hull. There was another craft in the background. A boatyard somewhere. The young man held a pipe in his hand. As he had just seen him do. It was little more than a sketch, but it told him a lot. A framed photograph of a young midshipman was on the opposite side. It looked exactly like Ransome as he must have been, but it was not him.

The door swung open and then slammed shut.

Ransome sat down heavily and stared at his pipe. 'Jesus Christ, how much more can we take of this?'

He glanced at the photograph. 'My kid brother. That was taken at *King Alfred*.' He smiled suddenly; the mood changed again. 'A million years ago. He's a full-blown subbie now!'

For those few seconds Hargrave saw them both. The boy and the sketch, like one person.

He said, 'I was looking at the drawing, sir.'

'Oh, that.' Ransome dragged some papers across the desk. 'I'm going to be away all day tomorrow. Lieutenant Commander Gregory,' he gestured with the unlit pipe, 'he drives *Ranger*, will take over as senior officer in my absence. I've left all the notes on the rest of them, two smaller fleet minesweepers and the trawler.

They're at sea with a group from Portsmouth. A joint exercise. But we shall remain here to complete a few repairs. Unless the country is invaded, or a new delivery of Scotch is announced, in which case we shall slip and proceed to search for it!'

He became serious. 'I'd also like you to go over the charts. We don't carry a navigator as such, it's mostly up to you and me.'

Hargrave felt on safer ground. 'I was assistant pilot before –'

Ransome eyed him for a few seconds. 'Thousands of miles of ocean, right? If you were a mile out at the end of it, you'd soon correct it, I expect?'

'Yes, sir.'

Ransome nodded slowly. 'On this job thirty yards is all you'll get.' He let his words sink in. 'Further than that,' he slapped out the loose tobacco into his palm, 'you're bloody dead.'

He changed tack again. 'Your old man is a rear-admiral, I believe?'

Hargrave nodded. 'I went to see him.'

Ransome looked at his pipe and decided to change it for another. *I'll bet you did*, he thought. Hargrave was much as he had expected, although he had been surprised that a regular officer should have been sent to replace David. Unless – Hargrave had been found unsuitable for submarines. That was hardly surprising, in that elite service within a service. Did someone high up, his father for instance, see the minesweeper as a chance of a quick promotion?

'I suppose you wanted a destroyer?'

The shot made Hargrave flush but Ransome grinned. 'I know *I* did. The last thing I wanted was the chance of getting my arse blown off minesweeping.' He gestured vaguely. 'But it's important. I expect you've had that rammed down your throat at the training base until you're sick of it. But it's true. Without us, nobody sails. If we fail, the country will be squeezed into defeat. It's that simple. The swept channel runs right around these islands, an unbroken track, into which the enemy throws every device he can dream up. Tyne, Humber, Thames, from Liverpool Bay to the Dover Straits, we sweep each and every day, no matter what. There's no death-or-glory here, no line-of-battle with flags and bands playing.' His eyes fell on his brother's picture and he

15

felt his muscles contract. In his last letter Tony had been full of it. Appointed to the Light Coastal Forces. A motor torpedo boat. God, his mother would love that.

He added, 'We sweep mines. It's a battle which started after Dunkirk and will never stop until –' he shrugged. 'God alone knows.' He made up his mind and wrenched open the little cupboard, and placed the whisky bottle and two glasses on the desk.

Hargrave watched as he broke the seal. His stomach was empty, he had been on a train for hours, but something made him understand that the drink was more than a gesture. It was important to Ransome.

Ransome tilted the whisky around the glass. 'Well, Number One?'

Hargrave smiled. 'I'll try and be a good one.'

'You'll do better than that.' He frowned as the phone rang and he snatched it up even as voices and slamming doors vibrated through the hull.

He said quietly, 'Signal from the tower. The bastards have just opened fire.'

Hargrave found that he was on his feet, his hands clenched at his sides. It was like being naked, or left as a helpless decoy.

Ransome said, 'They spot the flashes from Cap Gris Nez. It takes just over forty seconds for the shells to arrive.'

Hargrave looked down at him and saw that the glass in Ransome's hand was empty.

The roar when it came was like a shockwave, as if someone had beaten the side of the hull with a battering ram.

Ransome waited; there were four explosions somewhere on the far side of the town.

He said, 'The flashes are the only warning. At sea you can sometimes hear the fall of each shell, but *after* it's gone off.' He poured another glass of neat Scotch. 'Bastards.'

There were no more explosions but when Hargrave looked through the scuttle he saw a far-off column of smoke rising across the clear sky. Like a filthy stain. There would be more grief now. Like the young sailor called Tinker.

He picked up his glass. The whisky was like a blessed relief.

'May I ask where you will be tomorrow, sir?'

Ransome was staring at the photograph of his brother.

'Your predecessor's funeral.'

Hargrave looked at the door but sat down as Ransome said, 'Please stay. I'm celebrating. I've had this ship for a year today.'

He held out his glass and waited for Hargrave to clink it with his.

Ransome said quietly, 'I wish —'

Hargrave saw the brief blur of despair in the grey eyes. Like something too private to share. He waited but Ransome said, 'Here's to David.' Hargrave guessed it was his predecessor.

Ransome felt the neat whisky burning his throat but did not care. He never drank at sea, and only rarely in harbour. After tomorrow, David, like all those other faces which had been wiped away, would fade in memory.

He thought of the youth called Tinker, his wretched tear-stained face as he had listened to him, needing him. A travel warrant, a ration card for his journey home. Except that there was no home any more. Like a beautiful ship as she hits a mine and starts to roll over. An end to everything.

He looked hard at his glass. 'I — I don't want to go. But I must. He was my friend, you see.'

Later, as Hargrave unpacked his belongings in his new cabin, he thought about the interview.

No, it was not what he had expected. Nor was Ransome like anyone he had ever met before.

As darkness fell over Dover Castle the air-raid sirens wailed, and people everywhere went to the shelters or huddled beneath stairs with their loved ones and their pets.

Aboard the fleet minesweeper *Rob Roy*, Ian Ransome sat at his desk with his face on his arms and slept for the first time in weeks.

# 2

# *. . . and Men*

Lieutenant Hargrave was not the only replacement to be joining the fleet minesweeper *Rob Roy* before she was once again ordered to sea.

On the following Monday afternoon with a fine drizzle making the moored ships gleam like glass, Ordinary Seaman Gerald Boyes stood on the wall and stared across at the ship he was about to board.

The leading patrolman who had escorted him from the gate pointed with his stick and said importantly, 'Good record. Swept more mines than you've 'ad 'ot dinners, my lad.'

Boyes nodded, but was too polite to suggest that the harbour wall was probably the closest the leading patrolman had been to the sea.

Boyes was a slim, pale youth of eighteen. He had a kind of frailty which now, as he stared at his new home, was at odds with his set expression of determination.

At school he had been something of a dreamer, and usually his thoughts had been on the sea and the mystique of the Royal Navy. His parents had smiled indulgently while his mother had set her hopes firmly on a local bank where Boyes's father had worked for most of his life. While many of the people he knew in the unassuming town of Surbiton on the outskirts of South London had been stunned by the swiftness of events, Boyes had seen the declaration of war as something like a salvation.

Throughout his boyhood, at a respectable grammar school

18

which his father occasionally mentioned had 'been worth all the money it cost' him, Boyes had found his escape in magazines, the *Hotspur*, the *Rover* or the *Adventure*. There was rarely a time when they were without a story or two about the navy, the officers of the dashing destroyers in particular.

Boyes had volunteered for the navy as soon as he was seventeen. His mother, having seen his determination, had been tearfully proud. 'You'll soon be an officer, you see, Gerry.' He hated being called Gerry. 'With your background and education, they'll be crying out for your sort.'

The training to begin with had been hard, but always Boyes had seen his guiding light beyond the discipline and the foul language which at first made him blush to the roots of his hair. Until he realised that it was his innocence which was really the target. He watched the occasional appearance of the officers. Some seemed positively elderly, brought back from retirement, and others with the single wavy stripe on their sleeves seemed like young lords of creation.

His mother had been right about one thing. He had been officially listed as a C.W. Candidate, a potential officer, and sent to sea for three months in a sleek, brand-new destroyer. Another world again, working alongside tough, experienced seamen who for the most part had left him in peace with his so-called posh accent, even tolerated his efforts to fit in. At the end of three months, spent mostly in and around Scapa Flow in readiness to escort and protect the huge battleships there, he had been sent to Hove in Sussex, where he would begin his officer's training after a brief series of interviews. He had been wildly excited, and had even met some of the boys who had joined up with him, several from his own district at home. It had all ended there. It was still almost impossible to grasp. It was so brutal, so unfair.

The senior officer had merely said, 'You may get another opportunity later on.' He had looked genuinely sorry for the pale-faced youth with the feverishly bright eyes. 'We need volunteers in this war. We can't all be officers, you know.'

Back home for a few days before returning to the barracks for drafting to another ship. His mother had been upset. Or had she been humiliated, shamed because of his failure? His father had muttered sternly, 'Their mistake, son, not yours.' None of it was much help. Boyes had returned to R.N.B. Chatham and almost immediately had heard about the growing demand for men in the minesweeping service.

As a petty officer at the drafting office had cheerfully remarked, 'Good for you, lad, join the navy and see the world. Volunteer for minesweepers and see the next!'

With unbelievable dedication Boyes had entered the mine-sweeping course at the shore establishment, HMS *Lochinvar*. The need to prove himself, or to lose himself in danger, he neither knew nor cared.

He examined his feelings as he stood on the harbour wall, the light drizzle bouncing off his cap and oilskin, his kitbag leaning beside him in a puddle.

How did he feel? Not afraid, nor even elated. Just glad to be *moving* again, doing something which would wipe the shame away. He had heard the old hands talking about minesweepers. True guts, they said. 'You wouldn't get *me* in that bloody regiment —'

Boyes turned, but the leading patrolman had gone. He gathered up his kitbag, little suitcase, gas mask and the joining chit which he had produced several times on his way here to prove what he was doing and why. The train had been delayed for several hours because an air-raid had caused a derailment somewhere. He had been crammed in the overloaded train with sleeping soldiers and sailors, the air thick with tobacco smoke and crude jokes.

Boyes made his way across the brow to the inboard ship. It was high-water, and the crossing was reasonably safe.

The gangway sentry pulled his bag aboard for him and grinned as Boyes explained that he was the new replacement.

He said, 'Never 'ave guessed, would we, Bert?'

The quartermaster pointed to *Rob Roy*. 'Shouldn't join 'er, matey, they're killing 'em all off!'

They both laughed as if it was a huge joke.

Boyes eventually arrived on the other ship's wet deck and saw a chief petty officer watching him from beside the quartermaster's little folding desk.

'Well, nah, my son? What are all we then?'

He had a Cockney accent you could sharpen a knife on, although Boyes did not understand that. But he did recognise the crossed torpedoes and wheel on the man's lapels, his air of jovial authority. He was the coxswain, a kind of god in every small ship-of-war.

'Ordinary Seaman Boyes, sir.'

The coxswain's heavy brows came together to make a dark bridge across his battered nose.

'Not *sir*, my son. Call me Cox'n. I run this ship.' He grinned. 'Me an' the Old Man, that is.'

He became businesslike. 'You're in Three Mess.' He gestured to a seaman by the guardrail. 'Take 'im down. Then bring 'im back to me to get 'is part of ship, an' that.'

Boyes eyed him thankfully. There was something reassuring about the coxswain. His face looked as if it had been in many brawls, but his eyes were steady and not unfriendly.

Chief Petty Officer Joe Beckett, the *Rob Roy*'s coxswain, asked offhandedly, 'Age?'

'Eighteen, si – I mean Cox'n.'

'Gawd. Another wot's too young to draw 'is tot. Makes yer sick.'

Beckett watched the slight figure being led to the forecastle. Already lost. He frowned. Not for long. Not in this ship. There was no room for passengers.

He saw the new first lieutenant approaching and toyed with the idea of avoiding him around the funnel, but sighed and stood his ground. Between them they had to manage the ship. He thought of the new lad, Boyes, sent to replace a seaman who had gained promotion and been drafted to an advanced course ashore.

The navy was like that. All comings and goings. He glanced aft towards the shining new paint where the previous Jimmy-the-One had been cut down. All goings for some.

Joe Beckett often considered his own entry into the navy. A London Eastender from Hackney, he was one of seven children. It was a bloody wonder his mum and dad had found the time, he thought. His dad was more in prison than out of it, and two of his

21

brothers had begun thieving at Marks and Spencer's and Woolworths almost as soon as they had got their first pair of boots. They were likely as well known at the Hackney nick as his father by now.

So Joe Beckett had joined the navy at the age of sixteen. He had done well, despite several demotions and *bottles* at the defaulters' table in one ship or another. He was now thirty-six, one of the *old bastards* as they called him behind his back. It was a joke when you thought about it. His upbringing had been hard and without too much love. But it had taught him to take care of himself, as his face and scarred knuckles showed if anyone was stupid enough to challenge his authority. Now, as coxswain, he was as high as he would rise. Here in the fleet minesweeper he ran just about everything. A word in the right ear could shift a man from a miserable look-out position to a snug station elsewhere. Over half the ship's company were too young to draw their rum. That was a bit difficult. Rum and tobacco, 'ticklers', were the currency of the lower deck. He almost smiled. Not far different from the nick after all. And as coxswain he was also responsible for discipline, a sort of judge and policeman in one. How his old dad would have liked that!

At action stations, entering or leaving harbour, and at any other occasion when his seamanship and hard-won knowledge were required, Beckett was on the wheel, thick and thin. He had been sunk once, wounded once, and three times recommended for a decoration. Like Christmas, it was always still coming.

He watched the new first lieutenant as he paused to speak with Mr Midshipman Davenport. Unlike some of the regulars, Beckett admired the Wavy Navy reservists for most of the time. Many of them, like the RNR ex-trawler skippers, were professional seamen, and others, like the Old Man now, had done something before they joined up. Were not too proud to chat about that other world which had probably gone forever.

He was not happy about the new Jimmy. Strait-laced, and from a bloody cruiser at that. Beckett had been an A.B. in a heavy cruiser, had been weighted off for punishment for pitching a petty officer over the rail. Fortunately it had been in Grand Harbour, Malta, where you were more likely to be poisoned than drowned. Cruisers, like the carriers and battlewaggons, were floating barracks. Not for Joe Beckett. He scowled as he saw the white flash of Davenport's winning smile. Beckett had decided within a week of the midshipman's joining the ship that he could well be the reason for himself being disrated, busted as low as was possible.

Even when he considered it calmly over his tot, Beckett had reached the conclusion that if Davenport had sailed with Bligh in the *Bounty* the mutiny would have happened a bloody sight earlier.

He touched his cap in salute as Hargrave approached him.

' 'Ad a good tour, sir?'

Hargrave brushed down his sleeves. 'Been right over her, stem to stern.'

The midshipman drew closer. 'I could show you the radar, sir?'

Beckett tried not to look at him. *A real little prick.*

He said, 'Watch out fer wet paint, sir.'

Hargrave frowned at a smear of grey on his trousers. '*Thanks.*'

Beckett added, 'New ratin' 'as just joined the ship, sir. I've put 'im in Mr Morgan's division.'

Their eyes met. 'I'd like to be told first, Swain.'

'You wasn't 'ere, sir.' Beckett met his gaze coldly. 'We was one short, so to speak.'

The tannoy snapped the tension.

'D'you hear there! D'you hear there! *Up spirits!*'

Beckett tucked his clipboard beneath his arm and watched Hargrave walk briskly towards the bridge, the midshipman falling into step to keep up.

'Stand fast the 'oly Ghost!' he muttered. 'By Christ I've never needed a bloody tot more!'

The Chief and Petty Officers' Mess was about the same size as the wardroom, although less conventional. There was a small bar at one end where a seaman in a white jacket was acting as messman, and ranged behind it were souvenirs from various pubs scattered from Leith to Gibraltar. Beer mugs, ashtrays stamped with pub or brewery names, photographs of various groups at darts matches, regattas or just a good booze-up. There were a few dazzling pin-ups too, one even signed by a well-known madam in Gosport.

Beckett sat at the mess table which had been cleared of their supper, a meal of baked beans, tinned sausages, and great wads of toast made with fresh bread from the town – a real luxury.

He glanced at his companions. He and Dai Owen the C.E.R.A. were in fact the only members rated as chief petty officers. The rest were petty officers, heads of various departments, the backbone in any class of warship. Masefield, the P.O. sickberth attendant, known as Pansy, the closest thing to a doctor carried in *Rob Roy*, was bent over a letter from his mother, one delicate hand shading it from the others, like a schoolboy in an exam. Topsy Turnham, a dark-chinned, stocky figure with twinkling blue eyes, was the chief boatswain's mate, the *Buffer*, a direct link between the seamen and the first lieutenant. He was poring over some photographs of a full-breasted girl he had found somewhere. Beckett smiled grimly. He did not know how the Buffer managed it. He was married and had a home in Chatham, but always seemed to have his feet under the table with some bit of crumpet wherever he was based. A stoker P.O. lay snoring gently in his bunk behind a half-drawn curtain; otherwise the mess was empty. Kellett was doubtless fussing around his wardroom, and the others were ashore until midnight.

Beckett gazed at a mug of beer on the table. The lull before the night's storm. He would be almost glad to be at sea again. You felt so bloody helpless stuck in harbour, and the Jerries only twenty miles away. About the same distance as Margate. It didn't do to look at it like that.

It was a good mess, he thought. They had their bad moments, but that happened in any small ship where you lived in each other's pockets. But in bigger ships you found all the brains, whereas in *Rob Roy* the other key jobs were carried out by leading hands, just kids, some of them.

Beckett looked up sharply. 'Turn up that radio.'

The messman obliged so that the cool, precise tones of the BBC announcer intruded into their small, private world.

'And yesterday our forces advanced still further westwards along the Libyan coast, supported by units of the Mediterranean

24

Fleet. Some pockets of resistance were dealt with on the outskirts of Tripoli, but the advance continues.' The announcer's voice reminded Beckett of Hargrave. He could have been describing a cricket match. In his mind's eye Beckett could see it clearly. He had taken part in the evacuation of the army from Greece and Crete in the bad days. Ships sunk on every hand, exhausted soldiers, no air cover. A real foul-up. He had seen the battleship *Barham* explode and turn turtle after a U-boat had penetrated the destroyer screen and fired a salvo of torpedoes. *Barham* had been Beckett's first ship before the war. When he had been an O.D. like Boyes. He gave a sad smile. Well, not really like him.

His friend the C.E.R.A. glanced at him across the table. 'Remembering, Joe?'

'Yeh.' He downed the beer and signalled the messman. 'Turn that stuff off, or find some bloody music!' He faced his friend. He liked Owen, a man with a dark intelligent face, the engine-room's centre-pin. A bloody good chap. He smiled again. For a Welshman.

He said, 'I'm almost scared to think about it, Dai. These advances in North Africa. After all the setbacks and losses. Can we really be on the move this time?'

Owen shrugged and glanced at the bulkhead clock. Soon time for engine-room rounds. It would never do to let the Chief get there before him.

He said, 'Well, at this rate, Joe, we'll have Rommel's bloody Afrika Korps with their backs to the sea before the month's out. There's nowhere else for the buggers to go, see?'

Topsy Turnham folded his photographs and placed them in his wallet.

Beckett said, 'You should keep a bloody filing-cabinet for all your bits of skirt!'

Turnham beamed. He was quite ugly when he smiled.

'Jealous, Swain? I can't 'elp it if they finds me irresistible now, can I?' He was a Londoner too, from Stoke Newington, not that far from Beckett's manor.

Masefield glanced up from his mother's letter. 'What's the new Jimmy like?'

Beckett shrugged. 'Not your type, Pansy. Real old school tie.'

Owen grinned. 'Might be *just* his type then, see?'

Beckett conceded, ' 'E knows 'is stuff all right. You couldn't catch 'im out on the nuts and bolts of the ship. But I dunno, Taffs, 'e's no *warmth*. A proper cold bastard.'

Owen changed the subject. 'The Old Man's at the funeral today then?'

'Yeh. I 'ate burials.' He reflected. ' 'Cept at sea o' course. That's different. A bit of spit an' polish, a few words and splash, old chummy's gone for a last swim. A good tot and a tuck-in afterwards, well, you can see the point o' *that!*'

The tannoy intruded. 'D'you hear there! Air-raid warning Red. Short-range weapons crews close up. Duty part of the watch to muster.'

'*Sods!*' Beckett groped for his cap and a full packet of duty-free cigarettes. ' 'Ere we go a-bloody-gain!'

The mess emptied except for the P.O. sickberth attendant and the sleeping stoker.

A few minutes later the sky above Dover and beyond was lit up by bursting flak like hundreds of bright stars which touched the clouds and made them glow from every angle. The crump-crump of anti-aircraft guns from the batteries on the cliffs and inland, and then the sharper clatter of cannon-fire as some of the ships joined in the barrage. Whenever there was a lull they could hear the familiar drone of bombers, passing over, perhaps for London again.

Beckett disdained a steel helmet, a *battle-bowler*, and tugged his cap more tightly across his forehead.

The Jerries might be nearly thrown out of Africa, he thought savagely, but maybe they hadn't heard that at this end of the war.

Ordinary Seaman Gerald Boyes sat at the mess table and looked around his new home. Number Three Mess was a grand name for one scrubbed table with a bench on one side of it, and the cushioned lockers opposite which fitted against the ship's forecastle plating. There were the usual shelves packed with attaché cases, cap boxes, and life-jackets in easy reach, and two sealed scuttles, tightly closed against the darkness outside.

At the head of the table, Leading Seaman Ted Hoggan, the acting gunner's mate and killick of the mess, was engrossed in darning a seaboot stocking, his eyes screwed up with concentration. Some hammocks were slung, their owners, mostly watchkeepers, apparently able to sleep despite the blare of music from the tannoy and the noisy conversation from the mess opposite, where a game of uckers was in full swing.

Hoggan eyed Boyes thoughtfully. 'You can sling yer 'ammock over there on them 'ooks, lad. Young Tinker is ashore for a spot o' leaf.' He gestured with the seaboot stocking to a small oval hatch in the deckhead where Boyes had struggled down with his bag and hammock. 'When Action Stations goes you fly up that ladder like a bat from 'ell, see?'

Boyes nodded. He had changed into a sweater and overalls, apparently the rig except for those on watch in harbour. If anything it made him feel more of an intruder. The other seamen who lounged about writing letters, yarning, or watching the uckers game, wore overalls scrubbed and cleaned so often that they were pale blue, almost white in the harsh deckhead lights. Boyes's were still dark, regulation colour. He concentrated on the leading hand, a real-life seaman. Tough, with a wind-reddened face, and a snake tattooed around one thick wrist.

Hoggan had returned to his darning. 'Just keep yer nose clean, an' do wot you're told. If you wants to know summat, ask *me*, got it? Don't 'ave no truck with the officers.'

'Why is that, er, Leading —'

'Call me 'ookey.' He tapped the killick on his sleeve. 'You're Gerry, right?' He did not see Boyes wince. 'Well, there are officers and officers, Gerry. Some are better than t'others, of course, but deep down they're all bastards.' He gave a slow grin, 'I should know. My boss is Mr bloody *Bunny* Fallows, the gunnery officer 'e calls hisself. Nice as pie one minute, the next, phew! Specially when he gets pissed.'

A seaman who was stitching a new leather sheath which he had fashioned for a formidable-looking knife, said, 'Which is all the bleedin' time in 'arbour!' He glanced casually at Boyes. 'You a C.W. candidate?'

Boyes flushed. 'Well, no, actually.'

'No, *actually*,' the other man mimicked him and brought grins from the others until Hoggan said quietly, 'Leave it, Sid.'

27

The seaman shifted along the bench and touched Boyes's sleeve. 'No 'arm done.' He grinned. 'You're not old enough to draw a tot yet?'

Boyes shook his head. It was a question he was asked quite a lot.

'Well, you come round for sippers tomorrow, eh, Gerry?'

Hoggan watched them, pleased they had accepted the youth. It was not his fault, the way he spoke.

He said, 'Yeh, meet Sid Jardine, a *real old sweat*, eh? Must be twenty-one at least! Roll on my bloody twelve!'

Boyes wondered when it would be prudent to sling his hammock. He was not very good at it yet. Even in a big destroyer there had not been room enough, especially for a C.W. candidate, a potential officer.

He glanced with interest at his companions. Most of the mess were ashore, on a 'short run' as Hoggan had explained. They might return aboard by ten o'clock either in silence or fighting drunk. After ten they would arrive back with an escort of the naval patrol. Boyes wondered what his mother would make of these men.

'*Tea up!*' An elderly seaman with three stripes on his sleeve banged down the ladder with a huge fanny of tea.

Hoggan put down his darning. 'Teaboat's alongside!'

What sort of craft was that, Boyes wondered?

The old seaman glanced down at Boyes and then filled a cup of typical sailors' tea, almost yellow in colour from tinned milk, and so much sugar you could stand a spoon in it.

' 'Ere, this one's free, son!'

The sailor called Jardine exclaimed, '*Free*, Stripey? Do my ears *deceive* me?'

Another called from the opposite mess, 'Better keep your overalls on in your hammock when that old bugger's about!'

Boyes had heard much the same banter before. He took the sweet, sickly tea and thanked the three-badged sailor for it.

He did not care any more. He was accepted. The rest was up to him.

The chief petty officer Wren from the Welfare Section stood beside the khaki-coloured car, and watched the young sailor called Tinker as he stared at the ruined house which had once been his home. She was a severe-looking girl, with her hair set in a tight bun beneath her tricorn hat. It was not that she did not care, but she had seen too many broken homes and shattered marriages to let it reach her any more.

She said, 'The bomb hit the front of the house.' She gestured with her cardboard file. 'There was a whole stick of them right across three streets. They were both in bed. They wouldn't have felt anything.' She watched his silent anguish. 'I checked with the A.R.P. people and the Heavy Rescue chaps.' He gave no sign and she said, 'The police too.'

Tinker stepped amongst the rubble and peered up at one bare wall. The same striped wallpaper, a pale rectangle where one of his pictures had hung. Next to his old toy-cupboard. His eyes smarted again. His own little room.

The rest of the housefront lay at his feet. He heard the car engine turning over behind him and clenched his fists tightly. Bloody cow, couldn't wait to be off! What did she know?

Something like panic gripped him. He had nobody, and nowhere to go! It was like a nightmare. All the fear and tension of minesweeping was nothing by comparison.

He said quietly, 'I had to see it.'

She nodded. 'Very well. The salvage people have all the recovered property in store in case —' She did not finish it.

Tinker remembered a time, one month after he had joined *Rob Roy*, when they had sighted an airman in a dinghy. He had turned out to be a German, shot down in the Channel, and almost overcome by exposure and exhaustion.

Tinker had been one of the hands to go down a scrambling-net and pull the airman on board, who had fetched him coffee laced with rum. He clenched his fists tighter until the pain steadied him.

'I wish I'd killed the bastard!' he whispered.

He heard footsteps on the fallen fragments and the Wren call sharply, 'Not this way, sir!'

Tinker swung round, hurt and bewildered by the intrusion. He stared and thought his heart had stopped completely.

Then he was running, his cap fallen in the dust as he threw

himself into the arms of a man in heavy working-clothes. *'Dad! It can't be!'*

The chief petty officer Wren gaped at them. 'But I was told you were dead! They said you were both in bed!'

The man clutched his son's head tightly against his chest and stared fixedly at the remains of his house.

'She was in bed right enough! But the other bastard wasn't me!'

He lifted his son's chin. 'Pity I wasn't here in time. Come, we'll go to Uncle Jack's.' He turned the youth away from the house. 'But then it seems I was never here when I was needed.'

The Wren watched them walk away without a backward glance.

Her driver said, 'Wasn't your fault, Miss. There's more to this bloody war than bein' blown up.'

She slid into the car and adjusted her skirt.

It sounded like an epitaph, she thought.

# 3

# No Safe Way

Lieutenant Commander Ian Ransome sat behind his small desk and tried to relax his mind. The cabin looked bare as it always did prior to leaving harbour. Books secured on their shelves, his gramophone records carefully wedged in a drawer with newspaper between them. It was a trick he had learned after his first collection had been broken when a mine exploded almost alongside. He was dressed in his old seagoing reefer; the wavy stripes on the sleeves were so tarnished they looked brown in the glare of the desk-lamp.

Outside it was early morning, with a lively chop in the confined waters of the harbour. He felt the deck tremble gently and knew the Chief was already going over everything with his assistant engineer.

The tannoy again. 'D'you hear there! Special sea dutymen to your stations! Close all watertight doors and scuttles, down all deadlights!'

Another departure.

The cabin even felt different. It always seemed as if you were leaving it behind like part of the harbour. Until *Rob Roy* berthed or anchored again, the minute sea-cabin abaft the wheelhouse would be his refuge. He wore his favourite roll-necked sweater, his trousers tucked in his old leather seaboots. Fresh socks, some of the thick ones his mother had made. It might keep her mind off the other side of the war which had taken her two sons to sea.

Ransome patted his pockets although he barely noticed his

31

usual precaution. Pipe and tobacco pouch, plenty of matches. He glanced at the cabin door behind which hung his duffle-coat and cap, binoculars, and a newly laundered towel to wrap around his neck.

His glance fell on the drawing of himself which Hargrave had remarked upon. It all came crowding back as it had yesterday at poor David's funeral. The weather had been bright and fresh at the Hampshire village where the family lived. Ransome had not met any of them before. It was strange, he thought. War was like that. Someone who become a true friend, a bond as close as love; yet when he had been smashed down by cannon-fire it made Ransome realise he knew so very little about him.

The tannoy squawked, 'D'you hear there! All the port watch, first part forward, second part aft! Stand by for leaving harbour!' A brief pause; Ransome could hear the boatswain's mate's breathing on the tannoy. He sounded cold. 'Starboard watch to defence stations!' More noise this time, thudding feet, the dull bang of another watertight door or hatch. Men hurrying to familiar metal boxes. Not looking at each other just yet. Probably thinking of their last letters home. Like his own which had gone with the naval postman an hour ago.

He tried not to think about the funeral any more and imagined Hargrave as he coped with his new ship getting under way, or the curious stares from the men who were still remembering David in his place. So many things. But it did not work.

There had been several women of varying ages, most of them in black. David's father had been there, but had not looked a scrap like him. Another surprise: David's mother had apparently remarried. That explained it. The clergyman had spoken of David's sacrifice; several people had been quietly weeping. There were two others in uniform, both aircrew from the RAF who had apparently been at school with David. They had looked uncomfortable – embarrassed perhaps? They had most likely been to too many funerals in their trade. The next time . . .

He unhooked the drawing of himself and held it to the lamp. The rest of the cabin was in darkness, the deadlights screwed shut when he had been roused with a cup of tea by Kellett, the P.O. steward.

It had been after the funeral, the coffin hidden by freshly dug earth, a man rolling up a borrowed Union flag. Handshakes, David's mother murmuring something to him. 'So glad you were here, Commander.' It had sounded so formal, but he had said nothing. Was she really glad, or would she be thinking of her dead son, wishing he and not David had been the unlucky one this time?

The girl had been with her family. A slight figure with her long hair in a pigtail which hung down her school blazer.

Ransome's heart had given a leap. It was impossible, and yet — He studied the drawing again, remembering exactly how the girl had walked into his father's boatyard in Fowey, her sketch-pad under her bare arm, pausing to ruffle the head of Jellicoe the cat, who had been drowsing in the summer sunshine on an upturned dinghy. Like the girl at the funeral, she must have been about thirteen then. He slipped the picture into the oilskin bag and laid it beside his gloves.

But the schoolgirl had turned to stare at him when David's mother had been speaking. She had not been at all like Eve. He almost heard her name again in his thoughts.

How could she be? That had been in that other world before the war, when every summer had been full of sunshine and promise. The last time he had seen her had been in the summer of '39. He bit his lip. Four years back. In war it was a bloody lifetime.

The telephone above his bunk gave a sharp buzz. The one on the desk had gone, in a drawer too probably. Symbolic. The link with the land was cut. Almost.

He picked it from its cradle. 'Captain. . .?'

It was Sub-Lieutenant Morgan, his Welsh accent very strong over the wire. He had entered the navy by a roundabout route, and had first been in the merchant service where he had obtained his ticket. He had transferred to the navy and had started all over again. He was a junior sub-lieutenant, and yet was qualified in navigation and watchkeeping, and could in time have a command of his own. He would be hard to replace.

'Signal, sir. *Proceed when ready.*'

Ransome asked, 'What's the forecast?'

33

'Freshening wind from the south-east, sir. Not too bad, isn't it?'

Ransome smiled and put down the handset. He said that about every sort of weather.

The desk was throbbing more insistently now and he could picture the other minesweeper alongside, the complicated mass of wires and fenders which still held them both netted to the shore.

Hargrave would be down soon. What did he really think about his new job?

He thought of that last meeting with the girl called Eve. She and her parents had come to Cornwall to a cottage over the water in Polruan. They apparently borrowed it every year from a friend. He knew it was ridiculous of course, he still did, but he had always looked forward to the school holidays when people filled the villages and seaports, or hiked across the cliffs and moorland. Always she had brought her sketch-pad with her. Shy at first, they had become close while she had told him of her ambition to become a proper artist. He could see her clearly in her faded shorts and shirt, her long dark hair tied back from her ears, her eyes watching him while he had explained about building boats. The yard was owned and run by Ransome's father, who had moved there in the twenties from a smaller Thameside yard. Fowey with the village of Polruan on the opposite side of the little estuary had been exactly what he had wanted for his craft, for his two sons to follow in his footsteps, although Tony had still been at school then himself. Ransome felt the old twinge of jealousy he had known when he had seen his brother walking and chatting with the bare-legged girl. The same age; it had seemed natural and yet . . .

He stood up, angry with himself for allowing the memory to unsettle him. He *was* ridiculous. God, he was ten years older than she was.

He thought of the girl at the funeral; she had been standing as Eve did when she was trying to fix a subject in her mind's eye for her sketching.

Ransome always remembered that last meeting. He had been driving a potential buyer for one of his father's fishing boats to

34

the station in the yard's pickup van, and had met Eve with her parents waiting with their luggage. The holiday had been cut short. Ransome had not been sure which had surprised him more.

Her parents had not been unfriendly but had kept their distance. He had been surprised that Eve had not told him her father was a clergyman; or that she was leaving on that day.

She had been in her school uniform, something he had not seen before, and he knew she was hating him seeing her like that, embarrassed, when they had always shared each other's company like equals.

Her father had said, 'I expect the next time we meet, whenever that may be, you will be married, eh?'

Ransome had seen the girl look away, her mouth quivering. The schoolgirl again.

The train had whistled in the distance and Eve's mother had said, 'So we'll say goodbye, Mr Ransome. Ships in the night.' She had watched her daughter, had been aware of her bitter silence.

'Say goodbye to Mr Ransome, dear –'

She had held out her hand solemnly. 'I shall never forget –'

Her father had peered at the incoming train. 'Ah me, holiday friendships – where would we be without them?' He had been eager to go.

Ransome had watched the porter putting the luggage in the compartment. He had felt his mouth frozen in an idiotic smile. What did he expect? And yet his heart had been pleading. *Please don't turn away. Look at me just once.*

Eve had swung away from the door and had run towards him, then she had reached up and kissed his cheek, her inexperience making her skin flush like fire.

'Thank you . . .' She had stared at him, searching his face, her eyes already pricking with tears. 'Think of me sometimes . . .' He had never seen her again.

There was a tap at the door and he snapped, 'Yes!'

Hargrave stepped over the coaming, his eyes wary.

Ransome sighed. *He'll think I'm rattled already. Halfway round the bend.* 'All set, Number One?' He saw Hargrave flinch, as unused to the title as he was to giving it to someone other than

David. He also noticed he was wearing a collar and tie.

'Both parts of the port watch ready for leaving harbour, sir. Starboard watch closed up at defence stations.' He forced a smile. 'I hope I've remembered everything.'

Ransome unwound, muscle by muscle. It was a whole lot harder for Hargrave, he thought. He would learn. Or else.

He slipped into the duffle-coat and dragged his cap tightly over his unruly hair.

'Would you like to take her out?'

He saw it all on Hargrave's handsome features. Uncertainty, knowing that every eye would be watching him. Knowing too that he could not refuse. It was probably unfair, but they had to start somewhere.

Hargrave nodded. 'I'd like to, sir.'

Ransome glanced around the cabin. Would he ever set foot in it again? He thought of David, the earth rattling on the plain coffin. It was over.

He slammed the door.

'We'll do it together, Number One.'

Ordinary Seaman Gerald Boyes groped his way aft along the guardrail, his feet catching on unfamiliar ringbolts and other unmoving projections.

He looked at the sky and the fast clouds and shivered despite his thick sweater. He had slept well, wrapped in his hammock with the other gently swinging pods, and had not awakened once, even when the returning liberty men had crashed down the ladder, banging their heads against the hammocks and giving a mouthful of abuse to anyone who objected.

The other hands in the quarterdeck party to which Boyes was assigned stood around the coils of mooring wire and the huge rope fenders which were ready to supplement those already hung between the two steel hulls.

It was not like the mess, he thought. Here he recognised no one. He saw the quarterdeck officer, the squat and formidable Mr Bone, hands on hips as he discussed something with his leading seaman. Boyes tried to mingle with the other vague shapes, better still, disappear. He told himself not to be so timid.

36

Tomorrow and the day after he would get to know all of them. The ship's company of the destroyer where he had done his sea training had been double that of *Rob Roy*'s.

A seaman lounging against the steel door beneath the after four-inch gun straightened up. He had a handset to his ear, but stood to attention as he acknowledged the call from the bridge. 'Aye, aye, sir!' He looked for Mr Bone. 'Single up to back spring and sternrope, sir!'

Boyes was almost knocked off his feet as the figures were galvanised into action.

Guttridge, the leading seaman of the quarterdeck, a swarthy-faced young man with curling black hair, snapped, 'Cut them lashings off!' He peered at Boyes, 'You're new!' It sounded like an accusation. 'Well, shift yer bloody self.'

Boyes fumbled with the lashings around the nearest mooring wire, and his cap fell to the deck.

Mr Bone was old and ungainly but he was across the quarterdeck in a flash.

'*You* – what's yer name?'

Boyes stammered it out.

Mr Bone growled, 'One of *them*, are you.' He bustled away.

Boyes heard yells from forward as the other wires were let go from the ship alongside. He felt lost and humiliated, and sensed some of the others grinning at him.

A familiar voice said roughly, ' 'Ere, put these gloves on, *Gerry*.' It was the seaman called Jardine who had mimicked him in the mess. 'There's often loose strands in these moorin' wires. Don't want you to 'ave yer lily-white 'ands damaged, do we?' Then he chuckled. 'Don't mind the Gunner. He don't like nobody!' He pulled out the fearsome-looking knife Boyes had seen him measuring against his new sheath and expertly cut away the spunyarn lashings. 'One day he'll tell you all about 'ow he was a hero at Jutland.' He lowered his voice as Mr Bone bustled past. 'Jutland? It was a bloody picnic compared with what this tub went through last year.' He did not explain.

The deck began to tremble and Boyes saw the backspring rise up and tauten like an iron rod.

Leading Seaman Guttridge, called Gipsy by his friends,

exclaimed, '*Jesus*, what's the Old Man up to?'.

Another voice said, 'It ain't him. It's the new Jimmy takin' us out.'

Mr Bone snapped, 'Slack off the spring! Stand by sternrope!' He gestured into the gloom by the boat davits. 'Chief Bosun's Mate! More fenders down aft! Chop-bloody-chop!'

The Buffer appeared with some extra seamen and Jardine grinned. 'Poor old Buffer, he won't like that, gettin' a bottle in front of the lads! I 'spect he was out on the batter again last night, the randy old sod!'

Boyes watched the Buffer hanging over the guardrail to point where the extra fenders were to be placed as the hull began to angle away from the *Ranger*, so that the two sterns seemed to be opening like one great hinge.

Jardine said, '*See?*' He watched happily as the Buffer snarled at a seaman for not putting the right hitch on a fender.

'If you lose that fender, you'll spend the rest of the war payin' for it!' He certainly sounded out of sorts.

Jardine nodded. 'Anything in a skirt. Like a rat up a pump, 'e is.'

It was still too dark for him to see Boyes blush.

The communications rating called, 'Let go sternrope!'

Men ran amongst the jutting objects, the wire clattering inboard behind him where it was overpowered and lashed down like an endless serpent.

The hull was still swinging out, and when Boyes glanced up towards the bridge he saw the first lieutenant leaning right out to watch the remaining mooring wire.

No matter what, he thought. I'll be like that one day.

Froth and spray burst up around the low stern and Jardine said, ' 'Ere we go again then.'

'Let go aft, sir!'

Mr Bone watched the last wire snaking inboard through its fairlead and snapped, 'Take this message to the first lieutenant.' He thrust out a folded piece of paper to Leading Seaman Guttridge. 'We need a new wire afore we comes in again. Might as well break it out of the store now, right?'

Guttridge showed his teeth in a grin and looked even more like a gipsy.

He gestured to Boyes. 'You—Useless Eustace! Take it to Jimmy the One!'

Jardine winked. 'Take it off yer back, Gerry. They don't mean no 'arm.'

Boyes hurried along the side deck, watching out for more obstacles until he reached the first ladder to the bridge. He felt that he understood what Jardine meant. They might use the way he spoke or his lack of experience as a butt for their jokes. Sooner or later they would turn to another newcomer. Either way, they had accepted him.

'Where are *you* going?'

Boyes gripped the ladder to prevent himself from falling as the hull heeled unexpectedly to a sharp turn. It was the midshipman, whom he had not seen before.

'I've been sent to the bridge, sir.'

A shaft of frail sunlight broke through the clouds and brought out the colour of the dazzle paint on the bridge. But Boyes could only stare at the frowning midshipman.

He exclaimed, 'Good heavens, it's *you*, Davenport!'

It was amazing, he thought dazedly. Davenport was about his own age, and they had been at the same school in Surbiton, in the same class for most of the time.

Davenport looked as if he had been hit in the face. He seized Boyes' arm and dragged him past the starboard Oerlikon mounting where a seaman gunner was already strapped in his harness and testing his sights against the land.

Davenport asked wildly, 'What are you doing here?'

It was such a ridiculous question that Boyes wanted to laugh. He replied, 'I was drafted—'

Davenport did not let him finish. 'You failed your C.W., did you?' He hurried on like an actor who has only just been given his lines. 'I can help you. But if they know we grew up together, I shall have to keep out of it.'

He straightened his back as a petty officer hurried down the ladder.

'And call me *sir*, next time!' Then he gripped his arm again, his voice almost pleading. 'Really, it will be better for your chances.'

Then he lowered himself to the deck and Boyes stood there

unmoving while he took it all in. A friend in the camp? He doubted it; in fact he had never really liked Davenport at school. All the same . . .

He reached the bridge and handed the paper to a boatswain's mate. The latter said, 'I'll see Jimmy gets it. Things is a bit fraught up 'ere at the moment.'

Boyes took a lingering glance around the open bridge. The rank of repeaters and telephones, a leading signalman with his glasses trained on the tower ashore, a look-out on either side, some officers grouped around the compass platform, the occasional murmur of orders up and down the wheelhouse voicepipe.

An officer in a soiled duffle-coat, his binoculars dangling from his chest, brushed past him. Then he hesitated. 'Who are you?'

Boyes recalled Mr Bone's tirade and answered cautiously, 'Ordinary Seaman Boyes, sir.'

The officer nodded and gave him a searching glance which Boyes could almost feel. 'Oh yes, the replacement.'

He unexpectedly held out his hand. 'Welcome to *Rob Roy*.' Then he walked aft to peer down at the quarterdeck.

Boyes whispered to the boatswain's mate, 'Which one is that?'

The man laughed. 'That's the Guv'nor. The Old Man.' he nudged him roughly. ' 'E won't shake yer 'and again if you meet 'im across the defaulters' table.'

Boyes barely heard him. The young officer was the *captain*.

Boyes's day was made.


'Cox'n on th' wheel, sir!' Beckett's voice sounded harsh as it echoed up from the wheelhouse directly below the bridge.

Ransome nodded to the vague shapes of the watchkeepers, then made his way to the tall, wooden chair which was bolted to the deck behind the glass screens.

Around and beneath him he could feel the vessel moving restlessly against the other minesweeper alongside, caught the acrid downdraught of funnel-gas as the wind buffeted the bridge.

It was darker than he had expected, the sky still grey beyond the fast-moving clouds.

He settled himself in the chair and tightened the fresh towel around his neck. He recalled something his father had said on mornings like this. *Spring in the air – ice on the wind.*

Voicepipes muttered around the bridge and he watched as familiar figures and faces took on personality. Shapeless in duffle-coats, but he would know any one of them in pitch-darkness.

The leading signalman, Alex Mackay, his cap fixed firmly to his head by its lowered chinstay, binoculars to his eyes as he watched the harbour for unexpected signals. They would be unlikely to get any, Ransome thought. As soon as they quit harbour they faced death in every mile. But you had to accept that. Accordingly, the minesweepers' comings and goings were taken for granted. *Routine.*

And if the air cringed to a sudden explosion and you saw one of your group blasted to fragments, you must accept that too. The navy's prayer, 'If you can't take a joke you shouldn't have joined', seemed to cover just about everything.

Standing by the wheelhouse voicepipe's bell-shaped mouth, Lieutenant Philip Sherwood stood with his gloved hands resting on the rail below the screen, one seaboot tapping quietly on the scrubbed gratings. He gave the impression that he was bored, indifferent to anything which might be waiting outside the harbour.

Sub-Lieutenant Tudor Morgan, the assistant navigator, crouched on the compass platform, using the spare moments to examine the gyro repeater and take imaginary 'fixes' on dark shapes ashore.

Ransome glanced round towards the *Ranger* alongside, pale blobs of faces watching while the hands stood at the guardrails handling the mooring wire and fenders, ready to cast off.

Above *Rob Roy*'s bridge their most valuable addition, the radar lantern, like a giant jampot, glistened in overnight damp or drizzle. It was their 'eye', all-seeing but unseen. Not even a dream when *Rob Roy* had first slid down into salt water some six years back.

Ransome wanted to leave the chair and prowl around the bridge as he always did before getting under way, but knew Hargrave would take it as a lack of confidence. He saw the heavy machine-gun mounting abaft the funnel swivel round, the six

41

muzzles moving in unison as its crew tested elevation and training. The two four-inch guns and a single Oerlikon on either side of the bridge completed their *official* armament. Ransome recalled Hargrave's surprise when he had seen some of the sailors cleaning an impressive array of light machine-guns which ranged from Vickers .303's to a couple of Bren guns. The previous skipper had taken *Rob Roy* to Dunkirk and had helped to rescue several hundred soldiers. When Ransome had assumed command and had asked the captain much the same question as Hargrave, he had replied, 'The army seemed to forget their weapons when we landed them in England.' He had given a wink. 'It seemed a pity to waste them, eh?'

Feet clattered on a bridge ladder and Ransome heard Sherwood mutter, 'God, I didn't know it was a black tie affair! A bit formal, what?'

Ransome shot him a glance to silence him and saw Hargrave taking a last glance at the forecastle deck where he had been speaking with Bunny Fallows, who was standing in the eyes of the ship near the bull-ring while he waited for Hargrave's order.

Ransome wondered what Hargrave thought of the sub-lieutenant. A temporary officer he might be, but he could not be faulted at his job. Beyond that he was a bloody menace, Ransome had decided. He was one of his small team he would not be sorry to lose.

Fallows would be waiting for just one seaman to make a mistake, and his clipped, aristocratic voice would be down on the man's head like a hammer. Fallows was really two people. At sea he was the perfect officer, with both eyes firmly set on the next step up the ladder of promotion. In harbour he often drank too much, and had been warned several times for abusing the hands when he could barely stand. As Campbell, the Chief, had once wryly commented, 'On the bridge he's a real little gent. When he's awash with booze I seem to hear the accent of a Glasgow keelie!' It was unusual for Campbell to make personal remarks about anyone. He certainly had Fallows' measure.

The loud hailer on *Ranger*'s bridge gave a shrill squeak, then Ransome heard the unmistakable tones of her captain, Lieutenant Commander Gregory. A good friend over the months they

OUNDLE INTERNATIONAL FESTIVAL 1998    01832 272026

Is Sponsored By BARCLAYS STOCKBROKERS

FRIDAY   17 JULY 1998
OUNDLE PARISH CHURCH

8.00pm

# NIKOLAI DEMIDENKO

Sponsor: PERKINS FOODS PLC

Ticket £7.00

Unreserved Seat          Ticket No 18

To be Retained

Performance Ticket Printing 01260 270164
No Refunds/Exchanges

had been sweeping together, but one you would never really know in a hundred years.

'Did you have a party last night?'

Ransome glanced at Hargrave as he spoke to Morgan while they stooped over the hooded chart-table. It *was* taking Hargrave far too long. *Rob Roy* should have been through the gate by now. Even to mention it would throw him off balance, and might discourage him from asking advice when it could prove to be vital. For all of them.

The magnified voice added, 'I suppose your ship is aground on gin bottles? I can give you a wee push if you like!'

Some of *Ranger*'s seamen grinned broadly.

Lieutenant Sherwood muttered, 'Stupid bugger!'

Hargrave crossed the bridge. 'Ready to single up, sir.' He seemed oblivious to the banter alongside.

'Carry on, Number One.' He tried to settle down in the chair. It was a strange, uncomfortable feeling he had never experienced before. It was like having an unknown driver take the wheel of your new car.

'Single up to backspring and stern rope!'

The dark figures came to life on the forecastle, and Ransome heard the scrape of wires along the steel decks, the throaty bark of the Gunner (T), Mr Bone, from the quarterdeck, his personal domain when the ship moored or got under way.

'Stand by wires and fenders!' Hargrave looked even taller on the starboard gratings as he watched the activity on both ships. He was going to pivot the ship round, using *Ranger*'s hull like a hinge. There was not enough room ahead to make a simple turn. Men scampered aft with extra fenders, and Topsy Turnham, the Buffer, could be heard threatening death to anyone who scored the new paint. 'Stand by!' Hargrave gestured to Morgan. 'Warn the wheelhouse!'

Ransome leaned forward to watch the ship's forecastle deck, like a pale spearhead in the feeble light.

Bunny Fallows cupped his hands. 'All clear forrard!'

Hargrave glanced briefly across the bridge at Ransome, but he did not turn. Hargrave waited for his breathing to steady. 'Slow astern port.'

The deck responded instantly and a steady froth of disturbed water surged away from the stern. The remaining spring took the strain, the Buffer and a leading seaman watching the wire tightening as the ship put all her weight against it. Turnham growled, 'Slack off there!' Or, 'Watch that bloody fender, man!' The bows began to swing outwards away from the other ship, from which came a muffled, ironic cheer.

Wider and wider until the two ships angled away from each other at about forty-five degrees.

Ransome cleared his throat, and knew that he was gripping his unlit pipe so tightly that it might snap unless Hargrave stopped the ship.

Hargrave called, 'Stop engines! Let go aft!'

'All clear aft, sir!' The boatswain's mate holding the bridge handset licked his lips. He must have been sharing Ransome's anxiety.

Hargrave nodded. 'Slow ahead together. Port twenty.'

Ransome did not raise his voice. 'Back the port engine, Number One.'

Their eyes met and Ransome smiled. 'I know from near misses that this corner is tighter than it looks.'

Hargrave lowered his mouth to the voicepipe but kept his eyes on Ransome. As if he wanted to see what he really meant, or if it was a criticism.

'Slow astern port!'

Back came Beckett's reply. 'Port engine slow astern, sir. Twenty of port wheel on!'

The ship moved very slowly beneath the shadow of the wall, whilst in the shadows astern the other minesweeper was already casting off her lines, her screws churning the water brilliant white against the weathered stone.

Ransome nodded. 'I've got her, Number One.' He moved to the voicepipe. 'Slow ahead together. Follow the markers, Swain.'

He looked at Hargrave. 'Best to leave it to the man on the wheel. Joe Beckett is the best there is. You can lose precious minutes by passing and repeating orders.' He touched his sleeve. Hargrave's jacket felt like ice. 'That was well done.'

Hargrave stared at him. 'Thank you, sir.'

The tannoy intoned, 'Hands fall in for leaving harbour! Attention on the upper deck, face to starboard!'

When Ransome looked again, *Ranger* was in line directly astern, her hull beginning to shine as the light grew stronger. The seagoing ensign, patched, tattered and grubby from funnel smoke, flapped stiffly from the gaff, and already most of the wires and heavy rope fenders had vanished, stowed away until the next time.

Ransome raised his powerful glasses and studied the undulating silhouette of the land. South-east England, which had had just about everything thrown at it. Blitzed, bombed, shelled, and nearly starved on more than one occasion when the convoys had been cut to ribbons in the Atlantic long before they had been close enough to face the lurking hazards of enemy mines.

'But not invaded.'

'*Sir?*' Hargrave looked at him.

Ransome glanced away. He had not realised he'd spoken aloud. He said, 'It's never stopped. We sweep every day, whether there's anything to sweep or not.' He smiled sadly as he remembered the ladies in black at the funeral, the schoolgirl in her blazer with a cardboard gas-mask container hanging from her shoulder. 'For as the King once said, how else do you know there's nothing there?'

The bows lifted and made the uneven lines of men on forecastle and quarterdeck sway like drunken sailors waiting for the liberty boat. It was as if the sea was already groping into the harbour to find them. To take them back where they belonged.

Ransome moved the gyro compass repeater and found he no longer wanted to talk. But he said, 'Fall out harbour stations. We'll exercise action stations and test guns in fifteen minutes.'

He heard Morgan whispering behind him. When to make the first turn. The course to steer. The latest wrecks to be checked against the chart. Above their heads the radar kept its silent vigil, and once into deeper waters the Asdic would begin to sweep the darkness beneath *Rob Roy's* pitted keel.

Ransome had seen it so many times, and yet it was always new. He smelt cocoa, 'kye' as the Jacks called it, and felt his stomach contract. He had slept like the dead, and was regretting the whisky it had taken to do that for him.

As he stepped down from the compass platform his hand brushed against the picture in his duffle-coat pocket. If anything went wrong this trip, he would still have that.

He tried not to think of the funeral, and of the boy called Tinker he had sent on compassionate leave.

A young seaman appeared on the top of the ladder, and was speaking with the boatswain's mate. A new face.

Behind him he heard Hargrave ask, 'Are the hands always dressed like that when we leave harbour?'

Morgan made to reply but Sherwood's voice was sharp and incisive.

'What, no swords and medals, Number One?' His voice was quieter as he swung away. 'It's not a cruiser. There's no safe way in this job!'

Ransome frowned. There was bad friction there. He would have to do something about it. But first he crossed to the young seaman, who had apparently carried a message to the bridge.

'Who are you?' It was not much, but it was the best he could do.

In line ahead the two fleet minesweepers pounded out of the harbour, their tattered ensigns making them appear strangely vulnerable.

They were back in the war.

# 4

# Battleground

Ransome half-turned in his chair and took a steaming cup from the boatswain's mate. Eight-fifteen. It was tea this time. As he sipped it, feeling its hot sweetness drive away the last of the whisky, he watched the horizon as it tilted slowly from side to side as if to slide *Rob Roy* back towards the land. It looked as if it was going to be a better day after all, he thought. Still heavy patches of cloud, but the sky above was blue, and when he looked towards the land he saw sunshine on the cliffs, the light reflecting from house windows. Bed-and-breakfasts in those far-off days, now billets for the army, every man doubtless aware of the enemy's nearness. It looked peaceful for all that, except for a cluster of barrage balloons, probably towards Walmer and Deal. Like basking whales, placid in the sunlight.

He felt the deck lift and dip down again, and found that he was on edge with a kind of eagerness to see the rest of the flotilla again. Actually it was only half the full group, as the fleet sweepers were working in these waters mainly to back up the many other vessels, ex-fishing trawlers, and the even smaller motor minesweepers, *Mickey Mouses* as they were nicknamed.

When the whole flotilla of eight ships was together they carried the Senior Officer aboard. Now he had to be content with his office ashore, a gaunt, former holiday hotel which had had its windows blown out so many times they used plywood and sandbags instead.

He smiled as he thought of the Senior Officer. Commander

47

Hugh Moncrieff, a proper old salt from the Royal Naval Reserve, was always good company, but Ransome was glad that his trips to sea in *Rob Roy* were rare these days. For he had been in command of this ship until handing over to Ransome. Even during the simplest manoeuvre you could feel Moncrieff's eyes everywhere, no doubt comparing, remembering how he would have performed it. Moncrieff had begged to be returned to a seagoing appointment so many times that even the Flag Officer Minesweeping was getting nasty about it.

Ransome glanced around the bridge. Hargrave had the forenoon watch, and was busily checking the chart. Davenport the midshipman was beside him, supposedly learning from his betters. He was unusually silent, Ransome thought. Sub-Lieutenant Morgan was staring ahead, ever watchful. The others, a signalman and two lookouts, also kept their eyes outboard, back and forth, their glasses sweeping an allotted arc, while overhead the radar, which had already reported the rest of the flotilla on a converging course, watched for anything they might miss.

The ship was at defence stations, with the short-range weapons permanently manned, and the remainder of the hands working about the upper deck, whilst aft the minesweeping party were busy preparing the float and otter for lowering once the sweep was begun. He could picture Mr Bone directing operations, although it would be Hargrave's job when they started in earnest. What had got Bone into sweepers, he wondered? They did not normally carry a torpedo gunner, so he must have volunteered. A hard, unyielding man who should have been at home with his grandchildren.

Hargrave stood beside him. 'Alter course in five minutes, sir.'

'Very well.' Ransome groped for his glasses as he saw some men on the forecastle pause to peer across the port bow.

Hargrave said, 'When I came on watch some of the off-duty hands were hanging about, a few even sleeping near the funnel for warmth.' He shrugged. 'I'd have thought they'd be glad to use the extra messdeck rather than that.'

Ransome raised himself in the chair and levelled his powerful glasses. The tide was on the turn so it was closer to the surface, like a slimy, abandoned submarine.

'Take a look, Number One.'

Hargrave fetched his glasses from the chart table and stared hard on the bearing.

Ransome watched his profile. 'That's a destroyer, HMS *Viper*, an old V & W class from the Great War.' He remembered the nausea when he had first passed near the submerged wreck; the sea was even shallower then. He had been in his first mine-sweeper, an old Grimsby trawler with an RNR skipper who seemed to feel his way about the Channel by the smell of it.

Ransome heard himself say, 'She hit a mine and went down in fifteen minutes.'

He waited for Hargrave to look at him. 'You mentioned the hands' "rig of the day" when we left harbour, right? And just now you wondered why they prefer to shiver on deck rather than go below? The *Viper*'s commanding officer was a thoughtful man. He sent half his company below to change into their number ones for a run ashore. They would waste less time that way. You can see how near home she was when the mine caught her.' He did not hide his bitterness. 'For weeks we had to pass that wreck, and at low water, until the Royal Marine divers could hack their way into her you could see their faces at the scuttles, arms moving in the water as if they were still trying to get out. Those old destroyers had no escape-hatches then, and the scuttles were too small to climb through.'

Hargrave lowered his glasses. It was as if he had seen it for himself.

'I – I'm sorry, sir. It answers both my questions.'

Later, as the other ships lifted from the sea, Leading Signalman Mackay climbed to the bridge and took over from his assistant. It was as if he knew. A lot of the old hands were like that. Men like Beckett, and the chief boatswain's mate. They were always nearby when their extra skill might be needed.

Almost at once a diamond-bright light began to blink across the grey, heaving water.

Mackay was using his old telescope. It had been his father's; he in turn had been a chief yeoman of signals in the peacetime navy.

'From *Firebrand*, sir. *We were getting lonely.*'

Ransome watched the rising pall of smoke as the leading ships drew nearer. *Smokey Joes* they called them, and no wonder. More veterans from the other conflict, and just about the only coal-fired warships still afloat.

He said, 'Make to *Firebrand. Take station as ordered.*' His mouth softened only slightly. '*Follow father.*'

Hargrave was watching him. 'Your last command was one of those, sir?'

Ransome nodded. He could still feel the devastating impact when the mine had caught them halfway along the side of the forecastle. It was like being pounded senseless although he could not recall hearing any sound of the explosion.

He answered slowly, 'Yes. The *Guillemot.*' His eyes were distant while he studied the other minesweepers as they started to turn in a wide arc. 'Good ships in spite of the coal. They could manage seventeen knots like *Rob Roy*, with a following wind anyway.' He smiled, the strain falling away. 'And we never lost a man.'

Hargrave watched, feeling his hurt for the ship which had gone down under another captain. They had picked up only two. He thought, *You never lost a man, you mean.*

Ransome raised his glasses and waited for the third vessel to harden in the lenses.

He said, '*Firebrand* and *Fawn* are twins, but the rearmost ship is *Dryaden*, an ex-Icelandic trawler.'

'I gather they're a bit cramped, sir?' He suddenly did not want Ransome to stop, to shut him out as he had that morning.

Ransome studied the *Dryaden*'s perfect lines, her high raked stem and a foredeck which would ride any sea, even a hurricane.

'This one is a thoroughbred, Number One, not like my old tub. They just threw out the fish and pitched us in. Not like *Dryaden* at all. She was taken from the Icelanders when our patrols caught her smuggling diesel and stores to U-boats.' He nodded again. 'A fine piece of shipbuilding.'

Hargrave remembered the pencil drawing in Ransome's cabin. 'Was that your line, sir?'

'My father owns the yard. I was beginning to get the hang of designing boats.' He heard the girl's voice as if she had called out on the wind. *Show me what you do. Please.*

50

He said, 'Fix our position again, then make the turn, Number One.' He waved towards the salt-smeared glass screen. 'We lead, the others follow in echelon.' Ransome forced a smile. 'Just like you learned in training, eh?'

'What about *Dryaden*, sir?'

His eyes hardened. 'She drops the dan buoys to mark our progress. They call her the *blood-boat*. No need to stretch the imagination for that, is there?'

As Hargrave returned to the chart Ransome listened first to the radar reports, then to the starboard look-out as he called, 'Fast-moving craft at Green four-five, sir!'

The short-range weapons moved their muzzles on to the bearing until the gunnery speaker barked, 'Disregard! All angels!'

Ransome watched the low hulls as they flung up great wings of creaming spray. M.T.Bs, back from the other side, making for their base, probably Felixstowe. How many had they lost?

He tried not to think of Tony, always the one in a hurry. Falling from a horse, capsizing a sailing-dinghy, everything was a great game to him. He listened to the throaty, animal growl of engines. He would find this a very different kind of game.

He heard the leading signalman say contemptuously, 'There they go, the Glory Boys!'

Ransome turned. 'Maids-of-all-work maybe.' His voice had an edge to it. 'We're just the charwomen, so let's bloody well get on with it!'

He slithered from the chair, angry with himself and knowing why, angry too at the hurt on Mackay's open features.

He leaned over the voicepipe. 'Cox'n?'

'*Sir?*' As usual, Beckett was ready.

'Half ahead together!'

Beckett repeated the order, then. 'Both engines half ahead, sir. Revolutions one-one-zero.'

Ransome moved to his gyro repeater and stared through the V-sight while he steadied the compass with the azimuth circle.

He said, 'Starboard ten.'

He ignored Beckett's voice in the pipe as he watched the bright flickering colour of the dan buoy's flag creep across the sight.

'Midships.' He licked his lips. *I must not get rattled.* Bad memories meant death. *'Steady!'*

Beckett would be down there peering at his steering repeater as it ticked round in the sealed wheelhouse.

'Steady, sir, course zero-two-zero.'

Ransome could just make out the next dan buoy's flag beyond this one. The breathing-space.

'Steer zero-two-two.'

He straightened his back. 'Pipe the minesweeping party aft, Thomas!' To Hargrave he said, 'Ready?'

Hargrave tugged his cap over his forehead. At least he had discarded his collar and tie, and wore a white sweater instead.

'When you are, sir.'

Ten minutes later Ransome hoisted the signal *Out sweeps to starboard.*

As the leading signalman and his mate watched the flags streaming out from the yard Ransome said simply, 'Didn't mean to bite your head off, Mack.' He turned to watch the other ships acknowledge the signal and so did not see Mackay's pleasure, or Midshipman Davenport's disapproval.

Ransome searched the sky too. If it was fine for sweeping so was it for aircraft. Originally one of the minesweepers had hoisted a tethered barrage balloon in case they were pounced on by a single fighter or dive-bomber.

It had its drawbacks. For it had acted as an accurate marker for the German guns across the Channel.

He thought of Hargrave's face when he had told him about the sunken destroyer *Viper.*

Feet clattered on the deck below, while heavy gear was dragged aft by the Buffer's party. At the big winch the P.O. stoker and Mr Bone would be watching the sweep-wire, hoping or dreading as the mood took them. Hargrave was with experts. He should be all right.

He climbed on to his chair as Morgan took over the watch.

*And why not? You shouldn't have joined etc. etc.*

The boatswain's mate put down his handset.

'Sweep's out and runnin', sir!'

Ransome dug out his pipe. Now the waiting game began.

Petty Officer 'Topsy' Turnham banged the palms of his thick leather gloves together and said cheerfully, 'Sweet as a nut, sir!'

Hargrave watched the fat, torpedo-shaped float with its little flag cruising jauntily through the water. He had to admit that it had gone much more smoothly than he had dared to hope. He glanced round at the sweeping party as they secured their gear yet again without the need for any comment or order from anyone. And that was the real difference, he decided. On the mine-sweeping course they had all been novices. For every manoeuvre ashore and afloat they had constantly changed places with one another, taking, then giving orders, enduring confusion and caustic comments from their instructors.

In *Rob Roy* the business of putting out the sweep-wire had gone like clockwork. First the heavy Oropesa float, which had required manhandling clear of the side while it was lowered outboard. All available men were piped aft to assist, and Hargrave knew that any error of judgment could mean at best a crushed hand, or someone's arm pulped between the float and the ship's side. Next the otter-board, a clumsy device which looked something like a farm gate, with toothed and explosive wire-cutters, and finally, at the end of the Oropesa sweep and closest to the hull, was the *kite*, which like the otter would hold the sweep-wire beneath the surface at the required depth and veer it some forty-five degrees out and away from the ship's quarter.

Now, as the black balls were hoisted to masthead and starboard yard to show any stranger which side the sweep was dragging, *Rob Roy* and her consorts were on station in an overlapping line, in echelon.

The ship felt heavier in the water, which was not surprising with five hundred yards of stout wire towing astern.

Hargrave said, 'How is it in rough weather, Buffer?'

The petty officer rubbed his chin with the back of his glove. It made a rasping sound.

'Dicey, sir. It's when th' wire snares somethin' you gotta be all about. You can't *see* nothin' in a drop of roughers, and the bloody thing can be right under yer counter before you knows it!'

He winked at the petty officer stoker who was controlling the powerful winch.

'Old Nobby 'ere was blown right off 'is last ship.' He raised his voice above the din. 'Blew the ruddy boat right out of yer 'and, didn't it, Nobby?'

The other P.O. gave a grim smile. 'Coulda been worse,' was all he said.

Hargrave thought of the disciplined world of the cruiser. It was impossible to compare with this one, amongst men who never seemed to take death and disaster seriously. Not openly at least.

Hargrave returned his gaze to the Oropesa float as it appeared to bound across the water like a pursuing dolphin. He had seen the incoming M.T.Bs, just as he had watched a flight of Spitfires when they had lifted from the land like hawks, before taking formation and heading towards France and the enemy. They were fighting, hitting back.

'And we keep this up all day, Buffer?'

Turnham glanced at him, enjoying the officer's despair. 'Aye, we do, sir. Up this way, drop our dan buoys in case some careless geezer decides to take a short cut through the swept channel an' misses it like, then back to do it all over again.'

Hargrave wanted to remain silent and not display his uncertainty by asking questions. But the Buffer was a professional seaman, and a regular of the old style, although you would hardly think so to see him in his patched jacket with its faded red badges, and a cap which looked as if he slept in it.

He persisted, 'And at night?'

Turnham gestured savagely at a seaman who was casually coiling some wire.

'Not *that* way, you numbskull! Like I showed you!' He seemed to realise what Hargrave had said. 'Well, sometime we 'ave to sweep at night.' He grinned at a sudden memory. 'We 'ad some Yankee brass 'ats visitin' the flotilla a while back, and one of 'em says we'll soon 'ave the know-how to sweep in pitch-darkness.' He shook his head. 'The Old Man gives 'im a saucy look an' says, we bin doin' that for months, *sir*.'

Hargrave knew that the Buffer was quite a bit older than Ransome. Old Man did not seem to fit.

The leading seaman called, 'All secure, sir.'

Turnham nodded. ' 'E's a good 'and, sir. Bit too much mouth, but knows sweepin' inside out.'

Hargrave heard feet on the deck and saw the gunnery officer striding aft with one of his men hurrying to keep up.

Bunny Fallows would take some getting used to, he thought. Like now, for instance. He was wearing a bright balaclava helmet on his trim red hair, and on the front of his headgear he wore a large knitted rabbit. It seemed out of character for an officer who spent his time trying to be more pusser than any gunnery officer at Whale Island. At the same time Hargrave sensed that if Fallows was no good at his job the *Old Man* would get rid of him. It was an odd mixture.

Turnham had seen his glance, and had guessed what he was thinking. He would have liked to add his own twopennyworth, but he knew better than to push his luck. Nobody on the lower deck, and in the petty officers' mess in particular, had any time for Fallows. A good woman would snap the little bugger in half.

Instead he said, 'We're due for a spot of leaf soon, sir.'

It was the first Hargrave had heard of it. 'Really?'

Turnham almost licked his lips. 'Six days up the line with a nice little party.' His eyes gleamed at the prospect. 'Beats cock-fightin' anytime!'

Hargrave turned and looked up at the bridge as the signal lamp began to flash towards the other ships.

He said, 'They've sighted wreckage ahead.'

Turnham strode aft and called to his team. 'Stand by on the winch, wreckage ahead!'

The leading hand called Guttridge eyed him with surprise. 'I always thought you said you can't read morse, Buffer?'

Turnham showed his teeth. 'Can't neither, Gipsy. But the new Jimmy can!'

The telephone buzzed in its case below the gun and the communications rating called, 'From the bridge, sir. Wreckage ahead!'

Turnham grinned even wider so that he looked like a small ape. 'We *knows* that, sonny! The first lieutenant told us!'

Hargrave dug his hands into his pockets and looked away. He did not belong here. He must not allow himself to fall into the trap. And yet he knew that Turnham's obvious pleasure at knowing something before being told by the bridge had made him feel just the opposite.

The wreckage was no hazard to the sweep-wire; it was all too small and scattered for that.

Turnham watched the pathetic remains drift down either beam: broken planks, some charred, a few lifebuoys, great disconnected patches of oil, and a solitary deckchair.

He said, 'Last convoy that went through, I 'spect, sir.' He shaded his eyes and added, 'No dead-uns though, thank Gawd. We got no room for corpses in this ship. The convoy's tail-end Charlie would 'ave picked 'em up.'

The watches changed, soup and sandwiches were carried to the gun crews while the work continued with a new dan buoy to mark each section as they swept it.

Planes passed occasionally overhead, some of them probably hostile, but today nobody was interested in the staggered line of minesweepers.

Hargrave knew that he was being watched by the men working around him, and tried not to show any emotion or surprise when he saw the extent of this largely unknown war. The masts and upperworks of so many ships which had been mined, shelled or torpedoed in sight of safety. The wrecks were marked on all the charts, but seeing them like this was totally different from a dry correction in A.F.Os. Some had tried to struggle into the shallows to avoid blocking the swept channel, others had run amok, on fire and abandoned, to line the channel like gravestones.

Turnham occasionally pointed out a particular wreck which *Rob Roy* had tried to help, or from which they had taken off survivors.

Hargrave was stunned to find that he felt cheated, as if all the promise and training at Dartmouth, and later when he had served in two different cruisers, had been a complete waste of time. That until he had joined this slow-moving, poorly armed ship he had seen nothing and done nothing of any use.

Wrecks, stick-like masts, and mournfully clanging green buoys to mark those which lay in deeper water – it was a battleground, no less than the broad Atlantic.

The communications rating called, 'From the bridge, sir. Take in the sweep.'

Hargrave looked at him without seeing him. *All we do is clean up the mess, and leave the fighting to others.*

By dusk they had swept the channel six times without finding a single mine. For Hargrave it had been a long, long day — and his first lesson.

Ian Ransome wriggled his muffled body against the back of his bridge chair and began to wipe the eyepieces of his binoculars for the hundredth time. It was bitterly cold on the open bridge and against the moonlit rim of a cloud he could see the starboard look-out's hair ruffling in the wind like grass on a hillside. Like most of the watchkeepers, the look-out disdained to wear any form of headgear. Some sailors swore that it hampered the faint sound of danger, and others hated to wear their steel helmets anyway, no matter what Admiralty Fleet Orders had to say about it. Some six months back *Rob Roy* had been under a surprise attack from an aircraft, and their only casualty had been a seaman whose nose had been broken by his companion's helmet rim as he had ducked for cover.

Ransome fought back a yawn. It was three in the morning or thereabouts, and the ship was still closed-up at action stations. At night their duty was to patrol the swept channel, not to look for mines but to watch out for any stealthy intruder or aircraft trying to drop them.

The worst part was over. An hour back they had received and acknowledged the brief challenge of the eastbound convoy's wing escort. It was amazing when you thought about it. One convoy forging around the North Foreland, with no lights, hugging one another's shadows like blind men, and they would soon pass another convoy coming down the east coast. Because of the narrowness of the swept channel between land and their own huge minefield, the convoys would have to gridiron through each other. No lights, and only a few with radar, and yet Ransome could recall only one serious collision.

He listened to the slow, muted beat of engines and pictured Campbell and his men sealed in their brightly lit world. Almost everyone else was above decks, huddled around the gun mountings and shell-hoists, trying to keep awake, praying for the next fanny of steaming kye and some damp sandwiches.

*Fawn* and *Firebrand*, the two Smokey Joes, had returned to base to re-bunker; they would be back on the job tomorrow.

Now, at reduced speed, *Rob Roy*, followed by the vague blur of *Ranger*'s silhouette with the Arctic trawler *Dryaden* somewhere astern, continued their patrol in the area known as Able-Yoke, a huge triangle off the North Foreland which commanded the approaches to both of the major rivers, Thames and Medway.

The eastbound convoy's escort commander had reported one straggler, an elderly collier in ballast. He could not spare anything to watch over her, so she must make her own way into the Medway once she was *round the corner*, if she could not complete her repairs in time to rejoin the convoy.

There was a faint blink of light from the shaded chart-table and Ransome heard Sub-Lieutenant Morgan explaining something to the new replacement, Ordinary Seaman Boyes. He was in his division, and Morgan obviously thought he would be better employed at action stations helping with charts than fumbling around an unfamiliar ammunition hoist. Boyes was obviously keen and intelligent, and even though his chance of a temporary commission had been dashed by the bald comment, *Lacks confidence. Unlikely to make a suitable candidate*, he might have something to offer on the bridge.

Lieutenant Sherwood was officer-of-the-watch, although Ransome liked them to change round regularly so that they knew each other's work. *Just in case*. It did not do to dwell on it.

Sherwood was speaking into the voicepipe now.

'Watch your head. Steer one-nine-oh.' Then there was Beckett's harsh reply.

Sherwood was a strange man. He shied away from close relationships. Poor David was the only one who had got along with him, and then not too close. He was a loner in more ways than one. His parents and sisters had been killed in the first months of the war during an air raid. Although he never mentioned it, Ransome guessed it was his reason for his dedication to his work, and why he had volunteered for the most dangerous assignment of all in the first place.

Midshipman Davenport's voice echoed up another pipe from the automatic pilot in its tiny compartment within the wheelhouse.

'Plot – Bridge?'

Sherwood grunted. 'Bridge.'

'C-7 buoy abeam to starboard, one mile, sir.'

'Very well.' Sherwood peered round for Morgan. 'Get that?'

All as usual. Ransome wanted to walk about and restore the circulation and warmth to his limbs. But any movement might break their concentration. And yet if he stayed in the chair he might nod off. It had happened before.

A feeble light winked abeam, one of the buoys still marking the channel. Many were extinguished for the duration, and even the helpless lightships had been strafed by enemy fighters so that most of them were withdrawn from station. Those which remained were a godsend, and were presumably left alone because they also aided the enemy.

It felt as if the ship was without purpose and direction as she moved slowly into the darkness, an occasional burst of spray her only sign of movement. There were destroyer patrols, old V & W's like the poor *Viper*. Sloops and others from years back, even peacetime paddle-steamers which had carried carefree passengers from Brighton and Margate were employed in the grim work of minesweeping and inshore patrols.

Why were they never prepared?

'Radar – Bridge!' Surprisingly it was Hargrave's voice.

Ransome picked up the handset. 'Captain.'

'I think we've picked up the straggler, sir. Green four-five, two miles.'

Ransome said, 'Keep me posted, Number One.'

They should have spotted the straggler earlier; doubtless in one of the new destroyers they would have done. But here in the channel, with shadows and static bouncing off the land, they were lucky to see anything.

So Hargrave was using his time to familiarise himself with the ship's defences. It was a start.

Ransome said, 'Prepare recognition signal, Bunts. Warn 'A' Gun.'

He heard Fallows's sharp voice acknowledging the order from the bridge and pictured him near the gun in his ridiculous balaclava.

The other convoy would be heading along the Suffolk coast about now. Full hulls destined for other ports to be offloaded into heavier ships for the next part of the obstacle race. The Atlantic, the *killing-ground* as the sailors called it, or deeper to the south – the Indian Ocean, anywhere.

The convoy might wait for a night-time dash through the narrow seas, or if they were fast enough might risk the daylight, aircraft, Cap Gris Nez guns and all.

Ransome slid from the chair and moved to the opposite side of the bridge. Shafts of pain shot through his legs with every step and he swore silently while he waited for the cramp to go away. He stood on the steel locker which held the spare signal flares so that he was able to train his glasses above the smeared screen. He felt the wind across his cheek, the rasp of the towel, now sodden with spray, against his neck.

No sign of the straggler yet. And yet the moon was up there, glinting around some of the clouds, making an occasional silver line on the horizon.

Above the bridge, Hargrave crouched over the senior radar operator's shoulder and stared at the revolving, misty shaft of light until his eyes throbbed. Like a badly developed film shot underwater, he thought. Little blips and smudges abounded, but he had already taught himself to recognise the unchanging out-line of the coast, unchanging except that it quivered in the strange light as if about to disintegrate.

Booker, the operator, said, 'With the new sets, you can pick out individual buoys no matter what back-echo you get.' His voice was gentle, a New Zealander from Wellington. How had he found his way here, Hargrave wondered?

Booker added, 'Watch the ship, sir.' He gestured with a pencil. 'She's almost up to that buoy now. Better tell the Old – I mean the captain.'

Hargrave hesitated. 'The buoy looks too big.'

Booker chuckled. 'It's marking a wreck, sir. Upperworks of the tanker *Maidstone*.' He glanced at his clipboard of wrecks and unusual marks in the channel, so that his eyes shone green in the twisting phosphorescent glow. 'Why, sometimes at low water —'

He broke off as Hargrave snatched up the handset. 'Radar — Bridge!'

It seemed to take an age for Ransome to answer.

'Sir, the wreck buoy at Green four-five. We've picked up the upperworks . . .'

Ransome sounded calm. 'Impossible, Number One, it's high water now —'

Then Hargrave heard him shout, 'Starshell! Green four-five! Range four thousand yards!'

Booker stared at the set, then he exclaimed, 'Jesus, sir! It's moving!'

The E-boat must have been idling near the wreck buoy, taking its time after the convoy had passed, neither wishing to be seen nor to engage. The unexpected arrival of the lonely straggler must have taken the E-boat completely by surprise, as with a crashing roar of power it surged away from the buoy, ripping the night apart with its Daimler Benz engines.

Ransome pounded the rail with his fist. '*Open fire!*'

The gun below the bridge recoiled violently and seconds later, with the echo of the explosion still rolling across the water, the starshell cast its blinding light across the scene, making night into day. It was all there, the rising jagged wash of the E-boat as it increased speed away from the land, twin splashes when two torpedoes hit the water and tore towards the helpless collier.

'All guns open fire!'

The air cringed to the rattle of Oerlikons and machine-guns, the vivid balls of tracer lifting away from the ship and then from *Ranger* astern to plunge down on the fast-moving E-boat.

The explosions were dulled by distance, but the giant waterspouts that shot up alongside the collier told their own story.

'Radar — Bridge! E-boat steering oh-seven-zero! Losing contact!'

Ransome thrust his hands into his pockets as the moon broke

through the clouds, so that when the starshell died they would miss nothing. The collier was going down fast, the single, spindly funnel tearing adrift and lurching over the side with one of the loading derricks. They could hear her anchor cable running out, the explosions had probably done that, and in the arctic moonlight Ransome saw the rising wall of smoke and steam. One torpedo at least must have found the old ship's engine-room. Nobody would get out of there. He thought of Campbell; he would be listening, understanding better than anyone. Scalded to death as the sea roared in.

Ransome shook himself. 'Scrambling nets at the double! Signal *Ranger* to stand off and cover us!' He craned over the voicepipe, his eyes on the reflected ripple of flames as the other ship caught fire.

'Swain! Close as you can! Dead slow both engines!'

'Aye, aye, sir!'

He heard the tinny rattle of the ceasefire gong and imagined the E-boat racing away like an assassin. Forty-two knots against *Rob Roy*'s maximum of seventeen. He felt the bitterness welling up inside him.

'Stand by to come alongside starboard side-to.' He watched the other ship loom from the darkness, the familiar crackle of flames, tiny pathetic figures running, but to where? At least she wasn't a tanker. The whole sea would be ablaze by now.

He leaned over. 'Starboard a point, Swain. *Steady* now.'

He heard Hargrave beside him. 'Well done, Number One.' He kept his gaze on the other ship as men ran forward with the Buffer to wedge fenders into place for the impact. It would have to be quick.

'I – I'm sorry –'

'Don't keep apologising. You saw a flaw in the picture.' Hargrave had obviously been expecting to be blamed in some way.

Ransome said tersely, 'Stop together! Port ten!'

The ship was towering above the starboard anchor now. They could all smell the fire, the charred paint, even hear the jubilant roar of inrushing water. A ship dying.

'Get up forrard, Number One. Fast as you like. She's going to roll over. Haul those poor bastards on board!'

Minutes dragged like hours, and a fire-fighting team dashed into the bows as flames licked over the fairleads and made some of the seamen leap to safety.

To Sherwood, Ransome said, 'The E-boat was lying low. You know what that means?'

Sherwood's pale features shone with the orange light from the fires, his eyes like twin flames.

'She was dropping mines, sir.'

Ransome craned over the screen and saw Hargrave signal with his hands.

He snapped, 'Half astern together! Wheel amidships!'

Slowly at first and then with sudden desperation *Rob Roy*'s screws thrashed the sea into a surge of foam as she backed away from the sinking collier.

Ransome heard the thunder of heavy equipment tearing adrift and smashing through the hull, saw the old bows rise as she began to turn turtle. Whoever had been left behind would stay with her.

Hargrave clambered into the bridge. 'Eight survivors, sir. Two badly burned. The P.O.S.B.A. is coping with them.'

They both watched as the ship dived in a welter of leaping spray and acrid smoke. She did not have far to go, and hit the seabed with such a crash that it felt as if the minesweeper had run aground.

Ransome said, 'Stop together.' To Sherwood he added, 'Resume course and speed.' He looked at Hargrave. 'All right?'

'One of them was nearly burned alive, sir. How can they —' He broke off as a dark figure handed Ransome a signal flimsy.

Ransome held it beneath the chart table's hood and said quietly, 'We shall begin sweeping at 0500, Number One.' He watched Hargrave's astonishment. 'What did you expect, a medal?'

He looked at the rising welter of flotsam from the vanished collier.

'All part of the job. Now take over while I try and outguess the Krauts.' He hesitated by the chart table. 'Nothing moves until we say so. If that's any comfort, Number One?'

Hargrave heard someone retching and knew it was young Boyes.

63

They had been in action just moments ago, tracer tearing the night apart while a ship had blown up before his eyes. Now even the moon had gone into hiding, ashamed perhaps for all of them.

Again it was like being cheated. There would be no call to arms, men facing their front to defy the enemy.

Just the cold signal. *Begin sweeping at 0500.*

Hargrave stepped up beside Ransome's tall chair and leaned against the screen. Below by 'A' Gun he could hear a man whistling as he sponged out the muzzle.

Afterwards he thought it was like a lament.

# 5

# *Next of Kin*

The weeks which followed Hargrave's arrival on board *Rob Roy* were an unending test to his ability and patience as first lieutenant. The strain of minesweeping was double-edged; day after day the routine never changed, sweeping from first light to dusk and often patrols during the night. And yet while there was both boredom and frustration the anxiety of waiting for the unexpected was always there.

Four days at sea, then perhaps one or two in harbour, when tempers flared, or the gripping, suppressed fear erupted into drunken fights ashore, with the inevitable queue at the first lieutenant's defaulters' table the next day.

Convoys threaded their way back and forth through the narrows and around the newspapers' beloved Hellfire Corner. The enemy continued his relentless attack by air, by E-boats, and by bombardment. Men, usually cheerful, disappeared on compassionate leave to return red-eyed and despairing. In some ways it was wrong to have them back, for their private grief, the loss of a wife or family, made them slipshod in a job where carelessness could mean sudden death.

Only from that other war in the Middle East came daily news of success and advances where before there had been retreat and chaos.

The almost legendary Eighth Army, which had been the last line to stand between Rommel's crack Afrika Korps and the conquest of Egypt, had never stopped hitting back. The infantry must have marched and fought all the way from El Alamein, following the coast through Libya and on into Tunis itself. There had been no stopping them. Now, if the news reports could be believed, the enemy's retreat had turned into a rout. The once unbeatable German desert army was hemmed in near Cape Bon. After that, there was nowhere else to go but across the water to Sicily or Italy. All those months, famous names of places like Tobruk and Benghazi, which had changed hands so often it was said that the wretched inhabitants kept pictures of both Churchill and Hitler in their cafés until they were certain who was the victor, were a part of history.

Hargrave watched the resentful faces across the defaulters' table. One of them had been the young seaman Tinker who had returned from leave overdue after fighting a losing battle with the M.P.s. Joe Beckett, the burly coxswain, had told Hargrave in private, ' 'E's a fine lad, sir, never no trouble, but you know 'ow it is, like. 'Is dad was always away puttin' up aircraft 'angers, and his mum was 'avin' it off most of the time with an A.R.P. bloke.'

Hargrave had replied, 'It's no excuse. You should know that, Cox'n.'

Beckett had glared back at him. ' 'Cause I'm a reg'lar, is that wot you mean, sir?'

'Partly. And because you are expected to maintain discipline too!'

They had barely spoken since.

The lower deck buzz about leave, or leaf as Topsy Turnham called it, proved to be faulty, so that when the news did come it ran through the whole ship like a tonic.

Hargrave heard it first from the captain when he mounted the bridge to take over the forenoon watch.

Ransome was leaning back in his chair, as if he never left it, letting the warm breeze ruffle his hair, his grubby duffle-coat wide open while he stared up at the sky. It was strange to be steaming ahead of their consorts with no tell-tale black balls hoisted, or the Oropesa float skimming above the water far out on the ship's quarter.

Somewhere to port lay the great expanse of the Thames Estuary, but the land in the early sunshine was merely a purple blur. No Channel guns to watch and estimate their positions, and some chance of an early warning of any sort of air attack.

Ransome greeted him with, 'What it is to feel the sun, Number One!' He stretched his arms and gave a huge yawn. In those few seconds he looked like a boy again, Hargrave thought.

'And another thing.' Ransome groped in his pocket. 'Just had a signal. The flotilla is to enter Chatham Dockyard at the completion of the next sweep. Just think, a proper refit for once!'

Emotions chased one another across Hargrave's features. A chance to see his father perhaps, to obtain a transfer, a different appointment somewhere.

'That's good news, sir. I hope it reflects on the defaulters' table.'

Ransome wedged his pipe between his teeth and regarded him gravely. 'There's responsibility on both sides of that table, Number One.' He changed his mood with the subject. 'I might have guessed why the Boss is taking us out of Able Yoke. We'll be nice and close to Chatham on this sweep.'

Hargrave tried to concentrate on what he was saying. *Rob Roy* and the others had been ordered to sweep another sector of the war channel, to the east of Shoeburyness. There had been no explanation, and Hargrave thought it was more likely because they were short of sweepers as usual, rather than caring about *Rob Roy*'s proximity to Chatham for a refit.

Ransome said, 'I want to begin the first sweep at noon. Make a signal to that effect to the group.'

'Something up, sir?'

'A fast southbound convoy. The RAF are laying on a bit of hostility over the other side to keep their minds occupied. So it's obviously important. Put the word about the ship, although I expect most of the lads knew of the leave before I did. It may not be a long break this time so make sure that the ones with the farthest to go leave first. The rest can have local leave, so take every case on its merit. But no defaulters' grudges, Number One.' He watched him, his eyes level. 'All right?'

Hargrave nodded and climbed on to the compass platform to check the course which required to be steered in this powerful offshore current. He saw Morgan watching him, the way he dropped his eyes when he saw him.

Hargrave gestured to the signalman. 'Write this down, Bunts. To *Ranger*, repeated to the rest of the group —'

He looked at the glassy swell as it tilted the hull more steeply in the path of the sunshine.

*They dislike me for my ideas on discipline, do they? The sooner I'm off this damned ship the better!*

In the wheelhouse beneath Hargrave's feet, Ordinary Seaman Boyes was carefully polishing the glass of the automatic plot table. By day, the thick black-out curtains which separated it from the rest of the bridge were lashed up to the deckhead. It made the place seem larger, and with the windows and scuttles clipped open Boyes sensed a new atmosphere, relaxed and cheerful.

Reeves the chief quartermaster, a ruddy-faced leading seaman with two good conduct badges on his sleeve, watched the tape of the gyro-repeater as it ticked a fraction this way or that, to be corrected effortlessly by his hands on the wheel. On either side of him a telegraphsman stood by his engine-room and revolutions speed control, but they were chatting quietly, telling jokes but careful not to stand too close to the voicepipe's big bell-mouth.

By the opposite door which opened on to a bridge wing, Topsy Turnham the Buffer was expertly splicing a signal halliard and muttering fiercely, 'Bloody green 'orns, they don't teach 'em nothin'!' But he obviously enjoyed showing off his skills.

The chief quartermaster asked casually, 'Wot you doin' when we gets leave, Buffer?'

Turnham's eyes twinkled. 'Nice little party up the line, I got.' He did not see the others exchange winks. 'Tender as a boiled owl, she is —'

Boyes listened while he concentrated on his polishing. *Sharing it.*

'I shall come back a new man!'

'Make sure she don't give you summat else to bring back with you, Buffer!' They all joined in the laughter until Hargrave's voice echoed down the pipe.

'Less noise in the wheelhouse! Report to me, Reeves, when you're relieved!'

Reeves lowered his head. 'Christ Almighty!'

Turnham scowled and straighted his battered cap. 'Leave Jimmy to me. I've just about 'ad a gutful of '*im*!'

One of the telegraphsmen grinned. 'Ain't that the truth?'

Dead on noon the four fleet minesweepers hoisted their black balls and took station on the leader, like sheep responding to a familiar shepherd.

The sky remained clear, and apart from the deep unbroken swell, the sea was without malice.

Boyes went to the bridge to join Sub-Lieutenant Morgan by the chart-table, while Lieutenant Sherwood took several fixes from the gyro-compass to make certain *Rob Roy* was exactly on course. Boyes took it all in, from the clatter of Leading Signalman Mackay's Aldis lamp, to the regular reports from the W/T Office, or from the quarterdeck as the sweep streamed away on the starboard quarter.

Most of all he watched the captain as he moved occasionally from side to side, or levelled his glasses on the next astern. *Ranger* had signalled that she had lost a dan buoy overboard and had requested time to recover it. Now she too had her sweep in the water, but was following astern of the two coal-burners. At this slow speed, that same black smoke would come gushing on to *Rob Roy* once they turned to sweep in the opposite direction.

Mackay had remarked to a boatswain's mate, 'Just about due for a bloody refit, the lot of us, me especially!'

Ransome had thrown off his duffle-coat and was sitting sideways on his chair. He saw Boyes watching him and said, 'Settled in?'

Boyes nodded and blushed. 'Aye, aye, sir.' He grew redder as Morgan grinned and Sherwood exclaimed softly, 'Another admiral, no less!'

Ransome smiled. 'Ignore it.'

Boyes was stunned at being spoken to like this, and the fact that even Sherwood, a man who was said to be a bit 'round the bend', seemed able to accept his presence.

He replied, 'Yes, sir. I – I'm still not quite sure what happens when the sweep goes out, but –'

The look-out yelled, '*Mine*, sir! *Green four-five!*'

The others ran to the side, glasses trained, all humour gone.

'Make a signal to the group, Bunts! *Mine to starboard!*'

He ignored the clatter of the lamp's shutter, the bright stabbing light of the next ship's acknowledgement. Flags soared up to the yard, and Boyes could feel the tension like a vice closing around his heart and lungs.

'Clear the lower deck!' Ransome raised his glasses again. 'Tell the Gunner (T) to check all watertight doors.'

Sherwood said tightly, 'Must have just broken adrift. There's still some cable on it.'

A voice murmured in the pipe. 'Cox'n on the wheel, sir.'

Ransome watched the mine; in the powerful lenses it was huge and obscene. It was within the scope of the sweep-wire, but might well pass over it somewhere in the middle. 'Signal *Dryaden* to open fire as soon as the mine's clear.'

He saw Boyes staring at him, his eyes filling his face.

'Your question, Boyes. *This* is what happens.'

Boyes was to remember that for a long time to come.

Down aft with his sweeping party Hargrave hung over the guardrail and stared at the mine. It was imagination but it seemed to be swinging towards *him*.

Turnham said, 'Stand by on the winch, Nobby!' Then to Hargrave he added sharply, 'Clear the quarterdeck, sir?' It did not sound like a question.

Hargrave nodded and heard the leading hand telling the others to move into the shelter of the superstructure.

Turnham said, '*Fawn*'ll put a few shots into the bloody thing. If not, the blood-boat'll fix it.'

He shaded his eyes to look up at the signal halliards. No order to withdraw sweeps. With a drifting mine so close it could be fatal.

Hargrave felt his mouth go quite dry, like a coat of dust. He could not tear his eyes from the mine, half-submerged, turning slightly to reveal its pointed horns. Just a playful touch from one of those and –

The mine seemed to hesitate, then spiralled round in a complicated dance.

Someone called, 'It's free, sir!'

Turnham saw the first lieutenant give a great sigh. Do him good, he thought savagely. Nearly shit himself that time.

Hargrave did not even know or care what the Buffer thought at that moment.

He was remembering his first meeting with Ransome, his crisp comment about accuracy of navigation. *Thirty yards. Further than that you're bloody dead.* He could almost hear his voice as he watched the mine dropping slowly astern. With the ships in echelon, *Fawn*'s overlapping sweep would either pick up the drifter, or marksmen would do the job. Some mines made a fantastic exploding column of water; others, once punctured by small-arms fire, sank in silence to the seabed.

Mackay's lamp began to stammer again from the bridge.

Hargrave turned to read it. What happened next was blurred, unreal like a nightmare.

The explosion flung him from his feet, so that he collapsed over the depth-charge rack with the Buffer on top of him.

He struggled frantically to his feet, vaguely aware that the winch was hauling in the sweep, that the ship was leaning forward, sliding from a great wave-crest which seemed to be thrusting them through the water like a surf-board.

He stared wildly at the ship astern. Through belching smoke he caught a brief glimpse of buckled plates and dangling frames; her bows had completely gone, torn off by the force of the explosion. She was already dropping back, the other ships fanning out to avoid a collision.

The tannoy bellowed, 'Away sea-boat's crew! Stand by scrambling nets!'

It was already too late. Hargrave found that he was bunching his fists so tightly that they throbbed with pain while he stared at the stricken ship. One of their own. The front of the bridge was caved in like wet cardboard, and he knew that the threadlike scarlet lines down the plating were in fact blood. Everyone on the bridge must have been wiped out.

The communications rating shouted, 'Bridge, sir!'

Hargrave took the handset, his whole body quivering, out of control.

'This is the captain.' He sounded miles away. 'Take in the

71

sweep. I have told *Ranger* to take charge. Go with the whaler and see what you can do.'

Hargrave wanted to scream. *For God's sake, why me?* He did not recognise his own voice. 'Very well, sir.'

On the bridge, Ransome returned the instrument to the boatswain's mate. He saw Sherwood's pale features, the way he was staring astern like someone stricken by fever.

Ransome said, 'The mine's remaining cable must have snared something and pulled it into *Fawn*'s side. She was an old ship.' He wanted to shrug, but felt too drained to move. 'She stood no chance.'

As if to confirm his words Mackay called, 'She's going, sir!'

Ransome walked to the gratings and stared at the other vessel's blunt hull as it began to rise up in the midst of her own wreckage. The bows had dropped completely off, and her forepart, what was left of it, was already hidden. The funnel was still gushing smoke as if she was at full speed, while her abandoned Oropesa float wandered aimlessly nearby as if it had suddenly gone blind.

He saw the whaler pulling through the smoke, Hargrave standing in the sternsheets, the Buffer at the tiller.

Huge bubbles, horrific because of their size, began to rise around the sinking hull, where men thrashed about in oil and coaldust, and others floated away as if asleep.

Ransome had known her captain, Peter Bracelin, a mere lieutenant, very well. He was to have been married in the summer.

There was a great sigh from the watching seamen and stokers as with a sudden lurch the *Fawn* dived, her unused Carley floats and rafts tearing free when it was already too late to help anyone.

Ransome said, 'Stop engines.' He looked at Sherwood. 'Pipe the motor-boat's crew away; it'll save time. Some poor bastards might still be out there.'

Sherwood watched him, his pale lashes covering his eyes. 'And then, sir?' He already knew the answer.

Ransome walked to his chair and seized it with both hands. *It could have been us. It should have been.*

He said, 'We will carry on with the sweep, what else?'

Sherwood gave what might have been a smile.

'Indeed, sir. What else.'

When Ransome made himself look again there was only the usual slow whirlpool of filth and debris to mark the passing of another victim.

He said, 'Tell W/T to prepare a signal for their lordships.'

He watched the whaler pause on the swell, willing hands reaching down to drag some gasping survivors to safety.

Tomorrow or the next day there would be the usual curt communiqué in the newspapers, one which would only affect a few people when compared with the whole, mad world.

It would end in the usual way. *Next of kin have been informed.*

Ransome ran his fingers through his hair and felt his mind cringe.

*It's not enough*, he wanted to shout. But then, it never was.

Commander Hugh Moncrieff RNR, the flotilla's Senior Officer, slumped in the other chair and watched Ransome pouring brandy and ginger ale into their glasses.

Around them the little ship murmured with unusual sounds, strange voices of dockyard maties and their foreman, equipment being winched or dragged aside with tackles. One scuttle was blacked out by part of the basin wall, beyond which Chatham dockyard sprawled out towards the barracks.

The four ships had entered the basin this morning after the usual tortuous manoeuvring through the yard. It looked more like a scrapyard than one which worked day and night to repair and patch up the ravages of war, Ransome thought.

He sat down and pushed a glass towards Moncrieff. 'Sorry it's a Horse's Neck, sir. There's not a drop of Scotch aboard until I can have a word with the supply officer.'

Moncrieff sat back and pretended to study the glass. It was a bit early in the day for both of them, but what the hell. He watched the strain on Ransome's face, the dark shadows beneath his level grey eyes.

'Cheers!' Moncrieff said. He was a thickset, heavy man with a circlet of pure white hair around his tanned head. His reddened face was a mass of wrinkles, with deep crow's-feet around his eyes. Dressed in his naval reefer jacket with its three intertwined gold stripes, with a bright patch of medal ribbons above the breast pocket, he looked every inch the old sea-dog. You would have known him for that even if he'd been wearing a pin-striped suit in the City.

Moncrieff said, 'Got a fast car as soon as I read the signal. Bad show about *Fawn*. Still –' He did not finish it.

Ransome tasted the brandy's fire on his tongue. He felt that it was his first time off the bridge for years. He had not even found time to bath and change before Moncrieff had bustled aboard.

Ransome glanced at the envelope he had put aside for Moncrieff. The full report. He supposed it would be filed with all the others, and then forgotten. In war it was best to forget.

Moncrieff said, 'You've done wonders with *Rob Roy*.' He nodded firmly. 'Smart as paint. I see you've not been able to get rid of that rascal Beckett?' He kept his right hand deep in his pocket while he tilted his glass with the other. 'What about this Hargrave chap?'

Ransome smiled wearily. 'Settling in, sir.'

Moncrieff frowned so that his twin white brows were joined like a rime of snow.

'Bloody hope so.' He looked round the cabin. 'God, I do miss her.'

He had shown less emotion when his wife had died, Ransome thought.

Moncrieff was one of those men you rarely heard about. He had been everywhere and done just about everything. A deck officer in the Union Castle Line, he had fought pirates in the Malacca Strait when he had been a mate aboard some clapped-out tramp steamer, had sailed in the Fastnet Race, and had been in so many obscure campaigns that even his medal ribbons seemed a part of a world long gone.

'Anyway.' He made up his mind. 'I'm putting *Ranger*'s captain in charge during the leave period. He was the last commanding officer to have any decent time ashore.'

Ransome thought of Lieutenant-Commander Gregory, *Ranger*'s captain. He had hurried aboard within minutes of docking in Chatham, just ahead of Moncrieff.

He had said, 'But for that bloody dan buoy, *Ranger* would have been astern of you, as always.' He had looked round despairingly, which was rare for him. 'God, it would have been us!'

Ransome had replied, 'We all think that, James, every bloody time. So forget it.' He smiled sadly. He was a fine one to talk.

Moncrieff saw the small smile. It did not reach the eyes, he thought. A man would only stand so much. Command of any ship, battle-cruiser or M.L., took its own toll of a man's last resources. This small offering of leave might do the trick. It must help anyway.

Moncrieff asked, 'Where will you go, Ian?'

Ransome shrugged. 'Home, I suppose. I've not had much time with my parents since I got *Rob Roy*.'

He did not want to talk about it. He asked, 'Are you going to tell me why we're here, sir?'

Moncrieff's bright eyes twinkled and almost vanished into folds of crow's-feet.

'Cheeky bugger, Ian.' He offered the empty glass. 'Fill this up, eh?'

Ransome did as he was told. In some ways Moncieff was more like a father than his Senior Officer. But God help him if he had bumped the dock wall as they had moored. He had seen Moncrieff's keen stare as he examined the ship for possible damage, *neglect*, he would call it.

Then Moncrieff said, 'It's Top Secret, of course.' Their eyes met.

Ransome waited, wondering how he would react, preparing himself.

Moncrieff said, 'It's the Med. We're going to need a lot of fleet minesweepers out there. So that's what this overhaul is all about. You'll not get much opportunity later on.'

'That's nothing new, sir.'

They both smiled. Then Moncrieff added, 'In *Rob Roy*'s case, it'll mean a couple of new gun mountings. Two pairs of Oerlikons instead of the two singles, and a few other bits and pieces. No need to bother your head about that just now.'

Ransome pictured it. More guns meant extra hands. The ship was already overcrowded; they all were.

'You and *Ranger* will be carrying doctors too.'

Ransome nodded slowly. Doctors were rare in small ships. He said, 'We're going to invade, sir? The other way round for a change?'

Moncrieff frowned. 'I've said nothing. Keep it to yourself, but yes, I think an invasion is in the wind. Sicily is my guess.'

There was a tap at the door and Hargrave poked his head around the curtain.

'Come in, Number One.'

Moncrieff nodded. 'How d'you do?' As usual he did not remove his hand from his pocket to take Hargrave's as he made a half-attempt to offer it.

Ransome marked his expression. He would see it as a snub, or rudeness from another reservist. In fact, Moncrieff rarely showed his hand except to throw up a casual salute. He had lost his three middle fingers in an air attack at Dunkirk. His hand was like a crude pair of callipers. It was fortunate that he was left-handed anyway.

Moncrieff said bluntly, 'You think sweeping a bit of a let-down, eh?' Then he shook his head, 'No, your C.O. *didn't* tell me anything. I guessed it.'

He warmed to his pet theme. 'There was a time, when this war started, when reservists were outnumbered by the regular navy. Looked down on in some ships, I would say. Well, as you now know, that situation has fortunately changed. All these young men you work with joined up for one thing only, to fight the Hun – not to make a nice comfortable career for themselves, right?'

'I didn't see it like that, sir.'

'Good.' Moncrieff glanced at his empty glass. ' 'Cause if you did, I'd remind you that but for these Wavy Navy chaps and old codgers like meself, Mr bloody Hitler would have run up his flag over Buck House two years ago!'

Ransome felt sorry for Hargrave and asked, 'What did you want, Number One?'

Hargrave took the question like a lifeline. 'It's the base padre on the telephone, sir.' He looked at Moncrieff. 'About a service for *Fawn*.'

Moncrieff struggled to his feet. 'Yes, I forgot. I suppose it

76

won't hurt to have a few words with God. Can't help poor Peter Bracelin though.'

He turned and stared at Ransome. 'You've earned a rest, fifty times over, Ian. So use it. Lose yourself. Leave this little lot to me.' He held out his uninjured hand and shook Ransome's very gently. 'And don't worry about *Rob Roy* either. She's my next of kin now.'

They went on deck together and watched a khaki ambulance pulling away from the brow. The last of *Fawn*'s survivors who had died while the ship had headed up the Medway.

All told, *Fawn* had lost thirty of her company.

They had all worked together for many months, a lifetime in any war. They would be sadly missed. So would *Fawn*. Ransome saluted as Moncrieff strode heavily across the brow. *Poor old Smokey Joe.*

He said, 'Get the people away on leave, Number One. The cox'n and leading writer will help you. They know what to do.'

'I was wondering, sir —'

Ransome watched him calmly. *Invasion.* It was like seeing it in bright painted letters a mile high. The *where* didn't much matter. They only had to care about the *how*.

He said, 'I'm afraid you'll have to forget it, if you were about to ask me about leave, Number One. I need a good officer here in my absence. And, well, let's face it, Number One, you've only been aboard a dog-watch. Right?'

Hargrave gave a rueful grin. 'Understood, sir.'

I doubt that, Ransome thought. He said, 'It's ten days. I'll see what I can do for you.'

That evening Ransome left the ship. It felt like no other time. The emptiness, the stillness, the voices and daily routine already like another memory.

He waited in the dusk and looked down at her. Tomorrow she would stand upright in dry-dock.

Ransome turned and walked quickly towards the gates. But that was tomorrow.

# 6

# *Up the Line*

The train from Waterloo's mainline station seemed to wait for ages before it eventually moved off. Unlike the first part of the journey from Chatham when the train had been filled mostly with sailors, this one was crammed almost to bursting-point with a strong proportion of all three services.

Gerald Boyes was fortunate and had a window-seat, although with anti-blast netting pasted across the glass it made little difference, except that he was only being squashed from one side. It was a corridor train, and that too was packed. Boyes noted that he had not seen a single civilian climb aboard, or maybe they had been no match for the wild stampede of servicemen, partly rushing to avoid losing a precious minute of their leave; also by sheer weight of numbers some had hoped to crash through the handful of military policemen and railway inspectors to prevent anyone from discovering they had no tickets.

There had been a brief hit-and-run air-raid on London, someone said. Another complained that the train was too overloaded to move. Boyes glanced at his companions; curiously they were all sailors although he did not know any of them. It never failed to amaze him that they could sleep instantly, anywhere, and without effort.

He had seven days' leave. His stomach churned with both excitement and uncertainty at this unexpected break. He had tried to sleep on the slow, clattering journey from Chatham through the Medway towns and finally to London. It was different from the last leave when he had been so full of hopes for his chance of getting a commission. He could still feel his mother's disappointment, as if it was some kind of slur on her and the family. But the events of the past weeks had changed him, although he could not understand how. When he had tried to sleep on the train he had found no peace, but had relived the terrible moment when he had seen *Fawn* explode and disintegrate. The survivors hauled aboard, some coughing and gasping, black with coal-dust and oil, others horribly burned so that had he wanted to look away. As a boy he had always imagined that death in battle had dignity. There had been none there on *Rob Roy*'s deck as Masefield the petty officer S.B.A. had knelt amongst them, working with dressings and bandages, his expression like a mask.

One badly wounded man had looked up at Boyes when he had carried fresh dressings from the sick-bay.

His face had been scorched away, with only his bulging, pleading eyes left to stare at Boyes. For that brief moment Boyes had felt no fear. He had wanted to help the dying man without knowing how. The Gunner (T) had dragged a bloodstained cloth over the man's face and had barked, 'Can't do nothin' more for this one.' But even he had been moved by it.

Boyes glanced down at his uniform. Next time he would find a way of buying a proper, made-to-measure jumper and bell-bottoms like the real sailors wore. He turned his cap over in his hands after making sure that he was the only one awake. He had rid himself of the regulation cap tally with the plain *HMS* embroidered in the centre. He held it so that it caught the afternoon sunlight even through the dirty, net-covered window. In real gold wire, he had bought it from *Rob Roy*'s leading supply assistant, whom the others called Jack Dusty for some reason.

He felt a shiver run through him. *HM Minesweeper*. Pride, a sense of daring, it was neither. Or was it?

The corridor door jerked open even as the train gave a sudden lurch and began to move from the station.

Boyes glanced round and saw a girl in khaki peering in, a second girl close behind her.

She said, 'No seats here either. God, my feet are killing me!'

She glanced along the sleeping sailors. 'Looks as if they've all died!'

Boyes stood up, clinging to the luggage rack as the train tilted to the first set of points.

'Take mine.'

The girl in the A.T.S. uniform eyed him suspiciously, then said, 'A proper little gent, eh?' She gave a tired grin and slipped into his seat. 'I'd give you a medal if I had one.'

Boyes struggled out into the corridor where men clung to the safety rail across each window, or sat hunched on their suitcases. The lavatory door at the end of the corridor was wedged open and Boyes could see some soldiers squatting around the toilet, shuffling cards with grim determination.

'She wasn't kidding either. Poor Sheila has been on the move for days.'

Boyes faced the other A.T.S. girl for the first time. She was wearing battledress blouse and skirt, her cap tugged down over some dark, curling hair. She was pretty, with an amused smile on her lips, and had nice hands, both of which she was using to grip the rail as the train gathered speed.

'Had a good look, sailor?'

Boyes felt his face flushing uncontrollably. 'Sorry, I –'

Her eyes lifted to his cap and she gave a silent whistle. 'Mine-sweeping – is that what you do?'

He nodded, his skin still burning. 'Yes.' He wanted to sound matter-of-fact, casual even. 'It's just a job.'

She wrinkled her nose. 'I can imagine.'

She had very nice eyes. Not blue, more like violet. She was older than he was, he decided. By a year or two. But who wasn't?

She asked directly, 'You going back?'

He shook his head. 'No. Some leave.'

'Lucky you. I've just had mine.'

She had an accent he could not place. He asked carefully, 'Where do you come from?'

'Well, Woolwich actually.' She watched him challengingly. 'Where did you think, then?'

'*Sorry* –'

She gripped his arm. 'Don't keep apologising. It's the way I talk. Like you – we're different, OK?'

80

Boyes was losing his way fast. 'Your family – what do they do?'

She watched him again. He was just someone to pass the time with. They would never meet again. And yet she knew he was not like anyone she had met. Not because he had given Sheila his seat, or because of his careful, posh accent. She shied away from it. Not again. It was too soon.

'My dad's on the docks. Makes good money with the war on, and that. Most of it goes against the wall, but that's life, right?'

'Can I ask, where are you going?'

She shrugged. 'In the park, near Kingston. Know it?'

He nodded. 'My home's in Surbiton. Quite close.'

She said, 'I belong to an ack-ack battery there. God, I wish I was in the bloody Wrens. I'd give anything to see the sea every day instead of a lot of randy gunners and the deer!' She laughed. 'Did I shock you?'

'N – no. Of course not.' He stared through the window. It was not possible. They were almost there.

He stammered, 'I'm Gerald Boyes. Maybe we shall –'

She touched his arm, then dropped her eyes. 'I'm Connie.' She peered past him and said, 'I must wake her up. We're getting off here too.'

The next moments were lost in confusion as the train came to a halt and disgorged a living tide of uniforms on to the platform.

She said quickly, 'I've only been here a month. I was in North London before. I suppose you know your way around in these parts?'

The other girl exclaimed, 'Where's my bloody cap?'

The girl called Connie laughed and pointed to her respirator haversack. 'In there, you goof!'

Sheila said, 'I see they've sent the old Chevvy to fetch us.'

She stood discreetly away as Boyes said, 'Here, this is my address. If you ever want –'

She stuck the piece of paper in her blouse pocket. 'You're a real card, you are!' But her eyes were suddenly warm, vulnerable. 'Maybe. We'll see, eh?'

The two girls hurried away towards a camouflaged lorry where some others in A.T.S. uniforms were already sorting out their bags and parcels from home.

Boyes walked slowly down the slope from the platform. Apart from all the uniforms it had not changed much. Shabbier, but so was everywhere else.

He would walk the rest of the way to his home, steeling himself as he went up St Mark's Hill, just as he had that morning on his way to school when he had been dreaming of being accepted for early entry into the navy.

He had known that church on the hill for most of his life, and had sung in the choir there because of his mother's insistence.

But that morning it had been quite different. When he had passed the last houses he had looked for the church tower and steeple, a landmark thereabouts. There had been nothing but the steeple left standing; a German bomb had wiped the rest away. It had felt like an invasion, like being assaulted by something obscene. He shivered, as he had done when the *Fawn* had finally dived to the bottom.

Then he gripped his case and walked into the sunlight. He turned once to stare after the lorry but it had already swung out on to the main road, and he thought he could hear the girls singing some army song.

A real girl. And she had liked him.

He caught sight of himself in a shop window and tipped his cap to a more jaunty angle.

*Home is the sailor.*

Lieutenant Philip Sherwood paused on the steps of the club and waited for his eyes to grow accustomed to the darkness. He breathed deeply like a farmer returning to the land; even in wartime it was still London. Bombed, battered and rationed, with traffic groping up St James's Street towards Piccadilly, the night sky already criss-crossed by early searchlights, nothing seemed able to take away its personality.

He half-smiled. Like the old club he had just left, where he had dined alone in the high panelled room with its portraits of stern-faced bankers and businessmen.

His father had put his name down for membership years back when he had left school for Cambridge. His grandfather had been a member there too.

Just now he had asked an elderly servant if the club had ever been bombed.

The man, in his Pickwick-style brass-buttoned tailcoat, had given a wry smile while he had glanced at some equally old members who were sleeping in their chairs, faces hidden by their newspapers.

'It is my belief, Mr Sherwood, Hitler wouldn't dare!'

Mr Sherwood. Even that sounded old and quaint. Sherwood was twenty-six and had been in the navy since the beginning. His father had wanted him to wait a while. The business would not function without a younger head in the boardroom. Anyway, the war would be over by Christmas. That was four years ago.

In the club's elegant entrance hall hung one huge chandelier, unlit now because of the black-out and power cuts. But it was a chandelier which had once been the pride of London's clubland.

It had been made, or *built* as they called it in the profession, by one of the oldest chandelier companies, Sherwood's.

It had gone during the first devastating fire-blitz on London. They had all been there, that was the worst part, his father, mother and two sisters, helping after hours, to pack some of the antique, priceless pieces which would be sent into the country for the duration. The whole street had been demolished, and the blaze had been so terrible that the firemen had been unable to fight near enough to save anyone still inside.

It was still hard to accept that life could change so completely and remorselessly. Sherwood had left the affairs of his family in the hands of a solicitor who had been his father's friend and a cousin from Scotland he hardly knew. He could not face going back to the family home outside London in the quiet suburbs. Sherwood's had always kept a small flat in Mayfair, for foreign buyers and the like. By some miracle it had so far avoided both the bombing and being commandeered for some deskbound warrior from Whitehall, so Sherwood stayed there whenever he was able to reach London. To many people the city was a rambling maze; to Sherwood it was sheer escape, and could have been a desert island for all the notice he took of those around him.

An air-raid siren began its nightly wail, rising and falling above the growl of traffic, with barely a passer-by glancing at the sky. It was all too commonplace. To think about it could bring nothing but dread and despair. You just kept going.

Sherwood could see beyond the thousands of servicemen of so many nationalities who thronged the cinemas, pubs and dance-halls in search of momentary enjoyment. He saw instead the people, as they went about their daily affairs almost unnoticed. People who set out each day for the office or shop by any form of transport left running after a night's air-raid, not even knowing if the place of work would still be standing when they reached it. And at the end of their stint, returning home again, with that same gripping fear that it too might have been wiped away in their absence.

They were the real heroes, he thought. Without their courage under fire, all the sea battles and tanks in the world could not keep this island going for long.

He thought suddenly of Hargrave, their first meeting in the wardroom. *Confrontation*. His question about fear, his own reply about its only coming when there was an alternative. It was terribly true, but how could anybody like Hargrave understand?

Sherwood knew he was being unreasonable. Once he had tried to contain it. Now he did not care any more.

After his family had been killed he had returned to his ship and straight away had volunteered for mine disposal. He had been in *Rob Roy* about nine months. He had not expected to be alive this long when he had first volunteered for what they called the most dangerous work in any war.

His mind lingered on fear. That was the strange part. With him it was no act. He really did not feel it. He had supposed that one day he would either crack up completely as some had done, or make a stupid error which in the blink of an eye would have solved everything.

A dark figure seemed to slide from a doorway and he heard a girl say, 'Hello, love, d'you feel like a go?'

Sherwood quickened his pace, angry at the interruption, the intrusion into his solitude.

She insisted, 'Anything you like, and I'm clean!'

Sherwood caught the scent of strong perfume and sweat.

He snapped, 'Bugger off!'

She yelled after him. 'You stuck-up bastard! I hope they get you!'

Sherwood swung round. *'What did you say?'*

He heard her high heels tapping on the pavement as she ran into the jostling figures and disappeared.

Sherwood walked on more slowly, his hands deep in his raincoat pockets.

Perhaps he should have gone with her. He almost laughed out loud. Probably end up in Rose Cottage, as they called the officers' V.D. hospital.

He looked up and saw the tiny pinpricks of bursting flak. Soundless from here. The searchlights were groping across some clouds; it all seemed quite harmless, unreal. It was south of the Thames somewhere.

A voice said, ' 'Ere we go again. Let's find a shelter.'

The crowd seemed to be thinning, and Sherwood found himself walking past the Ritz, beside Green Park. He had often walked there with his sisters.

He clenched his fists together in his pockets. *Leave it. They've gone. You can't bring them back.*

*Crump – crump – crump –* the familiar sound of shell-bursts, nearer now. More casualties, more smashed debris where streets had once stood and survived the years.

Like the times when he had been sent to deal with the para-chute mines dropped on congested towns and seaports. Every street was always cleared beforehand. Just the *Unexploded Bomb* sign, his rating assistant, and utter desolation. As if every living thing had been spirited away.

He had never got over the feeling that he was intruding. The *Marie Celeste* atmosphere of meals from precious rations left steaming on tables, letters half-read or partly written. Mantel-pieces with their framed pictures of dear ones in uniform. Sons, husbands, lovers. And always below the tell-tale damage, the huge, deadly mine hanging from its parachute.

*Intrusion.* That summed it up better than anything. What war was all about.

A voice said sternly, 'Just a moment, sir.' A policeman in a steel helmet stepped from his little sandbagged observation post.

Sherwood peered at him through the gloom, saw the helmet reflect a couple of the shell-bursts. It was strange, but you never got used to seeing a London bobby in a tin hat.

'Yes?'

The constable said, 'Air-raid, sir. There'll be some shell splinters dropping about soon. It's not safe to walk the streets. Your cap won't stop the stuff.'

Sherwood thought of the ships he had watched being blown up or strafed, of *Fawn* and her broken, pathetic survivors.

He replied, 'It's the war, I expect.'

He walked on and the policeman muttered to himself, 'Another bloody hero!'

By the time Sherwood reached the street where the company flat was installed he had guessed that the raid was heading further away, to the City or East London perhaps.

He heard the far-off crash of bombs and the familiar rumble of collapsing buildings. As he climbed the stairs to his flat, the streets came alive with other sounds. It was like a mad symphony, he thought. The clamour of fire-engine and ambulance gongs, taxis roaring down side-streets, not with passengers this time, but towing small pumps as a part of the auxiliary fire service. It was as if the whole of London was putting its weight against the enemy. Nobody was spared. And yet when another smoky dawn laid bare the ruins, these same ordinary people would go about their daily tasks. *Make the best of it.*

Sherwood threw his cap on the bed and prepared himself for the night. He took a bottle of gin from a cupboard, one glass and a rare lemon he had brought from the ship.

Then he hung his jacket on a chair and glanced around the flat. As it was in Mayfair, he supposed it was worth a fortune. But it was for visitors who came and went without caring too much about the decor. It was dull, without personality.

He swallowed half a glass of neat gin and bit back a cough. Then he switched off the lights, opened the black-out curtains across the window, and seated himself in a comfortable chair to watch the progress of the raid. He heard the occasional clink of a splinter on the roof or in the street and thought of the policeman's warning.

Another ambulance dashed through the unlit street, its bell clanging violently. Some terrified soul would awake in a hospital bed. He grimaced and took another drink. Or not, as the case might be.

He did not remember falling asleep, but awoke with a jerk, his mind clearing instantly despite the gin, his reflexes tuned like those of a wild animal.

For a brief moment he imagined the building had been hit by a bomb or an incendiary. There were fires flickering beyond the window, and he heard a sudden crash and knew that was what had awakened him. But the glow of fires was several miles away. The noise seemed to be from the flat next door. He drew the curtains, then something fell against the wall and he heard a woman cry out; then a man's voice, blurred and indistinct, but full of menace.

Sherwood ran from the flat, wishing he had picked up a weapon. It must be a robbery, or some burglar who had been disturbed on the job. He had had no idea that the other flat was occupied. He stood breathlessly on the landing, gauging the distance as he stared at the closed door.

Then with only the briefest thought of the consequences he hurled himself at it. It flew open, the lock flying across the room so violently that the two occupants froze stock-still, like figures in a waxworks.

Sherwood was used to making up his mind in a split second. It did not need a genius to work out what had been happening. An army officer's tunic with red staff tabs on the lapels lay on the floor, and the bedside table was filled with bottles and a soda syphon. The scene was set.

Sherwood looked first at the man, a big, wild-eyed individual in khaki shirt and trousers, his eyes almost popping with surprise, then fury as he realised what had happened.

The woman lay propped against the wall, one leg bent under her, her blouse torn from one shoulder, a smear of lipstick or blood beside her mouth as if she had been hit, and hit hard.

Sherwood took it all in. She was very attractive, and half out of her mind with terror. He also noted she was wearing a wedding ring.

She called, 'Help me, *please!*'

Sherwood found that he was so calm he wanted to laugh. And it was not the gin.

He asked, 'Whose flat is this?'

'What the hell is that to do with you?' The man lurched towards him. 'I'm living here, and —'

Sherwood reached out and helped the woman to her feet. 'Are you all right?' But he kept his eyes on the army officer.

She thrust her foot into a shoe which had fallen under a chair.

'I came because he was going to tell me about —' She hesitated. 'About my husband —'

The man glared and then laughed. 'She *knew* what it was all about!'

He seemed to realise that Sherwood was partly dressed in uniform. 'You a bloody sailor?'

Sherwood said quietly, 'Go next door. It's open. Just walk in. You'll be safe there until the raid's passed over —'

'Don't you bloody dare to burst in here giving orders! When I've finished with you —' He got no further.

Sherwood lashed out hard and hit the man in the stomach. It was like exploding a bag, he thought. He just folded over, retching and choking, his face contorted with agony.

Sherwood said, 'You shouldn't drink so much, *old chum.*' He picked up a chair and smashed it across the reeling man's shoulders, so that pieces of wood and fabric flew in all directions.

He was aware of two things. That the young woman was pulling at his arm, pleading with him to stop. The other was that he knew he wanted to go on hitting the man until he was dead.

She did not resist when he guided her to the flat next door.

He said, 'Make yourself comfortable. I'll try to get a taxi, or walk you home if you like.' He heard the man lumbering around in the other room, the crash of glass and the loud flushing of a toilet.

He said, 'See? He'll live.' He watched her as she sat in the chair by the window. 'Do you want to tell me about it?'

She was not listening, but trying to drag her torn blouse across her shoulder.

Sherwood picked up her coat and bag where she had dropped

them when he had slammed the door. Perhaps the man in the other flat was telling the truth, that she had gone there for a bit of fun, which had got out of control. She was quite pretty, he thought, about his own age. He gropped for a handkerchief and dabbed the corner of her mouth. She winced but did not pull away.

She said in a small voice, 'I lost my husband some time ago.' She was staring at her hands, anywhere but meeting his eyes. 'In the Western Desert.' She spoke in clipped sentences, like parts of an official communiqué. 'He was in the infantry. First they said he was missing. Then they discovered he had been —' She looked away. 'Killed in action.'

'I see.' Sherwood sat very still opposite her, the blood-stained handkerchief held between them like a talisman. 'Go on.'

'I'd met Arthur —' her voice hovered on the name. 'The man next door, when his regiment was in Dorset, my home. He knew my husband, and quite recently he telephoned me to tell me he was stationed in London, that he had discovered something about my husband's death.'

Sherwood nodded. He had noticed that at no time had she revealed her husband's name. As if just to speak it aloud after what had happened would destroy even a memory. It was all she had now. So he was not alone after all.

'So naturally I — I came up on the train. He'd said that there would be others here —' She looked up suddenly and stared at him.

'I thought you were going to kill him.'

Sherwood smiled. 'Wish I had, now.'

'I intended to find a hotel, you see.'

Sherwood considered it. The raid seemed to have moved on, but the A.A. guns were still cracking away, the emergency vehicles as loud as ever in their combined protest.

'You'll not be able to find anywhere now.' He studied her impassively. 'Stay here.' He saw her eyes widen with alarm and added, 'No problems. This is a flat owned by my father's company.'

'Suppose he found out?'

'He's dead.' Sherwood stood up suddenly. 'They're all dead.

So you see —' He looked back at her and saw that she was crying without making a sound.

'I'm sorry. I didn't realise —'

Sherwood heard the man groan again through the wall. *I'll bet his bloody wife doesn't know what he's up to.*

Sherwood said, 'Look, I'll tell you what. You sleep here tonight. I can doss down in the chair, or find somewhere else if you'd prefer.'

She stared at the wall. 'No. After what you did, I —'

Sherwood waved her words aside. 'Tomorrow we'll go out for breakfast. I think you can still get a good one at the Ritz. There's nothing here.'

She was looking at the wall again. 'What about him? Won't he call the police and get you into trouble?'

'I wouldn't think so, not him. It might make too much of a scandal.' He tried to hide his bitterness. 'And trouble is no stranger to me anyway.'

'I don't know what you must think.'

He said gently, '*I think* you are a very pretty lady, but too vulnerable for the likes of *Arthur* next door.'

She kicked off her shoes and Sherwood felt a pang of envy for the man who had known her, who had died in the Western Desert. He could even envy the scheming bastard next door who had tried to rape her.

She said, 'You're very kind to me. And thank you for what you just said.'

He smiled and held out his hand. 'I'm Philip Sherwood, by the way.'

She saw his jacket hanging from a chair. 'Navy. I'm so glad.'

He did not ask her what she meant. Perhaps it was because her dead husband who had loved and known her, but made the mistake of marrying in war, had been in another service.

Sherwood went into the tiny kitchenette while she used the bathroom. He heard her climb into bed. It must seem a far cry from Dorset, he thought. Suppose there was another air-raid? They might be found together, like poor Tinker's mother had been discovered.

He downed another glass of neat gin. *So nobody lives forever.*

The excitement, the strain of the past months, and the gin took their toll, and within minutes he was fast asleep, slumped across the kitchen table.

He did not hear the wail of the *All-Clear*, nor did he feel the girl come to the kitchen and cover his shoulders with a blanket.

They had both learned a lot about themselves; if not each other.

# 7

# 'When Are You Going Back?'

Ian Ransome paused outside the boatyard gates and removed his cap to allow the lively Channel breeze to drive away the discomfort of the journey. There was a hint of haze above Gribbin Head where it thrust itself out into the sea like the bastion of some ancient fortress: a sign of an early summer perhaps.

He turned and looked through the sagging wire gates, then up at the big board which stated, *Edward Ransome and Sons, Boatbuilders*. The sign was flaking, and Ransome felt a touch of sadness for his father. He was carrying on as best he could, and from the din of saws and hammers within the yard, there was more than enough work to do. *Edward Ransome and Sons*. Now, one was sweeping mines, the other doing heaven knew what with torpedoes and deadly cannon-fire.

He walked through the entrance and stared in wonderment at the activity on every hand. Not graceful yachts or stocky fishing-boats, but hulls that looked more like giant egg-boxes than anything that floated.

A voice said, 'Bit of a come-down, eh, Mr Ian?'

Ransome swung round, then seized the rough hand of the yard's foreman, Jack Weese. Ancient yet timeless, as much a part of the boatyard as any frame or timber in it. Ransome knew he must be well into his late sixties, but he seemed exactly the same, as he had always looked. Heavily built, his shoulders rounded by stooping over every sort of craft from dinghy to ocean-racer, he was wearing a spotless white apron, and of course his cloth cap.

The latter was occasionally changed at Christmas-time when one of his offspring presented him with a new one.

Weese said, 'Landing-craft – infantry jobs.' He eyed the nearest with distaste, his eyes wrinkled against the glare. 'Bloody things. Still, it's a living.'

'I didn't know you were building them, Jack?'

Weese shrugged and eyed him keenly. 'Bless you, Mr Ian, they're throwing 'em together all the way from here up to Lostwithiel. For the Second Front, whenever that's going to be.'

Ransome fell into step beside him while Weese pointed out the various stages of construction, and all the strange faces who had been brought to work on the landing-craft.

'They don't know what an apprenticeship is,' he said scornfully. 'Just give 'em a hammer and nails, that's about their style!' He added, 'You look a bit bushed, if I may say so.'

Ransome smiled. 'As you say, Jack, it's a living.'

They paused by a small jetty and Ransome asked, 'Where is *Maggie May?*'

She was an old tug, very small, which his father had used first on the Thames, then down here for local jobs, towing timber to the yard, or moving craft to difficult berths. Like Jack, she was a part of it from the beginning.

He recalled his mother's horror in what Churchill referred to as 'the Dark Days' when she had discovered that the elderly tug was missing from the yard.

One of the local coastguards had told her, 'Mr Ted's gone to sea in the old girl, Missus. You know he's always wanted to.'

Ransome recalled the touch of pride and love he had felt when the news had reached him.

His father had taken the little tug with some of the fishermen from Fowey and Polruan, and of course Jack Weese, to a place over the other side called Dunkirk. It was still a miracle they had survived, let alone brought off some fifty soldiers in two trips.

Jack Weese said quietly. 'Your lot have taken her *for the duration*. I hope they looks after her.' He sounded like a man who had lost an old friend.

Ransome nodded. 'What about my –'

Weese cheered up and grinned, his eyes vanishing again.

'Your *Barracuda*? God, I've fought harder for her than me bloody pension!'

They walked through the litter of rusting metal and wood offcuts until Ransome saw the long hull resting on stocks, her deck and upperworks covered by patched tarpaulins.

*Barracuda* had been his dream. She was a big motor-sailer of some forty-six feet, one he would cruise in, and if necessary live aboard when the time came.

When not working on plans for his father and learning more about the craft of boat-building, Ransome had spent his spare time and the long summer evenings working on his boat. The hull had been overhauled, and some of the inside accommodation completed when Ransome had been called to make use of all the training he had done with the peacetime RNVR. She had stood here ever since, and Weese had indeed fended off the greedy approaches of Admiralty agents who toured the ports and harbours around Britain in search of vessels which might be thrown into naval service. A sort of press-gang, as Weese put it; not to be tolerated in Fowey.

The agents had insisted on taking *Barracuda*'s two diesel engines for war service in some harbour-launch or other, but the hull was still safe.

Weese watched as he crouched under the canvas awning, reliving all those dreamy days when he had come here. Ransome ran his hands along the curved planking. Old, but a proper boat, a thoroughbred. The girl had come here to watch, to sit with him, or just to sketch. He straightened his back, and looked across the harbour to the village of Polruan on the opposite side. The little houses banked street upon street, the pub by the jetty where the tiny ferry chugged back and forth. He had taken her to the pub once. She had been too young to go inside, but they chatted together on the benches near the jetty. A slim, sprite-like girl with long hair who had put away a Cornish pasty from the pub as if it was a mere crumb. He remembered her eyes while she had listened to him; her bare knees had usually been scratched or grubby from exploring the water's edge and this same boatyard.

'Memories, Mr Ian?'

'A few, Jack.'

Weese waited for him to re-tie the tarpaulin. 'When are you going back?'

Ransome grinned. Everyone said that, as soon as you came on leave. 'A week. I can spare that.' His inner voice said, *I need it*.

Weese said, 'Mr Ted's over in Looe Bay today. He'll be here before dusk.' He watched Ransome's profile. 'A freighter was torpedoed off the Knight Errant Patch a week back. There's some quite good timber washed ashore. Pity to waste it.'

Ransome slapped his shoulder. 'Years ago you would have been a wrecker!'

He hesitated, then asked suddenly, 'You remember the kid who used to come here in the school holidays? She sketched things – pretty good too.'

Weese nodded. 'I remember her. Her dad turned out to be a Holy Joe, didn't he?' His eyes became distant. 'She *did* come here again.' He was trying to fit it into place, so he did not see the sudden anxiety in Ransome's grey eyes. 'Same cottage as the other times.' He bobbed his cap towards Polruan. 'Your brother, Mr Tony would know. I think they went to a dance together over at St Blazey when he joined up.'

Ransome replaced his cap with care and tried to stifle his disappointment. *What is the matter with me?* Eve would be Tony's age. But it hurt him all the same.

'I'll go up the house and see my mother.' He groped in his gas mask haversack, which contained several items but no respirator, and handed a tin of pipe-tobacco to him. 'Duty-free, Jack. Have a good cough on me!'

Weese took it but watched him uncertainly. He had known him all his life, first on the Thames, then here in Cornwall.

Some of the lads had commented on it at the time. Cradle-snatching, that kind of remark. Weese had not realised that it had gone any deeper.

And now this. He studied Ransome as if for the first time. He was the same person underneath. Friendly but reserved; he had been quite shy as a boy compared with his young brother.

Now look at him, he thought. Fighting the bloody war, a captain of his own ship, but still just the same uncertain kid who had wanted his own boat.

He said, 'I reckon Vicar'll know. They were as thick as thieves during that last visit.'

'Thanks, Jack.' He turned towards the houses. 'I'll see you tomorrow.'

Weese shook his head. 'By the old *Barracuda*, no doubt!'

Ransome clipped the haversack shut and wished he had brought Eve's drawing with him. It was all he had, all he was ever likely to.

As he walked slowly past the familiar houses bathed in the afternoon sunshine he thought about the torpedoed freighter, the casual way Weese had mentioned it. So even here, the war was never far away. Right now some U-boat commander might be picking his way through a minefield, his periscope's eye watching this green sweep of land. Thinking perhaps of his own home, wherever that was.

His mother looked older, he thought, but hugged him with her same vigour.

'You've no meat on your bones, son! They don't feed you enough!'

Ransome smiled. Another misunderstanding, he thought. It was said that the cooks in Chatham Barracks threw away more spoiled food every day than the whole town got in rations.

She was bustling about, happy to have him home. 'I'll soon take care of *that*!'

Ransome saw the two photographs on the mantelpiece above the old fireplace where they burned logs in the winter, and his father had told unlikely ghost stories.

'Heard from Tony, Mum?'

She did not turn but he saw her shoulders stiffen. 'A few letters, but we did hear from one of his friends that his flotilla . . . whatever you call it, has gone to the Mediterranean.'

Ransome tried to remain calm. So much for security.

She was saying, 'I thank God the war's nearly over out there.'

Ransome groped for his pipe. The Mediterranean was about to erupt all over again. How could he even hint that *Rob Roy* would soon be going there too?

She turned and studied him. 'How is it, dear? As bad as they say? I think of you both all the time –' She bowed her head, and he took her in his arms to comfort her as her bravery collapsed.

Later that evening as Ransome sat at the table and faced an enormous dinner with his parents, the war intruded once again.

His father had switched on the wireless to hear the news. It was all much the same as Ransome had heard before he had left the ship. Until the very end when the urbane tones of the BBC announcer made the brief announcement.

'The Secretary of the Admiralty regrets to announce the loss of His Majesty's Minesweeper *Fawn*. Next of kin have been informed.'

It was a long time before anyone spoke. Then his father said flatly, 'She was one of yours, Ian? I'm so sorry.'

As night closed in over the little harbour Ransome mounted the stairs to his room and stared at the fresh curtains, which his mother must have made for his visit so that it would always look as if he had not really been away.

He had changed from his uniform into his oldest shirt and flannel trousers and lay on the bed for a long time, the window open to listen to the breeze, the querulous muttering of some gulls who slept on the roof.

He thought about the *Fawn*, of another gathering somewhere with more women in black to mark that curt announcement.

Perhaps he would sleep again and dream of the sun across his back while he worked on the boat's hull. Maybe in the dream she would come once again.

Lieutenant Trevor Hargrave sat at Ransome's little desk and leafed half-heartedly through the latest batch of signals and A.F.O.'s. Wrecks and minefields to be re-checked or inserted on the charts, new regulations about the issue of Wrens' clothing, revised designs for ship-camouflage, instructions for firing parties at service funerals. It was endless.

He listened to the muffled chatter on the tannoy speakers, the obedient gales of studio laughter, another comic programme to give a lighter side to the war.

It was strange to feel the ship moving gently again after being propped in dry-dock, her decks snared by electric cables and pipes while the dockyard completed a hasty overhaul of the lower hull before refloating her. Tomorrow she would be warped out to the gunwharf for re-ammunitioning, and for further inspections by the armaments supply officers and fitters.

Now at least they were a ship again, the deck empty of boiler-suited dockyard workers who seemed to spend more time idling and drinking tea than working.

As Campbell had dourly commented, 'If it's not screwed down, the buggers will lift it!'

The whole fleet knew about survival rations looted from Carley floats and boats while a ship lay in the dockyard. There were worse stories too, of dead seamen trapped below after being torpedoed, being robbed of their watches and pathetic possessions before they could be cut free from the mess.

Hargrave glanced around the cabin until his eyes settled on the drawing. It was unsigned, and yet he had the feeling that Ransome's unwillingness to discuss it meant there was much more behind it.

The ship's company were either on home leave, or ashore locally, leaving only a small duty-watch on board for safety's sake. Tomorrow the next batch would be packed off to their wives and mothers. More the latter in this youthful company, he thought.

He toyed with the idea of going to the wardroom. Bunny Fallows would be there, the Chief too probably. The rest were away. Even Mr Bone, whose home was in nearby Gillingham, was absent.

Hargrave decided against it. Campbell was friendly enough but kept very much to himself. Fallows, well – he stopped his thoughts right there.

The tap at the cabin door was almost a welcome relief. It was Petty Officer Stoker Clarke, a tough, dependable man who was said to have survived the sinking of his last ship by being blown bodily over the side after the explosion had sent most of his companions to their deaths. He was the only petty officer aboard, with Leading Seaman Reeves, the chief quartermaster, to assist him.

'What is it, P.O.?'

Clarke stepped warily over the coaming and removed his cap.

'It's Ordinary Seaman Tinker, sir.'

Hargrave picked out the youthful sailor's resentful face from his thoughts.

'Not back from leave again? I told the commanding officer that –'

Clarke shook his head. 'No, he's back aboard, sir. He's request-in' to see you. *Personal*.'

Hargrave said, 'I'll see him when I take requestmen and defaulters tomorrow, after we've cleared the dock.'

Clarke eyed him stubbornly. 'He says it's urgent, sir.'

'What do *you* think?'

Clarke wanted to say that he would have kicked the lad's arse clean through the bulkhead if he had not respected his anxiety. But he said, 'I wouldn't have bothered otherwise, sir.' He made to leave.

Hargrave snapped, 'I've not finished yet!'

'Oh?' Clarke eyed him calmly. He had suffered too much, gave too much each day to conceal it, to put up with officers like the Jimmy who always seemed to want to go by the book. 'Thought you had, sir.'

'Don't be impertinent.' He knew he was getting nowhere. 'So fetch him in now, all right?'

Clarke withdrew and found the young sailor waiting in the passageway. In his best uniform he looked even more helpless, he thought. Tinker was a good lad, always cheerful and willing to learn. Or he had been once. The whole ship knew about his mother playing open house while Tinker's dad was away. Nobody joked about it. There were too many men in the navy who might be wondering about the faithfulness of their loved ones at home. Especially with all the Yanks and hot-blooded Poles running about the country.

'He'll see you.' Clarke straightened Tinker's neatly pressed 'silk' which was tied beneath his blue collar. 'Keep yer 'air on, my son. Just tell 'im what you told me, an' no lip, see? Or you'll end up in the glasshouse, and you won't like *that*!' He gave his arm a casual punch to ease his warning. 'I wouldn't like it neither.'

Tinker nodded. 'I'll remember, P.O.'

He stepped into the cabin and waited by the desk. The first lieutenant looked much younger without his cap, he thought.

Hargrave glanced up at him. 'Well, what's wrong?' It sounded like *this time*.

Tinker said, 'My dad, sir. He's been out of his mind since — since —' he dropped his eyes. 'If I could be with him. Just a few more days. I'd make up for it later on, I promise, sir.'

Hargrave sighed, 'But you've just had leave. Would you make another man give up the right to go home so that you can get extra time in his place?'

Tinker was pleading. 'Able Seaman Nunn has offered, sir. He's got nowhere to go, not any more.'

Hargrave frowned. Another undercurrent. A home bombed, or a wife who had been unfaithful.

He said, 'You see, it's not in my province to offer you something beyond the bounds of standing orders. Perhaps later on —'

The boy stared at the carpet, his eyes shining with tears and suppressed anger.

'Yes, I see, sir.'

Hargrave watched him leave and grimaced. Tomorrow he would telephone the welfare section and speak with the Chief Wren there, unless —

He almost jumped as the telephone jangled on the desk.

He snatched it up. 'Yes? First lieutenant.'

There were several clicks, then a voice said, 'Found you at last, Trevor!'

Hargrave leaned forward as if he was imagining it.

'Father? Where are you?'

The voice gave a cautious cough. He probably imagined there was a Wren on the switchboard listening in to their conversation.

'Next door at R.N.B. Thought you might care to join me for dinner. There are a couple of chaps I'd like you to meet. Very useful, d'you get my point?'

'It's just that I'm in charge here.' He stared around the cabin as if he was trapped. 'The captain is —'

'Don't say any more. Have one of your underlings take over. God, it's only spitting-distance away, man!'

It was unlike his father to be so crude. He must have been drinking with his friends. Hargrave felt a surge of envy, the need

Thanks again
your splendid
hospitality.
Please place several
stars opposite my
name in your
visitors' book.
Very best wishes.
Malcolm.

Dr & Mrs Heywood,
Magdalene House,
Glapthorne Road,
Oundle,
Northants.

PE8 4JA

"The Brixham Trawler "Myrtle" built in 1881" from an original by Falmouth Marine Artist Tony Warren
Tony Warren Prints 01326 565849. © John Warren 1994.

DEVON & EXE
2 NOV
93

to be with career officers senior enough to free his mind from the drudgery and strain of minesweeping.

His father was saying, 'If any little Hitler tries to get stroppy, just tell him to ring *me*.' He gave a husky chuckle. 'But to ask for *Vice*-Admiral Hargrave now!'

Hargrave swallowed hard. 'Congratulations, I mean —'

'I'll tell you at dinner. Must dash.' The line went dead.

Hargrave leaned back, his hands behind his head. It was not all over after all. Strange, he had not expected it would be his father who would ride to the rescue.

Outside in the passageway Petty Officer Clarke said, 'Well, we tried, Tinker. Be off to your mess, eh?'

Clarke watched the slight figure move to the ladder. Poor, desperate kid. He glanced at the door and swore savagely.

With some alarm he imagined that he had uttered the words aloud because the door opened immediately and the first lieutenant strode from the cabin.

He saw Clarke and said, 'I shall be ashore, at R.N.B., this evening. Sub-Lieutenant Fallows will do Rounds with you.'

'Aye, aye, sir.' He tried again. 'About young Tinker, sir.'

'Look, it's over and done with. Young he may be, but he knows the score as well as any three-badgeman. So there's an end to it, P.O.!'

He strode aft towards his quarters.

Clarke nodded slowly. 'That's *bloody right*, sir. 'E comes to you for 'elp and you tells 'im to sling 'is 'ook. While you go an' stuff yerself in the barracks wardroom!' If only the coxswain was here, he thought. He'd have probably sent the kid ashore without asking anybody's permission. But he was the only one who might get away with it.

Clarke went to his mess and said to the sailor on duty, 'Get me a wet. I don't care wot, I don't much care 'ow. Just get it!'

The man did not bother to remind the petty officer it was only four in the afternoon.

Clarke called after him, 'An' you can join me! I don't feel like sippin' alone just now!'

The sailor came back with a jug of what Clarke guessed was hoarded tots.

He felt better already. 'Ta, very much.'

The man grinned. 'I just 'eard that Mr Bunny Fallows is gettin' tanked up already.'

Clarke paused in mid-swallow. 'Christ. I'd better get down aft a bit sharpish. Jimmy's ashore tonight.'

He found Fallows in the wardroom, squatting on the padded club fender by the unlit fire, a large drink in his hand, his face almost as red as his hair. He was just a youngster, probably not even twenty-one. God, he'll look like something from Skid Row when he gets to my age, Clarke thought.

'Yes, what is it?'

Clarke wished that the Chief, his own boss, was here. He never got in a flap, never pushed his stokers to do what he had not done himself a million times.

'The first lieutenant's compliments, sir, and —'

Fallows gave a knowing grin. 'Come on, man, spit it out! This is not a court-martial, y'know!'

He was already losing his posh accent, Clarke noticed. He thought, *It's a pity it's not yours.* He said, 'He's going ashore this evening, sir.' He watched the glass empty in one swallow. 'I'm to do Rounds with you, sir.'

Fallows considered it for several seconds. 'Righty-ho, can do! Got fuck-all else on tonight anyway.' He tapped his nose with the empty glass. 'But tomorrow, that's something else, eh?' He gave a little giggle.

Clarke breathed out with relief. Drunk or sober, he could handle the red-haired subbie. He had expected him to fly into a rage like he often did. That was something he could not manage, not after the Jimmy's behaviour.

He withdrew and heard Fallows yelling for the messman.

Later after a hearty supper of shepherd's pie and chips, Petty Officer Clarke was sitting alone in his mess, a glass at his elbow while he wrote a letter to his wife in Bromley.

The chief quartermaster tapped at the door and said, 'The first liberty men are comin' off, P.O. Seem quiet enough. Shall I tell the O.O.D.?'

'Hell no, I'll come up meself.' He reached for his cap and heavy torch. The latter was useful in a darkened ship; it also came in handy to pacify a drunken liberty man.

He added, 'Our Bunny's smashed out of 'is mind. God knows what the Jimmy will have to say.'

Reeves grinned. 'Who cares, eh?' They walked out on deck. It was almost dark, with gantries, ships' masts and funnels standing against the sky like jagged black shadows.

The men returning early from local leave would either be broke or disillusioned by Chatham's shabby hospitality. A sailors' town, where landladies charged them good money for the privilege of sleeping three in a bed with a cup of weak tea and a wad of bread and dripping before they plodded back to the barracks. Men serving in ships preferred to come back early. Like *Rob Roy*'s people; she was their home.

Leading Seaman Reeves said, 'I was a bit surprised about Tinker.'

'I wasn't.'

'No, I mean that Fallows allowed him to go ashore after what you said.'

'*What?*'

The chief quartermaster fell back a pace. 'Thought you knew, P.O.!' He forced a smile. 'No skin off your nose. Bunny is actin' O.O.D.'

Clarke looked away towards the brow as the first lurching figures groped across.

'I wasn't thinkin' of that. It's the kid I'm bothered about.'

Reeves shrugged. 'Well, you told him, so did Ted Hoggan the killick of his mess. So wot else can you do, I asks you?'

The liberty men glanced around on the darkened deck to make sure there was no officer present, then made their way forward to their messdeck. One said thickly, 'That bird you picked up, Fred – she was so *ugly*! I know you've never been fussy, but God, 'er *face!*'

The other man mumbled, 'You don't look at the bloody mantelpiece when you poke the fire, do you? Well then!'

Reeves groaned, 'Sailors, I've shot 'em!'

It was nearly midnight when Hargrave eventually returned on board. It had been something of a triumph to share the evening with his father's friends. Both were flag officers, and one was well known for his appearances in the press and on newsreels.

Even the thought of returning to *Rob Roy* had seemed unimportant.

His father had spoken to him privately before he had left barracks.

'Ours is a true naval family, Trevor. Things might have been different in the ordinary way, but we must think of the future, eh?'

By 'things' Hargrave knew he had been referring to the fact that he had had three daughters. He was the only male to follow in the family footsteps.

'War is terrible, we *know* that, Trevor. But when it's over, all these other chaps will go back to their proper jobs again – the navy will be just a memory, an experience in which they will be proud to have made a contribution.' He had leaned forward and tapped his knee, his breath smelling hotly of brandy and cigars.

'So we must use the time to benefit ourselves, and of course the service. It's why I want you to get a command, not bugger about in a damn great cruiser, don't you see? You were found unsuitable for submarines, and I can't say I'm sorry about that, and you've not time to make up the experience anywhere else but in small ships like *Rob Roy*. As a regular executive officer you stand out. Be patient, and I promise you a chance to walk your own bridge within months!'

Like speaking with the two flag officers, it was as if Hargrave had been lifted a few feet higher than he had been before. Provided he could stay in one piece, and that applied in any ship, he would have his father's promise to sustain him.

To his surprise he found the Chief alone in the wardroom drinking black coffee.

'I thought you were staying ashore for the night, Chief?'

Campbell looked at him coldly. 'Lucky I changed my mind then, isn't it?'

'What's happened?'

Campbell stood up and walked to the fireplace. 'I had to do Rounds. It's not my job, Number One.'

'Look –' Hargrave could feel his irritation rising. 'This isn't a bloody trade union, not yet anyway! Any officer should be capable of –'

'It's not a question of being capable.' Campbell faced him angrily. 'This ship has a fine reputation, everyone knows that. I came back on board to find the Acting-O.O.D. smashed out of his mind, spewing his guts up over the side, and the officer responsible ashore at the barracks! So be good enough not to lecture *me* about capability!'

Hargrave snapped, 'I think we've both said enough.'

The Chief strode to the door. 'And Ordinary Seaman Tinker's adrift, by the way.' He vanished, leaving the curtain swirling in his wake.

Hargrave sat down heavily. 'Bloody hell!' He saw the messman watching from the pantry hatch. 'Horse's Neck!'

'Bar's shut, sir.'

'Well, *open it*!' He stared hard at the deckhead. Nothing must spoil it. Tinker had deserted. Perhaps it was inevitable. He would speak with Petty Officer Clarke about the facts.

He took the glass from the messman. 'Thanks.'

The man eyed him anxiously. 'Mr Fallows's mess chits, sir.'

'What about them?'

'He's not signed for his drinks.'

'I see.' The distinguished faces of the admirals at dinner were already fading, out of reach. 'Leave it to me.'

Just a few more months and all this would be behind him. Tomorrow he would sort out Mr Bunny Fallows. But that could wait.

A command of his own. It was still uppermost in his thoughts when he fell asleep.

Ian Ransome stared at his reflection in the mirror and automatically adjusted his tie. The house seemed so quiet, as if it was waiting for him to go.

His father stood by the door, one arm around his wife's shoulder.

He said, 'Six days, Ian. That's all you've had.'

Ransome watched his own expression in the glass as he might a face across the requestmen's table.

He had worked hard on *Barracuda*, and the weather had remained fine, so that each night, after going over to The Lugger

105

for a pint with his father, he had fallen into bed, and had slept undisturbed. Something he had not believed possible.

Then there had been the telephone call. He was required on board. He had made his last visit to the boat, had touched the smooth hull with affection, even love.

Old Jack Weese had watched him. *It's breaking his heart*, he had thought. *For once, he doesn't want to go back.*

Ransome wanted to tell his parents all about it, but he knew he would crack up if he did, and that might finish his mother.

Now, in pressed doeskin uniform with the single blue and white medal ribbon, a crisp clean shirt which his mother had washed and ironed for him, he was back in the role again. The naval officer. The captain of *Rob Roy*.

His mother said again, 'Surely someone else could manage while you were away, dear?'

His father tried to change the subject. 'I'll run you to the station in the van. It'll not be breaking the patrol rationing regulations. I've got some gear to deliver there.'

Ransome looked round the room, half expecting to see the old cat Jellicoe. But he had long gone, and was buried with the other pets in the special place they had chosen as youngsters.

He recalled the same feeling when he had left his day cabin to go to the bridge on that day. Then too he had glanced around. *Was it the last time?* As it had been for *Guillemot* and *Fawn*?

He faced them and smiled. 'Off then. Might be back before too long.'

His mother watched him. 'I've packed some sandwiches for you.'

'Thanks.' He gazed at them fondly, despairingly. Going back. *I don't want to go.*

He thought of the telephone call, the unknown voice of an officer at Chatham.

It had been discovered early in the morning. A young seaman, doing extra work as a man under punishment, had been inspecting the air-raid shelters, checking each one to make certain that all the light bulbs were working. He had apparently run gasping to the main gates to call the officer of the guard, nearly beside himself with terror.

He had been standing on a bench in one of the long, underground shelters when he had felt someone watching him.

He had turned to stare into the face of Ordinary Seaman Tinker. He had been hanging from an overhead girder.

Ransome said, 'Don't forget to write.'

He kissed his mother and walked from the house, without looking back.

# 8

# *Full Day*

Commander Hugh Moncrieff sat behind his desk in a temporary office above the dockyard and puffed heavily on his pipe.

'It was good of you to come, Ian. When did you get in?'

Ransome stood by a window and felt the sun's warmth on his face. He did not feel tired now, but it would hit him later in the day. He watched an elderly destroyer in a nearby basin, stripped of almost everything as she underwent the indignity of a hasty refit and a conversion to a long-range convoy escort. Once a sleek destroyer which age and service had overtaken. Now sans everything. A great cloud of red rust hovered over her eyeless bridge, and the air quivered to the thud of rivet guns.

He replied, 'Early morning, sir. There was a raid on Plymouth yesterday. All the trains were in a real potmess.'

He thought of Hargrave standing across his desk in his small cabin; he had looked strained and unusually pale, as if he had not slept since Tinker's death.

Moncrieff said slowly, 'I half-expected you'd ask me to get Hargrave transferred.'

'It was not entirely his fault, sir.' Was that really what he thought? 'Circumstances, bad luck, a bit of everything. I'd not see him damned because of that.'

'Thought you'd say as much – hoped so anyway. We lost two more sweepers while you were on leave. On the East Coast run. So we'll be shorter still of experienced officers and men.'

Ransome smiled. 'That's one way of looking at it, sir.'

'The *only* way, Ian. If we go on like this —' He did not finish it. Instead he brightened up and said, 'The flotilla's being made up to full strength, one extra in fact.'

'Oh?' Ransome turned and looked at him. 'Newcomers?'

Moncrieff tapped out his pipe. 'Both foreigners so to speak. One from the Free Dutch navy, the other Norwegian. Both pretty experienced I'm told. I'll let you have all the guff later on today.' His eyes gleamed. 'Still top secret, but you'll be moving westward as soon as the leave period is completed.'

'May I ask where, sir?'

'You may not.' He chuckled. 'I've laid my hands on some Scotch for you, by the way. It should be aboard *Rob Roy* by now.'

He became serious again. 'That boy Tinker. He'd probably have done what he did anyway.'

'I know that, sir. But he needed to talk —'

'And you blame yourself for not being there. God, Ian, you drive the ship, you're not a wet nurse for everyone in her! Tinker's a war casualty as much as any other. When I think of some of the things that go on while we're at sea it makes me heave!'

Ransome smiled. 'Now, about these extra people?'

The old sea dog grinned hugely. 'Safer ground, eh? Well, you're getting a doctor. So is *Ranger*. There'll be four extra hands for gunnery, and I have to tell you that a new sub-lieutenant is supposed to be arriving today too.'

Ransome stared at him. 'What shall I do with them all, sir? Stuff them in a magazine hoist?'

Moncrieff pulled a huge dog-eared ledger towards him and frowned. Ransome guessed that he had probably been fighting off his other captains with equal determination.

'Your midshipman, Davenport, will be leaving in a few months when he gets his first stripe, won't he? The new sub will be doubly useful then. I see that at least two of your leading hands are due for promotion, and several others are awaiting advanced courses ashore.' He wagged his pipe at him severely. 'At this rate you'll be glad of every experienced Jack you can hold on to. They're building a whole new bunch of sweepers to replace the losses, and *they'll* be bleating for trained hands too. Supply and demand — it all amounts to that, my young friend!'

Ransome looked out of the window again. He was right of course. More ships, new faces, but the same deadly war to prepare them for.

He pictured Fallows as he had seen him an hour ago. Very grave-faced but quietly confident. He knew very little about Tinker's death, if he had, etc. etc. — No, Tinker had not approached him about leave, and in any case he had been given to understand that the first lieutenant had already refused it.

Ransome wondered about that, but Fallows had lost no time in clearing his own yard-arm.

'Still brooding, Ian?'

Ransome smiled at the dusty glass. Old Moncrieff could read his mind. It would be good to have him along when they left for the Med.

'Oh, I was just thinking, sir.'

'The first lieutenant went over to R.N.B. to meet his father, *Vice*-Admiral now, no less! Something anyone of us might have done. There was after all, science's latest triumph, the telephone, if things got out of hand.' He tapped his thick fingers with the pipe-stem. 'The Chief was aboard, so was Sub-Lieutenant Fallows, and the Gunner (T) was due back in the early morning. There was the duty-part of the watch, plus a very experienced P.O.'

Ransome looked at him fondly. He had certainly done his homework. 'I know, sir. I suppose it's my failing.'

Moncrieff glanced meaningly at the clock. 'I've got to see *Dryaden*'s C.O. in a minute. But I shall say the same to him, and I'm sending his chief stoker away on a well-deserved course for promotion, and he won't care much for that either!' He held out his left hand. 'Your failing, Ian?' He looked at him searchingly. 'It's what makes you the best I've got.'

By the time he had returned to the ship Ransome had decided to speak with Fallows again, to try and fit in the missing piece.

He waited on the dockside for several minutes as he studied his little ship, his gaze taking in the new double-mountings of twenty-millimetre Oerlikons, an extra winch down aft and a powerful-looking derrick which had replaced the old one. New paint, even a different motor boat in the davits; they had certainly pulled out all the stops. Probably Moncrieff, he decided.

He walked quickly down the steep brow and saluted, then glanced at the duty-board by the quartermaster's lobby. Apart from Lieutenant Sherwood and the Chief everyone appeared to be aboard.

He nodded to the chief quartermaster, the ruddy-faced Leading Seaman Reeves, the public's idea of the true sailor, with his silver chain and call tucked into the deep V of his jumper.

'All quiet, Q.M.?'

Reeves watched him warily. 'Very, sir. The new doctor's aboard, and the extra subbie will be joinin' this afternoon, earlier than expected.'

Ransome looked directly at him. 'What about Tinker?'

He shifted his feet. 'We're all sorry about 'im, sir. Nice kid, 'e was, too.'

'What do you think happened?'

'He requested to go back on leave to be with his dad, sir, his old woman bein' dead, like.'

Ransome waited. 'And?'

'Well, it was refused, sir. Like I told the first lieutenant after it was reported, I was on the gangway when Tinker went ashore. I asked 'im about it, and he said it was local leave, he wasn't in the duty-part of the watch, y'see, sir. He told me that Bun – I mean Mr Fallows gave him permission.'

'And you didn't think to check on it?'

Reeves swallowed hard. 'It was a bit difficult –' He saw Fallows's scarlet face when he had gone down to the wardroom later to tell him what had happened. P.O. Clarke had been with him.

The sub-lieutenant had been beside himself with fury, and barely able to stand.

'How *dare* you speak to me like that? Stand to attention when you address an officer, damn you!'

In fact Fallows had been the only one unable to stand upright.

'I did not *see* this wretched fellow Tinker, nor did I give him fucking permission to go ashore, *see*?'

Reeves had been amazed to hear his voice. Like one of their Scottish stokers on a binge.

Ransome nodded. 'How was he dressed? Did he say anything?'

Reeves frowned. 'I saw that 'e was carryin' nothin' but 'is gas mask, sir.'

'Which was why you imagined he was going on a local run ashore?'

Reeves faced him. 'There was somethin', sir. He said, "They don't really care, do they?" or somethin' like that, sir.' He dropped his eyes under Ransome's grey stare. 'I – I'm just sorry I can't 'elp any more, sir.'

Ransome looked up at the tiny masthead pendant above the radar jampot.

'I think you have, Reeves. Now put it out of your mind, O.K.?'

Reeves stared after him and exclaimed, 'Christ, what a bloke!' He looked at his hands, expecting to see them still shaking. Young he might be, but the skipper knew every bloody thing in this ship!

When stand-easy was piped, the tea-boat was already passing out mugs of tea in exchange for pence or barter, soap perhaps for the dhobying firm who would wash a sailor's blue collar better than any housewife, tobacco or 'ticklers', and of course *sippers* of rum from those who were old enough to draw their tot.

Around the scrubbed table of Number Three Mess, the seamen sat in quiet contemplation. They sipped their sickly tea and watched Ted Hoggan, the killick of the mess, as he placed the dead sailor's few personal effects on the table. It was not much, Boyes thought as he sat wedged between Jardine and a seaman named Chalky White, who had developed a nervous tic in one eye over his months of minesweeping. A new cap with gold wire inscription, a pusser's knife or 'dirk' as they were known, a hand-made ditty-box from which Hoggan, as their senior, had removed some personal letters and a photograph of Tinker himself as a boy at HMS *Ganges*.

It was the first time Boyes had come up against something like this. He could sense its importance in the faces around him, tough, hardened ones for the most part, who had seen and suffered experiences he could only guess at.

Jardine leaned over and whispered, 'We'll raise a few bob from this lot, see? Then we 'as somethin' to remember the lad by, an' 'is people will 'ave a bit to put towards – well, *things*.'

Boyes nodded and opened the flap on his belt where he kept his money.

Jardine saw the ten-shilling note and said fiercely, 'Not that much, Gerry lad! It's a sort of token. Not a time to show off 'ow much you got.'

Hoggan tapped the table. 'Well, mates, this here is a pretty good ditty-box – what do I hear?'

And so it went on until the table was cleared. Boyes sat staring at the knife which he had bought for two shillings. It was exactly a twin of his own, and yet it seemed special, had belonged to a boy like himself whom he had seen only for a few minutes before he had walked away from life.

Leading Seaman Hoggan tipped his tin on to the table and counted the contents with great care.

'Four pounds, one an' a tanner, lads.' He looked at each of them in turn. 'What d'you think?'

Someone said, 'His old woman's gone west, 'ookey, an' to all accounts 'is dad 'as 'it the jar since.'

Boyes looked at their expressions, half-expecting them to laugh or dispute such a casual summing-up, but they were all deadly serious.

Hoggan nodded. 'My thoughts too, Dick.' He scraped the coins into 'is tin again. 'We'll keep it –' he glanced at his world, Number Three Mess. 'For the next one of us, eh?'

They all nodded and emptied their mugs as if it was a kind of salute.

Hoggan looked at Boyes and gave a sad grin. 'Learnin' somethin', kid?'

Boyes nodded. 'Yes, thank you, Hookey.'

Nobody mimicked him this time.

Hoggan patted his arm. 'You can take Tinker's locker an' sling yer 'ammock on 'is 'ooks from now on, Gerry.'

Boyes stared around at the others and did not know what to say. Such a simple thing, some might say, but to Boyes it was like being awarded a medal.

To close the proceedings the tannoy bellowed, 'D'you hear there? D'you hear there? Out pipes, hands carry on with your work!'

Tinker had been popular in the mess, indeed throughout the whole ship. But Boyes somehow knew that his name would not be mentioned again.

*Rob Roy*'s officers stood or lounged around the small wardroom and waited for lunch, the event of the day.

Lieutenant Hargrave sat in a well-worn leather chair and stared at a copy of the *Daily Mail*, although he found that his eyes remained unmoving more often than not.

He was still dazed by Ransome's acceptance of his report. He had missed out nothing, had even admitted that he blamed himself for keeping Tinker from going ashore.

Ransome had listened without interruption and had said, 'You'll know better next time. If it's any consolation I think he might have done it anyway. In view of your full, and I believe honest report, I think you acted correctly.'

It was probably the closest they had ever been, Hargrave thought. But he had no doubt of Ransome's attitude if anything like it occurred again.

He glanced at the others, standing with drinks in their hands, bored with their stay in the dockyard while they waited for the rest of the leave party to return.

The Chief had just come in; he was wearing his best uniform, quite unlike his seagoing rig of boiler-suit or an ancient reefer with ragged and tarnished lace.

Bone the Gunner (T) sat massively on the fender and contemplated a large tankard of beer, his bald pate shining in the deckhead lights. For although they were out of dry dock, the scuttles were still masked by the jetty wall and *Ranger* on the outboard side.

Hargrave stared at Fallows until the sub looked at him, flushed, and glanced away. As well he might, Hargrave thought. He was even drinking tomato juice. At least Sherwood was still ashore, so there would be no friction for a while. Hargrave's eyes sparked with sudden anger. *If he comes the old soldier again I'll cut him down to size, hero or not.* He heard the midshipman's incisive voice as he discussed his prospects of promotion with the Chief.

Campbell kept his alert face impassive. 'I suppose being an old-school-tie type, you'll soon be up the ladder, eh, Mid?'

Davenport sighed. 'Well, it *helps* of course. My father wanted me to go into the army.' He added vaguely, 'One of the household regiments, actually.'

Campbell glanced at Hargrave, then walked across to him. 'Drink, Number One?'

They eyed each other like duellists, then the engineer said, 'If you will forget it, I can.' He lowered his lanky frame into another chair and signalled to Petty Officer Kellett. ' 'Nother Horse's Neck, or whatever it is, for the first lieutenant!' He regarded Hargrave curiously. 'What did the Old Man say?'

Hargrave put down the newspaper. 'Nothing much.' His own surprise was clear in his voice. 'In his place I think I'd have hit the roof.'

The Chief grinned. 'Well, you ain't, *sir*!' He raised his glass. 'To a new start, wherever it takes us.'

Hargrave leaned forward. 'Have you heard something?'

Campbell glanced across at Davenport, who was trying to interest Fallows.

'Sometimes I feel I'd like to beat the shit out of that pompous little snob!' He seemed to recall the question and tapped his nose with his glass. 'I've got friends over in the stores. They're breaking out shorts and fair-weather gear for the flotilla.'

Hargrave smiled. 'In that case it could be the Arctic.' They both laughed.

At that moment Sub-Lieutenant Morgan, who was O.O.D., drew back the curtain and entered with another young officer wearing a single wavy stripe on his sleeve.

Hargrave stood up to greet the new arrival. 'Sub-Lieutenant Tritton? I'm the first lieutenant.'

He had noticed that both Morgan and the newcomer had been in close conversation when they had entered the wardroom. They must have known each other elsewhere. The navy's way.

Tritton looked around. A pleasant, youthful face, with a ready and innocent smile.

'I'm glad to be here, sir.' He glanced at Morgan. 'I was a snotty in his last ship. One of the reasons I volunteered for mine-sweepers, as a matter of fact.'

Fallows said irritably, 'Don't swing the lamp yet!'

Bone peered across his beer. 'What's yer name?' For the Gunner (T) he was being remarkably friendly; his trip home must have done him some good.

'Actually, it's Vere.'

Bone nodded sagely. 'That's a queer sort of 'andle to 'ave!'

Tritton looked at his friend. 'Most people call me Bunny.'

Hargrave heard Fallows choking on his tomato juice and said, 'Welcome to *Rob Roy*.' He added, 'Funny, we already have a Bunny in the mess.'

'Really, sir?' Tritton's eyes were like saucers. 'Well, of course we do breed quite quickly.'

Morgan slapped Fallows on the shoulders. 'All right, Bunny? Cough it up, eh?'

By the quartermaster's lobby Beckett heard the laughter and thought suddenly of Tinker. *Heartless bastards.*

The Buffer hurried along the side-deck and beamed at him. He looked even more like a monkey, Beckett thought.

'Time for yer tot, Swain. I'll tell you about the party I picked up when I was up the line.'

Beckett grinned. 'Why not?' Tinker was forgotten.

Lieutenant Philip Sherwood wrenched open the door of a First Class compartment and stared with distaste at the occupants. He tried the next, where to his surprise there was a corner seat by the corridor. In the navy you learned to cherish privacy, even lying on a table with your cap over your face.

He slumped down and turned up the collar of his raincoat. It was early morning, with the clattering, lurching journey to the Medway towns and Chatham still stretching ahead.

It had been cool, icy even when he had left the flat in Mayfair. For once no sirens had split the night apart, and the barrage balloons, floating high above the beleaguered city, shone in faint sunlight, although on the ground it was still as dark as pitch. Sherwood had left early so that he could walk all the way to

Waterloo. He had not realised how out of condition shipboard life had made him. He thought of the woman he had left sprawled across the bed, sleeping as if she was dead. Maybe when she awoke, she might wish she was.

Sherwood closed his eyes as an air force officer smiled across, as if he was about to open a conversation.

Sherwood thought of their night of passion. He was still not sure how it had begun. In her case it had been a release probably. He had taken her to hotels and restaurants she had only heard about. Even a red-tabbed general had turned to stare when a head-waiter had called Sherwood respectfully by name. It had reminded him of the staff officer he had knocked down with a chair. He still could not believe that he had changed so much.

Working within a hair's breadth of self-destruction, defusing mines and sometimes huge bombs with delayed-action booby traps, he had taught himself to empty his mind of everything but the job, and the one after that. Even of fear, for himself and for others.

It had simply happened. He could place no time or exact reason. That final evening they had walked back to the flat, across Berkeley Square, then along Hill Street.

She had not spoken about her dead husband, and he had said nothing further about his family.

Once she had caught him looking up at a chandelier in one hotel restaurant, and he had found himself telling her about the company.

She had watched him closely as if she had been trying to remember every feature of his face.

'What will you do when the war's over, Philip?'

He had heard himself say, 'Over? It'll go on for years and years. I try not to think about it.'

Once their hands had touched across the table and he had found himself holding her fingers, as her husband must have acted.

Perhaps that had done it, he thought.

When they had returned to the flat last night they had stood in the centre of the room without speaking.

Then he had remarked, 'No sirens yet. We'll get a good sleep for once.'

117

She had been unable to look at him. 'Don't sleep in the kitchen. Not tonight, Philip.' That was all.

He had held her without yearning, lifting her chin to look into her eyes, to see a pulse beating in her throat like a tiny, trapped creature.

It had started like a brushfire, and had ended with them both sprawled naked and breathless across the bed. He had hurt her; she had not had a man since her husband had gone overseas. She had cried out in pain and in a wild desire which neither of them had expected. Just once, when she fell asleep on his shoulder, she had spoken his name. *Tom.* It was a secret Sherwood knew he would keep.

Later he had stood by the window and waited for the first hint of morning. The clink of a milkman's basket, a policeman's boots on the pavement below. Men and women had died, probably in their thousands, while they had been making love in this room, he had thought. But that had been somewhere else.

He thought desperately, *I must not see her again. I can't. Any connection now would make me careless and unaware.* It might also break her heart.

Her name was Rosemary. It was better to leave now, brutally and finally. They had had their precious moment, both of them. In war that was rare indeed.

Ransome leaned on one elbow and plucked his shirt away from his chest. With the deadlights screwed tightly shut for another night alongside the dockyard wall the air felt clammy and unmoving, in spite of the deckhead fans and a breeze from the Medway.

He stared at the pile of ledgers and files through which he had worked with barely a break, but could find no reward in what he had done. As if the day had been empty.

Dockyard reports to check and sign, signals to read, orders from the Staff Officer Minesweeping, from even higher authority at the Admiralty, which all had to be examined; *translated* was a more apt description.

Dockyard foremen had come and gone, and his own heads of departments, from the first lieutenant to Wakeford the leading writer, once a physics master at a grammar school, had all visited this cabin to increase or diminish his workload.

Now it was done. Even a personal letter to Tinker's father, although he wondered if it could make any difference to him. Had he acted correctly with Hargrave? No matter what he had told old Moncrieff he still felt some lingering doubts.

But the other rumour was now a fact. *Rob Roy* and the flotilla would soon be heading for the Mediterranean, to a real war, where it would take every ounce of skill and endurance to carry out the work for which this class of warship had been designed. It would not just be 'putting up with it', a conflict of boredom punctuated occasionally by stark and violent death and destruction. It was no time to start changing the team around. He had met the new sub, Tritton, a likeable youngster who probably saw the dangerous grind of sweeping mines as something glamourous. Fallows might have to leave soon when his promotion was announced. He might end up as somebody's first lieutenant. Better them than me, he thought. *But he did know his job.* In war that was vital, at the top of the stakes. In another year, there would be even more eager, barely trained amateurs filling gaps left by the Fallows of this world.

He thought about his brief meeting with Surgeon Lieutenant Sean Cusack RNVR. He had not been what he had been expecting. If small ships were fortunate enough or otherwise, to carry a doctor, they were usually little more than medical students with stripes on their sleeves. He pictured Cusack as he had sat opposite him that afternoon in the other chair. In his thirties, with dark, almost swarthy features and the brightest pair of twinkling blue eyes he had ever seen.

He had said in reply to Ransome's question, 'I got fed up with the R.N.H., and one damned barracks after another. I am in the navy, so why not a ship, I asked myself?' He had chuckled at Ransome's surprise. 'It's the Irish in me, I suppose.' Then he had said with equal candour, 'There'll be a lot of stress in a job like this one, eh?'

He had sat back in the chair, his head on one side like a watchful bird. It had made Ransome feel defensive, unguarded.

He had replied, 'I suppose that's true. You tend to think death

119

is the only enemy, that you can cope with all else, like a sort of god. When you discover you can't, it leaves you raw. Vulnerable.'

'Like the boy Tinker I've been hearing about.' The blue eyes had barely blinked. 'Perhaps I could have helped. I have some experience in that field.'

Ransome had made some excuse and the new doctor had departed.

He reached down to the cupboard and took out one of Moncrieff's bottles of Scotch. He poured a full measure and added a dash of soda. The first today. What would Cusack have made of that, he wondered?

The ship felt quiet and still, with only occasionally footsteps on deck, and the creak of rope fenders between the hull and *Ranger* alongside.

A full flotilla, with more new faces, different characters to know and understand.

They might be working with the fleet, taking part in an invasion which must not fail. If it did, all the sacrifices which had left a bloody trail from Dunkirk to Singapore, Norway to Crete, would be wasted. There would be no second chance. If they put a foot back into Europe, no matter where, it must advance. Otherwise it would not be a question of a retreat, or a *strategic withdrawal* as the war correspondents optimistically described them. It would mean an inevitable defeat. He thought of his parents as he had seen them on this last leave. No, it must not fail.

There was a tap at the door and the doctor looked in at him, his eyes everywhere as he took in the piles of papers and files which filled the desk and part of the deck too.

'And there's me been enjoying meself with my new comrades, sir!'

'What is it, Doc? Your cabin not to your liking?'

Cusack stepped into the light. 'I'm such a fool. I completely forgot in all the excitement of joining the ship today!' He held out a letter. 'This was given in my care at the gates, to hand to you. To be sure, you'd have got it faster if they'd entrusted it to a blind man!'

He watched as Ransome took the letter and examined it without recognition.

Cusack said, 'A woman's hand, I'll wager, sir.' He nodded. 'I'll be off to finish unpacking and to put my *strange* S.B.A. straight on a few facts of life.'

Ransome looked at the handwriting. It was addressed correctly, c/o G.P.O. London, but the writer had upgraded his rank to Commander. Somebody's wife or mother trying to dodge the rules and red tape, he decided.

He said, 'Thanks, Doc. One thing before you go.'

The doctor's eyes fell hopefully on the Scotch but Ransome asked, 'Are you from the north or the south of Ireland?'

Cusack pretended to be offended. 'No true Irishman comes from the *North*, sir!' He withdrew quickly.

Things might be very different with him around.

Ransome glanced at the bulkhead clock. An early night, a drink in *Ranger*, or a walk along the wall to clear his thoughts.

Orders would be arriving tomorrow.

He looked at the unopened letter and noticed it was postmarked Plymouth.

Something made him reach for his knife and he slit it open.

First he turned the neatly written letter over and then he felt a chill run down his spine. It was signed, *Sincerely, Eve Warwick*.

The ship, his worries, everything seemed to fade as he read it, very slowly and carefully. He should have known, although he had never seen her handwriting before; ought to have guessed, even though he had never trusted too much in fate.

Sentences stood out from each page as if lit from beneath. *I have thought about you since we last met. Worried about you more than I could tell anyone. I went to see your funny boat. Imagined us sitting there in the sun, and you answering all my daft questions. I saw your brother Tony –*

Ransome raised his glass to his lips but it was empty.

*I wanted to know what you were doing, how you were–*

Ransome reread it a third time. He could see her smile, her sadness too. Hear her voice in the writing.

Once or twice he glanced up at the drawing on the bulkhead. She was in Plymouth where her father was now a canon. He stared at the date. It had taken several days to reach here.

He sat bolt upright in the chair, recalled how the train had been held up by another raid on Plymouth.

They were used to them down there. Like Coventry and London, Portsmouth and Liverpool.

But he could not push the anxiety from his thoughts. Now he knew what it felt like to worry about someone who was as much under fire as any serviceman.

He examined his feelings, and was surprised but grateful that he no longer felt foolish because of his – he hesitated over the word. *Love* – how could that be?

Eventually, the question still unanswered and the letter lying open in the lamplight, Ransome took time to fill a pipe of tobacco.

It had been a full day after all.

# 9

# *Victims*

The three weeks which followed the minesweepers' departure from Chatham were the busiest and probably the most maddening Ransome could remember.

The ships steamed west through the Channel, dodging a sudden and concentrated bombardment from the Cap Gris Nez guns and arriving eventually in Falmouth. There they joined up with the rest of the flotilla, the first time they had all been together for months.

Apart from the newcomers, the Dutch minesweeper *Willemstad* and the very useful additional heavy trawler *Senja* from the Free Norwegian navy, the other ships were quite familiar. But in the time they had been apart, transfers, promotion, even death in a few cases, meant different faces and minds to contend with.

Commander Hugh Moncrieff, true to his fearsome reputation, kept his brood hard at it during every hour of daylight, and quite often during the night watches. They steamed around Land's End and into the Bristol Channel where Moncrieff threw every exercise and manoeuvre in the book at them, and many which he had apparently dreamed up on the spot. He was in his element. He even cajoled the C-in-C Western Approaches to lend him a submarine on one occasion to break through the flotilla's defences in the role of a U-boat.

With half of their number still sweeping, the rest of them had carried out repeated attacks on the submarine until she eventually surfaced to make the signal, '*You've given me a headache. I'm not playing with you any more!*'

Each ship's company must have cursed Moncrieff until his ears had burned, but Ransome had felt the old pride coming back, the feeling perhaps that the minesweepers were no longer the drudges of the fleet.

It must have been even more difficult for the two foreign captains, he thought. Both the Norwegian and the Dutchman were skilled and experienced, but had been used more for local escort work than chalking up kills in the minefields.

Moncrieff had remarked on one occasion, 'No matter, Ian, they've got the edge on the rest of us.'

Ransome knew what he meant. Like all the servicemen who had left their countries in the face of German invasion, they wanted only to fight, to free their homelands, and rejoin those they loved.

It was hard to imagine how it must feel, to know that a wife or family was in occupied Europe or Scandinavia. If news of their work alongside the Allies reached the Gestapo there was little doubt of what might happen. The bang on the door before dawn. Humiliation, agony, oblivion.

The flotilla even found time to work with the army, covering landing craft in a mock invasion along the Welsh coast, repeating signals for a mythical bombarding squadron.

As Beckett had complained, 'Gets more like a bleedin' circus every day!'

Then, when even Moncrieff was apparently satisfied, the flotilla returned to Falmouth.

Ransome had written a letter to Eve Warwick, but either there had been no time for her to reply or she had had second thoughts. In Falmouth, he decided to telephone her at the number shown on her letter. He presumed it was a vicarage, and waited, rehearsing like a teenage midshipman, planning his exact words should Eve's mother or father pick up the telephone.

In fact, he was unable to make any contact. He thought again of the air-raids, and called the switchboard supervisor.

She had said wearily, 'The telephone at that number is out of action.' When he had persisted she had snapped, 'There *is* a war on, you know, *sir*!'

Curiously, it had been Moncrieff who had unknowingly presented a solution.

'I've been summoned to the C-in-C's office at Plymouth, Ian.' He had attempted to conceal his rising excitement. 'Bit of a flap on apparently. I was asked today about our readiness to sail. I told them, God help any of my skippers who isn't!'

So the rumour was gaining even more substance. Moncrieff added, 'The real thing this time. I want you to come with me. As my half-leader you might find the trip useful. You're used to the blood-and-guts of war; down in the command bunkers they see all that as mere statistics.'

Ransome had left Hargrave in charge. He had not warned him about responsibility again. If he had not learned his lesson, he never would now.

Hargrave had asked politely, 'Is something on, sir?'

'Yes, Number One. I can't tell you yet, but if you've any mail outstanding I suggest you take some time to deal with it.'

Perhaps Hargrave already knew; maybe his father had told him?

Moncrieff had been provided with a staff car and Wren driver for the trip, and as they roared through narrow lanes then on to the main road to St Austell, Ransome was conscious of the closeness of the home where he had spent just six days of his leave.

Moncrieff must have read his thoughts. 'I shall be a couple of days at least with Staff Officer Intelligence, Ian. You could take some time off. It might be a long while before you can again.'

Ransome had experienced something like guilt. *I might never come back at all.* He knew that he could not leave this time without at least trying to see the girl. But he said, 'I might take you up on that, sir.' It only made him feel more guilty.

Moncrieff slept for most of the journey, waking suddenly as the car pulled into a roadside inn where he had arranged for them to take lunch. The Wren driver declined the invitation to join them and Moncrieff said, 'Pretty little thing.'

Ransome thought he had never looked so wistful.

They reached Plymouth in time for tea, and while Moncrieff went off to make his number with the staff officer on duty, Ransome took advantage of his freedom to begin his search.

As he made his way through the city he was appalled by the

125

extent of the damage. Great areas of buildings wiped out, streets marked only by their chipped kerbstones and pavements, the rest a blackened desert where people had once been born, gone to school and learned to fend for themsleves.

An air-raid warden directed him to Codrington House, the address she had given, and had assured him that it had missed the bombing. *So far*. Ransome had asked him why he should be so certain that one particular building amongst so many had survived.

The man had regarded him curiously. 'Well, it's a sort of halfway-house – like a hospital, isn't it?'

A taxi eventually took him there. It must have been quite beautiful in its day, with a long, gravelled drive curving amongst fine oaks to a pillared entrance, and a fountain around which cars, and at one time, carriages made their entrances and exits.

Now the grass was untended and the walls flaking, while the fountain was still filled with dead leaves. The once-impressive entrance was almost hidden by sandbagged barriers.

A woman of severe appearance in a grey costume watched him enter and asked, 'May I help?' It sounded like *what do you want?*

Ransome was at a loss. 'I understood that the Warwick family lived –'

She changed instantly, removing the mask and replacing it with welcome. 'Oh, Canon Warwick? Of course! Is he expecting you?'

'Well, no –' Ransome glanced round as three women in dressing-gowns accompanied by a tired-looking nurse crossed the great hallway. 'What is this place?'

She studied him, her eyes moving from his single medal ribbon to the rank on his sleeves. He looked far too young for both, she thought.

'Canon Warwick has an official role here as well as his relig- ious duties.' She waved her hand as the little procession vanished into another door. 'Evacuee children, bombed-out families, people who have lost everything and everyone –' She shrugged. 'I don't know what we would do without him.'

'If I could leave a message –'

'Nonsense.' She picked up a telephone. 'He's in the building. What name is it, please?'

The girl spoke from the entrance doors. 'It's Lieutenant Commander Ransome, Mrs Collins.'

Ransome swung round and stared at her. How long she had been there he did not know. Like those times in the boatyard. Watching. Listening to his words.

She did not move as he strode toward her, and only when he put his arms around her shoulders did she show any emotion.

'I can't believe it. Your letter. Now you.'

He kissed her on the cheek, conscious of her warmth, the touch of her hair against his face. Like that other impetuous kiss when he had seen her leave. For the last time.

He said, 'Sorry about this, Eve. It was just a chance, so I took it.'

She slipped her hand through his arm and guided him towards the door again. The birds were still singing, and there was sunlight clinging to the treetops.

He wanted to look at her properly, but she held to his arm as if to prevent just that.

She said, 'I've dreamed about this. I wanted to write.' She shrugged. 'I was a bit afraid, I think. But when I got your address I made up my mind. I sat with the paper in front of me for hours.' She swung round and faced him, her hands in his. 'I was frightened you might have changed. When you answered my letter I knew –' She reached up and touched his hair. 'You look wonderful.' The slight catch in her voice gave away the lie.

He said, 'I've thought about you so much. My little girl in shorts and pigtails.'

She smiled. 'Not any more.'

Ransome studied her slowly. It *was* like a dream. Four years, and yet she was not so different. She wore a shirt and overall trousers, the latter daubed with dried paint.

She said, 'If I'd only known –' She ran her hands across her forehead to brush away some strands of hair. 'I'm a mess!' Then she laughed, with relief, or with joy, perhaps both.

'How long can you stay? I am sure they'll ask you to when –'

There was a footfall at the top of the steps and her father hurried down to meet him.

'It is *good* to see you, Mr Ransome – or should I call you Captain?'

127

He looked older, his face drawn to give him cheekbones where there had been none.

Ransome shook his hand. 'I hope you don't mind, Canon?'

'Call me Simon, eh?' He looked around at the trees and some more aimless figures. 'One does what one can of course.' He did not continue.

Instead he said, 'You must eat at our table. Things are a bit chaotic here, have been since the vicarage was destroyed. But still, God's work cannot wait for the war-damage repairs, eh?'

He looked at his daughter. 'You are a bit flushed, dear. Go and tell them we have a guest for dinner.'

Ransome tried to protest, but it was to no avail.

They walked together across the coarse grass where there had once been an elegant lawn. Canon Warwick wore a long black cassock with a small crucifix hung about his neck. His eyes were everywhere, probing, almost fanatical.

'It's been bad here?'

Warwick considered it. 'Bad enough. It is an unending flow of people, searching for hope, loved ones, refugees in their own way as much as those who clogged the roads in Holland or Greece.'

He changed the subject. 'Not married yet? That does surprise me.'

Ransome looked away. *I love Eve. I always have, and always shall.*

But he said, 'There's never enough time for anything these days.'

Warwick seemed satisfied. 'Eve's been a real blessing since her mother –'

Ransome started. 'She's not –?'

Warwick tucked his hands into his cassock and shook his head. 'Betty had a lot of bad luck, poor dear. First the vicarage was bombed and she had a slight stroke. Then later on she was in the town at her stall – she helps the W.V.S., you know, selling tea and buns to the sailors, that kind of thing. There was a hit-and-run raid, and a bomb fell near to her little stall. Most of the servicemen who were queuing to be served were killed or badly maimed. It really upset her. She's still not herself.'

Ransome pictured the dead servicemen. It had probably upset them too.

128

He asked quickly, 'What does Eve do?'

'My daughter?' He smiled gently. 'She shares her love of art with some of the patients here. But maybe you didn't know she could paint and draw?'

Ransome thought of the picture in his cabin. 'Yes, I knew.'

'It's worthwhile work.' He nodded to emphasise it. 'If she left to join one of the services, I'd be in a sorry state, I can tell you.'

'Is that what she wanted to do?'

Warwick did not seem to hear the question. He said, 'I'll show you the kitchen garden – we are almost self-supporting here.'

It was a difficult meal, Ransome thought. And yet he would not have wanted to be anywhere else.

Eve's mother, a frail, vague lady who seemed to laugh a lot, but looked very near to tears when she did so, fired questions at Ransome from start to finish.

And all the while he was conscious of the girl who sat opposite him, her eyes rarely leaving his as he tried to paint a picture of his ship, of *Rob Roy*'s people. Although he answered her questions they were all directed at the girl named Eve.

The canon's wife looked fondly at her husband. 'He is so busy, Mr Ransome. He never spares himself for the good of others.'

Warwick jerked from his thoughts. 'Which reminds me. I have two hospital visits to do tonight.' He glanced at the clock. 'May I offer you a lift, Commander?'

Suddenly Ransome felt the girl's shoe press against his foot, saw the sudden anxiety in her dark eyes.

He heard himself reply, 'It's all right. I'm at the R.N.B. Devonport tonight at least. I can manage.'

Why was it he could not bring himself to call him Simon as he had requested?

'Well, if you're sure –' He fumbled for his watch. 'I've asked the porter to attend to the black-out, my dear.' He smiled at his wife, but his eyes said that he was elsewhere. 'I'll be off then. Very nice to meet you again after all this time, er –' Then he was gone.

Ransome helped the girl to clear away the table. To Mrs Warwick he said, 'A fine meal. Made me feel really at home.' But she had fallen asleep in her chair.

In the kitchen, which appeared to be stacked with every kind of ration from powdered milk to corned beef, she faced him.

'I'm sorry. You didn't hate it too much, did you?'

He held her at arms' length. 'Of course not. *I* was sorry to hear about your mother. Your father feels it badly.'

'Oh, you noticed?' She studied him sadly. 'Many wouldn't.'

He tried to laugh it off. 'Believe me, my girl, when you command even a little ship in this man's navy, you either learn fast about folk or you go under!'

She did not smile. 'What you said — am I really *your girl*? Like it was, all that time back?' She shook her head so that her long hair flowed across her shoulders. 'I'm not a child any more. Please don't treat me like one.'

Then she pressed her face into his jacket and shook; the sobbing seemed to burst out of her in a flood.

He tried to pacify her, stroked her hair, held her against him, but it was to no avail.

Between sobs she whispered, 'You mustn't laugh, but I have always loved you. I dreaded seeing you in case you had met someone else.' She leaned back and stared at him, blinking tears from her eyes. 'You haven't, have you?'

'No. Of course not.' It came out so simply it was as if he had shouted his love from the housetops.

He added, 'I'm a lot older than you —'

She hugged him and shook her head again. 'I'm nineteen. Two days ago. So you see, I'm catching you up!'

They walked into another garden, the dishes abandoned.

It was a starry night, with a warm breeze to ruffle the leaves. Somewhere a wireless set or gramophone was playing a lilting Spanish tune, and a small night creature ran through the grass; searching for food, trying not to become it.

In the darkness it seemed somehow natural, he thought. His hand on her waist, her head against his arm.

As they walked he told her more stories about the people he served with. Moncrieff, the ancient mariner; Sherwood who had been with a famous firm which had built chandeliers. He left out the pieces about Sherwood's grief, which was slowly driving him mad. About Hargrave's ambition, for himself rather than the ship, of Midshipman Davenport who bragged to everyone about his upper-class upbringing, when in fact he had been to the same modest grammar school as young Boyes. Or about Fallows who had probably been the last link with life when Tinker had killed himself. Now Fallows was the haunted one because he could remember nothing at all about what had happened.

Above all, he told her nothing about the danger they faced every time they went to sea. Danger and death were things they knew about in Plymouth. For centuries. Since Drake had routed the Armada, and Nelson had sailed for the Nile, since the little *Exeter* had sailed home to Plymouth after beating the German *Graf Spee* into self-destruction. And now the bombing. Even here, on the outskirts, amidst the ageless oak trees you could smell the rawness, the scorched and shattered buildings. Oh yes, they knew all about that.

She said softly, 'We didn't choose the time, Ian. It was held out to us. *For* us.' She looked up at him, only her eyes reflecting the stars. 'It was not our choice!'

As if to some silent signal they both turned and looked through the trees towards the house. It was in darkness with all the black-out shutters and curtains in place.

She said, 'I'll have to go in soon.' The words were dragged from her. 'Mother doesn't like to be alone if the sirens start. Everyone goes down to the shelters now.' He felt her shiver and tightened his grip on her shoulders. 'I don't know if I'm really doing any good here.'

'I'm quite sure you do.' They walked across the grass again and he said, 'I'll be at the Royal Naval Barracks all tomorrow, maybe longer. My boss is having a few meetings with the top brass.'

'Can I ask where you'll be after that?'

He looked away. 'Overseas. For a while. I shall write as often as I can.'

'Yes, *please*.' Her voice sounded husky. 'Tell me your thoughts. Share them with me.'

They stood by the gates and Ransome wondered if he would find a taxi. Otherwise it would be a long hike back to the base.

She said, 'I'm not afraid any more, Ian. It seems so right. I feel as if a great weight has been taken away. You can't possibly know.'

131

She looked along the drive. 'I must go. She'll come worrying otherwise.'

Ransome turned her towards him. 'I wish it was broad daylight. I want to look at you all over again.'

She tilted her head, then wiped her cheek with the back of her hand. 'Kiss me. *Please.*'

Ransome touched her mouth with his. A quick, innocent kiss, like that time at the railway station.

She said softly, 'I'll get better.' She stepped away. 'I'll make a fool of myself any minute.'

Ransome turned once and thought he saw her standing beside the gate's tall pillar. Then she was gone.

He walked down the road, hearing the breeze in the trees, catching the first breath of the sea as he topped the hill. *Waiting.* Always waiting. Like a great force which could be evil or kind as it chose for the moment.

He did not have to walk for long; a jeep full of military policemen pulled up beside him.

One redcap asked, 'Where are you goin', chum?' Then, as he saw the gleam of gold lace, 'Care for a ride, er, sir?'

They dropped him at the gate of the barracks and vanished into the night in search of drunks or deserters.

Ransome found his small room, his shaving kit and spare shirt still packed on the bed. There was a flask too, some of Moncrieff's Scotch.

He sat on the bed and thought about her face across the table, the warmth of her lips, the strange sense of fate or destiny which they both felt, and no longer challenged.

If he stayed another night he would try to take her out somewhere. Away from the sea, from people. Just walk and talk as they had once been able to do.

He looked at the flask and smiled. He no longer needed it.

The Staff Officer, Operations, an RN commander, greeted Ransome warmly.

'Good of you to call, Ransome. I feel I already know you pretty well. You and your flotilla have made quite a mark on the map!'

He sent for tea and biscuits and gestured towards a huge wall-chart of the Mediterranean.

He said cheerfully, 'Nice not to see any bloody swastikas on the North African coast any more, eh?'

Ransome waited while a neat little Wren brought a tray to tea to the room.

The S.O.I. said, 'It's to be Sicily, but I think you already know that?' He stood up and walked to the chart. 'Combined Allied invasion, with a vital role for the supporting squadrons.' His finger moved to Gibraltar. 'We've got quite a fleet here already. Big chaps, all of them. It will be no surprise to you that they can't even move an inch without you clearing the way for them. How does it make you feel – proud?'

'Useful, sir.'

'The main supporting flotillas will be combined, so that there are no foul-ups like we've had too many times in this war. Like the rest, you will have to be ready to change roles at a moment's notice. We must get the 'brown jobs' on to dry land, Ransome.' He eyed him grimly. 'If they get thrown back this time, well –' He sipped his tea instead of spelling it out.

He continued after a glance at the clock. 'A flag officer has been appointed solely for that task.'

Somehow Ransome knew who it was going to be.

The commander said, 'Vice-Admiral Hargrave. Good chap, knows his stuff.'

Ransome thought about it. It should not make any difference who it was. Yet somehow he knew that it did. He wondered where Moncrieff was, why he was not sharing this meeting.

'So be prepared for sailing orders, Ransome. You'll be routed with a convoy, that's about all I can tell you.' He grinned and looked human. 'About all I know!'

'Will Commander Moncrieff still be our senior officer, sir?'

The man pouted his lower lip. 'I was coming to that. Moncrieff is a fine sailor, but –'

Ransome stiffened in the chair. It would break his heart.

'He's used to the home patch, the War Channel, moulding a lot of fishermen into minesweepers. The Med is different. The flotilla will be commanded by a small destroyer, a headquarters ship

133

which can direct and divert as the occasion arises.' He softened his voice. 'Commander Moncrieff will be in control until Gibraltar. That's it, I'm afraid.'

Ransome did not remember much else of the interview. He found a lieutenant waiting for him by the operations room, who explained that Moncrieff had already returned to Falmouth. A car was provided for Ransome, and a signal had already been sent to the flotilla to announce his time of arrival there. So there would be no walks away from the sea.

Moncrieff wanted to be alone, to face up to the decision in his own way.

The same Wren was leaning against the staff car, and opened the door for him as he approached.

He tried to smile. 'Home, James.'

She studied him and liked what she saw. She knew all about Ransome; most of the girls at the Wrennery did.

Past the saluting sentries and the neat sandbags, Ransome watched her gloved hands on the wheel as she steered the big Humber with reckless enthusiasm around a convoy of army lorries.

'How long have you been in the Wrens?'

She puffed out her cheeks and blew some hair from her eyes. 'Six months, sir. Does it show?'

'No. I was just thinking of someone.'

She grimaced. *Pity*. She said, 'My brother's in *Ranger*, by the way, sir.'

He looked at her. 'Who?'

'The subbie, John Dent.'

A face fell into its slot. A navy within a navy. Like a family, with its own pride and pain like any other.

They reached Falmouth in record time. The girl was still staring after him as he walked towards the jetty where a boat was waiting.

Hargrave was standing with the side-party as he climbed up from *Rob Roy*'s motor boat, the 'skimming-dish', while the boatswain's mates split the air apart with their shrill calls.

It was the one part of the job he had never got used to, or took for granted.

Hargrave saluted. 'Welcome back, sir.' He looked relaxed and pleased about something.

As they walked towards Ransome's quarters Hargrave said, 'Orders have just arrived, sir.'

Ransome smiled. The S.O.I. must have known that even as they were talking together. *In case I got killed on the road, perhaps?*

Hargrave added, 'Commander Moncrieff is aboard. Sorry, sir, I forgot.'

'How is he?'

Hargrave was surprised at the question. 'Er — much as usual, sir.'

So he had said nothing.

Moncrieff was sitting in the cabin, his legs crossed while he thumbed through an old log-book.

He looked up and shrugged. It made him look as if he was in pain.

'He told you?'

'Yes, sir. I can't say how bad I feel about it.' He watched the disfigured hand resting on the open log, like a pair of crude callipers. It was his old log. When he had still been in command.

'The admiral is probably right. I'm too old for new tricks. I'm a sailor, not a bloody robot. No doubt the new senior officer will have it at his fingertips. Conferences and meetings all the time, that kind of caper.' He smiled at some old memory and added, 'You know what I think? From the ashes of today's conferences will arise the phoenix of tomorrow's fuck-ups!'

Then he said, 'Your orders are here. You're under twenty-four hours' notice. I'd like to see all the commanding officers this evening, sometime in the dog-watches. I don't want to make a *thing* of my immediate future. We've still got to reach Gibraltar, you know.'

'I understand.' He looked at the clock.

Moncrieff grinned. 'I thought you'd never bloody well ask. Yes, young man, I'd relish a large drink *right now*!'

Ransome glanced round the cabin. He was glad Moncrieff would be using it on his last passage in *Rob Roy*. Ransome would spend most of his time on the bridge or in his sea-cabin there.

135

It would be bitter for Moncrieff all the same, no matter how he tried to disguise it.

Later, with the other nine commanding officers packed into the wardroom, he had seen no weakening in Moncrieff's aggressive enthusiasm or his ability to tell all of them what he needed from them; what he expected.

Moncrieff said afterwards, 'I'll be ashore tonight, Ian. See you an hour before we leave harbour.' He studied him thoughtfully. 'You're looking better. You'll tell me why, when you want to, I expect.'

By eight bells that evening every man in the flotilla had been told about sailing orders. Bags of letters would be going ashore in the morning, all carefully censored, just in case. Like the humorous posters you saw in canteens and bars. *Be like dad, keep mum!* Or a sailor shooting his mouth off to his girl-friend with a barely disguised Hitler or Goering crouching under their table.

After North Africa, the Germans and their Italian allies would be expecting an attack. They could not guard the whole coastline from Greece to France. But just one hint . . .

There was a tap at the door. Hargrave stepped in and asked, 'I was wondering, sir, would you join us in the wardroom? They would all appreciate it.'

Ransome smiled. 'Of course. We may be a bit busy later on.' He would go ashore and telephone from there. His parents too.

He glanced up as Leading Telegraphist Carlyon hovered outside the open door. 'Come in, Sparks.'

To Hargrave he said, 'After you've had your meal, Number One, all right?'

Neither of them noticed Carlyon's stricken expression.

Ransome took the signal flimsy from the telegraphist's hand. Hargrave smiled. 'Don't tell me it's cancelled after all.'

Ransome reread the neat printing. It was like hearing a voice. He said quietly, 'It's my brother. He's been reported missing, presumed killed.'

He recalled her voice. Was it only last night? *It was not our choice.*

Hargrave looked at Carlyon and jerked his head. As the rating left he asked, 'What can I do, sir?'

136

Ransome thought of the boatyard. His parents must have been told about the same time as he had been with Eve.

He replied, 'You're doing it right now.' He glanced at the old personal log which Moncrieff had left behind.

'I've seen a lot of people just lately whose lives have been knocked about.' But in his heart he was screaming. *Not Tony. Not him, for Christ's sake.* His voice was flat and unemotional as he said, 'We still have a war to worry about. Deeper than that, we have *this ship* and the eighty-odd people who depend on us because they have no choice either.'

Hargrave watched him, stunned by it. Unable to think clearly.

'I – I'll tell the others, sir.'

'*No.* I'll come down as I said I would.' He stared at the slip of paper which had changed everything. 'It's nobody's fault.'

Hargrave tried not to glance at the framed photograph, of a midshipman who looked so like Ransome. Just a boy. It made the war stamp right into the cabin like a monster.

Ransome looked up from the desk. 'Just leave me a while, Number One. I've a couple of phone calls to make.'

As the door closed silently behind him the ship seemed to withdraw too.

He remembered his stupid jealousy when Tony had taken her to a dance, of his perpetual eagerness to get the most out of life. He picked up the telephone, and after a lot of clicks he was connected to the switchboard ashore.

*What shall I say to them? They'll expect me to come home, when I belong here, now more than ever . . .*

*I must speak to Eve. Tell her I can't see her until . . .*

He ran his fingers through his hair and stared at the signal until his eyes stung.

Aloud he said, 'Oh dear God, *help me!*'

The operator coughed. 'The number's ringing for you, sir.'

It happened all the time, every day. Others had had to cope with it. If he could not contain his despair he was not fit to command. Men would die, and it could be his fault because –

He heard the familiar voice in his ear and steeled himself.

'Hello, Dad, I've just heard about Tony     .'

# 10

# *To the Deep*

Ordinary Seaman Gerald Boyes gripped the ready-use chart-table for support and watched as the side of the upper bridge dipped steeply in the heavy swell. It was as if the great shark-blue procession of rollers was climbing over the ship before *Rob Roy* skittishly lifted her stern and pitched over on the opposite beam. It was all so new and breathtaking he could barely drag his eyes from it.

The bridge was filled with all the usual watchkeepers, but no one seemed to be paying him much attention. He had cleaned the chart-table, sharpened the nagivator's pencils and checked the bulb in the tiny, hooded bracket which by night was concealed by a canvas screen. It was halfway through the forenoon watch, the little ship lifting and plunging, hanging motionless for seconds or so it appeared, before attempting a different position.

Boyes glanced at the captain's chair in the forepart of the bridge behind the glass screens. It looked wrong to see it empty. Ransome was always there, had been for the long four days from Falmouth into the vastness of the Atlantic before joining up with an impressive convoy.

Boyes had sensed new excitement and tension as the ships had been rounded up like sheep, chased and harried by powerful fleet destroyers before forming into columns for the long haul to Gibraltar. Boyes, in his duty of acting-navigator's yeoman, felt privileged to pick up the rumours which circulated every watch amongst the élite on the bridge.

It was a convoy to rouse anyone's attention, he thought, but the escort had been equally exciting. A heavy cruiser as well as the destroyers, and bang in the middle, a carrier. Not one of the big fleet ones, like the famous *Ark Royal* or *Illustrious*, but a stubby escort-carrier. A merchant ship's hull with a wooden flight-deck, a *banana boat* as some of the old hands called them. But the little escort-carriers had changed the whole face of every convoy lucky enough to enjoy their protection. No longer were there great areas of ocean where air-cover could not reach or be provided.

A Focke-Wulf Condor, one of the huge long-range maritime bombers, had found the convoy the second day out. But the sight of three Seafires being scrambled from the carrier had soon sent the enemy racing for home. Whereas before, these same aircraft would circle a convoy, day in, day out, just beyond the range of the guns, and all the while homing U-boats on to a helpless target.

They had not seen another enemy plane after that incident.

The ships in convoy were all big ones, including two troopers, ex-liners, and several fast freighters, their decks and hulls crammed with tanks, crated aircraft, and other vehicles. No wonder they had taken such precautions. Far out into the Atlantic, zigzagging ponderously in response to irate signals from the commodore, then around Biscay and south into warmer waters. Some of the sailors, especially those on the open bridge, were already sporting healthy-looking tans.

Boyes glanced at his companions. Lieutenant Sherwood was the O.O.W., with the new sub, Tritton, assisting him. Leading Signalman Mackay was studying the *Ranger*, which was steering a parallel course some four miles away, the rest of the mine-sweepers divided between them in two lines.

It was strange to see the ocean so deserted, Boyes thought. Just yesterday the convoy had increased speed and had gone on ahead. Each ship had been capable of much greater haste than the sweepers, but they had all kept together until the worst part of the passage was astern.

By glancing at the vibrating chart Boyes knew that neutral Portugal lay some two hundred miles across the port beam; they should be passing the invisible Lisbon about now. It was the furthest he had ever been in his life.

He looked at the empty chair again. Everyone knew about the captain's brother. Occasionally Boyes had watched him, had found himself searching for some sign of grief or anxiety. He had discovered nothing but a remoteness, something respected by the other officers.

He thought about the radar plot beneath his feet in the wheelhouse. The chief quartermaster, Reeves, was on the wheel, while Beckett was down below somewhere dealing with some requestmen. It never seemed to stop. Midshipman Davenport always managed to avoid him. It was as if they belonged to a separate society. Difficult at any time in the two-hundred-and-thirty foot hull.

He found himself thinking back to his leave again. His mother saying how she had seen young Davenport in his officer's uniform. *So smart, so dashing*. She could have had no conception just how much it had hurt.

And then, out of the blue, had come *the great adventure*. One evening when he had been having tea with his parents the telephone had rung.

Boyes's mother had bustled away, and his father had murmured, 'If it's another bridge-party I shall really do some extra fire-watching to get out of it!'

But she had returned, her eyes questioning, even suspicious. 'It's for *you*, Gerry.' It had sounded like an accusation. 'A girl!'

Boyes had hurried to the door. Over his shoulder he had heard his father ask mildly, 'Who was it, dear?'

'Someone who met our son. Sounded rather common –'

Boyes had not even noticed.

The girl named Connie had sounded very easy and matter-of-fact over the phone. Boyes had had virtually no experience of girls apart from the school dance once a year. His arrival on the lower deck of a fighting ship had made him flush with embarrassment, even if half what the others said was true.

She had said, 'You're not doing anything then?'

'N – no –' he had imagined his mother listening through the closed door. 'I'd been hoping, actually –'

She had laughed. 'You naughty boy!'

He had felt himself flushing all over again.

140

'What about the pictures? There's a good one on at the Regal –'

When he had remained tongue-tied she had added, 'But if you've something better –'

'No. I'd love to.'

'In an hour then.' The adventure had begun.

The cinema had been packed, mostly with servicemen and their girls, so that when a cracked, much-used slide was thrust across the screen to announce that an air-raid warning had been sounded, there had been a great bellow of protest. 'Get it off!' Plus whistles and derisive laughter. She had leaned against him in the cinema, until halfway through the main film when he had put his arm around her shoulder.

As the light blazed from the screen, he had seen her looking at him. Surprised? Curious? But then Boyes knew nothing about women.

Afterwards they had walked to the square in Kingston where the army had thoughtfully sent a truck for its army girls, a sort of liberty boat to get them back to camp safely.

They had stood in a shop doorway, and to hurrying passers-by it was just another sailor on leave with a girl in khaki. To Boyes it was something else. But he had had a sense of disappointment, not in her but in himself.

He had asked desperately, 'May I see you again, Connie? Please?'

She had watched him, her eyes bright despite the black-out.

She had expected the usual wrestling-match in the cinema, a groping hand, the sense of shock when it touched her. Boyes was different. God, he was so different.

'You've never had your own girl, have you?'

He had hesitated. 'Not before.'

She had wanted to hug him. To weep for his innocence, his old-world sense of honour.

'I'm free tomorrow, if you like.'

They had met in the warm afternoon, and had gone into a pub by the river for a drink. He had told her about the navy, about the ship, and all the while she had watched him, her bright lips around the straws in her port-and-lemon, her other hand close to

141

his across the table. She had taken him to another cinema, a smaller one than the Regal, one which had been known as a flea-pit in his schooldays. It had been practically empty, and she had led him to the back row of seats. They were in pairs.

She had whispered, 'Must have been a right lot of lovers in your neck of the woods, Gerry!'

During an interval he had blurted out, 'I'm off tomorrow, Connie.'

She had straightened up, her eyes suddenly anxious.

'Already? I thought –'

He had said, 'I've loved being with you so much. I can't tell you.'

She had waited for the lights to dim. 'Kiss me.'

He had tried, but had pressed his face into her hair. 'Sorry.'

She had stood up. 'Keep my seat warm. I'm going to the Ladies.' She had reached out and touched his mouth. 'It was sweet. Just need a bit of practice.' But she was not making fun of him.

For a time Boyes had imagined she had left by one of the fire-exit doors, but then he saw her hurrying up the aisle and felt her sink down beside him. He put his arm round her and kissed her again. She had her hand behind his neck and had pulled him against her, so that their mouths were locked until she opened hers and touched his tongue with hers. She had taken his hand and moulded it to her body. Her tunic had been unbuttoned, and he had felt the fullness of her breast through the shirt, her heart thumping as if to break free.

She had spoken into his ear. 'I got rid of the army-issue in the Ladies.'

He slipped one of the shirt buttons open and touched the bare skin beneath. Then another button until he had held her breast in his hand, the nipple hard between his fingers.

She had been gasping. 'Don't stop, Gerry! Oh, for God's sake!'

He had felt her reaching for him in the same wild desperation, finding and gripping him until he could barely control himself.

When they had finally left the cinema and made their way to the same square where the army lorry was waiting, he had hugged her again.

She had pushed him away, her voice breathless. 'Not here! Not like those others! Next time –' She had kissed him hard on the mouth, then had run through the night to the throbbing lorry.

Afterwards he had realised that he could not remember the name of the film or anything about it.

Sometimes now he would touch himself as she had done, and relive the moment when he had slipped his hand into her open shirt.

'*Ranger*'s calling us up, sir.'

Mackay's voice shattered his dream and made him stare around the bridge like a stranger.

The leading signalman's mouth moved in time to the diamond-bright signal lamp across the heaving swell.

'*Wreckage in the water at one-six-zero degrees*, sir.'

Sherwood nodded. 'Better tell the captain.'

'I'm here.' Ransome strode from the ladder and climbed into his chair to reach for his binoculars. 'What was that bearing?'

Mackay called, 'From *Dryaden*, sir. *Shall I investigate?*'

'Negative.' Ransome ignored the clatter of the Aldis lamp. 'Alter course to close. Inform *Ranger*.'

'What's up?' Moncrieff lurched heavily across the bridge. He looked as if he had just woken up.

'Wreckage, sir.' Ransome looked at him as if expecting an argument. *Dryaden* was better suited for these tasks. The point of her being here at all.

But Moncrieff merely said, 'Right-oh.'

Boyes dodged aside as Sherwood crouched over the gyro repeater.

'Port ten. *Steady*. Steer one-six-five!'

Up the voicepipe came Beckett's harsh acknowledgement. 'Course one-six-five, sir.' He had taken the wheel without being called.

Boyes made himself small in case anyone ordered him from the bridge. Another drama. And he was part of it.

Ransome said, 'Full revolutions.'

Boyes saw Sherwood glance at the captain's back, the slightest rise of one eyebrow. But that was all.

As the revolutions mounted the ship headed slightly **away** from her consorts so that Boyes was able to see them from a different angle. Third in line, *Fawn*'s sister-ship *Firebrand*, an old Smokey Joe, was puffing out black clouds against the clear sky. It had caused quite a lot of friction with the convoy's escort commander, until Moncrieff had seized the loud hailer and had told him to mind his bloody manners.

Hargrave had appeared on the bridge now, and raised his glasses to peer over the screen at the drifting spread of flotsam. Remnants from another convoy perhaps?

Ransome tried to lean back in the chair and relax his mind and body. Why had he taken *Rob Roy* from the formation when the trawler could have managed? Moncrieff would have been justified to question his decision.

It was a distraction. Anything better than the brooding, the regrets, the pain. He knew it was getting into him more deeply, had noticed how careful the others had been to make themselves scarce or busy when he was near. It wasn't their fault, as he had tried to tell the first lieutenant. But it still didn't help. He felt himself leaning forward again, the old dryness at the back of his throat.

'Half ahead together.' Would anyone ever be able to sum up the cost of the war at sea? Ships and men, material and hopes, the very balance of fate for friend and enemy alike.

Hargrave asked, 'What do you think, sir?'

Ransome raised his powerful glasses again. It was all too familiar. Drifting timbers and odd fragments of canvas, packing-crates, an upended lifeboat, the whole sea littered with it. He trained his glasses on the capsized boat. He could just make out the port registry, Liverpool, painted on the hull. There was a lot of scum around the planking. It had been wandering with the aimless currents for a long time, probably weeks, the last reminder of a ship, perhaps a whole convoy which had fallen foul of a U-boat pack.

He heard a look-out remark, 'Not much left in that lot!'

He snapped, 'Well, keep looking! Any clue might be useful later on!'

He turned away, sick inside, angry with his inability to stay calm.

Sherwood said, 'There's a raft, sir. Red four-five.'

Ransome found it, his glasses taking in the scene as if he had actually been there. The roar of a torpedo, perhaps more, the sudden confusion, a shock of despair as the ship went over. This vessel may have been carrying explosives, and had been blown apart before the boats could be got away. Just the one raft. Low in the water, barely rising up to challenge each roller or trough. There were three figures on board. Spreadeagled across it, tied there like some grisly warning to those who risked the Western Ocean.

'Slow ahead together.' Ransome slipped from the chair and stood on the gently vibrating gratings. 'Send the sea-boat away, Number One.' Their eyes met. 'Tell the doctor to go too.'

'What is it, sir?'

Ransome wiped his glasses with a piece of tissue. 'Nothing. You go across with the boat, will you?'

Hargrave walked away and soon the tannoy barked, 'Away seaboat's crew!' Then, 'Slip the gripes, stand by for lowering!'

Ransome turned back to watch the little raft. Must have been quite a big ship to carry some naval personnel. He held the glasses fixed on the sprawled shape of the officer whose outthrust arm splashed in the sea alongside. Strained and sodden, but the single gold wavy stripe on the sleeve told its own story. The other two were seamen; one had lost a leg, and appeared to have been lashed to the raft by his companions.

'Out pins! Slip!' The whaler dropped smartly on to Rob Roy's falling bow wave and veered away from the side on the boatrope. As it was cast free, the oars dipped and sliced into the water, and Ransome saw Hargrave standing upright in the swaying sternsheets while Surgeon Lieutenant Cusack crouched beside the coxswain, the sunlight touching the scarlet cloth between his stripes like blood.

It would not be a pretty sight. Ransome glanced around at the others and saw the new sub, Tritton, fingering his own sleeve, as if he had seen himself lying there. Leading Signalman Mackay too, his expression a mixture of pity and hate. He had served in the Atlantic and knew the score well enough. Sherwood, eyes partly hidden by his pale lashes, his jaw very rigid as he watched

145

the compass. And the youngster Boyes, who had been staring at the flotsam until he felt his eyes on him. Ransome nodded to him. It was all he could offer. And yet Boyes seemed to symbolise everything as clearly as a bursting starshell. They all expected him, their captain, no matter how young and unprepared, to hold every answer.

Moncrieff said thickly, 'Not a nice job at any time.'

Ransome watched the whaler's oars still, the bowman reaching out warily with his boathook as the raft lifted sluggishly, then surged against the hull. They would hold their breath, pretend it wasn't really happening, while someone reached over and cut away the identity discs from those poor, broken corpses who had once been like Mackay and Tritton. *Like me.*

Someone, somewhere would have received a telegram, *Missing, presumed killed.* The three discs would wipe away any last hope for those who still believed in such things.

He said angrily, 'Signal the whaler to tow the raft alongside!' He knew he was speaking harshly, but could not contain it. 'At least we can remember them properly, for God's sake!'

And so it was to be.

It was the first time Ransome had been off the bridge for days. It felt like an eternity as he climbed down the two ladders, past the new Oerlikon mounting and grim-faced look-outs, and then along the side-deck past the whaler, now hoisted snugly in the davits again, the wetness of its recent excursion already dried in the sunshine. How different it all looked from down here, he thought. The men off-watch, clinging to stanchions and life-rafts similar to the one they had cast adrift to remain with all the other flotsam of war. Faces watched him, some sad, some stony, all familiar to him like his own family.

It was the same as all the other times, and yet not the same at all. The three shapes by the break in the guardrails, no longer without privacy or dignity, but safe under the clean flags. He heard a snapping sound and saw Cusack pulling off some rubber gloves. Leading Seaman Hoggan was standing with the burial party, the snake tattoo very obvious around one thick wrist as he whistled silently to himself. Two faces by the engine-room hatch,

Campbell the Chief, and Nobby Clarke, his petty officer, who knew all about losing a ship. Sub-Lieutenant Fallows, his mouth a thin line as he took charge of the party. He never wore his woolly rabbit any more, Ransome had observed. He was like a different person who was trying to find himself.

Ransome looked first to seaward where *Dryaden*, which oddly enough had the most modern Asdic in the group, ploughed around them protectively, the sunlight flashing on levelled glasses on her superstructure. Then he glanced up to *Rob Roy*'s bridge and saw Hargrave craning over the side to watch him, silhouetted against the sky.

Ransome removed his cap and opened the little book. It was so creased and worn he wondered why he had not obtained a new one. The three identity discs seemed to stare up at him.

*That was why it was different.* They were some of their own. Probably part of a naval gun-crew carried aboard a big merchantman. This was for all of them. *For us.* He made himself face it. *For Tony.* As he read the familiar prayer he glanced up occasionally as if to test his own strength, his own resolve.

He saw Able Seaman Nunn who had lost everyone in his family gripping the lines by the open guardrail, his face expressionless. Only his eyes told it all. Young Boyes sent down from the bridge with an extra flag, his face screwed up while he held on to the new knife which hung from his belt; beside him the tough seaman Jardine with an arm around the boy's shoulder.

No, he could not let any one of them down. Especially not now.

He glanced up at the bridge and instantly the last tremble of power began to die away.

Ransome read the last part from memory.

'We commend unto thy hands of mercy, most merciful Father, the souls of these our brothers departed, and we commit their bodies to the deep . . .'

The rest was blurred, wiped away. As he replaced his cap he saw that the deck was cleared, the flags being folded again. There was the clang of telegraphs, and as if emerging from a brief rest, *Rob Roy*'s screws beat the sea into an impatient froth once more.

While Ransome made his way forward to the bridge ladder he

pictured the three little bundles sinking slowly into eternal darkness. The sea was two and a half thousand fathoms hereabouts. Undisturbed.

When he reached the upper bridge he walked to the chart-table and saw that Hargrave had marked the burial for future reference.

Moncrieff was slouched in his chair. He watched him thoughtfully.

'Feel better now, Ian?'

Ransome faced him. 'Much.'

He was the captain again.

# 11

# *Gateway*

Ian Ransome gripped the rim of the motorboat's canvas dodger as the little hull bucked wildly over another craft's wash. The spray across his face was surprisingly cold despite the full, hazy sunshine, and it helped to drive away the strain of marshalling the minesweeping flotilla to their various buoys.

The whole anchorage appeared to be filled with ships, moored, anchored, or tied alongside one another at the mole, so that it gave the impression they might never be able to move again. Above it all, the towering bulk of Gibraltar made even the capital ships appear almost insignificant.

Ransome glanced at the ships as the boat tore between them. Famous names, battleships and cruisers he had read about as a boy, some he had even served aboard in the peacetime RNVR days during his annual training. He thought it unlikely that there had been such a gathering of naval force before. The troopships and ungainly landing-craft too, all bedecked with lines of khaki washing hung out to dry like drab bunting.

This was naval power, the machinery it took to sustain an invasion.

A long barge crossed the motorboat's bows and he heard Able Seaman Suggit, the skimming-dish's coxswain, swear between his teeth. The launch bore the markings of a rear-admiral. Nothing must stand in his path. No wonder leaders who held the real authority could not afford to consider men as individuals. Ashore they were flags on a map. At sea just a marker with your ship's name on it. To show that you were at least still afloat.

Like sweeping mines, he thought. You never knew what effect you were having on the whole panorama of war. You worked at it, you mourned when a friend blew up and men burned before your eyes. And yet in the front line you could still afford pity.

The coxswain said, 'There she is, sir!'

Ransome saw the anchored destroyer immediately. HMS *Bedworth*, one of the small, speedy Hunt Class destroyers which had been created at the outbreak of war to fill the gaps left by peacetime neglect and reductions. They carried no torpedoes and were used mainly for escort and patrol work. For their size they were heavily armed with four-inch and multi-barrelled weapons, and the *Bedworth* even mounted a single pom-pom right in the eyes of the ship, a bow-chaser which could singe the whiskers of even the fastest E-boat. The little Hunts had an impressive speed of thirty-two knots. She would run rings around her brood of minesweepers, he thought, but then who didn't?

'*Bows!*'

The bowman raised his boathook and held it above his head as the *Rob Roy*'s only motor boat scudded round and headed towards an accommodation ladder.

He wondered if Moncrieff was still aboard, or, as in Plymouth, if he had already left without a word.

A flight of Hurricanes roared low overhead and Ransome imagined the Spaniards across the water in Algeciras watching every movement, using a one-sided neutrality to keep their German friends fully informed.

Gib in peacetime had been a favourite calling-place for the fleet. A sailors' port then, today it would seem like Aladdin's Cave to the youngsters who made up most of the ships' companies that came here.

Ransome thought of his own company. Hardly any of them had been out of home waters before. Gibraltar never changed, with its blazing lights and garish cafés, its tiny shops and stalls filled as always with junk. To these young sailors it would seem like the treasures of the Orient.

It would be packed with servicemen now more than ever before. Like the Great War when the troopships had assembled here before the bloody carnage of Gallipoli. *The Rock*. Who held it, commanded the gateway to the Mediterranean.

The motor boat's engine coughed and went astern as the hook swept down on to the accommodation ladder to bring them together.

Ransome ran lightly up the side, feeling sweaty and out of place when he was confronted by the white-clad side-party, the O.O.D. in shorts that looked as if they had just been washed and ironed.

The lieutenant saluted. 'Welcome aboard, sir. We watched you enter harbour. Yours is a job I'd prefer to see from a distance.'

Ransome followed him to the quartermaster's lobby. Just a small hard-worked destroyer, some forty feet longer than *Rob Roy*. And yet in a strange way she felt twice as big.

He heard Moncrieff's voice before they even reached the door marked *Captain*.

'I don't give a bloody toss what they say, whoever *they* are, I think it's a damn stupid –' The rest was cut off as the lieutenant tapped on the door.

Another voice spoke. *'Come!'*

The lieutenant grimaced at Ransome. 'Good luck, sir.'

Ransome knew a fair amount about the new S.N.O. *A bit of a goer*, everyone said, an officer who had seen most of his service in destroyers, and latterly working with Combined Operations right here in the Med.

Ransome adjusted his expression and stepped into the cabin.

Commander Peregrine Bliss, DSO, Royal Navy, was young for his rank. He had a square, eager face and dark curly hair which with his deeply tanned skin made his eyes stand out like chips of blue glass. He thrust out his hand, his eyes crinkling as he gave a wide grin. 'At last, Ransome. Been dying to meet up with you. Take a pew.'

He glanced at Moncrieff. *'We've* been having a discussion.' Like the man, his speech was lively, like a sea breeze. Ransome could picture him without any difficulty at all, conning his destroyer through some hazard or other, his men hanging on his every word.

Ransome sat. 'I came immediately, sir. I have all the reports you asked –'

Bliss waved a sunburned arm. 'Hell, that can wait. We're on the move right now. Can't you feel it in the air?'

Moncrieff exclaimed angrily, 'I think it stinks!'

Ransome noticed for the first time that Moncrieff held a large tumbler in his good hand; it was almost empty.

Ransome looked away. God, what was the matter with him? It was only nine in the morning!

Bliss saw his glance and beamed. 'What about a Horse's Neck, eh?'

Ransome forced a smile. 'Not for me, sir. The sun isn't over my yard-arm at this hour, I'm afraid.'

Bliss nodded, his eyes amused. 'Good show.'

Ransome tried to stay calm. Bliss had no glass, nor had he any intention of joining Moncrieff or anyone else for a drink. What was the point? A little test to see if the new boy was up to it?

Ransome tried again. His nerves were worse than he had imagined.

He said, 'My people have been working hard together, sir. By August we shall have it off to a fine art.'

Moncrieff opened his mouth but Bliss snapped, 'My turn, I think!'

To Ransome he continued, 'There's been an advance of plans. The invasion of Sicily, Operation *Husky* as it is codenamed, will begin on July 10th.' The smile expanded into a confident grin. 'It will succeed.'

Ransome said, 'Two weeks' time?' He watched the grin and recalled when he had read to Tony about the Cheshire Cat in *Alice*.

Bliss nodded. 'This flotilla, and all other inshore forces involved, must ensure that the heavy supporting squadrons are on station to offer covering fire before the first landing-craft drops its ramp!'

A hundred details seemed to scramble through Ransome's mind. He sensed that Moncrieff had been protesting on their behalf; he also had the strong feeling that this was the original date as planned. The high command may have thought that security and the shortest notice possible to risk the news leaking out, was of more value than preparing the ships for what lay ahead.

Ransome said, 'We'll just have to manage.'

Bliss regarded him with some amusement. 'I like it, Ian. May I call you that?' He hurried on, 'Just two days on dry land, and we'll have the Krauts by the short and curlies!'

Ransome relaxed slightly. He had noticed that Bliss rarely appeared to wait for, even to expect an answer. But he was a live wire, right enough. He was disturbed to find that his sadness for Moncrieff was changing to pity. Where would his Phoenix fit in now?

There was a tap at the door and a sub-lieutenant glanced in at them. Like the O.O.D., he was an RNVR officer, so Bliss had no prejudice there at least.

'I beg your pardon, sir, but the commander's boat is already alongside.'

Bliss nodded. 'Very well.' He thrust out his hand to Moncrieff. 'I do hope we meet again, old chap.'

Ransome stared. Quite apart from the obvious insincerity he could scarcely believe what he had heard.

'You're not leaving *now*, sir?'

Bliss explained smoothly, 'There is apparently a shortage of places in available aircraft. Their lordships are keen for Commander Moncrieff to take over his new appointment without any delay.'

Moncrieff lumbered to his feet. '*New appointment*, Ian. It's a supply dump in Orkney!' He dropped his eyes and stared blindly at his maimed hand. 'A bloody stores clerk!'

Bliss had turned away to peer through a gleaming scuttle.

Ransome said quietly, 'I'd hoped to lay something on for you, sir. After all this time. To leave like this —'

Moncrieff gripped his hand. It was like a vice. 'No more, Ian — I can't take it, y'see.' He groped for his cap with its cherished peak of oak leaves. 'Just tell the others —' He seemed to regain some of his old power and added fiercely, 'Tell 'em I'm *proud* of them!' The power faded; Ransome saw it dying in his eyes as he added huskily, 'Look after the ship, eh? My old *Rob Roy*.' They walked to the door and Bliss and Ransome saluted as he clambered down into a harbour-launch alongside.

While the boat surged away towards the white buildings

ashore Moncrieff looked back only once. But he was staring at *Rob Roy*.

Bliss said absently, 'Last of his kind, I shouldn't wonder.'

Was it meant with contempt, Ransome thought?

He replied calmly, 'No better way to be remembered, I'd say, sir.'

Bliss made no comment until the 'skimming-dish' sputtered back to the accommodation ladder. He stood with his feet wide apart, his strong fingers interlaced behind his back as he stared gravely at the mass of assembled ships.

'You will meet the new vice-admiral tomorrow, Ian. He will want to speak with you, and your other C.O.s of course.' He turned suddenly and fixed him with a blue stare. 'But I command the group now and my head will be on the block if just one captain screws this up. Am I making myself clear?' Again, he did not wait. 'I am, how do you say, *unused* to failure.'

He saluted as Ransome climbed back into the motor boat. He had disappeared before the bowman had even cast off.

All the way back to *Rob Roy* Ransome tried to accept Bliss for what he appeared to be. A man of courage and ability; his record said all that and more. He knew that it was like to fight the enemy at close quarters and it was obvious that that experience plus his training as a regular officer made him a perfect choice for this task.

He was ruthless too; his attitude to Moncrieff and the hint of his displeasure if anyone else *screwed things up* left little to the imagination. But then you could not fight this kind of war with a book of naval etiquette.

*It was something else.* Ransome watched the ships passing on either side, guns being swivelled round in their turrets, seamen and marines working on deck and in the various superstructures. Like some vast iron hornet's nest waiting to be unleashed.

He nodded to himself. *That was it.* Bliss made it all sound so personal, as if nothing and nobody would be spared to make his part of the operation a success.

Ransome smiled inwardly. In the navy, that was not unique.

Later, as he was sitting in his cabin, Hargrave came to see him. Ransome glanced up and nodded to the other chair. He felt different now in his clean shirt and shorts. Like someone playing a part. As for Hargrave, he looked almost a stranger in white, although he was obviously quite used to it.

Ransome said, 'I should like you to organise a party for tomorrow, Number One. If you're short of anything, I'll sign a couple of magic chits for you to take to the Base Supply Officer!'

Hargrave watched him curiously. It was not just a change of uniform, he thought. He could picture Ransome's face right here in the cabin as he had read out the signal about his brother's death, and again when the three bodies had been tipped over the side.

If it was an act, it was very convincing. Or was he really able to put things like that to the back of his mind in the name of duty? Hargrave had had all that rammed into him from early boyhood as a cadet in the Royal Naval College at Dartmouth. He had actually believed it, just as his father had insisted he would, given time. But never once, from midshipman to lieutenant, had he ever expected to see it as a physical presence. He was seeing it now, and from a man who had been a civilian until the outbreak of war.

Ransome saw the look and thought he could guess what he was thinking.

He touched a sheet of notepaper on the desk. 'This was waiting for me.'

Hargrave nodded. 'The guardboat brought it shortly after you'd left, sir.'

'It's from the vice-admiral's secretary, no less. In it he "suggests" that a party given by us might be the best and most informal way for the admiral to meet our commanding officers.'

Hargrave replied quickly, 'My father said nothing of it to me, sir, and that's the truth.'

'Thank you. I never doubted it. But it *sounds* like a command all the same, so lay on the party, right? It might be the last for quite some time.'

He gave Hargrave a thoughtful glance. '*It's* been brought forward. Two weeks from now. Top Secret, but you should know in case –'

Hargrave stared at him. He had never considered it from that angle. That Ransome might be unable to retain command, that he could be injured, even killed, before the invasion began. He felt the sweat trickling down his spine. Surely that wasn't what his father had meant about a ship of his own.

Ransome said, 'Arrange shore leave for all but the duty-part of the watch, Number One.' He was formal again. 'I believe there are two men requesting to see me?'

Hargrave nodded. How did he know that already? 'Bad news from home for both of them, sir. I don't see what we can do about it now.'

Ransome half-smiled. 'I can *talk* to them. It's the least I can do.'

Hargrave stood and made to leave. 'The Chief wishes to discuss the new pumps with you, sir.'

'Ask him to come now, will you?'

As the door closed Ransome leaned back and massaged his eyes. It never ended. He thought of Bliss's words. *I command this group now.* He should have added, 'And don't you forget it!' Ransome recalled too when he had obtained his own first command, the poor old *Guillemot*. He had looked up the meaning of command in his dictionary. It had been quite an ancient version and one definition had been, 'To demand with authority.' It fitted Bliss rather well.

It was evening by the time he had dealt with the Chief and his problem of spare parts for the new pumps, seen the doctor about a seaman whom he had put ashore with the first signs of gonorrhoea, and finally made several operational signals both to the Admiralty and to the Flag Officer Gibraltar. He felt drained. The one redeeming fact about the luckless rating sent to the V.D. clinic was that he was a new hand, who had joined the ship at Chatham. He would certainly miss the invasion anyway, and might well end up in the glasshouse as payment for a few moments of doubtful pleasure.

He smoked his pipe, took a glass of Scotch and listened to one of his Handel records. The liberty boats squeaked their fenders alongside to mingle with the jubilant chatter of shore-going sailors, then came the pipe to clear up messdecks and flats for Rounds.

At times like these he was grateful for his privacy. He pictured Moncrieff arriving in England. No ships to visit, to be part of. How would he cope? Ships were all he knew, all he had left.

Eventually he knew he was ready. Very carefully he opened his writing-case, the one his mother had given him for his last birthday, and picked up his pen.

It was easier than he had dared to hope. It was not like writing to her. It was as if she was here, listening to him, or sitting with her bare legs tucked beneath her chin in the old boatyard where it seemed as if the sun had always shone.

*My dearest Eve, We did not have that walk together which I had promised for us, but I walk with you every day, and we are together . . .*

Apart from Sub-Lieutenant Fallows, *Rob Roy*'s wardroom was deserted. Even the old hands like Bone and Campbell who had little to say in favour of the Rock's attractions had gone ashore, and aboard *Ranger* tied alongside the situation was the same.

Fallows decided that he would go ashore tomorrow, perhaps before the wardroom party. He glanced down at the single stripe on his shoulder strap and considered his future. A second ring very soon now, but what then? You needed a push, a friendly word in the right places, and Fallows was not so much of a fool that he did not know his own unpopularity. But it had not been easy for him. He had nothing but determination and guts. Even the captain had seemed satisfied with his work and would have to say as much in his personal report.

He thought of the others. Bone and the Chief did not count, but young Morgan would do well because of his navigation qualifications if nothing else. Even the newcomer Tritton – just thinking of his name made Fallows burn with anger and humiliation. *Bunny* Tritton. He too seemed so full of confidence. Fallows had never got to know Sherwood, but then he suspected that nobody ever really *knew* him. On the face of it he should have had everything. He felt envy replacing his anger. Sherwood came from a prosperous family, should have had the world at his feet even after his family had been wiped out. *Suppose my own family were killed?* Fallows swallowed his neat gin and coughed.

He did not need to seek an answer, not if he had been in Sherwood's shoes. Sherwood had known the life Fallows had only dreamed about. Cruise ships, and luxury yachts, good hotels and women probably eyeing him whenever he passed; Fallows could imagine it all. With his background, and especially when he had tempted death to gain the George Cross, second only to the VC, he could have found a safe and comfortable billet anywhere he chose. And after the war, he would never have to work again.

Fallows avoided thinking of Hargrave. He had sensed his disapproval, dislike even, from the start. Another one who had it made, no matter how things turned out. A naval family, his father a flag-officer, and right here in the Med to offer a leg-up as soon as it presented itself – no, he would get nothing out of him.

He saw the duty messman watching him. He was a seaman-gunner named Parsons who chose to act as a steward rather than work another part of ship when not employed on 'A' Gun. As gunnery officer, Fallows had been instrumental in getting him what was both a soft number and a lucrative one.

'Another gin, Parsons.' Fallows never said *please* or *thank you* to a rating. He thought it was beneath him.

Parsons fetched the bottle and, while he measured the gin, watched the ginger-haired sub-lieutenant as a milkman will study a dangerous dog. The big shindig would be tomorrow. They would be working fit to bust, he thought. Ted Kellett the P.O. steward would have all his work cut out. He couldn't be everywhere at once. With the place packed with officers all downing free gins it would always be possible to fake a few records. There would be some bottles going spare, unaccounted for, and Parsons always knew where he could sell duty-free at the right price for a nice, handy profit.

He put down the glass. So Bunny was drinking again. That was something. He was a bastard, one of the worst Parsons had known, but he had eyes like a bloody hawk when he was sober.

Parsons began warily, 'I was wondering, sir, if we could clear up the accounts before the party?'

Fallows frowned, his train of thought disturbed. 'What d'you mean?'

Parsons had been a pub barman before the war in

Southampton. Like the milkman and the dog, he could usually spot the signs. He said in a wheedling tone, 'It's not me, sir, you know that, but the Jimmy the One has been riding all of us a bit over the mess bills, an' things.'

'*And?*' Fallows stared at him. He had not taken a real drink for so long it was making his mouth and tongue numb.

'Well, sir, you didn't sign your mess chits –'

Fallows slammed down the glass. 'What the bloody hell are you yapping about? I always pay my bills –' He contained his anger and asked sharply, 'When was this anyway?'

'In Chatham, sir. You'd been working very hard, and Jimmy the One landed you with extra duty –'

Fallows smiled gently. 'Don't crawl, man, it doesn't impress me!'

Parsons licked his lips. 'There's ten quid to cover, sir.'

'*What?*' Even Fallows lost his practiced calm. 'At duty-free prices, how the hell could that happen?'

Parsons persisted; it was all or nothing now. 'It was the night when young Tinker came down to see you, sir, when you told him –' He did not go on. There was no need to.

Fallows stood up and dragged at his short-sleeved shirt as if it was clinging to his body.

'I told him what?'

Parsons watched him. Just for an instant he had thought he had gone too far, chosen the wrong moment. But now . . . He said, 'Tinker asked to go ashore, sir, because of what had happened.'

Fallows sat down heavily on the club fender and pinched the crown of his nose between finger and thumb as he tried to remember, to make the picture form in his mind.

It was like a terrible nightmare. You knew it was bad, and yet you could never make any sort of form or sense out of it. He *had* been plagued by some vague, distorted memory about Tinker.

Parsons added, 'You shouted at him, sir.'

Fallows looked up. 'Did I?' The admission seemed to stun him. 'Then what happened?'

Parsons could scarcely believe it, but the old in-built caution flashed its warning. Like the drunk in the bar who takes one too many, who picks up a bottle, thirsting for blood.

'You were worn out, sir, like I told you. You shouldn't have been on duty that time.'

Fallows nodded like a puppet. 'That's right. I do remember. Number One –' He checked himself just in time, and asked curtly, 'What did I say to Tinker?'

Parsons took a deep breath. 'You told him he was *not* going ashore, that he was a disgrace to the ship and his uniform. Things like that.'

Fallows eyed him like a man who has suddenly lost his memory, afraid of what he might be or do. 'There's more?'

'You told him that his mother was an effing whore, sir, that it was the best thing that could have happened to her.'

Fallows stood up and walked to the side and back again. He felt sick, trapped by the nightmare he could still not recognise or break.

He said, 'I have to do Rounds in a moment.' He looked vaguely at the letter-rack. 'First I must go to my cabin.'

'About the money, sir.'

Fallows fumbled with his wallet. 'How much was it, ten pounds?'

Parsons took the notes. They were damp from the officer's sweat.

'Thank you, sir. We've all got to stick together in some things.'

But Fallows had thrust open the door of the officers' heads and Parsons heard him vomiting helplessly.

He folded the notes inside his paybook and smiled.

'Bloody little bastard!' He poured himself a tall measure of brandy and swallowed it in one gulp. As he topped the bottle up carefully with water he added savagely, 'Now you'll know what it's like to bloody well crawl, *Mr* Bunny!'

Unexpectedly, Vice-Admiral Hargrave stepped from the brow which crossed to *Ranger*'s deck and touched his cap to the ramrod stiff side-party. He paused to listen to the music, the muted buzz of voices from the wardroom skylight, and said, 'Sounds like a good party, Ransome.'

Ransome said, 'Sorry about the reception, sir. You caught us all on the hop, I'm afraid.'

The admiral smiled. 'I didn't expect a guard and Royal Marines band – I happen to enjoy informality!'

Ransome looked at the slender figure who followed the admiral across the brow. Like the admiral, she was all in white, the only touch of colour being the blue of her shoulder-straps; a second officer in the W.R.N.S.

'This is Second Officer Rosalind Pearce, by the way, my flag lieutenant and guardian angel.' He laughed loudly.

How like his son he was, Ransome thought. A bit heavier, but the same good looks, and the added confidence of age.

He looked at the girl. She was tall, almost the same height as her admiral, with dark hair showing beneath her neat tricorn hat, and serious eyes which were probably blue.

The vice-admiral added, 'She wanted to see all you rough, sea-going types anyway – another experience, eh?'

They glanced at each other. Ransome could detect a closer relationship, the sense of understanding.

He said, 'I'll lead the way, sir.'

The wardroom was packed, and the guests overflowed into the passageway and at least one neighbouring cabin.

Hargrave pushed through the throng and then saw his father. 'Welcome aboard, sir!'

Ransome saw his eyes shift to the girl.

Vice-Admiral Hargrave made the same introduction and again they looked at one another. Ransome suspected that the admiral said the same thing quite often. Explanation, or defence, he wondered?

Hargrave beckoned to a perspiring messman with a loaded tray.

'A bit of a mixture.'

She said, 'That one looks nice,' but her eyes were on Hargrave. Comparing, perhaps?

Ransome turned as a messman took the admiral's heavily oak-leaved cap from him. There was the true difference. The thinning hair, the deeper lines around his mouth and eyes. His immaculate white-drill uniform with its double row of decorations did not hide the slight belly either.

The vice-admiral nodded to the officers nearest him and said,

'At last we're shifting my H.Q. to Malta, Ransome. Exciting, eh? After all the disappointments and the blockades, we'll be back where we belong.'

The girl remarked, 'I'll not be sorry to leave that cavern under the Rock they loosely *describe* as our present H.Q.'

The vice-admiral grinned hugely. 'You wait till you get to Malta, my girl! That dismal tunnel at Lascaris may be bombproof, but it's like living in a sewer, believe me!'

Hargrave asked, 'How long have you served with my, er – with the admiral?'

She regarded him thoughtfully. In the hard deckhead lights her eyes were violet, very relaxed, like a cat's.

'Six or seven months, I think.' She had a low, well-modulated voice. Very self-assured.

A boatswain's mate appeared in the door and gestured to the first lieutenant.

'What is it?' Hargrave was irritated at the interruption, just as he was confused. His father had never mentioned the girl before. She was quite stunning, with the looks of an actress, and, he guessed, an intelligence as sharp as anyone he had ever met.

The seaman called above the din, ' 'Nother guest, sir! A civvy!'

The vice-admiral chuckled. 'Good old Jack, never changes, thank God.' He added, as he reached for a passing drink, 'My guest actually – you'll like him. He's Richard Wakely. Heard of him?'

Who hadn't? Right from the early days, the Phoney War as it was called by those who did not have to fight it, Richard Wakely had been a household name. As a BBC roaming journalist he had brought every aspect of the war to Britain's firesides. When England had stood quite alone he had rallied every heart with his stirring words. Even before Dunkirk he had toured the front lines of the British Expeditionary Force, and visited the unbreachable Maginot Line, where he had enthralled his massive audience when he had described the nearness of the enemy in the Siegfried Line; the *Huns* as he had called them. He had disappeared after Dunkirk for a time, and had carried on his broadcasts in the USA.

Then when Britain stood firm and her friends and allies rallied from all parts of the world, Richard Wakely came back. From a

Lancaster bomber above Berlin, or in the Western Desert even within range of German snipers there, he had told his listeners what it was like, regardless of the risk to himself.

It seemed strange that such a famous figure was about to enter their tiny, private world in *Rob Roy*.

The vice-admiral turned aside so that nobody else should hear. 'I want you to meet him because the people at home need to be told about your war for a change. Just be natural.' He added sharply, 'I didn't know *he* was coming too!'

Ransome saw Commander Bliss enter with the man he knew was Wakely. He heard the admiral mutter, 'I thought he was at that damned meeting!'

The girl replied indifferently, 'Must have finished earlier, sir.' She watched him, gauging his mood.

Ransome watched Bliss being greeted by the admiral. What was it? Something from the past? He had assumed that Bliss was his choice; now he was not so sure.

Ransome took Wakely's hand and shook it. It was surprisingly soft and limp.

Wakely looked a lot like his pictures. Tall, heavily rather than powerfully built, with wispy fair hair and a round, plump face.

'I am really looking forward to this, Commander Ransome!'

Bliss asked, 'Have I missed something, sir?'

The vice-admiral shrugged. 'Mr Wakely has agreed to keep us company while he gathers material for his next series of broadcasts.' He lowered his voice although it was quite unnecessary as the noise, which had faded at Bliss's entry, had mounted again. '*Operation Husky.*'

Wakely gave a childlike smile, 'All the way to Europe's soft underbelly, as Winston calls it!'

Bliss nodded approvingly. 'You honour us, Mr Wakely. I've often listened to your broadcasts.'

Wakely sipped what looked like an orangeade and blinked modestly. 'Then the honour is all mine, believe me.'

Bliss nodded again, this time to Ransome. 'Everyone here?'

'All the commanding officers anyway, sir.'

The vice-admiral dabbed his mouth with a handkerchief. 'I'd like to speak with them now.'

Bliss was saying, 'We'll do all we can to make you comfortable in *Bedworth* —'

Ransome held up his hands and the conversation began to die away once more. It was unfortunate because the vice-admiral's voice was made to sound unnecessarily loud.

'Richard Wakely is sailing with *Rob Roy* as it happens. It's all about minesweeping, and bloody time too if you ask me!'

Ransome saw Lieutenant Commander Gregory, *Ranger*'s C.O., chain-smoking as usual, nudge his companion, Stranach of the *Firebrand*.

Hargrave had placed himself beside the Wren officer again. They made a handsome pair, Ransome thought. Did he think so too? Or was he pondering on his father's morals, his mother and sisters in England?

Vice-Admiral Hargrave announced, 'You will be sailing very soon now to play an important part in a moment of history. Sicily is a stepping-stone and the pace will be hot and demanding. Our success will mean the opening of the Second Front, with all that that implies, and the end result, with God's help —'

Ransome saw the Wren officer's perfect mouth quiver very slightly in what could have been a smile.

Vice-Admiral Hargrave concluded, '— will be the eventual defeat of our enemies!'

They all applauded and the vice-admiral said softly to the girl, 'Pretty good, eh, Ross?' She nodded and clapped her hands with the others.

Ransome felt suddenly grateful as the admiral glanced at his watch. It was bad enough to have Bliss here with his face like thunder without the others sensing a rift between their superiors as Gregory had obviously done.

The vice-admiral seized a few hands. 'Malta, then. We shall all meet again before too long.' He smiled at Richard Wakely. 'I have some more people waiting to hang on your every word!'

Wakely shook Ransome's hand, his eyes distant. 'I'm getting the *feel* of it already.' He nodded firmly. 'I'm never wrong.'

Ransome accompanied them to the brow and wondered why the vice-admiral had chosen to board *Rob Roy* via *Ranger*. Perhaps he never threw away the chance to see and be seen.

The Wren officer turned to face him.

'It's been a pleasure, Commander.'

Ransome felt her gaze like an inspection. Outwardly cool and composed. But the admiral's use of her first name told a different story.

He returned to the wardroom and found Bliss in deep conversation with several of the commanding officers.

To Hargrave he said, 'It went well enough, I thought.'

Hargrave plucked at his shirt. 'All these people. Every mother's son seems to know about the invasion.'

Ransome thought about the peacetime Budget, when it was always touted as a total secret until the actual announcement in the House of Commons. And yet as his father had pointed out many times, there were hundreds who must have known the 'secret'. The secretaries, the financial advisers, and all the printers who produced the final budget papers. Like Second Officer Pearce and her staff, these officers and God alone knew how many others in Whitehall. There was no such thing as a true secret.

Bliss made his excuses and left. He seemed calm enough but his eyes were angry, like the moment he had been curtly put right about Wakely.

His boat was waiting on the outboard side and Bliss paused to say, 'If you have any problems, tell *me*, right?'

Ransome nodded. *Before telling the vice-admiral*, he might just as well have said.

Bliss added, 'So your Number One is the admiral's son?'

'Yes, sir.' It was a sounding remark. Bliss knew just about everything. Perhaps he and the vice-admiral were too much alike.

There was a commotion in the wardroom and Bliss said shortly, 'I'm off. Before the high jinks begin. Best to get it out of their systems now, eh?' It sounded vaguely like a threat.

Ransome paused by the wardroom where Petty Officer Kellett was hovering outside the curtained entrance.

He said anxiously, 'I'd like to offer you one of my special cocktails, sir.'

Ransome took the hint. 'Trouble?'

Kellett shrugged. 'Storm in a teacup, sir.'

Beyond the curtain, Lieutenant Philip Sherwood clung to the back of a chair and stared glassily at the mass of figures which filled the place. He had missed Bliss by seconds, having boarded *Ranger*'s deck from a passing launch.

He looked tousled and crumpled and there was a wine stain on his shirt, like dried blood.

'Well, well, well! A celebration or a wake, which must it be?'

Hargrave made to step forward but Campbell touched his arm. 'Leave it, Number One. He's never been like this before.'

Sherwood beckoned to a messman and took a glass from the tray without even looking at it.

'I am sorry I missed the party, I was elsewhere —' He swallowed the drink and swayed against the chair for support.

Someone called, 'For Christ's sake take it easy, or you'll spill a drop!' Another said, 'Don't anyone light a cigarette near him or you'll blow up the ship!'

Sherwood ignored the laughter and stared around with haunted desperation.

He said in a surprisingly clear voice, "If we are mark'd to die, we are enow to do our country loss: and if to live, the fewer men, the greater share of honour —"

He almost fell and then pivoted round as Ransome entered the wardroom.

Sherwood made a mock bow. 'Oops. I — I am so sorry, *dear* Captain, but I am slightly pissed —'

Surgeon Lieutenant Cusack stepped forward and caught Sherwood as he fell.

To the others he said, 'I think his party's over.'

Ransome looked around their faces, so different and yet suddenly bonded together, sobered by Sherwood's rambling quotation, which he had delivered like a prophesy.

As captain he was just another guest here in *Rob Roy*'s wardroom. It was not the time or the place to make a stand on Sherwood's behaviour. He had not seen him like it before, and tomorrow he would have to put it all behind him. Otherwise . . .

He nodded to the others and left the wardroom, but even when he reached the companion ladder there was still no sound to mark his departure.

He opened his cabin door and switched on the light. It seemed to shine directly on Tony's face.

Sherwood was not the only one, he thought. Nor would he be the last once they were through the gateway.

Chief Petty Officer Joe Beckett tilted his cap further over his eyes and stared up at the Rock, the strange shimmering haze which swirled around the summit like smoke.

The Buffer stood beside him watching the last of the NAAFI stores boats alongside, another taking aboard the final sack of letters from *Rob Roy* and *Ranger*.

Beckett said, 'Any more for the Skylark, Topsy?' He glanced at some of the seamen in their clean shorts and white tops. 'Soon be their old scruffy selves again, eh?'

The Buffer nodded. 'Big White Cheese come aboard last night, I 'ear?'

Beckett grinned. 'Yeh, an' you bloody missed it, scuttlin' about the Rock like a randy dog, no doubt!'

The Buffer shrugged. 'I've seen more admirals than young Boyes over there 'as 'ad 'ot dinners!'

Beckett savoured it. 'But 'e 'ad 'is Wren officer with 'im.' He blew a kiss. 'I'd rather be on 'er than the middle watch, I can tell you!' His grin faded as he took on his stern coxswain's expression.

'An' wot are all we, then?'

*All we* was one small, slightly built sailor who was being unceremoniously manhandled over the brow from *Ranger*, his frail body almost buried by hammock and kitbag, attaché case and gas mask respirator. His uniform was new and did not fit very well.

The Buffer gave a theatrical groan. 'Must be twelve years old, eh, Swain?'

'No more, and that's the truth!'

He beckoned the small figure over. 'Wot's yer name, son?'

'G – Gold, sir.'

'*Gold*, is it? Wot're you, a four-by-two or summat?'

It was all quite lost on the newcomer, who looked as if he might burst into tears at any moment.

Beckett relented slightly. 'You must be the replacement for whatsisname.'

The Buffer showed his monkey teeth. 'The one wot got a dose of clap!'

'Don't shock the lad, Buffer!' He looked severely at the sailor. 'Last ship?'

'This is my f-first, sir.' He peered around the busy deck, clattering winches, order and purpose, none of which he could recognise. 'I – I was supposed to be joining a c-cruiser, s-sir.'

The Buffer stared outboard. 'A stutter too, that's all I bleedin' need!'

Beckett touched the youth's shoulder and felt him jump.

'No sweat, Gold. You'll soon settle in, though as you can see with yer own mincers, this ain't no bloody cruiser!'

Boyes walked past and Beckett seized him like a straw. ' 'Ere, Boyes, take this lad to Number Three Mess and get 'im fixed up.' He winked. 'Veteran like you should know wot to do, eh?'

Boyes helped the new hand gather his kit. The deck was begining to tremble, and there was a stronger trail of smoke from *Rob Roy*'s single funnel.

Getting ready to slip from the buoy. Boyes shivered and glanced up at the bridge as if expecting to see the captain. But there was only a solitary signalman who was flashing his Aldis towards the shore.

'This way.' He picked up the hammock and led Gold towards the forecastle.

The Buffer shook his head. 'No experience. *None*. Wot do they expect us to do?'

Beckett made a few notes in his book about Gold's future. The machinery had already taken over.

He said abruptly, 'Try an' keep the poor little sods alive, that's wot!'

Boyes recalled his own despair when he had entered the lower messdeck. Now, with almost everyone aboard and standing up in the small, confined space, it was a picture of utter chaos.

Men were changing into the rig-of-the-day as all the ships would have to look right and pusser when they left harbour, not merely for the F.O.I.C.'s sake but also the ever-watchful

Spaniards. Some were trying to cram a last souvenir into lockers or kitbags.

Leading Seaman Ted Hoggan appeared to be the only one seated, at his usual place at the head of the table, apparently undisturbed by the packed bodies all around him, a rock in a tideway.

Boyes said, 'I'll show you where to put your gear. You'll not have a place to sling your hammock, of course. There aren't enough hooks in this mess.'

Gold nodded, then flinched as the tannoy squeaked and the boatswain's call shattered the air. 'D'you hear there! Special sea dutymen to your stations! *Away* motor boat's crew!'

Able Seaman Suggit, his mouth spurting crumbs, pushed up the ladder, cursing through his food. 'Bloody officers! Always want something!'

Boyes got to the table and waited for Hoggan to look up.

'New one for the mess, Hookey.'

Hoggan eyed the newcomer without any change of expression. 'You've put 'im in the picture, Gerry?'

Boyes nodded. 'I think so.' He turned to Gold. 'First sound from *that bell*, and you drop everything, run like hell for your action station, right?'

He did not see Able Seaman Jardine, the one who wore a wicked-looking knife in his hand-made sheath, give a broad wink, nor Hoggan's acknowledgement.

Jardine said, 'Take the advice of an *old sweat*, my son.' He clapped Boyes round the shoulder as he had beside the burial party. 'He'll see you right –'

He might have burst out laughing but the tannoy made them all look up.

'All hands! Hands to stations for leaving harbour! Stand by wires an' fenders!'

Hoggan thrust a partly darned sock into his locker and grabbed his cap.

He watched Boyes leading the new seaman up the ladder and smiled sadly.

'Here we go again –' But he was alone; the messes on either side of the deck were empty.

# 12

# *One of Their Own*

Sub-Lieutenant Tudor Morgan lifted his face from the wheelhouse voicepipe and squinted into the fierce glare. 'Steady on zero-four-five, sir!'

Ransome crossed to the opposite side of the bridge and grimaced as his bare arm touched the steel plating. It felt like an oven door.

He levelled his glasses above the screen and watched the flotilla taking station again for the next sweep, the hoisted black balls showing they were trailing their wires to port.

Their formation keeping was so good now that they could all have been connected by a cable, he thought. He moved the glasses along the echelon of dazzle-painted hulls, the occasional flash of colour from the little flags on their scurrying Oropesa floats. Then Ransome trained his glasses directly astern. How unreal it all looked. More like an ocean than the approaches to Malta. They had begun sweeping at dawn as they had the previous day; now it was halfway through the forenoon watch. There was no horizon, and the great expanse of water was like pale blue milk, rising only slowly in a shallow swell. The sky had no colour at all, and the sun, although covered by haze, shone brilliant white like a furnace bar.

The men working aft with the sweep wire or employed about the upper deck were almost naked, their bodies either brown or uncomfortably reddened in these unfamiliar surroundings. So different from the North Sea and the English Channel, Ransome thought.

It was almost impossible to believe that the purple blur barely visible astern was actually Malta, that these very waters had been fought over continuously since the retreat from Greece and the start of the real desert war against Rommel. The seabed was littered with wrecks, ships of every size, from carriers to tiny sloops, even China River gunboats which had been sent to bolster up the embattled fleet and had soon paid the price for it. Ships of Rudyard Kipling's navy against Stuka dive-bombers, E-boats, and crack Italian cruisers.

And now it was as if the war had never been. In the first dawn light they had headed past a vast fleet of minesweeping trawlers, of the kind which had kept the channels open around Britain since the beginning; many of them were veterans of that war, of Dunkirk and the ill-fated Norwegian campaign.

Ransome had been standing on the bridge, his first cup of tea in his hands as they had pounded through the scattered fleet of trawlers. It had reminded him of a picture his mother still treasured, of a Japanese fishing flotilla with Fujiyama in the background. The same unlikely sea and mist, the ships like models above their own seemingly unmoving images.

*Rob Roy* was steering north-east; the coast of Sicily lay about forty miles away. Just months ago this area had been dominated by the Luftwaffe, the killing-ground for any vessel which had dared to make for Malta with food and supplies. Overnight, or so it seemed now, all that had changed. Malta was relieved, new airstrips had been hastily laid there by the Americans so that daily fighter patrols could be maintained.

He heard Sherwood speaking with Morgan as they pored over the chart-table together. A good team now that they were at sea again.

Sherwood had apologised for his behaviour on the night of the party. Ransome had left it at that. Whatever had happened to throw Sherwood off balance seemed to be under control once more. That was part of his trouble. He held himself stretched out like a wire. He only appeared to be content when he was working.

Ransome looked aft to the quarterdeck and saw Richard Wakely with his cameraman speaking with Hargrave beside the new winch. He saw him smile as he put on a steel helmet, then point, squinting at the sky, while his cameraman recorded the moment. Even without using his binoculars Ransome could sense the first lieutenant's embarrassment as the little act continued. Necessary probably, but somehow cheap against those sailors who were watching, who had seen the real thing far too often. Was that the real reason for Vice-Admiral Hargrave's insistence that Wakely should be in *Rob Roy*? So that his own son could get some of the limelight, if any was ever left over by Wakely?

Ransome crossed to the forepart of the bridge and trained his glasses ahead. The sea was empty, rising and falling so slowly, as if it was breathing. Nothing. Not even a gull or a leaping fish.

But there were mines here, or had been until this massive sweep had been mounted. British, Italian, German, it was a veritable deathtrap for any ship too large to avoid them. Yet many had braved the minefields; submarines had crept through that silent forest of rusty wires with their obscene iron globes, to carry aid to Malta. They had had to lie submerged in the harbour throughout the day to avoid air attacks which could be mounted in minutes from both Sicily and the Italian mainland. Then at night they would unload their precious cargoes of fuel and ammunition, tinned food, and anything else they could cram into their hulls. Even their torpedo tubes had been used to carry vital supplies although it left the submarines without teeth for the hazardous journey back to base. Many did not make it.

*Rob Roy* alone had put up twenty mines in these waters so far; *Ranger* had swept three more than that. If you were lucky it was a whole lot easier than in the Channel, with its troublesome currents and fierce tides. Here at least it was non-tidal, and if you picked up a mine – Ransome did not continue on that train of thought.

He said, 'Another hour?'

Sherwood looked at him. His hair was even more bleached by the sun.

'Near enough, sir.' He glanced at the glistening water. 'Surely they must know what's happening?'

Ransome nodded. Probably what every Jack in the flotilla was thinking. The enemy, silent and unseen, must have known for weeks what to expect.

He replied, 'Four days from now.' He thought about the pack of intelligence reports and plans in his cabin safe. The sea was empty, and yet from Gibraltar and the battered North African ports where *Rob Roy* had refuelled, and from Alexandria in the Eastern Mediterranean, the huge fleet of landing-ships and their protectors was massing for this one-off assault on Sicily.

He added, 'They're probably more worried than we are.'

Richard Wakely appeared on the bridge ladder, his round face dripping with sweat.

'What a day, eh, Captain?' He mopped his features with a spotted silk handkerchief. 'Just a few more shots in case the light changes, I think.' He beamed to the bridge at large. 'I don't want to leave anything out!'

Sherwood had replaced the dark glasses he often wore on the bridge.

'You must have seen quite a lot of different types of action.'

Wakely smiled gravely. 'That's true, I suppose. I've been lucky.'

Sherwood asked, 'Did you ever run across a Brigadier de Courcey in the Western Desert, sir?' He seemed suddenly very intent. 'Alex de Courcey?'

Wakely mopped his throat vigorously. 'Can't say I have. But then I meet so many, y'know.' He looked at Sherwood for the first time. 'You know him?'

'Friend of my late father, actually. They used to shoot together.'

'I see.' He turned away. 'Must be off. Still a lot to do.' He called for his cameraman. 'Where *are* you, Andy?'

When he had gone Ransome asked quietly, 'What was all that about?'

Sherwood removed his glasses and polished them with his shirt. His eyes looked bitter.

'He knows who I'm talking about, right enough, or he should. Alex became a staff officer after he was promoted out of the tanks. He told my father all about Richard Wakely in the early days in France when he was a tank commander.'

'I take it you don't care much for him?' Ransome added sharply, 'Come on, spit it out, man!'

Sherwood glanced briefly at the nearest bridge look-out. The man was crouching by his mounted binoculars, his eyes protected from the glare by a frame of deeply tinted glass. He was apparently out of earshot.

'Wakely's a phoney, a complete fraud. Never went near the front line the whole time. After Dunkirk he shot off to the States to protect his precious skin.' He faced Ransome and gave an apologetic smile. 'That's what he said.'

Ransome climbed on to his chair and winced from the contact. 'You are too cynical by half.'

Sherwood glanced at the ladder as if he expected to see Wakely there, listening.

'That famous broadcast from El Alamein.' He shook his head. 'I'll bet he did it from his suite at Shepheard's in Cairo!'

They both turned as Leading Signal Mackay shouted, 'Signal from *Dunlin*, sir! *My catch, I think!*'

Ransome strode to the opposite gratings and steadied his binoculars against the slow roll.

He watched the stab of *Dunlin*'s signal lamp, the bright hoist of flags breaking from her yard.

'Signal *Dryaden* to close on *Dunlin*.'

Ransome ignored the clatter of the signal lamp, the stir of excitement around the bridge. *One more mine. Should be all right.* He shifted his glasses on to the graceful Icelandic trawler and saw the mounting white moustache of her bow wave as she increased speed, her marksmen already up forward in readiness to dispense with yet another would-be killer.

'There it is, sir! *Dunlin*'s quarter!' There was an ironic cheering from aft and Ransome wondered if Wakely's cameraman was recording the moment.

Leading Signalman Mackay was using the old telescope, his lips moving silently as he spelled out another signal.

'From *Scythe*, sir. *Senior Officer closing from the south-west.*'

Ransome waited for *Dryaden* to forge ahead until he could train his glasses astern again.

So Bliss was moving up to join them. He had been content to stay with the main force of minesweeping trawlers until now. A compliment or a snub, it was hard to say.

'From *Bedworth*, sir!' Mackay braced his legs wide apart. '*Aircraft approaching from the north!*'

Ransome let his glasses fall to his chest. 'Acknowledge.' His mind seemed to click into place, to remind him of Sherwood's earlier words. *They must know what's happening.*

He said, 'Inform the first lieutenant, recover sweep immediately.'

He stared at the red button below the screen, the metal around it worn smooth by all those other emergencies.

They might think he was losing his grip. Going round the bend at last. Plenty had.

He vaguely heard a cheer, then the rattle of small-arms fire as *Dryaden*'s marksmen punctured the released mine and sent it on its way to the bottom.

Too careful, or like the ill-fated *Viper*'s captain had been, too bloody confident for his own good?

He did not realise he was speaking aloud as he exclaimed, 'They can think what they bloody well like!' Then he pressed down the button and heard the shriek of alarm bells coming up the rank of voicepipes.

*'Action Stations! Action Stations!'*

The calm was shattered, the momentary interest of a mine made harmless forgotten, as the barebacked figures scampered to their stations, groping for anti-flash gear and helmets, making sure their lifebelts were tied loosely around their bodies.

All down the line the alarm was picked up, and Ransome felt the hull shiver as the new winch hauled on the sweep wire like an angler with a giant marlin.

'Short-range weapons crews closed up!'

'Coxswain on the wheel!'

'Main armament closed up.' The latter was Bunny Fallows' voice on the intercom, his Scots accent strangely noticeable.

So many reports for so small a ship.

Ransome dragged his white-covered cap from beneath a locker and tugged it across his ruffled hair.

'From *Bedworth*, sir. *Do not engage.*'

Sherwood muttered, 'Must be some of ours after all.'

Ransome felt chilled despite the unwavering heat. If there was such a thing as instinct, he had never felt so certain.

'Aircraft, sir! Red one-one-oh! Angle of sight –'

Ransome gripped his glasses until they hurt his fingers; he did not hear the rest. Did not need to.

There they were, not just two or three, but maybe a dozen or more, strung out against the empty sky in a fine curve, catching the sunlight like chips of bright glass.

'*Start tracking!*'

Sherwood was watching the tiny slivers with his binoculars. Young Morgan looked up from the chart-table. 'Heading for Malta, d'you think?'

Sherwood did not turn. 'Not this time. It's us they're after.'

Ransome said, 'Signal *Dryaden* to drop dan buoys *now*.' Someone would have to complete the sweep after this was over. He watched the leading aircraft, still without shape, as it began to turn, until it appeared to be flying straight towards him.

'Warn the engine-room. Full revs when I give the word.'

Richard Wakely's voice broke through the chilled concentration.

'What the *hell's* happening?'

Sherwood still did not take his eyes off the plane.

'Some good shots coming up, sir. We are about to be attacked.'

'Alter-Course signal from *Bedworth*, sir. *Steer zero-nine-zero in succession.*'

Ransome nodded. 'Bring her round.' It had been a near thing. If Bliss had not had a change of heart the whole flotilla might had ended up in a minefield with their sweeps snug and useless on deck.

'*Here they come!*'

'*Full ahead together! Starboard twenty!*'

Ransome felt the gratings bounding under his shoes. They were going to attack from astern, and use the sun's glare to best advantage. Pictures flashed through his mind. The old instructor who had said, 'Always watch out for the Hun wot comes out of the sun!' Of David down aft where Hargrave was, the suddenness of his death, the women in black, and the girl who had looked like Eve.

He closed his mind against all of them. This was his purpose for being. Nothing else must matter now.

'Midships! *Steady!*'

He saw Morgan crouched behind the gyro repeater, a boatswain's mate cocking one of the old stripped Lewis guns they had 'borrowed' from the army. Even the cook would be down there with the damage-control party or helping the doctor. There were no passengers in *Rob Roy*.

He thought suddenly of Moncrieff and his last words about the ship he had loved above all others.

Ransome pounded the rail beneath the screen as the revolutions continued to mount in time with the increasing vibration.

'Come on, old girl – for him if not for me!'

Of course the enemy knew. No minesweepers meant no invasion, not until they were ready to repel it.

Wakely called, his voice shrill, 'What shall I do, for God's sake?'

Sherwood smiled as he picked up the parallel rulers, which had jerked to the deck from the shaking chart-table.

'What about a nice hymn, sir?'

The wheelhouse seemed to shrink as the door was clipped shut, and all but the slitted observation panels slammed into place.

Boyes wedged himself in a corner by the plot-table, his eyes everywhere as he tried to form a picture of what was happening, what had begun with the sudden scream of alarm bells.

Midshipman Davenport was leaning over the plot and making some adjustments for a new chart. His shirt was plastered to his spine by sweat, and Boyes could see it dripping on the chart from his face. Beckett was on the wheel as usual, the quartermasters manning the engine and revolution telegraphs. A messenger crouched by the emergency handset, and through the bell-mouthed voicepipe by Beckett's head Boyes could hear much of what was said on the upper bridge.

He heard the captain call for full speed, the deft movements of the waiting hands near the wheel, then Beckett's harsh reply, 'Both engines full ahead, sir!'

Faintly through the open intercom he heard Fallows' voice. 'All guns load with semi-armour-piercing –'

Then the captain's intervention, curt but seemingly untroubled.

Fallows mumbled, 'Sorry, sir, I mean high-explosive!'

Beckett turned aside from the voicepipe. 'Poor old Bunny's lost 'is bottle!'

Boyes whispered, 'How many, d'you think, er, sir?'

Davenport peered at him, his eyes wild. 'How the hell should I know? Just shut up and wait for orders!'

Boyes found to his astonishment that Davenport's tirade left him unmoved. At the same instant he realised he was unafraid. That really did surprise him.

The captain's voice sounded different; he was speaking directly to the engine-room.

'I know that, Chief, but I want everything you've got. *Now.*' There was the merest hesitation, and he was heard to add, 'Bale out if I give the words. No heroics, right?'

Davenport opened and closed his fists, his voice thick with disbelief. *'Bale out?'*

Leading Seaman Reeve clung to a shuddering telegraph and said cheerfully, 'Better swim than fry, sir!'

Right aft by the second four-inch gun, Lieutenant Hargrave shaded his eyes in the glare to watch the damage-control party taking cover, the Buffer calling out last minute instructions.

It was getting harder to hear anything clearly. The wake frothing up from the racing screws had risen level with the deck, and spray surged over the sides as if they were sinking by the stern. He saw the other ships astern, some making too much smoke, others almost lost in haze and drifting spume. He saw *Bedworth*, her yards alive with flags, turning in a wide sweep, showing all the grace of a thoroughbred as she displayed her streaming deck, the guns already pivoting round to track the target.

He said aloud, 'There they are, Buffer! Port quarter!' He felt a catch in his throat. 'God Almighty!'

The Buffer sucked his monkey-teeth and watched the tiny, glinting aircraft through slitted eyes.

He saw 'Gipsy' Guttridge, gunlayer on the four-inch, looking down at him, like a member of some forgotten monastic order in his anti-flash hood. As he turned his controls effortlessly in his strong hands he was singing quietly to himself, the words set against a well-known hymn.

'Six days a man shall work
as long as he is able,
and on the seventh shall scrub the deck
and holystone the cable –'

They grinned at one another and the Buffer called, 'That's bloody true, Gipsy!'

The gunnery speaker crackled into life, 'Aircraft starboard quarter! Angle of sight three-oh!'

The gunlayer and trainer spun their polished wheels and Guttridge muttered, 'I just 'ope Bunny's got *that* bloody right!'

The speaker again. *'Barrage – commence – commence – commence!'*

Hargrave watched the other ships astern open fire, the sky suddenly filled with drifting balls of dirty smoke, then as the leading aircraft burst into view above their mastheads, the livid tracer and the steady thud-thud-thud of pom-poms added their weight to the barrage.

*'Shoot!'*

The four-inch recoiled violently and the breech was wrenched open, streaming cordite fumes before the shock-wave had receded.

'Gunlayer, target!' Then, 'Trainer, target!' And another sharp explosion cracked out towards the aircraft.

Hargrave heard a tremendous explosion, felt it punch against the hull like a ram, and saw a column of water beginning to fall. It looked as if it was right beside the third minesweeper, but they were still afloat, following in a sharp turn as *Rob Roy*'s rudder went over for a violent zigzag.

An aircraft just seemed to materialise right over Hargrave's head. It must have dived low after dropping a bomb, and he saw the stabbing flashes of its machine-gun fire, and gasped as the Buffer grabbed his arm and pulled him against the hot steel.

'Watch out, sir! That bugger's taken a real dislike to you!'

Hargrave tried to smile, but his mouth felt like leather. He saw the twin-engined plane roaring away ahead, pursued by bright balls of tracer, and one very near-miss from 'A' Gun. He even saw the black crosses, so stark on either wing, streaks of oil near the open bomb-bay doors.

He took a grip on himself. 'Nobody hurt?'

The Buffer pointed. 'They're attacking from both sides, sir!'

Hargrave saw Kellett, the P.O. steward, still wearing his white jacket, hurrying to the opposite side, a Bren gun cradled in his arms as he squinted at the sky.

The Buffer sighed. 'Where's the bloody RAF now that we needs 'em?'

'*Shoot!*'

Hargrave winced as another plane roared down through the gunsmoke. His ears throbbed as if they would never hear again, and his eyes felt raw from the constant firing.

*Brrrrrrr!* He heard the harsh rattle of machine-gun fire, and stared at the advancing feathers of white spray until the metal clanged and cracked across the deck like a rivet-gun.

One of the damage-control party was down, kicking wildly, blood everywhere, so bright and unreal in the hazy glare.

The Buffer yelled, '*Get that man!*' He glanced at Hargrave. 'You be okay 'ere, sir?' The he was gone, his stocky figure pushing men where they were needed, pausing to restrain the wounded seaman as 'Pansy' Masefield, his red-cross satchel bouncing from one hip, appeared from nowhere.

'Nasty, Pansy.' The Buffer grinned at the wounded man, whose eyes were filled with dread, like a terrified child's. 'But we've seen worse, eh?'

Masefield glared at him then beckoned to his assistants. 'Take him to the *real* doctor, chop-chop!' Then he patted the wounded man's face and said gently, 'You'll be fine, Jenner. I've stopped the bleeding.'

The hull swayed as the wheel went over again, and a great shadow swept above them like some nightmare seabird.

The Buffer looked for Hargrave. It was as if he had never moved. He turned to the plane again, even saw the bomb as it tumbled untidily from its belly.

He watched it with tired resignation. Why here, he seemed to ask. Why now?

From his position on the upper bridge Ransome saw the bomb too. '*Hard a-port!*' He gripped the voicepipe as the wheel went over and the ship seemed to reel to the thrust of screws and rudder.

'Thirty-five of port wheel on, sir!'

He heard men gasping and slipping as *Rob Roy* continued to pivot round, and he thanked God, not for the first time, that she had twin screws.

The bomb, which seemed to fall so haphazardly, suddenly righted itself and appeared to gather speed as it hurtled down while the plane, a Messerschmidt 110 fighter-bomber, bellowed low over the bridge, cannon-fire and machine-gun bullets raking the forecastle while the Oerlikons continued to pursue it with tracer.

The explosion felt as if the ship was being lifted bodily from the sea, and for a few seconds Ransome feared the worst, and prepared to stop engines before his ship charged headlong for the seabed. Then the towering column of water from the explosion fell. It was like something solid, as if the ship had been engulfed by a tidal wave.

He heard himself coughing and retching, trying to keep on his feet as water surged through the bridge and crashed to the deck below. As he wiped the spray and stinging salt from his eyes he saw a fireball suspended in space, then droplets of flame breaking away, to speckle the sea's face with bright feathers.

As his hearing returned he heard men cheering, and realised that the ME 110 must have been caught in the cross-fire even as the bomb had exploded so near to the ship.

Voicepipes crackled on every side and Ransome looked quickly to make certain his small team was still intact.

Sherwood was hanging on to the gyro repeater while Morgan was groping for the remains of his chart and scattered instruments. Leading Signalman Mackay was peering at his telescope and saw Ransome's glance. 'No damage, sir, thank God!'

The ship or his precious telescope, it was hard to tell.

'Bring her back on course!' Ransome wiped his sodden binoculars and peered astern. The aircraft were gone, the edge of their attack blunted at the sight of their companion's horrible end.

Cease-fire gongs were ringing, and he saw figures emerging from cover, as if dazed by their survival.

'Report damage and casualties.' Ransome looked at the sea ahead, the small fragments of the ME 110. There would be no survivors.

'First lieutenant for you, sir!' The boatswain's mate had put down his stripped Lewis, and Ransome noticed that there were several empty magazines by his feet.

'Captain here.'

'No damage aft, sir.' Hargrave sounded muzzy, a hundred miles away. 'One casualty. Ordinary Seaman Jenner. Not serious.' He hesitated. 'You all right, sir?'

But Ransome handed the telephone to the boatswain's mate and raised his glasses again.

The cheering had died away and some of the gun crews had left their stations to line the guardrails and watch.

Like a crude memorial, Ransome thought later. The forward section of a minesweeper seemed to rise amongst the others, pointing towards the white sun, the sea boiling around the hull like steam. Huge, obscene bubbles and a spreading blanket of escaping oil fuel. A ship dying. One of their own.

Morgan said huskily, 'It's *Scythe*, sir.'

Mackay called, 'From *Bedworth*, sir. *Senja will search for survivors.*'

Ransome nodded as he watched the upright hull, feeling the pain, wanting her to go, to get it over with. He could see her young captain, a mere lieutenant who had held the command for four months. Was he alive, he wondered? If so, how would he get over it?

'No damage below, sir. Engine-room request permission to reduce speed.'

'Very well. Half ahead together. Signal *Bedworth* and tell them what we're doing.' He spoke without emotion, as if he had none left to give.

Feet scraped on the ladder and Richard Wakely, his eyes almost bulging from his head, dragged himself into the bridge.

'Is it over?' He stared round, his chest rising and falling as if he was about to have a seizure.

Ransome said, 'For some it is.' He steeled himself as the broken ship began to sink very slowly, stern-first, tiny figures struggling in the filth of oil and worse while the big Norwegian trawler *Senja* manoeuvred almost against the wreckage.

Ransome gritted his teeth together. They should have had air

182

cover, but perhaps there was none to spare after all, or it was all being used to protect the troop convoys. The same German ME 110's had probably made a strike against those mine-sweeping trawlers they had seen in the dawn light.

Someone let out a sob as *Scythe* seemed to drop very suddenly from view. They heard several dull explosions, and more flotsam burst to the surface as if to torment further the gasping survivors.

Ransome turned his back and looked at his ship.

That violent turn had saved her. *This time.* Otherwise he and all the rest of them might be out there trying to keep afloat; waiting to die.

He saw Sherwood's eyes, Morgan's honest features twisted in pity and despair, Mackay gripping his telescope, his eyes smarting but not from the sun. *One of their own.*

The Buffer appeared on the bridge, his battered cap hiding his expression.

'Beg pardon, sir, but Jimmy – I mean the first lieutenant is askin' for orders. I think our phone 'as gone dead on us, like. The Gunner (T) 'as got one of his torpedomen on the job.' He looked around until his glance settled on Wakely.

'They've gone 'ome, sir.' He barely hid the contempt in his voice.

Ransome could feel the shock and despair closing its grip on all of them. It was often like that.

'Orders, Buffer?' He dragged out his pipe and prayed to God his fingers would not shake as he tamped down a fill of tobacco. 'We shall resume sweeping to port in fifteen minutes. What did you expect?'

Their eyes met, each man in his own way needing the other.

The Buffer grinned. 'From you, sir, nothin' but the best!'

Ransome looked away. They had come through again. *Nothing but the best.*

# 13

# *Husky*

The tiny chart-room which adjoined Ransome's sea-cabin was unbearably sticky and humid. Condensation ran down the sides and dripped from the deckhead to add to the discomfort of the officers who were squeezed around the table.

Ransome glanced through the solitary open scuttle. The light was strange, the sky like smoky bronze. He waited for the deck to lift, to roll uncomfortably to starboard in a steep corkscrew motion. Anyone with a weak stomach would know it by now, he thought.

It was like a warning, an omen. From first light the weather had started to deteriorate with a wind strengthening from the north-west. It was unusual for July – the one flaw in all the planning and preparations for Operation Husky.

It was now late afternoon and the wind had risen still further, so that the angry, choppy sea had changed to a parade of crumbling rollers.

How could they hope for any sort of success? With a heavy sea running many of the landing-craft would never reach their objectives in time; some could be swamped with terrible loss of life.

He glanced up at their intent faces. Hargrave, more tanned than any of them, always clean and tidy no matter what was happening. Sherwood, eyes hidden by his pale lashes, examining the chart with its transparent overlay of Ransome's secret orders, the coloured markers which had to be translated into action – into results.

Sub-Lieutenant Morgan, his body swaying easily to the sickening plunge and roll, had his pad already half-filled with notes. As assistant navigator he was directly involved. Surgeon Lieutenant Cusack was also present, his intelligent features and keen eyes recording everything. Beyond the bulkhead, voices murmured from the duty watch, clicks and groans of steel under pressure, the endless stammer of morse and static from the W/T office.

Ransome said, 'The first landings are due to take place at 2:45 tomorrow morning.' He felt his words move around the chart table like a chill breeze through reeds. Not some hazy plan any more, some grand design, but right here, and just ten hours away.

Sherwood said, 'They'll have to call it off, sir.' He looked up, his eyes searching. 'Won't they?'

Ransome pointed at the chart. 'Every flotilla and convoy is assembling at this moment to the east and south of Malta. It involves hundreds of ships, thousands of men. The RAF and the American Air Force have been pounding the enemy airfields and defences for weeks. Everything was set fair – the High Command allowed just twenty-four hours to cancel the whole operation or give the go-ahead.' He heard the wind howl around the super-structure, the blown spray lashing the bridge like a tropical downpour. It made a mockery of all the plans and hopes. 'If this wind holds out, the Americans making for the southern shore will be hard put to get their landing-craft in position.' His hand moved to Sicily's south-eastern coastline. 'Here the Eighth Army will land with the Canadians on their left flank. The Royal Marine Commando will go ashore to the left of the Canadians slightly earlier than H-Hour to seize vital objectives which otherwise might cover the landings.'

Hargrave rubbed his chin. 'I can't see it going ahead, sir.' He looked at the open scuttle and the strange, angry glare. 'It would be a shambles.'

Ransome nodded. 'It could be a greater one if they try to cancel Husky at the last moment, Number One. There would be even more confusion, some might not even get the signal on time and attack without knowing they were unsupported. And if the assault was delayed for another day, the landings would be ragged, ill-timed. I think most of us know what that would mean.' He let his words sink in. 'The Met people were caught with their pants down, but then so were the enemy.' He forced a smile. 'It's not much, but it's all we have. Our role is to give close support to the first wave of landing-craft under cover of a bombardment from the heavy boys.' He glanced at Cusack. 'You'll be dealing with the wounded if there are any — troops, sailors, anyone we pick up.'

Cusack nodded. 'I thought there was a catch in it.'

Sherwood smiled. 'Ain't that the truth!'

The others relaxed slightly. Ransome pictured those on watch, Fallows and young Tritton, Bone and Campbell, and all the rest. They had no say in any of it. They obeyed. It had to be enough.

Hargrave asked, 'When shall we know, sir?'

Ransome looked at the bulkhead clock. 'There will be airborne attacks on certain objectives, gliders and parachutists all with precise instructions on their objectives. They will be taking off from their bases in Tunisia this evening. After that —' He did not need to finish.

Instead he said, 'This is just a small ship, a minute part of what might be a great campaign. Most of our people are little more than boys. I'll bet that fifty percent were still at school when Hitler marched into Poland, and even after that. Give them all you've got. They deserve it.' He dragged a folded signal pad from his hip-pocket and flattened it on the chart.

'This is part of a signal from the C-in-C, Admiral Cunningham. I think you should hear it.'

He read it slowly, very conscious of the wind's deathly moan, the stillness around the table, the ship around all of them.

"On every commanding officer, officer and rating rests the individual and personal duty of ensuring that no flinching in determination or failure of effort on his own part will hamper this great enterprise."

He looked up, expecting some witty cynicism from Sherwood or Cusack, but it fell to the young Welshman, Morgan, to say what they were all really thinking.

He said simply, 'Like Trafalgar in a way, see? Nothing grand, just the right words —' He fell silent as the others looked at him.

Ransome said quietly, 'Tell your departments. I want, no, I *need* them all to understand —'

They filed out and Ransome sat for some time before opening his oilskin pouch and adding the last lines of the letter she might never read, or after tomorrow might never wish to.

Then he made his way to the upper bridge and watched the sea curling back from the bows, the spray bursting through the hawse-pipes and flooding the scuppers. Huddled shapes in oilskins, sweating despite the constant soaking, men at their guns and look-out stations. Men he knew.

The rest of the flotilla were like ghost ships in the bursting wave-crests and driven spray, the formation smaller now without *Scythe*. Already that seemed like a month ago instead of days. And tomorrow — what then? He saw *Bedworth* butting diagonally across the waves, her forecastle slicing through the troughs so that her solitary bow-chaser appeared detached from the rest of the ship as the foam surged around it.

He heard angry voices, the sharpness of resentment from men who were busy enough trying to prepare themselves for tomorrow. Richard Wakely stormed across the bridge, his shirt plastered to his body like another skin, oblivious to his hair, which was all anyhow in the blown spray.

'What are you doing, Captain?' He peered across the smeared screen. 'That's *Bedworth*!'

Ransome looked at him, feeling neither anger nor pity. 'It is.'

'I want —' Wakely clung to a stanchion as the bows dipped again, and water thundered past 'A' Gun and along either side-deck. 'I demand to be transferred to that ship at *once!*' When Ransome remained silent he shouted, 'You sent that injured sailor across to her! Don't deny that!'

Ransome thought of Ordinary Seaman Jenner. He had left the bridge to see him swayed over to the destroyer lashed in a stretcher. He might well lose his left foot. It depended how soon *Bedworth* had been able to transfer him to one of the big transports. But he would live. Ransome had taken his hand and had been shocked to hear the youngster plead despairingly, 'I don't want to go, sir! I'm with me mates here!' All that had happened, and he still wanted to stay in *Rob Roy*.

The memory touched his mind like a hot wire and he said sharply, 'He actually asked to stay aboard, Mr Wakely, did you know that?' He saw some of the watchkeepers turn to listen but did not care. 'God, I'd have sent you with pleasure, believe me, but the S.N.O. thought otherwise!' He waved his arm across the dripping metal, only then aware that he had forgotten to put on an oilskin. 'You wanted to see our war – well, that is precisely what you will be doing!'

Wakely stared at him as if he could not believe his ears. 'You don't know what you're saying! I'll see that you regret this!'

Ransome turned away. 'I hope so. That will mean that we've both survived. *Now get off my bridge.*'

He heard feet slithering down the ladder and then Hargrave coughed politely.

'I think he got the message, sir.'

Ransome breathed out slowly, and wiped his streaming face with his forearm.

Then he stood up on the gratings and held the top of the screen with both hands.

He said, 'Feel it? The wind's started to drop, Number One.' He had his head on one side like old Jack Weese did in the boatyard when he was gauging the day's weather.

He swung round and looked at the glistening bridge. It was like hearing a voice. The ship, perhaps?

He said, 'So it's on. No turning back.'

'You knew, didn't you, sir?'

'I'm not sure. Just a feeling.' He shrugged and repeated, 'Not sure.'

Leading Signalman Mackay watched the *Bedworth* just in case she might want to talk. He had heard every word, and earlier had seen the skipper leave his bridge to see the lad Jenner over the side.

*Of course he knew.* That was why *Rob Roy* was still afloat when so many others were so much scrap.

It made him feel better, and he began to hum a forgotten tune to himself.

By the time darkness finally closed over the flotilla the tension had become like something physical. Reports and requests whispered up and down the voicepipes and telephones, like

188

nerve-ends; and in each ship those ends led directly to her captain.

Ransome made himself remain in one corner of the bridge where he was within reach of the voicepipes, but able to watch the faint outline of *Ranger*, which was steering about two cables to starboard.

*Bedworth* had ordered the fleet minesweepers to form two small columns, with the big trawlers following up astern.

*Ranger*'s outline was little more than a jagged edge of lively spray around her stem, the occasional glassy shine of her hull as she rolled in a deep trough.

An hour earlier they had passed a slow-moving formation of landing-ships, butting through the choppy seas like huge, ungainly shoe-boxes. They were the first they had seen, and it was still hard to accept that the sixty miles of water between Malta and Sicily was probably packed with landing-craft, transports and heavily armed escorts.

Landing-craft of any size were difficult to handle even in calm seas. What it must be like for them in this wind, which had still not completely died, did not bear thinking about. They had had little chance to operate and manoeuvre together before as they had been needed for the build-up of men and stores, tanks and armoured fighting vehicles. Most of them were commanded by youngsters, RNVR officers like Sherwood and Morgan, who were standing side by side near the chart-table.

And what of the troops, Ransome wondered? Many of them must surely be sick from this savage motion, and in no fit state to charge ashore into God alone knew what the Germans had waiting for them. The tank crews would be in no doubt. When exercising with the army along the Welsh coast Ransome had heard a tank commander explain exactly what happened if one of their number would not start, or broke down at the moment of disembarking.

He had said with all the casual experience of a 23-year-old, 'You just shove the poor bugger ahead of you into the drink!'

'Radar – bridge.'

'Bridge?' That was young Tritton, the other Bunny, facing up to something he could barely imagine.

189

'*Bedworth* is taking up station astern. sir.'

Ransome nodded. 'I heard that.' Bliss was preparing to place himself in the best strategic position, where he could watch the supporting craft as well as the landing-ships when they eventually gridironed through to the beaches.

Ransome fixed the picture of the chart in his mind. He had studied it until he thought he could draw it blindfold.

As if to jar at his nerves the radar reported, 'Headland at three-five-zero. Ten miles.'

Ransome peered at his watch. 'Shut down all transmissions. This weather seems to have kept the Eyetie patrols in their beds, but the R.D.F. will still be working.' Somebody, probably Mackay, gave a chuckle. It was something.

Sherwood called, 'That will be Cape Passero, sir.' He sounded pleased. 'Right on the button.'

Ransome wished he could smoke his pipe. *Rob Roy* was leading her little pack and might be the first to come under fire. It was still better than groping blindly astern. The night could play cruel tricks on the watchkeepers. You would stare at the ship ahead so hard that it would vanish like a mirage. You might panic and increase speed to catch her, only to see her looming up beneath your stem. Terrible moments with the added knowledge that the vessel astern of you might well be charging in pursuit, her bows like a giant cleaver.

Ransome pictured his men around the ship. Hargrave down aft to oversee the guns there and take charge of damage-control. He would doubtless prefer to be here on the bridge, but the old lesson of too many eggs in one basket was never more true than in a ship at action stations. Mr Bone, grim and resentful, and no doubt clicking his dentures, would be ready to assist with anything but an act of God. And beneath all of them, Campbell with his team, sealed in their oily, thundering world, protected from the sea or a torpedo by steel plate little thicker than plywood. Fallows brooding over his mistake during the air attack; Cusack in the wardroom with his senior S.B.A., Pansy, waiting, probably as young Morgan had pictured it, as they had off Cape Trafalgar, their instruments rattling impatiently.

He thought too of Midshipman Davenport, with Boyes, manning the plot-table in the wheelhouse. Two boys from the same school, but a thousand miles distant from each other. After this, Davenport would be ready to pick up his first ring. But not in *Rob Roy*, which was just as well.

Sherwood said, 'Time, sir.'

'Very well.' Ransome crossed to the central voicepipe. 'Revolutions for half-speed, Cox'n.'

He could picture Beckett without effort, even though he had never seen him at the wheel. Part of his own strength, like Campbell and the horny Buffer.

'Revolutions one-one-zero, sir.'

Ransome made to move away but asked, 'All right down there, Cox'n?'

He heard a laugh. 'Yeh, sir, like bugs in a pusser's blanket!'

Ransome moved to his chair and leaned against it, feeling the deck shiver and sway with each thrash of the screws.

Less than ten miles. The enemy's coastal batteries could doubtless shoot this far.

He looked up as the stars as they flitted between the pale clouds. Like that moment at Plymouth, he thought, the darkened outline of Codrington House through the rustling trees. Her mouth against his, his arm around her shoulders. Would she know what he was doing? Could the fate or whatever it was which had brought them together, tell her that too?

'*Aircraft*, sir!'

Ransome swung round. 'Bearing?'

'Not certain, sir!' The man was swinging his powerful night-glasses in a full arc. 'P'raps I was wrong, but it *was* a sound.' He nodded firmly, 'I'm sure of it, sir.'

Ransome touched his arm as he passed him. The seaman was one of the best look-outs. It was why he was here on the bridge.

Sherwood joined in. On every ship heads would be twisting round, men dragging off helmets or woolly hats so that their hearing would not be distorted or tricked.

Sherwood suggested quietly, 'Bombers?'

Ransome stood away from the side and cupped his hands behind his ears. 'Shouldn't be. Wrong direction.' He stared at him through the darkness. 'Those gliders we heard about?'

Sherwood shook his head. 'No, sir. Too far out. They're supposed to be letting them off their towlines somewhere in a fifty-mile drop area inland, according to my notes.'

'Aircraft, sir!' The seaman lurched back from his night-glasses, and no wonder.

It was like some great bat, black against the stars and reaching out across the slow-moving ship as if about to seize her from the water.

Someone shouted, 'For Christ's sake, they've released them in the wrong place!'

Ransome felt his face stiffen as the huge glider passed directly overhead, the air rushing over its wings like a great wind through a forest. There was another glider directly behind it, swaying wildly as its pilot realised what had happened.

The strong headwind, a last-moment miscalculation, or inexperience; it was all too late now.

They heard the first glider smash into the sea, even saw the white spectres of spray as one of the wings was ripped away by the terrible impact. Ransome tried not to see it in his mind. The airborne troops packed inside, loaded down with weapons and equipment.

Tritton's voice broke into his thoughts. 'First lieutenant, sir!' He sounded shocked out of his wits, and huddled down as another glider tore overhead and then dipped heavily towards the water.

Ransome asked, 'What does he want?' When Tritton remained silent he shouted, '*Pull yourself together!*'

Tritton replied in a small voice, 'Requests permission to lower rafts and scrambling-nets, sir.'

Ransome turned away, his mind cringing as another glider hit the waves and flopped over in a great welter of spray. Men were dying, drowning, not knowing why or how.

He heard himself say, 'Denied! We are here to support the landings, not search for those who lost their way!' He did not recognise his own voice. 'One of the trawlers will carry out a sweep.'

Sherwood watched him, feeling his anguish and sharing it, perhaps for the first time.

Morgan whispered, 'God, what a decision to have to make!'

Sherwood saw some tiny pinpricks of light, far away abeam. Lifejacket lamps. A common enough sight to sailors. But to those poor devils it must be a moment of horror.

'Flare, sir! Dead ahead!'

Ransome stared across the screen and saw the red flare drifting like a drip of molten steel.

He wanted to think about it, what it meant; the Royal Marines already ashore, or the Germans at last facing the reality of attack. The bridge suddenly lit up, as if a giant torch had been directed over it. Faces and fittings stood out but left the rest in darkness. The horizon astern flashed again, like lightning or a great electric storm. Ransome waited, counted seconds as they did at Dover. Then he heard the far-off roll of heavy gunfire and almost simultaneously the express roar of shells passing overhead.

*Whoooosh!* Then the tell-tale blink of lights from the land as the first great salvoes found their mark.

Ransome tugged his cap more firmly across his forehead and stood high on the gratings. Falling further and further astern now, the abandoned airborne soldiers – those who had survived the crashes – would hear the huge shells ripping above them from the invisible bombarding squadron, and would know they had been forgotten.

It was a madness, more terrible this time because he could not control it, but the smashed and abandoned gliders were made suddenly meaningless.

'*Slow ahead together!*'

They were committed. In minutes now the first landing-ships in this sector would be passing to starboard.

Their madness was about to begin.

Hargrave clung to the shield of the after four-inch gun and tried not to blink as the horizon flared up again and again. It was still dark, and yet in the regular flashes the fragments of the whole stood out like parts of a crazy dream.

He recalled hearing Ransome's voice in the background when he had told poor Tritton his decision. Hargrave accepted it was the right one but still wondered if he would have done the same.

He had seen the great gliders hurtling out of the sky, some hanging on longer than their companions before smashing down into the sea.

Why should it seem different from any crashing aircraft? Men died every day. Hargrave rejected the argument immediately. What must those soldiers have been thinking when they realised the inevitable? All the training and preparation wasted? Or small, precious moments like the last farewell on some railway station or garden path? A wife, a child, a lover?

He winced as another massive salvo thundered overhead. There were battleships as well as cruisers back there. The navy he had been bred for. Great guns, order and discipline. The old flagship *Warspite*, the darling of the Mediterranean fleet, would most likely be adding her voice to the onslaught, and dropping her salvoes of some nine tons a minute on targets she could not even see.

The gun crew started to cheer as the pale silhouettes of landing-craft began to slide past beyond *Ranger*'s station abeam.

Hargrave snapped, 'Keep silent!', feeling their resentment but knowing that any second the communications rating might be passed an order from the bridge.

Between the thundering roar of heavy gunfire they heard the armada thrusting ahead, the choppy water surging against their blunt bows and ramps while the smaller, infantry landing-craft followed close astern as if afraid they might lose their way.

Once, just once, Hargrave heard the sound of bagpipes. What brave, crazy soldier could find the wind to play at a moment like this, he wondered? The next salvo blotted out the sound and Hargrave pictured the tanks lined up behind their steel doors, the air choking with fumes as they revved their engines. In the smaller, boxlike craft there would only be flesh and blood, eyes staring from beneath their helmets, bayonets fixed, legs braced for the moment of impact.

The Buffer appeared below him. 'I've spread the fire parties about.' He watched the lieutenant and wondered. 'Good idea of yours, sir.'

Hargrave had the great desire to yawn despite the gunfire. He dared not. Others had often told him it was the first sign of fear.

Gipsy Guttridge wiped his gunsight with his glove. 'Gettin' lighter already!'

The Buffer grunted. 'I remember once when I was in Sicily afore the war —' He broke off as the sea exploded in a towering spire of water between the two lines of minesweepers. '*Strewth!*'

The spray drifted across the deck and Hargrave spat out the taste of cordite.

The enemy had woken up at last.

The next pattern of shells fell to port. Hargrave gripped a stanchion as the wheel went over, and the deck began to shake to an increase of speed.

He peered astern and saw *Dunlin* following her leader while the others remained shrouded in darkness.

The communications rating had his headphones pressed against his ears and did not realise he was shouting.

'Why don't we shoot! Can't we 'it the buggers?'

Gipsy Guttridge twisted round on his little seat and gave him a pitying glare.

'Wot, with *this*?' He slapped the breech. 'Like a fart in th'wind against that lot!'

More explosions threw up great columns of torn water. Against the dull sea they looked like solid icebergs. They seemed much closer, and Hargrave guessed they were around the headland now, and felt the change in the motion as the sea levelled off.

He saw dark orange flashes from the land, the occasional glitter of tracer. Too soon for the landings, so it must be the commando, or maybe some of the airborne who had found their objectives after all. Shells continued to whimper overhead but only daylight would measure their success.

Someone muttered, 'I just 'ope they know wot they're doin'!'

Gipsy Guttridge grinned. ' 'Ear that, Buffer? Pathetic, ain't it? I seen more blokes killed by *our* admirals than the bloody enemy!' He looked defiantly at Hargrave's back, but the lieutenant did not rise to it.

Turnham said, 'Stow it, Gipsy, enough's enough!'

Hargrave was staring at the pale stars, the way they seemed to leave part of the sky in darkness. He felt his heart begin to thump.

It was the land, not an illusion. The high ground beyond the beaches which pointed north to Syracuse. They were that close. He gripped a stanchion as hard as he could while he assembled his thoughts. All the while, one stood out in his mind, like a voice yelling in his ear. If the captain fell today, he would be in command. *Can I do it?*

The Buffer seized his wrist. '*Down*, sir, for Gawd's sake!'

Hargrave watched the glowing ball of light as it tore across the sea barely feet above the water.

His mind had time only to record that it was a flat-trajectory shell, probably fired by an anti-tank gun of some kind, when it hit the ship like a giant hammer.

A man shouted incredulously, '*Didn't explode!* Went straight out the other side!'

Hargrave watched the second shell and waited for their luck to run out.

# 14

# *Who Is the Brave?*

Chief Petty Officer Joe Beckett shouted up the voicepipe, his eyes concentrating on the gyro repeater tape, 'Steady on zero-three-zero, sir! Both engines full ahead!'

Nobody else in the wheelhouse spoke now and the men at the telegraphs watched Beckett's hands on the polished spokes, and drew comfort from his strength while the hull quivered to the shock of falling shells.

Beside the plot-table Boyes gripped a fire-extinguisher bracket, as much to be doing something as to retain his balance. The ship felt as if she was moving at a tremendous speed, even though he had heard the others say often enough that she could barely manage eighteen knots with a following wind.

He stared at the others, their eyes and expressions illuminated only by the compass and indicator lights, although like the tense figures near him he had already noticed that the sky was lightening outside the bridge, the observation slits pale instead of black.

Beckett said between his teeth, 'Reckon they've landed by now, poor sods!'

Leading Seaman Reeves murmured, 'Don't feel all that bloody safe meself!'

Beckett roared, 'Close that door, you stupid oaf!'

The starboard door clanged shut again, and Boyes found himself forced painfully into his shrinking corner as Richard Wakely and his cameraman Andy crowded inside the wheelhouse.

Wakely peered anxiously round in the darkness. 'What's *happening?*'

Beckett bit back an angry retort and twisted the wheel a few spokes to hold the line steady on the gyro repeater.

It would do no good to take it out of Wakely, he thought. He was a *celebrity*, everyone knew that, and civvy or not could make a lot of trouble if he wanted to. He felt his stomach muscles tighten as the hull bounced to another explosion. Big shells from some Kraut shore battery. He gave a bitter smile. Or their own bombardment falling short of the target. He thought of Wakely again. *Shit-scared*. But how could that be, after all he was supposed to have done? Or was that just a line of bull, the sort that old Goebbels and Lord Haw-Haw gave out on the German radio?

Midshipman Davenport stared at Wakely. 'We're under fire, sir!'

It was meant to come out like it did on the films, but Davenport sounded near to breaking-point.

Wakely looked at the plot-table, then at the other figures near the wheel. 'If they're landing troops now, why are we still being fired at?'

Beckett snapped, *'Listen! –'* He nodded his head at the voicepipe. 'Up there on the bridge, they can tell you better than I can!'

Andy the cameraman unslung his heavy leather case. 'I'm going to get some shots as soon as it's light enough.' He was a small, rat-like man, everybody's idea of the downtrodden male, but there was no doubting his determination as he reached for one of the door-clips. He grinned. 'See you all later, gents – least I *hope* so!' Then he was gone.

Wakely exclaimed, 'Thinks he knows everything. Just because he was in Manchuria and the Spanish Civil War he imagines that –' He broke off and ducked as a voice came down the pipe. *'Tracer to port!'*

Boyes felt the hull jerk as the shell struck the side like a fiery bolt. He did not know it, but the shell punctured the plating as if it was paper and ripped across the upper messdeck and cracked through the opposite side without exploding.

Wakely cried shrilly, '*Get me out of this!*'

Beckett glared briefly at the midshipman. 'Keep that lunatic quiet, *Mr* Davenport! It's bad enough without 'im!'

The second shell hit the port wing of the bridge and ricochetted from the Oerlikon mounting before smashing into the wheelhouse. The rest, to Boyes at least, was unreal, a moment rendered motionless in time, as if his own world had stopped.

He realised that the shell had rebounded from two sides of the wheelhouse before exploding in a vivid white glare. He knew he was on his knees and thought he was screaming, the sound muffled by deafness. He felt the bite of broken glass in his fingers and knew the plot-table had been shattered to fragments; his shorts were sodden, and he wanted to cry out, to die before the agony came. He guessed from its sticky warmth that it was blood.

Beckett hung on to the wheel, his mind ringing to the explosion. In the beam of light from one of the repeaters which had had its shield blown aside, he saw Leading Seaman Reeves sliding down the steel plates, eyes wide and staring, his slow progress marked by blood until he hit the gratings and rolled over. Even in the poor light and trapped smoke he saw the hole in his back. It was big enough to put your boot inside.

Beckett felt a pain in his thigh and then the spread of fire running up his side.

But he did not fall, and the pain did not weaken his voice as he shouted, 'Wheelhouse – Bridge!'

Then Ransome's voice, very near, his lips against the bell-mouth. 'This is the captain!'

Beckett dashed sweat from his eyes and steadied the spokes as the lubber's line seemed to bend away from the gyro bearing.

'Men wounded down 'ere, sir!' The splinter in his thigh seemed to twist like a branding iron and he gasped, ' 'Oly shit! Sorry, sir, but I can't tell wot's up!'

Ransome called, 'Help on way. Can you hold the wheel?'

'Sir!'

'Bring her round. Steer three-five-zero.'

Beckett nodded. Was he the only one alive?

Boyes staggered to his feet, his mind clearing, sobbing uncontrollably as he realised that he was all right but for a cut hand. Wakely was pressed against the side, his fingers interlaced over his head, moaning and gasping, but apparently unhurt.

One of the telegraphsmen was on his knees and had turned over the messenger by the emergency telephone. He croaked, 'Bert's bought it, Swain.' His control cracked, 'Jesus, he's got no face left!'

Beckett snapped, 'You okay, Boyes?'

But Boyes was trying to drag Midshipman Davenport into a sitting position. It had been his blood which had soaked his shorts; in the strange light it looked black, solid.

'It's Mr Davenport!' He felt close to tears as he tried to make him comfortable. First Aid books had told him nothing about this. Davenport must have taken a shell fragment in the back, which had thrown him across the cowering Wakely and had consequently saved his life. He was probably dead. Boyes stared at him, the familiar features twisted into a mask, like the face of someone who had suddenly aged.

Beckett said, ' 'Old on, Boyes! Stiff upper lip, ain't that wot they say where you comes from?'

The door crashed open and Surgeon Lieutenant Cusack stepped over the broken table, his eyes taking it all in, his shoes skidding in blood.

He saw the man on his knees. 'Can you manage?'

The telegraphsman hung his head like an exhausted swimmer. 'Just about.'

Cusack nodded and turned away from the chief quartermaster's slumped corpse; only Reeve's bulging eyes held in a small beam of light seemed to cling on to life.

He saw Boyes and snapped, 'Don't lay him down.' He ripped open Davenport's shirt and threw it aside like a butcher's rags. 'In my bag. Two shell dressings!' He watched Boyes and added, 'You're doing just fine.' They both ducked as heavier shells thundered into the sea nearby, and they heard the falling water sluice over the bridge superstructure.

Cusack tilted Davenport's naked body forward and then pressed a heavy dressing over the wound. To Boyes he said, 'Here, tie these tapes. My hands are too bloody.' His eyes glinted as he looked up at Beckett's tall figure. 'You're a bit damaged too, Cox'n.' He shook his head. 'But you'll never break. Not you, man!'

Boyes said despairingly, 'Can't we lay him down now, sir? He's still breathing.'

Cusack listened to feet clattering up a ladder, someone hacking away broken fittings brought down by the shell. He answered quietly, 'You're a friend of his, are you, son?'

Boyes nodded without knowing why. 'We were at school together.'

It should have sounded stupid, Cusack thought grimly, with all hell breaking loose, and the ship liable to be straddled at any second. But it seemed to make all the sense in the world.

He said gently, 'He's dying. Drowning in his own blood. Stay with him. I'm needed elsewhere.' He tossed another dressing to the injured telegraphsman. 'Tie that on our man of steel, eh? I'll send someone as soon as I can.'

He touched Boyes's shoulder as he left. 'It'll not be long.'

Davenport opened his eyes and stared at Boyes for several seconds.

Boyes said, 'It's all right. I'm here. You were wounded when –' He realised for the first time that Wakely had somehow disappeared. 'When you were saving Richard Wakely's life.'

'Did I?' His head lolled on to Boyes's shoulder. 'Can't feel much. Never mind.' He tried to laugh and blood ran down his chin.

Boyes mopped it away with a rolled signal flag. 'Easy. You'll soon be safe.'

'Safe.' Davenport tried to look at him. 'Next time –' He broke off and groaned. 'You see me.' He was starting to struggle, as if he had suddenly understood but would not accept it. 'Sub-lieutenant, eh?' He closed his eyes. 'Oh, dear God, *help me!*'

It was several more seconds, while the ship tilted this way and that, and voices echoed from above and below like demented souls, before Boyes realised that Davenport had died.

Beckett called hoarsely, ' 'Ere, lend me a 'and, young 'un! You're the only bloke in one piece!'

The door was wrenched open again and the Buffer, an axe

gripped in his hand, stared at the scene without speaking. The great daubs of blood, the buckled plates where the shell had ricochetted around the wheelhouse before exploding as it had been designed to do inside a tank, and lastly at his friend hanging on to the spokes, one leg tied with a reddened dressing.

'Jesus, Swain, you managin' to 'old on? I'll get one of the lads from aft to relieve you!'

Beckett grinned at him fondly. 'Fuck off, you mad bastard. Get on with yer own job fer a change!' He gestured to Boyes, 'Me an' young Nelson is doin' very well!'

The Buffer showed his monkey teeth. 'Come round for sippers arter this lot, my son!'

Beckett retorted through his pain, 'He ain't old enough.'

The Buffer became serious for the first time. 'In my book 'e bloody is!'

Beckett said, 'Take the wheel fer a sec, Boyes.' He eyed him grimly. 'You *do* know wot to do?' He saw him nod. 'I'm goin' to fix this poor sod's bandage before things 'ot up again.'

Boyes cleared his throat and called up the voicepipe.

'Wheelhouse – Bridge!'

Sherwood answered immediately, his tone sharp, as if he expected the worst.

Boyes blinked tears from his eyes. 'Relieving the wheel, sir! Ordinary Seaman Boyes!'

Behind him he heard Beckett call, 'Only time they care is when they think you're bloody dead!'

Sherwood gave a brittle laugh. Beckett had a very carrying voice.

He said, 'The enemy has shifted target to the beaches. Hold her on three-five-zero until you're told otherwise.'

Boyes watched the gyro tape until it appeared to mist over. He felt sick and faint, his whole being rebelling against the touch and stench of death.

Above all he was conscious of a great feeling of pride.


Ransome trained his glasses above the screen and saw the land looming in the early dawn light, the sea criss-crossed with the wakes of other craft while closer inshore tall columns of water showed a regular concentration of artillery fire.

'Starboard ten.' He craned over the screen and stared down at the port Oerlikon mounting; it was pointing uselessly towards the quarter, the bright scar where the shell had smashed into it surprisingly sharp in the pale light. The Oerlikon gunner was squatting on the step massaging his head with both hands, seemingly oblivious to what was happening around him.

Ransome had called down to him immediately after the second shell had exploded beneath his feet in the wheelhouse, but the seaman had merely shrugged and spread his hands with disbelief. His guns were knocked out of action and yet miraculously he had been left untouched, apart from his headache.

Hargrave clambered on to the bridge, his face and arms streaked with dirt.

'Three killed and two wounded by splinters, sir.' He sounded out of breath.

Ransome waited as another massive salvo thundered overhead to burst somewhere inland. He could see the smoke now against the brightening skyline, like something solid which would never disperse. Fires too, with the more livid stabs and flashes from small-arms fire and mortars.

Ransome already knew about those who had died. It seemed incredible that anyone could have survived down there. The youngest and the most seasoned, Boyes and Beckett. If it was true what he had heard about Wakely it seemed a pity that others had fallen when he had done nothing to help them, but whimpered only for his wretched skin.

Hargrave said, 'Sorry about young Davenport, sir.'

They faced each other, each knowing that few people in the ship, if any, had liked the midshipman.

But he had tried, and with his eighteenth birthday hardly behind him, it was a bitter way to end everything. In his heart Ransome knew that in days, provided *Rob Roy* was spared, few would remember his name. Only at home in England – he closed his mind like slamming a door.

'Did you check the other damage?'

'Yes, sir. The messdeck was barely marked. No need to plug the holes at this stage. Too high above the waterline.'

They both looked up as two flights of fighter-bombers, their

RAF roundels like staring eyes in the strange light, screamed low overhead towards the land.

Perhaps the most marked change of all, Ransome thought. Air-cover, and plenty of it. Not sitting ducks – not this time.

Morgan looked up from a voicepipe. 'R/T signal from *Bedworth*, sir. *Two mines adrift to the south-west.*'

Sherwood grunted. 'Not surprised after that gale.'

Ransome nodded. 'Signal *Dryaden* to investigate. Right up her street.'

Hargrave smiled sadly. 'Pity to get your bum blown off by a drifter at this stage of an invasion.'

Sherwood's eyes widened in surprise. 'Did I hear a *joke* from our first lieutenant?' He strode over and offered his hand. 'I salute thee!'

Ransome watched the unexpected gesture, the way Morgan and even young Tritton appeared to relax, while Leading Signalman Mackay gave a great grin.

*Bedworth*'s signal lamp glittered across the water and revealed the great rolling bank of smoke which covered the slow moving landing-vessels like a blanket.

Mackay read, 'From *Bedworth*, sir. *Detach vessel to assist landing-craft which is out of command.*'

Sherwood murmured, 'Bliss likes to make signals, that at least is obvious.'

Ransome said, 'Signal *Dunlin* to assist. We will support her if required.'

A loud bang, familiar to all of them, made the air quake. *Dyraden* had found and destroyed one of the drifting mines.

Ransome watched *Dunlin* alter course away from *Rob Roy*'s straight wake and head towards the mass of landing-craft closer to the beach. As the light hardened it looked as if there was an impossible tangle of vessels with neither order nor purpose, landing-craft thrashing sternfirst from the beach, their box-like hulls higher now without their tanks and other vehicles, while others pushed ahead, following darting motor-launches with their bright pendants to mark their passage to a prescribed landing-place.

The gunfire was getting louder, and Ransome felt the air quiver to an unbroken artillery duel somewhere to the right of the beach. Probably the road to Syracuse, known to be heavily defended by crack German troops. If the Eighth Army could not break their line of defence the rest of the invasion would be left in stalemate.

'Half ahead together!' Ransome levelled his glasses again. There appeared to be fighting everywhere, grenades, tracer, with a fiery backdrop of falling bombs as the RAF and American planes battered away at the enemy's support lines and gun emplacements.

Hargrave murmured, 'I'll never forget this.'

Ransome did not lower his glasses, but watched as *Dunlin* swung broadside on near a large landing-craft.

'You still here, Number One?' He smiled. 'It's something I never thought I'd see either, as a matter of fact.'

The Buffer appeared on the bridge. 'Wheel'ouse cleared, sir. I've put two 'ands in there to 'elp the cox'n.' He sighed. 'But you know wot *'e's* like, sir, won't budge from that wheel!'

Ransome stiffened as two waterspouts shot up from the sea near *Dunlin*.

'*Hell!* They've got her ranged-in!' He beckoned to Mackay. 'Signal *Dunlin* to stand off immediately!'

More explosions made the sea boil and leap in bright columns through the drifting smoke.

Sherwood shouted, 'One of them hit the landing-craft, sir!'

Morgan called, '*Dunlin*'s captain for you on R/T, sir!'

Ransome ducked down and snatched the speaker from the boatswain's mate.

'Obey that order and *stand away*!' He pictured the man's face, one more lieutenant like *Scythe*'s C.O., called Paul Allfrey. He came from the Isle of Wight.

'I can't, sir!' His voice ebbed and flowed through the roar of explosions. 'The L.C.T. is full of wounded! Must get a tow-line rigged!

*Just when you thought that death was elsewhere.* Ransome snapped, 'Affirmative. We will assist you.' He ran back to the forepart of the bridge again. 'Signal *Ranger* to assume command. Then make a signal to *Bedworth*. *We are assisting*.'

He stared down at the side-deck and saw the corpses being lashed down under some bloodstained canvas. He knew them all. Reeves especially. A good man who had been hoping to take a petty officer's course.

'Get down there, Number One. The Buffer and the Gunner (T) will assist you. A towing job is never easy, and we've not much time.'

'*Oh God!*' Morgan clutched the rail and pointed as *Dunlin* took a direct hit just abaft her squat bridge. She was smaller than the other minesweepers, and the shell seemed to tear her upperworks apart in one blinding flash of fire. Falling debris, her mast and radar lantern hurled over the side and the sea pockmarked with falling fragments. Two more columns shot up in a tight straddle, and even above the roar of gunfire they heard the grating crash of splinters gouging through steel.

Hargrave had gone, and Ransome watched the gap between the ships narrowing.

'Cox'n?' He raised his eyes level with the glass screen. 'Bring her round to port. Hold her on a bearing with the L.C.T.'s stern.' It cut out the confusion of too many helm orders, and Beckett, injured or not, knew *Rob Roy*'s behaviour better than anyone.

'Slow ahead together!'

He heard shouts from aft, the grate of wires being manhandled along the deck.

Mackay lowered his telescope. 'From *Ranger*, sir. *Good luck.*'

Two more shells fell close to *Dunlin*, but it was impossible to measure the damage. *Dunlin* had stopped completely, and Ransome saw half of her motor boat dangling from the shattered davits. There was a lot of smoke, flames too, shooting from the foot of her single funnel. An old ship built for the Kaiser's war. It was asking a lot from her. Too much.

He thought of *Ranger* taking the trouble to make that short but so-important signal. Like old comrades, twins. He thought too of the Wren driver who had told him about her brother, a subbie, who was in *Ranger*.

Ransome strode across the bridge and gripped Tritton's arm. 'Take over the voicepipe.' He looked at him until the young sub-lieutenant met his gaze. 'I need to be where I can watch things.' He shook his arm gently. 'Don't worry about being scared. Most of us are, sometime or other.' He watched his words taking effect, hoped they would stay uppermost in his mind the next time, and the time after that.

Tritton nodded. 'Yes, sir. I'll do my best.'

Ransome pictured the scene as it must have been in the wheelhouse when the shell had burst into it. He was glad that young Boyes had come through. It was very important for some reason, as if he had become a mascot.

He listened to Hargrave shouting to his party. Thank God they did have good air-cover today, because he guessed Hargrave had stripped most guns of their crews to manhandle his tow-line.

Leading Signal Mackay said, 'I've got my bunting-tosser ready to pass messages aft if need be, sir.'

Their eyes met. Parts of a machine. The family. The Job.

'Good thinking. We'll try and tow her from her stern — it seems the bow door may be damaged.' He made himself take a few more seconds. 'You can shift your gear after this lot's over.' He saw the man's frown of surprise and added, 'Into the petty officers' mess.'

Sherwood grinned at him. '*Cheers*, Yeoman!'

Ransome leaned over the screen once more, glad he had told him. In minutes they might all be killed, but at least one man would know what he thought of him. Like poor Davenport, clinging on to his first gold stripe even in the presence of death.

'Stop together! Slow astern starboard!' He saw Leading Seaman Hoggan running across the forecastle, a heaving-line coiled and ready in his big hands. Once bent on to the tow-line they could get the L.C.T. moving until she was clear of danger.

A deafening bang rocked the bridge and Ransome saw a bright tongue of flame punch through *Dunlin*'s side.

Ransome shaded his eyes to watch the heaving-line as it snaked over the L.C.T.'s square bridge, where several seamen were waiting to seize it. He could feel *Dunlin* burning, the heat on his face like a noon sun.

Sherwood said flatly, 'She's going.'

Morgan called, 'Tow's going across, sir!'

Another explosion boomed against the hull and Ransome saw

tiny figures jumping into the sea, some clinging to injured comrades as their ship erupted into flames from bridge to quarterdeck. That big explosion must have been deep in her engine-room. No one would walk away from the there.

'Ready, sir!'

Ransome stared across at Tritton, his pale face framed against the smoke and fires of a dying ship.

'Slow ahead together.' He turned to watch the towing-wire rising from the water. *'Stop both engines!'* He bit his lip, made himself ignore the other minesweeper as she began to settle down, buried by fire.

'Easy now. Tell the Cox'n, minimum revolutions!' If they parted the wire now, the L.C.T. and then *Rob Roy* would fall under those guns. The towing-wire rose and tightened again. Ransome was banking on the L.C.T. being empty but for the wounded.

He watched, holding his breath, but the wire remained taut like a steel rod.

'Slow ahead together.' He glanced at Sherwood. 'Tell the Doc to stand by. They may not have one over there.'

Tritton swallowed nervously. 'Wheelhouse reports helm answering, sir.'

Ransome nodded and strode to the gyro repeater. 'Bring her round. Steer one-three-zero.' He smiled at Tritton's strained features. 'You can do it. Just like *King Alfred*, eh?'

A duller explosion rolled over the water and when Ransome glanced across he saw *Dunlin*'s keel rolling towards the sky, the screws stilled at last as she began to slide under amongst the struggling survivors.

Mackay licked his lips. 'From L.C.T., sir. *Have two hundred wounded on board. God be with you!*'

Sherwood said harshly, 'Put it in the log. *Dunlin* sank at . . .' He glanced away. 'Was it *worth* it?'

Ransome watched the L.C.T. yawing untidily astern and pictured the helpless wounded who had fallen almost before the landings had started.

He said to the bridge at large, 'For them it was.'

* * *

Ransome stood on a flat rock, and shaded his eyes to watch the motorboat as she zigzagged through a small brood of L.C.T.s to make her way back to *Rob Roy*. He felt strange, unsteady, standing on dry land, seeing his ship at anchor again for the first time since the invasion had begun.

Then he looked around the littered beach and marvelled that anybody had ever got further than the shallows. This same beach, which had been mined and covered by deadly cross-fire from several concrete emplacements, was a hive of activity, with shirt-sleeved soldiers digging and levelling the shell and mortar craters while the sappers laid fresh tapes to show the safe tracks for tanks and lorries, which arrived in a regular procession from incoming landing-craft.

In three days they had forced the enemy back, and as expected the Eighth Army had borne the worst of it, but had still managed to take Syracuse on the evening of that first day, and two days later the port of Augusta which gave the navy a useful base, a foothold from which future operations could be launched.

But the other side of the story was plain to see. Half-submerged landing-craft, pitted with holes or completely burned-out, abandoned tanks, and the tell-tale reminders of bayonetted rifles with helmets resting on them, to mark where some of the attackers had fallen.

The war made itself heard as it raged without let-up towards Catania, below the brooding presence of Mount Etna. But it was at a distance, and the regular sorties of aircraft which roared above the various beaches should make certain it remained so.

After that first day when *Rob Roy* had towed the damaged L.C.T. to the more experienced care of a fleet tug, the flotilla had been kept busy on duties which ranged from depth-charging a suspected enemy submarine, Italian or German it was never discovered, to carrying out more wounded, and keeping the beaches clear of obstruction.

They had suffered no further casualties, but there had been no slackening of vigilance, so that when not needed for duty the hands had fallen exhausted on deck, the memory of *Dunlin*'s end still stark in their minds.

Richard Wakely and his resourceful cameraman Andy had

seen none of the aftermath. A gleaming launch had arrived from one of the big cruisers while *Rob Roy* had been unloading more wounded into a hospital transport vessel, and Wakely had departed without another word. Off to another theatre of war perhaps, later to enthrall his audiences on the wireless and in the newspapers? It was unlikely he would ever forgive what had happened in *Rob Roy*. It certainly seemed as if what Sherwood had said about him was not just a rumour.

The cameraman, on the other hand, had taken a few moments to say his farewells. To the men he had watched and photographed in action, the petty officers' mess where he had been quartered, and lastly the bridge where he had apparently shot some of his best film.

'So long, Captain. Stay lucky. It would have been a privilege to meet you even if we'd stayed in dry dock the whole time!'

A small, undistinguished figure, yet somehow head and shoulders above the man he worked for.

An army lieutenant-colonel was squatting on a shooting-stick, smoking a cheroot. He smiled amiably.

'Come to stretch your legs, Commander?'

Ransome saluted. 'It still looks a mess here, sir.'

The soldier watched his men chattering to one another as they worked beneath the cover of some mobile A.A. guns. 'It'll take weeks to sort it all out. There are so many Italians deserting from their old ally and surrendering to us, or scampering off in civvies, I reckon Jerry must be browned off with the whole bunch of 'em!'

He turned as Sherwood sauntered along the beach, his hands in his pockets. 'You've got a good lad there, a great help until our experts came.' He smiled, some of the strain passing from his face. 'He caught some of my chaps in a bombed church just up the beach. You know how it is, looking for souvenirs. There was a dead Jerry in there, one arm sticking out with a really tempting watch strapped on it. One of my lads was about to 'commandeer' it when your lieutenant arrived. He apparently tied a line to the corpse, ordered my soldiers outside – much to their irritation according to the sergeant-major – then he pulled on the line.' He spread his hands. 'The stiff was booby-trapped. Blew down the church wall. Near thing!'

Sherwood joined them and gave a tired salute. 'Your own bomb-disposal blokes are there now, Colonel. Should be okay.'

Ransome watched him. That close to danger and yet Sherwood seemed so calm, almost disinterested. It was unnerving.

The lieutenant-colonel said, 'Anyway, I just wanted to thank you for all you've done in the past days. It will come officially, no doubt, *through channels*,' he became grave, 'but you and I understand. We do the job when the planners have finished theirs.' His gaze strayed around the beach, remembering, holding on to the images, the faces of those he had known and would never see again.

'No matter what, we made it come true, Commander. Together.'

Ransome slowly filled his pipe. 'I'll pass the word, Colonel.' He watched his hands and expected them to start shaking now that it was over. When had he last slept? When would he again?

'Well, well, we've found them at last!'

Ransome turned and saw a small procession of soldiers, most of whom were wearing Red Cross brassards and carrying stretchers. The officer who had spoken was a major, his face still smudged from the dawn action, his eyes red-rimmed as if looking through a mask.

The major said to his companion, a lieutenant, 'I just *knew* the British would have someone who smoked a pipe!'

They were Canadians, some of those who had landed to the west of Cape Correnti.

They all solemnly shook hands and grinned at each other.

Ransome handed over his pouch and both Canadians took out their pipes.

The major said, 'I'm going to be greedy, Commander. Most of the guys smoke fags, and all our pipe tobacco was lost in the attack.' He shook his head with mock sadness. 'That was a real disaster, I can tell you!'

The colonel said, 'This is Lieutenant-Commander Ransome, by the way. His ship towed out those wounded on the first day.'

The major studied him curiously. 'Ransome?' He turned to his lieutenant. 'Hey, Frank, why does that name ring a bell?'

The lieutenant paused, his unlit pipe halfway to his mouth. 'You know, the partisans.'

The major nodded. 'That's right. We flushed out some Sicilian partisans who'd been hiding from the Jerries up in the hills. Bandits more likely. They came to my boys so as not to get shot up by mistake.'

Ransome stood motionless and despite the unwavering, dusty heat, felt like ice.

The major continued, 'Just a coincidence, of course, but they'd been hiding some kid from the Krauts – a young officer some fishermen picked up a while back –'

Ransome gripped his arm. 'Where? Which one?'

The major did not understand but sensed the urgency, the quiet desperation.

'Go and get him, Frank.'

Ransome watched two stretcher-bearers descend the slope to the beach.

The major added, 'The partisans say he was wounded and they got a doctor from some village. He had to operate immediately, but had no anaesthetics apparently –' He broke off as Ransome ran along the beach.

'What is it?'

Sherwood said quietly, 'Don't ask. Just pray.'

They lowered the stretcher to the ground and Ransome dropped to his knees beside it.

With the greatest care he pulled the blanket down across a heavy, stained bandage, and gently brushed some sand from his brother's hair. Then, oblivious to the watching eyes, he put his arm round Tony's bare shoulders and hugged him for several moments, quite unable to speak.

His brother opened his eyes and stared at him, first without recognition, and then with disbelief.

Ransome whispered, 'You're going to be all right, Tony, I promise. *All right!*'

Sherwood said, 'It's his kid brother. Reported killed. He carried it with him day and night, but most of us never saw it.' He watched Ransome cradling the boy's head against his shoulder. 'We were all too busy thinking of ourselves.'

The lieutenant-colonel said, 'Leave them another minute, then take him along with the others to the field dressing-station.'

The Canadian major held a match to his pipe. 'And I thought they said miracles were out of fashion, eh?'

# 15

# *Aftermath*

Lieutenant Trevor Hargrave turned and touched his cap as Ransome climbed up from his sea-cabin.

'Starboard watch at Defence Stations, sir.' He waited while Ransome walked to the gyro repeater and wiped it with his glove before adding, 'Course is zero-seven-zero, revolutions for eleven knots.'

Ransome stretched his arms and fought the desire to shiver.

'Very well, Number One.' It was eight o'clock in the morning, with the forenoon watchkeepers scattered throughout *Rob Roy*'s private world, at their weapons or in the engine-room. Ransome had donned an oilskin over his old duffle-coat and had wrapped a dry towel around his neck, and yet he was still cold. Too long on the bridge; or perhaps he had been foolish to snatch a few moments to be alone in his sea-cabin, to enjoy the luxury of piping-hot shaving water, and a mug of Ted Kellett's strong coffee. His face felt raw from the razor and he questioned the sudden need, the importance attached to shaving on this particular day.

He moved to the chart-table and saw Sub-Lieutenant Morgan step aside for him.

Surely there should be a feeling of relief, of joy even at returning home?

He turned the page of the ready-use log while he held it close against the shaded lamp bulb. Eight o'clock in the morning, but it was almost as dark as night. He saw Sherwood's writing at the

214

close of the previous watch. The last day in November 1943. Perhaps time and distance were already making that other war seem unreal, the memories of Sicily and the months which had followed blurred, like mixed images.

Two months after the fear and excitement of watching the first troops surge ashore, the Allies had launched their second invasion, Operation Avalanche, on the Italian mainland, first on to the bloody beaches of Salerno, and later in a daring pincer-movement at Anzio. The enemy had been more than ready that time and every yard of the way had been fiercely contested. New weapons in the shape of glider-bombs had appeared over the landing-sites; controlled by parent aircraft they had been homed on to the heavier warships, many of which, including the battleship *Warspite*, had suffered casualties and damage. Another ship, the American cruiser *Savannah*, had received a direct hit, which had penetrated a turret and burst deep inside her hull, causing serious flooding and over a hundred casualties. The Germans, no doubt aware of their Axis ally's desire to declare a position of either neutrality or surrender, threw in everything they had with a total disregard for the rules of war. Two hospital ships, *Newfoundland* and *Leinster*, were bombed, although they were brightly lit to display their identity and purpose; the former sank with a heavy loss of life.

But *Rob Roy* and the remainder of her flotilla played no part in the Italian invasion. With her consorts she returned to the nerve-racking job of sweeping the channels and approaches around Malta, to make it safe even for the heaviest warships and transports once more.

Several minesweeping trawlers had been lost, but *Rob Roy*'s depleted flotilla seemed to recover the luck which had failed them when *Scythe* and *Dunlin* had gone down.

The orders to return to England had come unexpectedly. Even Bliss, who had dashed on ahead of the convoy in *Bedworth*, had seemed at a loss. The Mediterranean war was by no means over, and even now there were reports of the Allied armies being bogged down both by bad weather and reinforced German divisions, with little hope of an early victory. The flotilla had paused at Gibraltar to effect brief repairs before joining a small homebound convoy in the role of additional escorts, and Ransome had walked around his ship, sharing her tiredness as well as her pride in the part they had all played.

He glanced at Hargrave, his features deeply tanned against the dull backdrop of mist and drizzle, and the white scarf which showed above his oilskin. When he spoke to Morgan or one of the watchkeepers, his breath streamed from his mouth like smoke. The change in their circumstances was all around them, to the senses as well as the mind.

The convoy had dispersed northwards towards the Irish Sea. Just to think of it made Ransome's heart miss a beat. All those miles; the air-attacks, the frantic alarm bells in the night, the roar of mine and bomb, and now they were here at the gateway of the English Channel. Some five miles abeam was the ageless Wolf Rock lighthouse, which meant that the mainland of Cornwall was only about twelve miles distant.

He could feel it in the heavy rise and fall of the hull, the drifting spray and drizzle across the glass screen. Cold, chilling right to the marrow. The English Channel in winter.

He thought of Tony, remembering yet again that terrible moment of uncertainty and fear when he had turned down the blanket and had clutched his body against his own. Tony would be safely in hospital now. It had been a close thing; the wound in his side had been from a jagged shell splinter and was infected despite all that his rescuers could do. He had existed with the partisans in a small cave and had lived mostly on goat's milk and fish. It was all they had, and they had given it freely.

As far as Ransome had been able to discover, his brother was the M.T.B.'s only survivor. Perhaps one day Tony would be able to tell him what had happened.

Ransome climbed into his bridge chair and thrust his numbed fingers into his pockets.

After losing the convoy they had slowed down while *Firebrand* had carried out makeshift repairs to a stern-gland. Creeping along in the darkness there had been few who had not cursed the elderly minesweeper and her defects. For whatever was happening in Italy, the Germans were very active in the Atlantic, and on passage by their slow roundabout route they had sighted several abandoned wrecks and large patterns of flotsam. Convoys, or a solitary ship caught in a U-boat's crosswires: an insect in the web.

Ransome tried to ignore the spray and rain which ran down his face to soak into the towel. Coming back to another war, or to the one which they had left just months ago? Little was changed at home, he thought, except for one vital factor. Midget submarines, X-craft as they were called, had managed to penetrate deep into a Norwegian fjord where they had found and attacked the last great German battleship *Tirpitz*. The most powerful warship in the world, sister to the ill-fated *Bismarck*, she had remained the one real threat to the British fleet. While she lay in her heavily defended lair, protected by booms and nets, she was a menace to every convoy on the open sea. Heavy units of the Home Fleet were tied down in harbour or at Scapa Flow, just in case she broke out to ravage the supply lines with her massive armament.

A few midget submarines had achieved what others had attempted, and had laid their charges beneath her while she lay at anchor. Nobody knew for certain the full extent of the damage, because several of the tiny X-craft had been lost, and the surviving crews had been captured. But she might never move again. David and Goliath, with the odds somewhat worse, Ransome decided.

He thought of his orders for *Rob Roy*, to proceed to Devonport dockyard in company with *Ranger* to carry out a refit and overhaul. The others were being scattered to different yards where there was room for their needs.

Ransome considered his ship's company and how they had all been changed in some ways. Perhaps being far away from home, most of them for the first time, fighting alongside the real fleet, the big ships with their towering superstructures and battle ensigns. Strange and new. Their world had been grey seas and small ships, stubby trawlers and lean destroyers, tramp steamers and the Glory Boys of Light Coastal Forces. England under attack, shabby, rundown, defiant. A few Mediterranean skies and hot suns would work miracles here, he thought.

Plymouth. Where he had last seen her. Would she still feel the same? Was it wrong of him even to hope she would need him as much as he did her?

He had written to her whenever he had found the time, but had received no more letters from her. He was certain she would have put her thoughts on paper as he had tried to do in his own letters to her. They were probably following *Rob Roy* around the Mediterranean, to Malta and Alexandria and to North Africa. Minesweepers stood pretty low on the Fleet Mail Office's priorities.

'Char, sir?' The boatswain's mate handed him a heavy mug. Thick and sweet, the way only sailors could make it.

And how had it affected *him*, he wondered? Had he risen above the strain, the constant decisions, the need to exercise authority when his heart had directed otherwise? Would she see that in him too?

And he thought of the ones who would not be bothered either way. He had written to Midshipman Davenport's parents, and to the other men's families. Would it ever help? They might even blame him in some way for their lost ones.

*Dunlin* had been luckier than many, and had had just seven men killed. When Ransome pictured the final explosion that had blasted out her guts, it seemed like another miracle. Her young captain, Allfrey, from the Isle of Wight, had not been one of the survivors.

He heard feet on the deck below and knew that some of the men off watch were at the guardrails, looking for the land, seeing it as it would be, each to his own.

He thought of Sherwood's story, how he had demonstrated his chilling skills yet again with the booby-trapped German, of the cheerful Canadians enjoying their pipes once more, perhaps still unaware of what they had done for him. The lieutenant-colonel sitting on his shooting-stick, and the mad piper in one of the landing-craft; the lines of wounded waiting to be lifted from the beaches, suddenly so young and frail without their weapons and helmets.

The one extraordinary feature was the enemy. As in the war at sea, they had not seen the Germans at all. Always at a distance, ringed by fire, or laying down barrages of utter destruction.

He heard Morgan speaking into a voicepipe and knew he was talking to the plot below their feet. The youngster Boyes doing Davenport's job.

It was some beacon picked up on the radar, to be marked and compared on the chart. A link with home.

Ransome slid from the chair, aware of the stillness, the mist and drizzle. Shipboard noises, muted but for the creak of wet steel, the regular bleep from the Asdic compartment.

He glanced over the screen at the crouching lookouts, shining in their oilskins, their breath like Hargrave's. The port Oerlikons had never worked again to Fallows' satisfaction after being hit by the anti-tank shell. One more job for Devonport, 'Guz' as it was affectionately nicknamed.

Familiar shapes and outlines in the grey gloom. The hard man Jardine; Leading Seaman Hoggan, one of the stalwarts in this elite company; A.B. 'Chalky' White, who had a nervous tic in his eye; Gipsy Guttridge and all the rest. How did they feel? Ransome remembered Morgan's comparison with Trafalgar before the invasion. But there were no proud pyramids of canvas this dull morning to excite and warm the hearts of the watchers on the shore, had there been any. Not this time. Just eight small ships, tired and streaked with rust, dented from numerous encounters with jetties and mooring buoys, often in pitch-darkness.

Ransome looked up at the single funnel with its usual lick of smoke trickling abeam. He recalled what Commander Moncrieff had said after their last handshake.

He felt a lump in his throat. Well, they *had* taken care of her. One more time, *Rob Roy* was coming home.

Lieutenant Philip Sherwood withdrew his head and shoulders from the shielded chart-table where he had been peering at a signal pad and said, 'From C-in-C Plymouth, sir. Details of berthing tomorrow morning and arrangements for tonight.' He added as an afterthought, 'The dockyard ordnance people are coming aboard sometime in the forenoon.'

Ransome turned in his chair and winced. It was even colder, and beyond the bridge it was pitch-black, with only their sluggish bow wave to break the darkness.

A long day, and a strangely tense one, he thought. Only when they closed with the land to pass the Lizard, while the air was heady with the daily rum issue and some curious smells from the galley funnel, did he accept the reality of their return.

Then north-east with his own home, Fowey, somewhere to port, shrouded in gloom and mist; until like a disembodied island, the headland of Rame Head, guardian of Plymouth Sound and marked by a solitary winking buoy, passed finally abeam.

It was a nuisance to have to wait for morning, another day before he could take the ship into the dockyard. But it was a difficult entrance, past Drake's Island and through the narrows, a hard passage even in broad daylight.

'Tell Fallows about the gunnery thing.'

Sherwood nodded and resumed his position in the forepart of the bridge. It was odd about Bunny Fallows, he thought. He barely spoke to anybody these days; it could not still be pique over Tritton and Morgan's little joke. It was something much deeper, which gnawed away at him from within like a disease. Not fear then? It seemed unlikely. Fallows did not have the imagination to feel that kind of emotion. Sherwood pushed him from his thoughts and trained his glasses astern. *Ranger* was somewhere in their wake, the only one still in company. The rest were on their way to Chatham and Harwich, Rosyth and Tynemouth. Repairs, a lick of paint – then what?

He heard Morgan speaking quietly to the signalman. Would it mean a breakup of this company? Promotion, courses in various shore establishments, drafts to other ships to make way for green youngsters like Gold, and Boyes, who no longer seemed so youthful.

He glanced at Ransome's shadow framed against the glass screen. As if he never moved. *Rob Roy* and *Ranger* each carried a Render Mines Safe Officer. It was fortunate that the other R.M.S.O., like himself, held a watchkeeping certificate. It made the officers' watches on the bridge less of a strain, spread out instead of four hours on and four off without let-up. But the captain was always here. Everyone who visited the ship remarked how young he was to hold a command. Sherwood had told more than one, he bloody well needed to be young to keep from splitting into halves.

He shied away from thoughts of the girl he had met in London.

220

Rosemary. But she often came into his mind when he was unprepared and vulnerable. He was all that and more just now. He was coming home — to what? A big bank balance which he had done almost nothing to create, property which was filled with memories, and a background which was worth very little in a fighting war.

He recalled her question. *What will you do after the war?* And his own cynical reply.

He might leave *Rob Roy*; he was surprised that the idea seemed almost painful. Once he had believed it did not matter, that he could not care less. In that at least he must have changed. Ransome had probably done it. He remembered that moment on the Sicilian beach when he had understood Ransome's own anxiety, shared it; afterwards he had thought it was like being privileged to do so.

Even if he did not see her again, he might give her a call. He owed her an apology for the way he had acted after — again he closed his mind to it.

*I must not think like this.* Next week, or the one after, he might be called to examine some new enemy technique, a booby trap designed only for the likes of him. He smiled as he thought of the soldiers' resentment when he had ordered them from the bombed church. Their embarrassed grins afterwards, their stammered thanks for saving them from being killed or maimed. It did no good to think that some of those same men were probably dead anyway by now.

A slight shadow crossed the bridge and he heard Morgan report, 'Ordinary Seaman Boyes, sir.'

Then he heard Ransome say, 'I want you on the plot full-time, Boyes.'

A flurry of snow sifted over the screen and a look-out muttered, 'Jesus! Roll on my doz!'

Ransome continued, 'You've done well.' There was some mumbled response from Boyes. 'I shall see it goes in your papers.'

Boyes stared at the captain's silhouette, oblivious of the snow which froze on his eyelids and lips. In a small voice he whispered, '*Papers*, sir?'

He tried to remember each word as Ransome replied, 'I think

you should have another go, Boyes. A proper interview at least. How do you feel about it?'

Boyes could scarcely speak. It was everything he wanted, and yet to his amazement his first reaction was one of disloyalty to the men who had helped and guided him in the brutal kindness of the navy's lower deck.

'T-thank you very much, sir.'

Ransome said, 'We'll be entering the Sound within the half-hour, so get your charts tidied up. The dockyard maties will doubtless want to see Malta's efforts to repair your plot-table, eh?'

Boyes climbed down the ladder and saw Morgan's white teeth set in a grin as he passed. *Another go.* He had not really had one before. What would his mother have to say about *that*?

'All the port watch! First part forrard, second part aft, stand by for entering harbour!'

Boyes gripped the rail of the bridge wing, buckled by the shell which had cracked around the wheelhouse, killing, *killing*. He still found it hard to sleep; it haunted him like a nightmare which had no beginning or ending.

Leading Seaman Reeves, his eyes bulging with horror as if he had seen the shell coming, Davenport lolling against him, trying to laugh, and coughing out his blood while it drowned him. And the towering figure of the coxswain, tough, outspoken and unexpectedly kind. He still limped a bit from his wound, but was more afraid of being put ashore than any momentary pain.

When he had first come aboard he had been almost too frightened to speak. Bursts of anger born of strain, foul language and stories of conquests on runs ashore, blondes, barmaids and waterfront toms. They had been baiting him, testing his reactions. And yet at the sea burials it had been Sid Jardine who had put his arm over his shoulders while in their different ways they had shared the same grief.

If the captain could push his papers through it would mean leaving all this, and he knew that nothing would ever be quite the same again. As *Rob Roy* picked her way between the blinking buoys until she was met by a fussy harbour launch, there were others in her company who did not share Boyes's feelings.

Leading Seaman Gipsy Guttridge had been able to keep his wife out of his mind while the ship had been in the Med. Now he was back, and as he waited with the quarterdeck party amongst the well-used coils of mooring-wires, springs and rope fenders, he wondered what he would do when he faced her again. A laughing, bright-eyed girl with dimples. A friend had written to him once to tell him she was having it off with a pongo from the local army camp. He had confronted her with it but it had ended in passion in bed. And there had been another letter waiting for him at Gib, from the same 'friend'.

The Buffer brushed past and rasped, 'Jump about, old son, you look shagged out!'

Guttridge glared after him. It never seemed to bother the Buffer. If half of it was fact, he'd screw anything. He gripped the guardrail and turned his face into the freezing snowflakes.

*When I catch whoever it is, I'll do for them both!*

Alone at the wardroom table Sub-Lieutenant Fallows chewed half-heartedly on some corned-beef hash. He stared at the table-cloth, still soiled from the previous meal, then poured himself another mug of black coffee.

He could not remember needing a drink more. He swallowed hard; he could almost hear it being tipped into a shining, clean glass. What should he do? He glanced up as the messman padded through the wardroom. It was madness to feel guilt, or was it fear? But it was not Parsons; he would be on the forecastle for entering harbour.

*I must have been out of mind to give him money.* Fallows pulled out a tin of duty-free cigarettes and gestured to the mess-man to clear the table.

Parsons had explained that he would soon be leaving the ship, to go on an advanced gunnery course at Whale Island and pick up his leading rate. They would never see each other again.

Fallows wiped the sweat from his forehead although the wardroom was almost cold.

He should have seen it. Stood firm and stamped on the little bastard when he had first brought up about Tinker.

Fallows glanced at the single, wavy stripe on his seagoing reefer. He had not liked Davenport because he imagined he came from a better background than himself, but he understood how he had felt about getting on in the navy. Take the chance while it lasted. When he became a lieutenant he would feel more secure, and then — He stubbed out the cigarette and lit another without noticing. Parsons had asked for a loan at first, then another to tide over his domestic problems until he had completed the gunnery course.

He thought suddenly of his father in Glasgow, a belligerent, sneering drunk who had barely worked for years and had made all their lives hell.

'You'll never get anywhere with those stuck-up bastards! I know you too well, you'll fall in yer own shit before you get what you want!'

Nobody knew or cared what it had cost him to get where he was, or what that piece of tarnished gold lace represented to him. And despite all his care to cover up his humble background he had allowed a crawling rat like Parsons to sneak under his defences.

The last time they had been alone Parsons had explained in a hurt, wheedling voice, 'I feel as much to blame as you, sir. I should 'ave spoken out — an' wot if someone asked me about it sometime, wot then, eh?'

Who could he have turned to? Now of course it was all stark and clear. He should have gone to the commanding officer there and then. It might have damaged his chances of promotion, but it was better than admitting he had bribed a rating to conceal the truth, for that was exactly how it would look in the cold eyes of a court martial.

Fallows lived on his meagre pay and had no other funds. He had got into debt several times with his mess bills, and had borrowed at first to square the accounts.

With Parsons constantly pressing him — he shuddered; the word was *blackmail* — he had been forced to do some deals with a friend he had met in Alexandria. They had been at *King Alfred* together, but his friend had failed to become an executive officer. He had ended up as a paymaster-lieutenant in the naval stores there.

Dockyard paint which until then had meant nothing to

Fallows. It was merely slapped on by the ship's company or men under punishment whenever there was a spare moment.

But in Alexandria any kind of naval stores were big business. All Fallows had been required to do was sign for something which in fact was never delivered to the ship.

He had told himself a hundred times that Parsons was too implicated to cause any more trouble for him. He was a vindictive and unpopular man in the ship, but there were always those who would believe his story.

Surgeon Lieutenant Cusack entered the wardroom and slumped down in one of the battered chairs.

'You can smell the land!' He watched Fallows curiously as he remained pensive and silent. 'There were times when I thought I'd never see green grass again.'

Fallows stood up and looked at him without understanding. 'I must go.'

Cusack leaned back and stared at the deckhead, picturing the work above as wires scraped on steel, and seaboots thudded past the sealed skylight.

It had been an experience, and he knew he did not want to go back to hospital until it was over. He thought of the men he had come to know, their hopes, and perhaps above all their secrets. Cusack smiled grimly. He had a brother who was a priest in Galway; perhaps he would be more use here than a doctor.

Above them all Ransome stood high on the bridge step and stared down at the activity on deck. Merely shadows and shouts of command, but he knew *Rob Roy* blindfold if need be.

Water thrashed in the darkness and he saw one of Devonport's ancient paddle-wheeled tugs standing by, her bridge and forecastle white with driven snow.

'Stop port!' He heard Sherwood repeating the order, the instant response from the engine-room. 'Slow astern port!'

He watched, dashing the snow from his eyes as he gauged the slow swing of the stern towards the stone wall.

'Sternrope's made fast, sir!' That was Morgan.

'Headrope's being hauled over now, sir!'

'Stop port, slow astern starboard!' He pictured the hands hauling the rebellious wires and securing them to their bollards.

The deck rocked, and he heard the call for more fenders as they came reluctantly alongside. 'Stop together!'

He heard Hargrave's voice from the forecastle as he supervised the mooring. 'Out springs and breasts!'

Through the snow Ransome saw the blink of a signal lamp. A greeting, fresh orders; he was too tired to care.

'All secure fore and aft, sir!' Sherwood was looking up at him through the snow, his cap white against the wet steel.

'Ring off main engines, if you please.'

The deck shuddered and fell still as a low shadow passed slowly abeam, while the wary tug thrashed round with the ease of a London taxi. It was *Ranger* following their example.

Mackay called, 'Unusual signal, sir.' He controlled a chuckle. 'From the Wrens at the Signal Tower. *Welcome home.*'

Ransome stepped down. 'Tell them thanks, from all of us.'

But he was thinking of Eve. It was as if she had spoken those words just to him.

# 16

## *Lifelines*

Commander Peregrine Bliss, DSO, Royal Navy, tossed his oak-leaved cap carelessly on to a locker and sat down in Ransome's other chair.

'All quiet, Ian? He looked bright-eyed and fresh, his powerful hands resting in his lap as if unused to inactivity.

Ransome nodded. The first day in Devonport dockyard and it had been a full one. People to see, at least five tours around the ship with various dockyard officials and other experts, not least the business of getting the major part of the ship's company away on leave again. It was only months since their last leave, but it felt like years.

He replied, 'They say at least three weeks, sir. There's apparently quite a queue for repairs or boiler-cleaning.' He recalled Hargrave's face when he had left the ship. Hargrave was changed in some way, perhaps more than he had realised. He had seemed uncertain, and could almost have been reluctant to leave *Rob Roy* now that the chance had arrived. Ransome wondered if it was because of his father and the lovely second officer named Ross Pearce. When they all got back there would be more changes waiting for them.

Ransome said, 'I know I have to stay aboard, sir, but I *could* let Lieutenant Sherwood go. One officer for occasional duty is enough for me, and I do have *Ranger*'s Number One at my beck and call.'

Bliss examined his fingers. 'I sent word for Sherwood to stay.'

He looked up and flashed a white smile, like an impish schoolboy, but for his eyes. 'For a day or so. After that, well, it'll be up to you, of course.'

Ransome glanced at the list of names on his desk, a copy of the one he had already sent on board *Bedworth* for Bliss's consideration. He guessed he had not had time to read it yet. Bliss probably wanted Sherwood to transfer to another ship. Experienced watchkeeping officers were like gold, RNVR, or not. Once again Bliss proved him wrong.

'I read your summary of people for promotion and so forth. To some I can agree, others will have to wait.' He saw Ransome's expression and added, 'You can take it higher of course, but –'

Ransome said, 'There will be several overdue for advancement this time, sir.'

Bliss went off at a tangent. 'I see that you've started papers for Ordinary Seaman Boyes. I gathered he was washed out the last time?'

'He was not properly examined, sir.'

Bliss grinned. 'In *your* opinion. We must trust these training chaps. Surely they know their stuff.'

Ransome glanced down the list, seeing their faces, knowing them like his own family. He said flatly, 'I have put Boyes down for a Mention in Despatches.'

Bliss answered, 'Saw that too. Good thinking. No promotion board could very well turn down an interview with a chap who has a M-i-D, eh? He threw back his head and laughed. 'God, you are a crafty one, Ian. I'd have done the same myself!'

He glanced around the cabin and nodded, suddenly grave. 'Stout little ships. If I couldn't drive a destroyer I'd have one of these old ladies any day.'

'About Lieutenant Sherwood, sir –'

There was a tap at the door and Bliss said casually, 'Hope you didn't mind, Ian. A bit high-handed maybe, but I sent my snotty to dig him out when I came aboard.'

Their eyes met. A challenge. A threat.

Ransome called, 'Enter!'

Bliss said, 'Good show. I can explain to both of you together. It'll save time, eh?'

Sherwood glanced round for a chair and then leaned against the closed door. It was as close to showing his irritation at being summoned by Bliss as he could demonstrate.

Bliss regarded him impassively. 'I *know* you, Sherwood. Your record, and it's damn good.'

Sherwood sounded surprised. 'Thank you, sir.'

Ransome watched the pair of them. Sherwood was beginning to lose his Mediterranean tan already. It was strange that he always looked so pale, his skin, his hair, his lashes. Even his eyes, which were watching Bliss. Like a cat's, Ransome thought, deciding whether to purr or lash out with its claws.

'You've done some useful work in the flotilla too.' He wagged a finger. 'There isn't much I don't know.'

The guard came down. 'Really, sir.'

Bliss turned to Ransome. 'Fact is, Ian, we've found a new German magnetic mine.' He said to Sherwood without facing him, 'I believe you had a go at one last winter?'

Ransome saw the lieutenant nod, his defences falling slightly as his intelligent features recorded some memory – the mine, or another before it.

Bliss said, 'They found it in the Thames Estuary while we were in Sicily. Commander Foulerton said it was a more sophisticated version.' Then he did turn to Sherwood again. 'You know the name, I see?'

Sherwood nodded, a lock of fair hair dropping over his forehead. 'He was at HMS *Vernon* when I was there, sir. Taught me everything I know. A fine man.'

Bliss smiled gently. 'A regular officer too.' The smile vanished. 'Well, now we've found another one of the bastards, near Portland Bill, provided it hasn't blown up yet. It's being kept a close secret – we mustn't let Jerry know we've got one.' He glanced briefly at Ransome. 'Not yet anyway.'

In those flashing seconds Ransome saw Sherwood's face change again. As if he had seen a ghost.

Ransome said quickly, 'I don't see why we should –'

Bliss snapped, 'I can't send *Ranger*'s R.M.S.O., he's not got Sherwood's experience. Might just as well trundle some heavy-footed soldiery along!'

Sherwood asked quietly, 'You're asking *me* to go?'

Ransome interrupted, 'What about this Commander Foulerton — what does he suggest, sir?'

'Well, there you have it, Ian.' Bliss looked at Sherwood, his eyes hard. 'He was killed while he was handling the one in the Thames Estuary. The only information is what he passed over his telephone to an assistant. They had to keep his death hush-hush.'

Sherwood said softly, 'Christ!'

Bliss added, 'I wouldn't ask, but —'

Ransome picked up his pipe. Portland was one of the most important naval harbours on the South coast, about seventy miles from here.

He persisted, 'But he'd being doing other duties on board, sir. He'll need an assistant —'

Bliss didn't shift his gaze from Sherwood. 'I'll get somebody. I can't order you to go, Sherwood.'

Sherwood turned his cap over in his hands. He replied, 'You just did.' His eyes glittered in the deckhead light.

He looked at Ransome. 'I'll get my gear, sir. I don't want to take anyone I don't know. If Leading Writer Wakeford agrees I'd like him, please.'

Bliss stared. 'That's your writer, Ian — what does he know about it?'

Ransome was equally baffled but was determined not to show it. There was something so compelling and yet so sad about Sherwood that he knew there was no room for doubt.

Sherwood said calmly, 'Leading Writer Wakeford was an excellent physics and chemistry master in a good public school, or didn't you know that, sir?' He did not hide his contempt. 'But they said he was too old for a commission. What is he? Thirty-two? Not too old to get his arse blown off in bloody minesweepers, though!'

Bliss ignored the outburst, or perhaps he was so relieved that Sherwood had agreed to go that he had not noticed it.

Ransome nodded. 'Send for him.' He pictured the quiet leading writer who had acted as his helper, secretary, and shadow all the while he had been in *Rob Roy*. A withdrawn, gentle man.

Sherwood said, 'I've often discussed mines with him. He's got a very retentive mind.' He gave a bitter smile. 'But the navy doesn't seem to care too much about such trifles.'

Ransome nodded to him. 'I'll see you before you leave.'

As the door closed he said, 'I must disagree with you on this, sir.'

'*Why?* Because you know him, or because you need him here?' He watched him curiously. 'Or maybe it's because you think he's over the top already, too far gone to cope.' His tone hardened. 'I can't lament over personalities, Ian, not any more. God Almighty, I've seen enough youngsters get the chop — so have you. It's the bloody war, man, it doesn't help to look over your shoulder or to care too much. I *know*. I've been there and back a hundred times. He's probably the best man for the job, and right now he's the *only* man we've got available.' He leaned forward to emphasise each point. 'The Met people have promised good weather, or the best you can expect in winter. If the wind drops still further, Sherwood will have a fair chance. *But we must know!* The Allies will attempt to invade France next year, you can bet on it. With the Italian campaign slowing down to a crawl, they'll have to launch the landings whether they want to or not. Any secret weapon Jerry can create we must master before it drops in our laps.'

'I'd like to be there with him.'

Bliss's expression softened. 'I expect you would. But I need you here. I shall go with him. I know he hates my guts — better that than you worrying about him, eh?' He relaxed and smiled. 'Besides which, our vice-admiral, who, like the sick and needy, is always with us, will expect it.' He stood up and seized his cap. 'I'll go and rouse the driver.'

Ransome followed him out to the darkened deck. The first full day. What a way to end it. So Bliss had known all along that Sherwood would go; he had even laid on a car for the fast drive to Weymouth and Portland Bill.

They paused by the quartermaster's lobby and Bliss observed.

'It'll look good for the flotilla too, think of it that way!' Then he was gone.

Sherwood arrived eventually carrying a small bag. He had changed into old blue battledress and rubber boots, which

Ransome knew he always wore on these dangerous assignments.

Sherwood glanced up at the sky. 'No more snow then. That's good.' He sounded very cool. Almost disinterested. He faced Ransome and added quietly, 'Thanks for trying to put a spanner in the works.' He shrugged. 'It'll all be the same in a thousand years, I expect.'

They heard steps on the steel deck and Leading Writer Wakeford hurried into view.

'He agreed then.'

Sherwood smiled for the first time. 'Glad to go. You work him too hard, sir.'

Wakeford peered at Ransome and said, 'Sorry about this, sir, short notice, but I've done all the files you needed for the dock-yard and –'

Ransome gripped his arm. It felt like a bone through his raincoat sleeve.

'Just take care of yourself. I can't manage without you.' He stood away. 'That goes for you both.' He saluted. 'I want you back as soon as possible.'

Sub-Lieutenant Morgan, who was staying aboard as O.O.D., watched them go and said, 'Your writer left some letters, sir. It's as if he knew.'

Ransome shivered. There was no point in asking about Sherwood. He had nobody to write to. He doubted if he would anyway. There had been grief enough in his young life.

He said, 'It looks as if your promotion may be delayed a while.'

Morgan stared into the darkness but the two figures had vanished.

'Suddenly it doesn't seem that important, see?' He shook his head. 'It's always just around the next corner, isn't it, sir?'

He did not explain but Ransome knew exactly what he meant.

The Reverend Canon Simon Warwick stood with one hand resting on the huge stone fireplace and stared thoughtfully into the flames of a cheerful log fire. It gave only an illusion of warmth however, for this room, like all the others in Codrington House, were too vast to heat easily. Once away from the fireplace and the winter intruded like a chill breath.

232

He glanced at his wife, who was sitting with a local lady dressed in the uniform of the Women's Voluntary Service, of which Betty had been the most active member until the bombing.

Sometimes it was difficult to pick up the threads of God's reasons and reasoning, he thought.

The two women were checking their lists of promised gifts offered by local shopkeepers and farmers for the Christmas raffle.

Warwick was already thinking of Christmas, of how hard it would be to decorate this rambling house and brighten things up for the ebb and flow of evacuees and homeless people who stayed here.

But he was finding it hard to concentrate. He could hear the clatter of plates and cutlery from the dining-room where two evacuee volunteers were laying the table for dinner. He hoped the W.V.S. lady would leave before any of his guests arrived. He knew it was an uncharitable thought, just as he knew the reason for his inability to concentrate on Christmas.

But for the sound of cheerful chatter and clink of crockery, he knew he would hear Eve's voice from the draughty hallway, where the private telephone was situated.

He frowned. Seeing her face in his mind, the young lieutenant-commander, so self-assured, who seemed to think of little but his ship and the war. He had said a lot, but their eyes when they met across the table had told another story. Warwick had felt it then, something akin to jealousy, more like a suitor than a father.

She had answered the telephone herself. Warwick shied away from the thought which touched his mind like a raw nerve. Would he have summoned her, had he answered Ransome's call first? Or might he had made some excuse? It would only postpone, rather than prevent it. But the thought remained, unanswered.

The W.V.S. lady stood up and snapped her handbag shut. She was a square, competent woman, a local magistrate, and the widow of an old major-general who had died in the neighbouring village.

She thrust out her hand and said, 'Goodbye, Canon.' Her handshake was like her heavy shoes, firm, sensible.

Betty played uncertainly with her necklace.

'Well, er, – I'll see you to your car.'

Warwick bit his lip. They were old friends, but he knew Betty had nearly revealed that she had forgotten her name.

The door opened and Eve walked in. She wore her heavy fisherman's jersey, and her favourite trousers with the paint smears.

She hugged her arms across her body and shivered. 'I'm like ice!'

Betty smiled at her. 'How is he, dear?'

Eve looked fondly at her mother. 'He's all right, Mummy.' She dropped her eyes. 'I – I think he's had a bad time.'

The W.V.S. lady exclaimed, 'What's this, Betty? A secret love? I must say, I'm not surprised, what?'

Warwick said, 'He's someone we used to see when we were on holidays, before –' He did not go on.

The woman said knowingly, 'I see. Well, well!'

She crossed the room and put her hands on the girl's shoulders. 'He's a lucky boy!'

She replied, 'He's a man, not a boy. He commands a mine-sweeper.' It sounded like defiance, a defence against the trite summing-up and her father's constant refusal to accept that she had feelings.

Once her mother would have helped and understood. Now she seemed to wander, lost in her own thoughts, which nobody could share any more.

She said, 'I'm going up to have a bath and –' She looked down at her daubed trousers and remembered his smile when he had seen them, how he had recalled those other times in the boatyard, reminded her without making her relive them as a young girl, but as an equal. 'And change, I suppose.'

Warwick tucked his hands into his cassock. 'Good idea. Don't be long. Early supper tonight. In case there's a raid on Plymouth.'

The W.V.S. lady was still watching Eve, her flashing eyes when she had spoken out. Such a quiet girl, who rarely mixed. But something had changed her. It would make a new topic at the bridge party on Saturday, she thought.

Eve closed the door behind her and leaned against it, hoping that the heavy fisherman's jersey had hidden the thrust of her breasts and her breathing, which had still not settled after speaking with him. A bad line, but they often were nowadays. She had sensed the change in his voice, the careful way he spoke, as if each word was precious to him.

But nothing could take the real happiness away. He was back, after all the months and the days, and the hours; his ship was in the dockyard. It might have been anywhere, in Scotland or in the North of England, but *Rob Roy* had come to Plymouth. He had not told her in so many words, and she had had the feeling that many ears were on the line, fingers waiting to snatch away the hissing, noisy connection. By mentioning the gardens around this old house, he had made her realise where he was.

He could not say when he would see her. There were 'things' which had to be done. Again, she had felt the same sense of anxiety, that someone he cared about was in danger.

She ran up the great spiral staircase to her room. She did not even see the flaking paint, the rough notices pasted to the wall which gave directions about the nearest air-raid shelters, what to do in a gas attack, how to deal with an incendiary if one fell through the ceiling.

She arrived in her room and stood panting by the window before drawing the heavy black-out curtains. There had been snow, but most of it had melted.

Perhaps he would be home for Christmas? She threw herself on the bed and pressed the old teddy bear against her face.

She thought of his brother, the irrepressible Tony, who was still in the naval hospital. *He* was to be home for Christmas; he had written to her, had told her about meeting Ian in Sicily. It had taken several attempts before she could control her tears and read it.

She had made a point of visiting Fowey to see his parents. His father had hugged her warmly and treated her like one of the family. His mother had kept a polite distance, playing much the same role as the Canon downstairs. She had gone to see his old boat, the *Barracuda*, and the foreman Jack Weese had pulled her leg about sailing off with her before young Master Ian got home for good. It could all have been so different. She closed her mind to the other thought. That it might still change.

She opened a drawer and took out his precious letters, and lastly the big newspaper article written by the celebrity war correspondent Richard Wakely. It was very much like the broadcast, so that when she read and reread it she heard his familiar voice describing the scene just as he had witnessed and shared it. The shrill scream of Stuka dive-bombers, the roar of ships exploding, the troops fighting their way up the Sicilian beaches.

Richard Wakely had been right there beside Ian. Could have reached out and touched him. Wakely's cameraman had taken several action pictures, and one of them had been of Ian.

He had been looking up at the sky, pointing with one arm while smoke rose behind him like an evil presence.

She looked at the picture now. *Oh, dearest of men, I love you so.*

Wakely had finished his broadcast like the article, with his usual flourish.

'Together, that young captain and I had looked into the face of death, and come through yet again.'

She had written to the newspaper and had asked if it was possible to purchase a copy of the print of Ian's picture. So far there had been no response.

She walked into her small bathroom and turned on the taps. She saw the unopened jar of bath salts by the window. They didn't make it any more. As the lady in the shop had said wistfully, 'I expect it's used for explosives now!'

Eve would save it, as she had – She felt her face flushing and left the bathroom. Then she did something she never normally did. She locked the bedroom door, and stood in front of the wardrobe mirror for several tormenting seconds, while the hot water hissed into the huge bath like a pool of lava.

Very deliberately she opened a flat drawer at the bottom of the wardrobe and took out the nightdress. She carefully removed the little sachet of rosebuds and rosemary although their fragrance remained in the fine white silk, as it had for the two years since she had bought it. She smiled and held it up against herself while she watched the image in the mirror and remembered. She had almost emptied her post office savings account to buy it, in the days before rationing had made such luxuries beyond the reach of all but the very rich and the black market. She had taken two buses to go to another district and withdraw the money, in case the local postmistress might tell her mother what she had done.

She made up her mind, and pulled the jersey over her head and slipped the trousers down to her ankles.

Her heart was beating painfully; she kept her gaze on her own reflected stare as she tossed her underwear on to the bed and stood quite naked, with the nightdress held up to her chin. She would not put it on until . . .

Two years she had had it. She had known then, and before that, that she had wanted him. If he had turned instead to another, she would never have married. She did not know how she was so certain. She just knew.

Her mother called, 'Will you be long, dear?'

She smiled and carefully folded the sachet inside the nightdress before slipping it into its special bag.

'Ten minutes, Mummy!'

She walked, naked, across the cold room and into the steamy embrace of the bath.

Soon. They would make up for all things lost. Together.


The big staff car seemed to be hurtling into complete darkness. With the headlamps almost blinded by the regulation shields to prevent them being seen from the air, objects loomed out of the shadows as if the driver had lost control.

Commander Bliss muttered, 'God Almighty, I'm glad she knows the road!'

*She* was a leading Wren from the C-in-C's staff at Plymouth, a small, wiry girl who seemed to be enjoying the drive, a conflict between herself and the car.

Sherwood saw pale cottages, their small windows blacked out, crouched by the roadside, then gaps where the fields took over again, gaunt hedgerows which shone in the dipped beams from the melted snow, and once a horse staring over a gate, its eyes like bright stones in the glare.

Up to Exeter and away from the sea to Honiton in Devon, the windscreen wipers fighting a losing battle against the mud and slush thrown up from the road by other vehicles. Most of the latter were military, Sherwood noticed, huge lorries which seemed to fill the breadth of the unmarked road.

In the front seat beside the driver, Leading Writer Wakeford sat stiffly back in his swaying seat, and Sherwood got the impression he had both feet pressed against the floor – as well he might.

Sherwood kept thinking of Ransome's attempt to keep him from this unexpected assignment. He had heard about Wakeford's letters, which he had left in safe keeping, and wondered why he had not done the same. Just a note, a few words to try and explain why he had left her asleep, why he had not even written to her.

If this job went badly wrong . . . He glanced out of the streaked window so that he could avoid opening another conversation with Bliss. He seemed to speak of little else but The War, in capital letters. It was like being cooped up with the nine o'clock news, he thought.

The mine might easily explode. Something new could have been added. Bliss had stopped the car once to make a telephone call: when he had returned he had said that the mine was still intact. He had sounded almost relieved, as if it would have spoiled his record to lose it.

Sherwood thought of the girl called Rosemary, the way they had clung to one another, had demanded so much that they were totally spent.

A letter would have made it worse for her; that is, if she cared after what he had done.

He thought too of the men who shared his life in *Rob Roy*, a typical small ship's company. How long would they remember him if things went wrong? He forced a smile. Just a dog-watch, as the old sailors said.

He could picture some of them now, making their different ways to all points of the compass. The luckier ones would already be home, down at the local pub, or picking up the pieces of a broken marriage, discovering peace away from their messmates, from everything. Others might still be wondering what they would find. A gap where the house had once stood, sympathy, and a feeling of utter loneliness.

He thought of Rosemary again. She was alone. Could she

remember her husband, the soldier called Tom? Had she been loving *him* on that last, desperate night in Mayfair?

Sherwood heard his bag rattle behind the seat as the car lurched over to avoid a man pushing a bicycle. The man shouted something after them and the little Wren murmured, 'Stupid sod. Trying to get his name in the papers.' She seemed to remember her senior passenger and added, 'Sorry, sir.'

Bliss replied cheerfully, 'Just so long as we get there, eh?'

Sherwood thought of the two bottles of gin he had in his bag, packed alongside his instruments. That was what he needed right now. Oblivion. He recalled his feeling of disbelief when Bliss had told him about Commander Foulerton. It did not seem possible that it could happen to him. He was a genius. A quiet, unassuming man who had known more about mines than any other human being, be they magnetic or acoustic, dropped from the air, or laid by any ship which could slip through the defences.

As Bliss had been quick to point out, Foulerton had been a regular officer. But he had not mentioned that he had been a ranker, who had joined the peacetime navy as a boy, and had got there by his own sweat and intelligence. These rare characters who had climbed up to the quarterdeck the hard way were the backbone of the navy. He thought of *Rob Roy*'s engineer officer, John Campbell, and poor old Bone with his dentures and his stomach troubles. They had to stand aside now and leave the medals to younger men, but without them the fleet would never have put to sea.

He leaned forward, as if his mind had been triggered like a time-fuse.

'The sea. I'm sure I can smell it!'

The Wren called over her shoulder but fortunately never took her eyes from the twisting road.

'That's right, sir. That was Lyme Regis. We're in Dorset now. We should be there in an hour at this rate!'

Bliss said irritably, 'A few hours sleep then. I hope somebody has remembered to arrange our messing and accommodation.' When Sherwood remained silent he added, 'Well?'

Sherwood replied, 'I shall go to the place first.'

The Wren had up to then believed that Bliss was some kind of

V.I.P. Now she knew differently. The young, pale-faced lieuten
ant who rarely spoke or smiled was the one who counted fo
some reason. She had been told nothing, so it was obviously
important.

Bliss said, 'It's up to you, of course –'

Sherwood stopped it there. 'So it seems.'

Sherwood touched the girl's shoulder and apologised as she
jerked with alarm.

'Sorry.' He pointed ahead through the filthy windscreen.
'What's the next place?'

She said, 'Bridport, sir. We stop for a road-check usually,
provided the army or the Home Guard haven't all gone to the
pub!'

'I'd like to make a phone call from there.'

She seemed to sense the tension, the sudden determination in
his tone. 'Know just the spot, sir.'

Sherwood took out his wallet and felt the small notebook in
the darkness. Why had he taken her telephone number? What did
he think he was doing?

They swept through a checkpoint, waved on by some vague,
helmeted figures beside a sandbagged barrier.

Bliss said, 'We could have been bloody Germans for all they
know!'

The Wren was glad it was too dark for Bliss to see her grin. She
knew most of the personnel who mounted these checkpoints, and
few of them would care to stop one of the C-in-C's own cars.

She exclaimed, 'Here it is now, sir.'

Sherwood felt the car slew off the road and saw a small inn, its
weathered sign swaying slightly in the chill breeze. Like a scene
from *Treasure Island*, he thought.

Bliss said, 'Don't be too long.' It sounded as if he was trying to
reassert himself. 'I'll just go and pump the bilges while we're
here.' He peered at his watch. 'Why not snatch a pint? It's still
opening time, or near enough.'

Wakeford shook his head. 'Not tonight, sir, but thanks all the
same. Tomorrow, well, now, that'll be different.'

Sherwood touched his shoulder and opened the door. Probably too close to the truth for comfort, he thought.

As the two officers left the car and separated in the darkness the Wren asked, 'What's it all about?'

Wakeford shrugged. 'That's Lieutenant Sherwood. The one who was given the George Cross, remember?' He saw her eyes widen in the pale oval of her face. 'He's gone to phone someone. Probably thinks it's his last chance.'

She looked away. 'You make it sound like the condemned man.'

Wakeford sighed. 'He is, in a way.'

Sherwood in the meantime had found his way into a bar which was barely furnished, with six farm labourers and two dogs the only customers.

The landlord looked at Sherwood without curiosity. His old battledress with the tarnished gold stripes on the shoulders implied he was up to something. That was nothing new along this stretch of coast. It was safer not to ask.

'Telephone, Skipper? Roight through therr –' His accent was as West Country as Drake.

Sherwood sat on a small stool and held his book near a ship's lantern with an electric bulb shaped like an ancient candle. He dialled the number, then had to ask the exchange to help him. Then he had a crossed line, and he thought he heard a car door slam: Bliss displaying his impatience.

Sherwood tightened his lips. *Well, let him. He's not taking the risks*. A straightforward bed-and-breakfast-job for *him*.

A man's voice answered and Sherwood almost replaced the receiver. Then he remembered. She had said that she lived with her elderly parents.

'Er, could I speak to, er – Rosemary, please?'

There was a lengthy pause, as if the man was thinking about it. He said, 'It's a bit late, y'know!'

Sherwood felt the desperation rising like a flood.

'I must speak with her!'

'Now just hold on, whoever you are. My daughter's not –'

There was a muffled sound, and he guessed the telephone had been covered by somebody's hand.

When she spoke the line was suddenly clear. It was as if she was right here beside him.

'Who is that?'

He tried to explain. 'I had to speak to you. To tell you —' He got no further.

'Oh, Philip, where are you? I've been so anxious, so terribly worried. I thought you disliked me, that I'd done something —'

He said, 'Please. Listen to me. I have to leave right now. It's a job I must do.' Now that he had begun he could not stop. 'I'm not sure what's going to happen.' He heard her sharp intake of breath but hurried on. 'I just wanted you to know what you did for me, how happy those days together really were.'

She said, 'I know. I wrote to you several times, but —'

'They're still following me, I expect.' He heard the car toot its horn. 'I didn't want to hurt you, Rosemary, you've had enough, but I couldn't be so near to you without —' He stared at the telephone, his eyes smarting. He was doing everything he had sworn not to do.

She said, 'Don't hang up. Whatever it is, wherever you have to go, please take care, for me if nothing else — I must see you again, Philip.' She waited and added, 'Are you still there?'

'Yes.' One word, and he could barely get it out.

'I shall never forget either —'

Sherwood murmured, 'Goodbye, darling girl.' He put down the telephone and two pennies beside it before walking back through the bar. They were all still in their places. Only one of the dogs had moved.

He climbed into the car without speaking.

Wakeford asked quietly, 'All right, sir?'

Sherwood watched the bushes gathering speed again. 'Yes. Now it is.'

He did not speak again until the car rolled to a halt and the sea opened up to greet him like an old enemy.

It took Sherwood only a few minutes to gather all the facts he needed. The mine's parachute had snared itself on some sunken boat, a local fisherman's apparently. The wind was still without much power, but there was a hint of more to come, snow too.

In the back of an army fifteen-hundredweight Chevrolet, its red-painted wings marking it as one of the Bomb Disposal Squad, Sherwood studied the map, his breath mingling with that of two sapper officers, and a lieutenant from the naval base at Portland.

The mine was too close to the Chesil Beach, that strange ridge of stones which ran parallel to the coast, right down to the northern part of Portland Bill itself. It was an eerie place even in daylight, the graveyard for many ships through the centuries, although some were said to have been lured here by wreckers.

Now, with the breeze sighing against the wet stones, and the knowledge that the mine was just offshore on a sandbar, it would make anyone's flesh creep.

Sherwood said, 'It's low water. This has to be done quickly. If the parachute breaks adrift, or the mine is thrown up on this beach, we'll not get a sniff at it.' The two sappers nodded together. They had probably defused enough bombs and mines in their time. They would not be here otherwise. One said, 'We've rigged the line for tomorrow.' Sherwood lowered himself to the ground and sniffed the bitter, damp air. Tomorrow might be too late. Why did he think that? Was it because he knew his nerve would not last until then?

'It's got to be now. I'll need two good lights.' He laughed to break the sudden tension. 'The black-out will have to put up with it!'

'What's all this about lights?'

Vice-Admiral Hargrave, followed by two aides, marched down the beach.

Sherwood murmured, 'God, it's getting like a flag-day!'

The vice-admiral studied the map and then said, 'You're right, Sherwood.' So far he had not spoken to Bliss at all. 'See that it's done.' One aide hurried away. To the other he snapped, 'Tell the police inspector to get on with the evacuation. Those cottages up there, and anyone else who might —'

Sherwood was crouching beside his bag. 'Get blown up, sir?'

The vice-admiral chuckled. 'Sorry about that.'

Sherwood took Wakeford's thin arm and led him away from the others. 'According to the map there's part of a concrete wall which the Royal Engineers built here as an exercise. Run the telephone line up to that and keep out of sight.'

'Yes, sir.'

Sherwood touched his lips; they were bone-dry. 'Look, I can't keep calling you Leading Writer Wakeford, now can I, under these sorry circumstances. What's your first name?'

Wakeford looked at the beach. 'Horace, sir. A name I have always detested.'

It was suddenly very necessary to find and keep close contact with this gentle man. He would probably be the last one to hear his voice; would need to write it all down, so that the next poor idiot – He persisted, 'What did the kids at school call you behind your back?'

Wakeford seemed to brighten up. 'Stinky, sir, because of my job.'

'So be it.' Sherwood handed him his cap. 'The inshore sounds are a nuisance. I must be able to hear.' He gripped his arm. 'Off you go. If I say the word, hit the deck sharpish!'

Wakeford stared at him in the darkness. 'If, I mean, sir, how long?'

Sherwood picked up his bag. 'If the fuse goes, there's usually about twelve seconds to play with.'

Wakeford watched him stride down the beach where more anonymous figures hovered at the water's edge, while some stood in the sea itself, holding a small rubber boat.

Sherwood saw the sappers paying out a field-telephone line while they waded through the shallows, pushing the boat ahead of them. Once the tide began to turn it would be too late yet again. As he held on to the boat and sloshed through the water with the others, Sherwood tried to remember everything he had learned about this type of mine. Packed with over fifteen hundred pounds of deadly hexanite. Enough to knock down several streets, or demolish a cruiser.

A sapper switched on one of the lights, and Sherwood could imagine the consternation on the shore. It was so close it was startling, lying half-submerged, the torn parachute vanishing into the shadows of deeper water. The mine was cleaner than usual because of the sea. The one he had dealt with before had been grimy with black filth from the exhaust smoke of the plane which had unloaded it. He could see the identifying letters and figures shining in the hard beam, the way it appeared to roll about in the current. But that was only a trick of the light – otherwise he would be dead.

'All right, Sergeant, take your chaps off now.' The men moved back into the surrounding darkness.

Sherwood felt the sea breeze like ice on his face. He had tried to make it sound encouraging for Wakeford's sake. Twelve seconds. Maybe. But here the real difference was that there was nowhere to run, no empty house, or garden wall, or as in one incident, pressed against a railway embankment. That one had exploded and he had seen two complete railway carriages fly over his head as if they were paper kites.

He tested the telephone. 'D'you hear me, Stinky?' He made himself chuckle, although he felt as if the breath was being strangled out of him.

'Yes, sir.'

'Write this down. It's a Type Seven. That's the only classification we have to go on so far.' He measured it with his eye, moving the light an inch at a time until the beam was shining beneath the slopping water. 'About nine feet six long, I'd say.' He paused to tug his bag clear of the water on to a small hump of sand. The sea sounds seemed so loud out here. The tiny purr of the fuse would probably pass unheard. Not that it would make any difference anyway.

'I've found the fuse.' He fumbled for his special callipers, the ones he used to prevent it from moving and coming to life. He wiped the spray, or was it sweat, from his eyes. The callipers locked on to the keeping ring which held the whole fuse in position.

Sherwood rocked back on his heels. 'There's something wrong.' He did not realise he had spoken aloud.

'What is it, sir?'

'Not sure.' He peered into the water again. Was his mind playing tricks or was it already deeper?

'It's too easy, Stinky. All I have to do is unscrew it, just like the earlier models.'

Wakeford said, 'Be careful, sir.'

Sherwood smiled despite his raw nerves. *Careful*. Commander Foulerton had died trying to defuse one of these mines. He was a true expert, a professional. Otherwise, this mine might indeed be one of the easy jobs. Lucky to have been washed clean by the sea, to have come to rest the right way up.

Sherwood moved slowly along the mine, his free hand feeling it as if it was alive.

He returned to the fuse again and touched the keeping ring with his fingertips. A few turns, and the whole thing would slide out. Not easy, but not impossible.

It was then that his hand began to shake as if he had a fever. He put the light in his bag and gripped his wrist with the other hand. *For Christ's sake, not now!* He tried again. If they were on dry land, he would risk attaching a tackle to the hoisting flaps. As if to mock him the wind ruffled his hair, and part of the sodden parachute floated against his thigh like a shroud.

There was no more time. His whole body was quivering. What he had always dreaded more than anything.

He picked up the lamp again and began another careful inspection. A voice seemed to jeer at him. *You're putting it off. It's over. Why not give the brute a kick and end it all right now?*

He tried to cling to fragments of memory, like a man caught in a dying ship's final whirlpool. Her voice on the telephone. When was it, one, two hours ago? Was that all?

He pulled out the special spanner he had had made for himself at *Vernon*. Foulerton had probably used the original one.

He stared wildly at his flickering reflection in the water. *Hoisting flaps!* It seemed to scream out at him so that he almost dropped the lamp.

He spoke carefully on the field telephone. 'Stinky. This mine has hoisting flaps. They stopped using them eighteen months ago.'

'I – I don't understand, sir!'

'Don't try, old son.' He recalled his words to the Canadian major in Sicily when Ransome had run to the stretcher. 'Just pray!'

He lined up the flap with the fuse, tightened his spanner around it and then stared at the low clouds.

*Twelve seconds.* He put his weight on it. Nothing happened at first, then it scraped away from its new paint and began to turn.

He gasped, 'It's under the flap, Stinky.' He let the lamp fall into the sea by his boot, which had now filled with icy water. Another turn, and another. How much time would he have to know what was happening?

He shouted, 'It's here, under the flap. I'm doing it now.' He inserted the callipers and began to turn. Suppose Foulerton had seen it too, and this was the real booby-trap.

He yelled, 'Well, it's too bloody late now, you bastards!'

The fuse slid into his fingers, and the sudden silence seemed to probe his ears like fingers. He returned to the original ring and inserted the callipers. Inside the gap there was the second fuse, now made harmless by his discovery. But for some warning instinct the mine would have exploded at the first or second turn of the keeping ring.

He heard Wakeford calling, 'Are you all right, sir? Please answer me!'

He bent over against the mine and gasped into the telephone, 'Come and get me out of this! I – I can't move!' He vomited over the telephone and hurled it into the water.

Men were running through the water towards him, then someone put his arm round his waist and a voice shouted, 'Here, lend a hand! The poor bastard's done his bit for the night!'

Then there was Wakeford on the Chesil Beach, although Sherwood did not remember how he got there. It was no longer empty, but dark figures ran and bustled in all directions.

Commander Bliss reached out and took his hand. It was like a piece of ice.

Bliss said, 'I wondered what you chaps did. Now that I know, I'd still like to be told *how* you do it! That was a bloody brave thing you just did.'

Sherwood tried to speak, but nothing made sense. He was shaking so badly he knew he would have fallen but for the others holding him. The Wren driver wrapping a rug over his shoulders, laughing and sobbing at the same time, the vice-admiral thumping the beach with a walking-stick and booming, 'Well, how about that, eh?'

Wakeford whispered, 'What is it, sir?'

'Just get me away from here. Somewhere I can use a telephone.' Then he fainted.

Bliss said, 'Call up *Rob Roy*. Tell her captain. He wanted to be told at once, though we were all expecting it would be tomorrow.' He glanced up at the clouds as the wind whipped his coat against his legs. 'Then it would have been too late, I fear.'

He watched some soldiers carrying Sherwood up the beach towards the road.

'I don't know how many of those damnable things that lieutenant has made safe, but I swear to God, that one will be his last.' He looked out at the black water as if expecting to see it lying there, as evil and as patient as ever, but there was only the faint gleam where Sherwood had lost one of his lamps in the water, and the sigh of a tide on the turn.

When Wakeford returned to the car he found Sherwood sitting in the back, the rug still around his shoulders, his face hidden in his hands.

The Wren whispered, 'He was just sick again.'

Sherwood looked up; in the darkness his eyes were like holes. 'Telephone?'

'D'you think you should, sir?'

'Please.' His voice was very small. 'Help me.'

They found a telephone at the police station where the news of the mine had obviously been a lively topic since it had been dropped by an enemy aircraft one night earlier. The German pilot had probably jettisioned it because he was caught in a barrage, or being pursued by night fighters. They would never know.

Tomorrow the sappers would haul the mine from the sea and then it would be the boffins' chance to examine it.

Sherwood found himself in a small office with pictures on the wall of wanted criminals and missing persons.

Wakeford got the number for him, handed him the telephone and then withdrew. He tried to smile at him, to offer some encouragement, but all he could think about was the sound of Sherwood's voice on the field telephone, like a man staring at the rope or a firing squad.

Sherwood heard her voice immediately.

She said huskily, 'Somehow I knew you would phone. I had to wait. To be sure. Tell me what to do.'

Sherwood tried to clear his mind. 'I want to see you. Now. I – I need to –'

She said quickly, 'Where are you? I'll come at once.'

He tried to laugh. 'The police have offered to drive me, you see.'

She said, 'I shall be here, waiting. Don't do anything, just come.'

But Sherwood could not reply this time. His defences had finally broken down.

# 17

# *Reunions*

Ian Ransome stamped his feet on the stone flags to restore the circulation and watched the snow falling steadily from a dull grey afternoon sky.

Every so often he turned and looked at the massive abbey and the groups of people who were making their way towards it.

Many of them were in the uniforms of all three services; in fact they outnumbered the civilians. Some were accompanied by girl-friends, others walked purposefully and alone. There was no saluting although the ranks varied from army privates to at least one group-captain from the local air station.

Eve had chosen this place where they would meet for the first time since *Rob Roy* had entered the dockyard. That had been three days ago, with only their brief, sometimes anxious telephone calls to sustain them.

There was a concert being held at the abbey, musicians from Plymouth and some surrounding towns, plus a few in uniform. She had remembered that he enjoyed classical music, and had bought tickets for this one performance.

It was not just that. She had told him on the last telephone call, she wanted them to meet *on their own ground*. Perhaps she meant away from her usual surroundings, even her father? He had answered Ransome's calls twice and had been outwardly friendly, and yet Ransome felt his reserve; he was careful not to display too much warmth.

He glanced at his watch and saw the snow clinging to his

sleeve. He thought of Sherwood, what Cusack had said when he had gone to see him.

The astute Irish doctor had described finding him in the care of the young woman to whom he had gone directly after the incident with the mine.

'Before he never felt fear, y'see, because he no longer *cared* about living. He thought that his life, in its deepest sense, was finished, with only some driving force keeping him going, a determination to hit back at the enemy in a field he knew better than most.' He had shrugged and downed another glass of Ransome's Scotch. 'Then everything changed. He and this woman found one another, though that part was left suitably vague for my benefit, I suspect. Philip Sherwood did explain how it hit him when he was working on the mine. He thought of dying, and for the first time since his life had been smashed to pieces, he wanted, no, *needed* to live.'

Thank God Sherwood was not required for duty. He wanted to come back to *Rob Roy*, but Ransome knew inwardly that he was finished with his lonely encounters with mines and whatever the enemy could dream up, forever. Perhaps in his strange, distant fashion he wanted to share his change of fortune with the only people he really liked.

He heard a door closing behind him and felt a start of anxiety. Maybe she had changed her mind? Or she had been prevented from coming? A small bus rolled to a stop with slush dripping from its sides, and suddenly she was there, running towards him, her arms outstretched, oblivious to the other passengers and the grinning bus driver.

They clung together for a long moment, saying nothing, each reassured that it was really true.

Then she said, 'Shall we go inside?' She looked up at him, searched his face, and in those few seconds she saw it all. The shadows beneath his eyes, the small tight lines at the corners of his mouth. She wanted to keep on hugging him, to hold him as she would a child, and make the strain go away.

She asked, 'Perhaps you'd rather not? I — I mean they're not from Covent Garden or the Albert Hall. But I thought —'

Ransome put his arm around her shoulders and guided her

into the ageless shadows of the entrance, where he shook the snowflakes from his cap on to the worn stones. 'I'd *love* to, Eve. I can't tell you —'

A wizened usher guided them to their seats in one of the pews. The place was quite cold, but strangely moving with its flickering candles and air of timeless strength.

She pressed against him while he spread his greatcoat over their knees like a rug.

She whispered, 'No heating. To save fuel.'

A man in an unfamiliar uniform touched Ransome's shoulder. Excuse me, sir, but would you let this party into your pew?'

Ransome had wondered why the rest of the pew had been empty when the abbey appeared to be packed.

A line of young RAF officers filed past them, silent, and looking neither right nor left. The highest ranking one was a flight-lieutenant. They were all about Eve's age.

As the last one attempted to pass he knocked a prayer book from its shelf, stooped down and then handed it to Eve with a mumbled apology. He had been a good-looking youth, but now half of his face had been burned away. Just like wax, with a gleaming glass eye to complete the mockery of his survival. The others were much the same, burned, mutilated, and somehow embarrassed.

Eve said, 'Thank you. There's not much room, is there, in such a big place.'

Ransome saw the young pilot stare at her. Astonished that anyone who looked like her could treat him as if he were normal. Perhaps he had once had a girl like her, before —

Ransome saw a tear run from his remaining eye before one of the others pulled his sleeve and said jokingly, 'Come away, Bill, she's in the navy's care!'

What did each hour cost them? Yesterday's heroes.

Ransome felt her fingers digging into his hand. But she did not speak this time.

He glanced around. The wounded pilots still had the same need as the other servicemen here, he thought. Like an oasis, to help repair what they had lost.

The orchestra made itself comfortable, and while a senior lay churchman made a ponderous introduction there were all the usual exciting if discordant sounds of musicians tuning up.

It was a mixed Baroque concert, the Telemann violin concertos, and after a freezing fifteen-minute interval, a selection from Handel's *Water Music*. Eve had even remembered that, and Ransome thought of his small and dwindling collection of Handel records in *Rob Roy*. Too many explosions and near-misses had done for most of them.

And all the while he was very aware of the girl beside him, her warmth, the scent of her long hair, and when he glanced at her profile, the memory of those other times. Was it wrong to hope in wartime? Could it even be fair to profess love when each day the odds against survival mounted?

Then the concert was over, and they were outside in the snow again.

'I have to get back.' He hated each word.

'I know.' She thrust her arm through his as they walked towards the bus-stop. 'You warned me.' Then she turned and looked at him. 'I'm so happy, Ian. Just to have you with me. I shall never forget this, the concert –' her eyes dropped. 'Those poor airmen. Everything. I feel a part of it now because of you.'

Ransome had already been told about Richard Wakely's broadcast and newspaper article. He should have guessed. Wakely's image was far more important to him than trying to score points off the men who had been there, who had seen him grovelling and blubbering for his own skin. Perhaps in its way his was a kind of courage too. Being in contact with events which could strike terror and revulsion into you when you did not have to, because of duty, or whatever sent a man to war . . .

The bus floundered through some deep puddles and they climbed on to it. It was about twenty miles to Plymouth and yet it seemed to pass in minutes.

When they reached the outskirts of the city it was pitch-dark, with only the falling snow giving any sort of life to it.

She said, 'Thank you for meeting me at Buckfastleigh.' She shivered, although not from cold. 'Sometimes when you spend your days in and around Christianity it can become oppressive.' She smiled and wrapped her arms around his neck. 'But never with you!'

Ransome gripped her and wanted to blurt out everything, as Sherwood had probably done. As he held her against him he was very aware that she was no longer the schoolgirl, and he knew she understood what he was thinking.

She said, 'When can we meet? Please make it soon. I've been so worried, I've tried to be with you wherever you were. Then seeing your picture, hearing how it was –'

He replied, 'I'll call you tomorrow. Things on board should be in hand by then. I'll have to go and visit my parents – Tony will be home too, with any luck.' He looked at her, then kissed her very gently on the cheek, feeling the snow melt on his lips. 'Will you come with me?'

She nodded. 'We can look at your funny boat.' She was almost in tears.

'Don't be sad, Eve. I love you more than ever, at least I would if that were possible. I don't want to share you with anyone.'

She touched his mouth with her fingers. 'I know. Once I didn't dare to admit what I was thinking about you.' She shook her head. 'No, don't look at me! I never knew I could feel that way, so utterly wanton.'

Another bus groped its way towards them. She said breathlessly, 'I want you, Ian.' Then she kissed him hard on the mouth and ran to the bus. He watched her wiping the condensation off a window with her sleeve to wave to him as the bus headed away towards Codrington House.

Ransome thrust his hands into his greatcoat pockets and walked slowly into the deeper darkness, his whole being clinging to those last words. *I want you.* No demands or conditions, not even a doubt, without knowing it she had already given him the greatest gift of all. Her trust.

When he reached *Rob Roy* there was an air-raid warning in progress, two seamen of the duty watch were under arrest for being drunk and disorderly in a dockside canteen, and Vice-Admiral Hargrave had been asking for him several times on the shore telephone.

Ransome listened to Morgan's report and then touched his arm. 'Deal with it, will you. Then come to my cabin and listen to some music.'

Sub-Lieutenant Morgan watched him go below and smiled.

Like the cat that found the cream, he thought. And about time too.

Ordinary Seaman Boyes felt his heart quicken as a camouflaged Bedford three-tonner rolled into the station yard and spilled its khaki occupants on to the slushy snow. For a moment longer, he thought she was not there, and realised just how much he wanted to see her again. Then he saw her, her face lighting up in a grin as she pushed through the soldiers and A.T.S. girls from her battery who had been given a lift into town.

It was hardly like the West End, but he guessed that anything was probably better than gaunt army huts in Home Park across the river from where the battery provided A.A. support for the sky above London.

She let him kiss her and stepped back to look at him.

'How long have you been back, then?'

'Two days.' It sounded like an apology. 'I had to see the parents of one of our people in *Rob Roy*.' He looked at her, his eyes pleading. 'He was killed at Sicily.'

She put her arm through his. 'Never mind, Gerry. I'm taking you to a party. It'll be warm at least, and more important, it's free.'

As they walked she glanced at him. He had changed in some way. Not matured, that would be too simple; if anything he had seemed more defenceless when he had blurted out about someone who had bought it at Sicily. His face held a kind of desperation, made him look older.

They crossed a street near the riverside of Kingston-on-Thames, with the massive chimneys of the power station standing against the dull sky like abandoned lighthouses. He did not know where she was taking him. He had hoped to be alone with her, and recalled his mother's tone when he had telephoned the army camp to ask for her.

She had warned, 'Don't get into any trouble, that's all I ask.'

His father had murmured soothingly, 'Don't worry, dear. He's home now, and to all accounts he's earned a bit of leave.' He might just as well have saved his breath.

Boyes thought of his visit to Davenport's home. It was as if the midshipman's body was still in the house. Everything was so still and deathly quiet.

They had been civil enough, but when he had left he had had the feeling that Davenport's parents resented his being alive while their son lay fathoms deep in the Mediterranean.

Davenport's father had asked just once, 'Did he suffer? Was he able to speak?'

Boyes had replied as truthfully as he could. 'He didn't feel very much.' He thought of Davenport clinging to the talisman of his promotion even as his life had drained away.

Davenport's mother had asked almost sharply, 'How could you know that?'

Boyes had got to his feet and had answered without hesitation, 'Because I was with him. He died in my arms.' Before, he would have stammered and felt in the wrong. That at least he had left behind.

The girl dragged his arm around a corner, an ordinary street of Victorian houses. It could have been anywhere.

She stopped outside one of them. 'Here 'tis. Might be fun.'

A gramophone was cranking out dance music, and she led him into the sitting-room where several others were already swapping jokes and making steady headway into crates of bottled beer. The owner of the house was apparently a local butcher, who did quite a bit of business with the army in Home Park. His wife, a lively looking girl with dyed blonde hair and wearing, surprisingly, a bright party dress, was obviously a good bit younger than her husband, but they both made Boyes and the girl called Connie very welcome.

There was Connie's friend Sheila with a bombardier from the battery, and a massive quartermaster-sergeant whose contacts with the butcher had opened the way for this and perhaps previous parties.

A leading aircraftman and his girl, related in some unexplained way to the host, made up the party.

Connie settled down on a sofa beside him and took two glasses of beer from the table.

'Cheers, Sarge!'

The quartermaster-sergeant beamed at her and touched his ginger moustache. He nodded to Boyes. 'Up the navy!' Then he turned to his host and thrust another full pint into his hands. 'Come on, my son, drink up! It'll put hair on your chest!'

Connie giggled. 'You'd think it was *his* beer he's being so free with!'

Boyes tried to remember how much he was drinking. He did not usually drink, and was too young to draw his tot of rum as Beckett had often reminded him. The thought of the coxswain and his friend the randy Buffer touched him like a hot wire. The shell screaming and ricochetting around the wheelhouse, men dying, Richard Wakely attempting to hide under the table where Davenport lay bleeding.

Connie saw his expression. 'What is it, Gerry?'

He shook his head, not wanting to spoil anything. 'Someone walked on my grave, that's all.'

She did not believe him but said, 'I'm just going to powder my nose.' She waited for his eyes to meet hers. 'Remember the last time, you naughty boy!' Then she was gone.

Boyes could not remember how long she had been away, and for one awful moment imagined she had become irritated by his mood and had left, perhaps with somebody else.

He stared around the room. All but a table lamp had been switched off; Sheila and her bombardier lay in one another's arms, her stockinged feet curled over his massive army boots.

The leading aircraftman and his girl were trying to dance without cannoning into the beer crates and empty bottles.

Boyes blinked. Surely they hadn't drunk all that? Then he saw the butcher and knew that he must have consumed the bulk of it. Their host lay propped in a corner, his mouth open, his shirt and waistcoat sodden with spilled beer. He was out to the world.

The leading aircraftman and his girl left without speaking, so that only the quartermaster-sergeant and the butcher's wife remained in the centre of the floor, slowly gyrating but barely moving to the beat of the music.

The sergeant had his arm around her waist and was pressing her against him, while she clung to his neck, her body swaying even when the record came to an end.

Boyes noticed that her party dress was caught in the sergeant's uniform, but when they turned slowly once again he realised why the hostess had her eyes tightly closed. The sergeant's other hand was thrust up beneath her skirt.

Connie opened the door softly and quickly turned over the record. She looked at Boyes and held out her hand. 'Sorry to leave you with this lot, but I had things to do.' She pulled him to his feet. 'They won't miss us.'

She led the way up the stairs to a narrow landing and asked, 'Home for Christmas, d'you reckon?'

'Don't know.' He noticed that she did not look at him, and had the same bright nervousness as that time in the cinema.

She opened a door and waited for him to enter. He saw her lock it behind them, then turn to watch his reactions.

'I don't think they'll be wanting their bed, do you, Gerry?'

Boyes felt his mind in a whirl. Mixed feelings of uncertainty, even fear, ran through him; he could not even speak.

Connie came towards him and held his blue and white collar with both hands.

She said, 'You'll have to help, Gerry. You sailors seem to wrap yourselves up like herrings in a barrel!'

He pulled his jumper over his head and tossed it on to a chair. When he tried to hold her she evaded him. He heard himself say, 'I'm sorry, Connie. I've never –'

She nodded very slowly. 'I *know*. That's why –' She began to undress until she wore only her underwear and stockings.

She threw herself on the bed and watched him. 'I should be in pure silk, not army issue, for a moment like this.' She giggled.

Boyes sat beside her and touched her skin, then her breasts. She moved to make it easy for him, until she lay quite naked, surprised that she could feel shy while he finished undressing.

She rolled down the sheet. 'Slip in beside me. It's bloody cold in here.'

But still Boyes waited, without knowing why. A girl all of his own, her curly hair in disarray against the pillows, her breasts full and pink-tipped, as he had known they would be. He tortured his dazed mind a little longer, then climbed into the bed.

At any second someone might come banging at the door, no

matter what she believed, but nothing save this moment mattered, nothing but his Connie.

She lay back and felt his hands exploring her breasts, then down into her hair and her smooth thighs.

If he kept this up, neither of them would hold out for long. She reached out and gripped him, felt his body quiver as if he had received a shock.

'Come, Gerry!' She murmured against his skin but retained her hold of him. It was his first time, she had always known it would be, but there was no hesitation or disappointment after all.


Lieutenant Hargrave walked quickly across the hotel lobby and looked around at all the uniforms. It was the first time he had returned to the Savoy Hotel since his father had given a dinner party here when he had got his first ring. God, how long ago that felt.

Hargrave had come from their home in Hampshire, the same place he had known all his life. In fact, he had been born there. Old, comfortable and dependable – even with the grounds dug into vegetable gardens, with pigsheds kept as far away from the house as possible, it did not seem to have changed.

The hardest thing to stomach had been the gardeners who joined in the country's craze to *Dig for Victory*, even to be self-supporting in some cases. All the gardeners were Italian prisoners-of-war, with a foreman who was apparently a conscientious objector.

When he thought of the ships he had watched go down, men wearing the same uniforms as *Rob Roy*'s company, choking out their lives while they drowned in fuel, it seemed unrealistic and unfair.

His mother had explained that the vice-admiral was staying in London again now that his headquarters had shifted back to England. To be ready for instant briefings, to advise Churchill, to send ships and men wherever they might be needed. He wondered if his mother really believed all of it.

At the Admiralty he had been politely informed that the vice-admiral was on tour, after his return from the West Country where he had witnessed Sherwood's success with the mine.

'You can leave your number, sir.' Which meant that they firmly believed that if Vice-Admiral Hargrave had intended anyone to know the address of his private billet, he would have told them himself.

But an old messenger had whispered, 'Your father often drops into the Savoy for a drink after he's finished here, sir.' His watery eyes had lit up as Hargrave had put a pound note in his fist. 'Why, bless you, sir.'

Unknown to Hargrave he often sold tit-bits of information to junior officers in this way.

'May I help you, sir?'

The concierge regarded him gravely. He probably thought this was no place for a mere lieutenant, a regular or not.

'I was looking for my father.' He felt some of the others in the lobby watching him. He was suddenly angry with them and himself. His father would feel at home amongst them, he thought, there seemed to be no one less than a brigadier in the place. He continued, 'Vice-Admiral Hargrave.'

The concierge's eyes did not even flicker. 'I think *not*, sir. But I shall enquire right away.'

A small page marched through the throng of uniforms carrying a card on a stick. It read *Air-Raid Warning in progress*. Nobody took any notice. It could just as easily have been an announcement about a telephone call.

'Well, this is a surprise, Lieutenant.'

He turned, still angry, then caught aback by the girl who was watching him, her lips slightly parted in an amused smile.

Second Officer Ross Pearce looked anything but an admiral's flag-lieutenant. She wore a long dress of dark blue silk, and there was a diamond clip below one shoulder which must have cost a fortune.

'I hope it is a *pleasant* one?' She pouted, and although she was obviously well aware of the watching, envious glances, she was equally able to ignore them.

Hargrave began, 'I came looking for my father.'

'Oh dear. Well, I'm afraid he's not here.' She touched her lip with her tongue. 'I am not permitted to tell you where he is.'

Hargrave said, 'Well, I thought you *would* know!'

260

Her smile faded. 'I can understand your feelings, I *think*, but I do not have to tolerate your rudeness!'

Hargrave stepped closer. 'I'm sorry. I didn't mean to behave like a ten-year-old schoolboy, really. Could we begin again?'

He expected another rebuff and was surprised at his own surrender.

She was tall, cool, and extremely beautiful.

He added, 'It was just that I was expecting –'

She nodded slowly, her eyes examining him without curiosity.

'As I said, he's not here.' She gave a small shrug. 'But join me, if you like. You can tell me about *Husky*.' She mentioned it so casually she might have been on the beach in Sicily. 'I'd like that. All the reports, the despatches coming every hour to our H.Q. in Malta – well, it's not like the real thing, is it?'

A waiter hovered near her elbow, 'Shall I lay the table for two then, m'lady?'

She smiled at him. 'Please.'

Hargrave was floundering. *My lady*. 'I'm sorry. I wasn't told.'

'Does it make any difference? Anyway, the vice-admiral probably thought it less irksome this way. He likes to feel dominant – but I expect you know that?'

Hargrave did not know what to say. Her direct, challenging manner was like nothing he had experienced. He was in awe of her after just a few minutes, and yet strangely stimulated, as if the reason for his being here no longer counted.

She eyed the menu and said, 'Afterwards we can talk about you, and the command you hope to get. How does that suit?'

Hargrave had the feeling he was getting into something which was already out of control.


Ransome sat on the well-padded arm of a familiar chair and felt the warmth, and yet the unreality of his homecoming. His father, back to the blazing log fire, was in his favourite old sports jacket with the leather patches on the sleeves; Jack Weese held a pewter tankard of cider in his fist while he listened to the conversation, the reunion of a family he loved like his own. His wife was in the kitchen helping to prepare the Sunday lunch, which from what

Ransome had glimpsed through the door threatened to be a gargantuan one.

Occasionally he let his hand stray close to Eve's shoulder. She was sitting below him in the deep chair, and whenever she felt or sensed his hand close to her she would move slightly against it, or turn to glance up at him.

Ransome looked at his brother and wondered. Even after the months of treatment, and two operations to repair the damage left by a wound which had gone bad on him, he looked thin and very pale.

He was finished with M.T.Bs, he had already been told that. His first disappointment seemed to be behind him; now he was more concerned that the navy might find him unfit for any service at all. It seemed unlikely, but Tony had had plenty of time to brood about it, and what had done this to him.

He seemed as irrepressible as ever. He said, 'I mean, I'm fit enough – everything still works, as the bishop said to the actress!' He shot Eve an a apologetic grin. 'Sorry!'

She retorted, 'No, you're not.' Then, 'Can you remember what happened yet?'

Tony stared at his empty glass. 'Not really. We were working inshore, the skipper was hoping to catch one of Rommel's transports slipping out of North Africa.' He tensed and Ransome saw his fingers tighten around the glass like claws. 'There was a flash right under the bows.' He was speaking so quietly that they could hear the wind swishing against the windows. 'The next thing I knew, I was in the drink. I don't recall much else. Just vague pictures. A boat, the fishermen who later turned out to be partisans. Then there was the little doctor they brought from their village. He did what he could. I'd be dead otherwise.' He glanced up and realised his mother was in the doorway listening. 'Sorry, Mum.'

'Did you see the doctor again?' His father was looking at him as he might when he had been a child.

Tony lowered his head, as Jack Weese leaned forward and took away his glass.

'The Germans shot the poor little bugger when they pulled out.'

Ransome said, 'I shall never forget that day on the beach.'

Tony seemed to shake himself, to be glad of the interruption. 'And what about you?' His eyes moved between them. 'What have *you* been up to?'

She spoke first. 'We went to the concert at Buckfastleigh.'

Tony grimaced. 'Classics, eh? Seeing *Fantasia* at the local cinema is as close as I get to that kind of stuff!'

But his eyes asked, *Are you in love? Have you become lovers?*

Eve turned and put her hand on his. Ransome could feel the others watching, just as he could sense her quiet defiance.

'The sun's out, Ian. Take me to see the boat, *please?*'

His mother called, 'Don't be too long. I'm dishing up in half an hour.' She beamed at her two sons. 'Officers or not!'

Ransome put a short oilskin coat about her shoulders before they left. There were always several such coats around the house, used by the family and boatyard workers alike.

Outside they were met by bright sunshine, cold and hard, the air crisply clean. There was even a slight vapour of steam rising from some of the canvas-covered boats in the yard, the winter sun drying out puddles of overnight rain.

He put his arm round her shoulders and together they walked through the rough, untended grass, past the familiar boatsheds and slipways, scattered pieces of rusting engines, bilge pumps and other discarded clutter.

They said nothing until they had gone to the lower slope of the boatyard where *Barracuda* stood apart from all the rest, covered from stem to stern by a black tarpaulin. That too was steaming slightly, and Ransome felt a pang of sadness. Was she a part of the impossible dream too? She might stay here forever, rotting away, forgotten.

Then she turned and looked at him, her long hair whipping across her mouth so that only her eyes were clearly visible.

'Something's wrong, Ian. What is it? Please tell me. Remember our promise – no secrets.'

He gripped her gloved hands, and wanted to hug her.

'The refit has been cut to a minimum. We're on the move again.'

She said in a small voice, 'Not home for Christmas?'

'Not this time.' Try as he might he could not raise the dullness from his voice. In war why was one day different from another?

Well, *it was this time*. Four years of it, and he had never been at home for Christmas. It had not seemed that important before.

'*But why?*' The words were torn from her, so that she became the girl he had first met in this yard once again.

He thought of Lieutenant Commander Gregory's explanation when he had been told the same thing for *Ranger*. 'Can't give us a bloody minute, Ian. They think we're expendable, the whole damn lot of us!'

But he replied, 'We have to keep all the lanes open. With the war moving as it is, big ships will be sent where they're in the most advantageous positions.'

She hugged his arm with hers. 'For the Second Front?'

Ransome nodded. He glanced around the yard, remembering Jack Weese's contempt for the boxlike landing-craft they were building. There were only two half-completed ones here now. That was all the evidence they needed. The Allies were ready to move again, or soon would be when the weather improved. All the people who had been screaming and demanding a Second Front would get their wishes. How many more had to die to satisfy those who never endured the agony of battle?

She sensed his mood and faced him, her hands gripping his arms while she looked directly into his face.

'Nothing is going to keep us apart, Ian! Now it's my turn to help *you*.' She pulled him around the sleeping *Barracuda* and pointed across the estuary, towards the tiered houses of Polruan on the opposite side. 'We're not going to lose it now! Remember how my family used to stay at that cottage over there, every year? I used to think of nothing else, dream of the moment when I would be able to come and see you, show you my paintings and sketches. Once, I came but you were away training with the navy.'

'I didn't know, Eve.'

She did not seem to hear. 'I went back to Polruan and cried my heart out. My father probably thought I'd got myself into trouble.' She gave a laugh, so bitter than Ransome barely recognised it. 'How could he know even if he wanted to? That I was yours then, and I've never looked at another man!'

Ransome held her, felt her body trembling through the rough oilskin.

She said, 'You're a wonderful person, and you just haven't any idea, have you? The way you treat people, make them smile when there's precious little to grin about nowadays — it fills my heart. With love, with pride, everything!'

Ransome said, 'I was afraid to show how I felt about you. But you know now.'

Something in his tone made her turn towards him again, her eyes shining.

'I want to be married here, to be with you always, to come down the aisle knowing we both mean it, and when the church bells ring —'

Ransome held her more tightly. Even that was a brutal reminder. No church bells rang any more. Only if German parachutists were reported to be landing. Many bells had been sent to the war effort for scrap.

She was crying quietly against him, but said in a stronger voice, 'That's how it will be.' Then she moved away and stood on the edge of the slope, framed against the swirling current below, her hair streaming in the breeze. 'I just want to be with you.' She must have heard his steps through the wet grass and said, 'Not yet.' Her arm pointed across the Fowey River. 'I can see the cottage, next to the one with blue shutters. Is it empty?'

Ransome watched her shoulders, the way she was holding herself by force.

He said, 'Yes. Most of them were for holidaymakers. They're not suitable for the military either.'

Then she swung round, her eyes very large and bright, but not with tears anymore.

'One day, soon, could we —'

'Could we what?' He thought he knew, but dared not even imagine it.

She joined him on the slope and stood on tiptoe to put her face against his cheek.

'Have the cottage? Just for us? To make it come true?' She leaned back as he put his arms round her. 'It would be ours for just a while. Not some hotel room with all the remarks and leers. Just us.'

He pulled her closer. Was it her heart he could feel or his own?

'People will know. It's like that here.' When she remained silent he said, 'I must tell you, Eve, I don't know when it might be, but I would like it better than anything in this world.'

She walked towards the tarpaulined boat and reached up beneath the wet cover with her hand.

Ransome heard her say, 'Wish us luck, funny old boat.'

Then she ran to him again and whispered, 'Take care of yourself this time, dearest of men.'

Someone was calling from the house and Ransome said, 'Just in time. And yes, I shall take care.'

They walked back to the house, his arm around her shoulders as if it had always belonged there.

From the window Ted Ransome watched them coming down the path and asked, 'What do you make of it, Jack?'

'Fine pair.' Jack Weese raised his tankard in salute. 'God bring 'em luck!'

Tony, sitting in his chair, grinned, then winced as his savage wound made its presence felt again. He was rarely free of pain.

In his heart he had always known about Eve and Ian. He recalled with sudden clarity Ian's face, inches from his own, while he lay helpless on that damned stretcher.

It was hardly surprising, he thought, they were closer even than brothers.

As darkness closed in over Devonport Dockyard the rain returned, heavier than the previous night's, to make a mockery of the Sunday sunshine.

Sub-Lieutenant Robert 'Bunny' Fallows paused to fix his bearings, breathing hard, his head swimming after stopping at several bars. He had not gone on leave, although he was entitled to it. The idea of facing his home and all that it represented made staying aboard an easy choice, and as happened only too often he did not have the cash to spare for a hotel, something he had often dreamed about.

The blacked-out dockyard was always a trap for the unwary, drunk or sober, and Fallows had consumed too many gins to take chances on the maze of catwalks and bridges which separated the various basins from one another. The dark silhouettes of ships loomed out of the downpour, under repair or enjoying a complete overhaul as *Rob Roy* was supposed to have had. But all that was shelved. The minimum repairs possible, and already the dockyard workers had left the ship to work on something more important.

But Fallows, despite the ache behind his eyes and the sour sickness in his stomach, had other things uppermost in his blurred thoughts. That morning he had met Tudor Morgan and had been astounded to see he was wearing a second gold stripe on his working dress, several shades brighter than the old one.

He had been retained aboard instead of going on a long navigation course, but his promotion to lieutenant had unexpectedly come through all the same. Fallows still could not accept it. Although Morgan was a professional sailor who had started in the merchant service, their seniority was about the same, surely?

He grabbed a handrail and began to pull himself across another catwalk, on one side of him a yawning empty basin, the other containing the battered hull of a destroyer which had almost been sunk after an air attack in the Western Approaches.

He had confronted Morgan with it, but the young Welshman had merely suggested that the delay was due to some formality or foul-up along the line.

As he had drunk himself from bar to bar Fallows had considered it from every angle, until his mind throbbed like a drum. It had to be because of Tinker. That little bastard Parsons, who was leaving the ship anyway for a gunnery course and promotion to higher rate, must have told somebody. Spite, hatred, it did not really matter.

Fallows clung to a chain rail and stared up at the rain until it cleared his mind a bit.

Now they were going back to sea, to God alone knew what. Morgan promoted, while he remained a sub-lieutenant. Some of them would get a laugh out of that. Most of all his bloody father.

He saw a figure swaying towards him from another catwalk and he thought for an instant he was going mad.

Able Seaman Parsons straightened his back and wiped his mouth with his wrist. There was an acrid smell of vomit despite the steady rain: Parsons had also been drinking, saying various goodbyes to old shipmates before he left the flotilla for good to go on the course at Whale Island.

He saw Fallows and peered at him uncertainly. Then he bowed, his collar black with rain, so that his hat fell on the catwalk unnoticed.

'We shall say our farewells, eh, *Mister* Fallows?' He laughed, and almost threw up again. It was funny to see the officer's face. Even in the darkness he could make out the anger and the dismay.

Fallows exclaimed, 'You little bastard! After all I did, all I gave you!'

Parsons almost laughed, but said instead, 'Take it off your back, Bunny! All's fair in love and war, and you treated all of us like shit. *And* you know it!' When Fallows remained speechless, clinging to the rail for support, Parsons shouted, 'You're pissed, you useless git — but if one of *us* got tanked up you'd slap him in the rattle!' He leaned right over to get his eyes into focus.

Fallows said thickly, 'You told them what I said that night!'

Parsons could hardly believe it. 'Told *who*, for Chrissake? You were too drunk to say *anything* that night! Tinker never even spoke to you!'

Fallows wiped his face and yelled, '*You're lying!* I gave you money —'

Parsons sneered. 'So what?' He waved his arm over the dock-yard. 'You'll remember me after this, eh?'

It was all a blur. Fallows stepped forward, intent only on hitting him no matter what the consequences might be. Parsons gave a high-pitched giggle and ducked away. The chain which joined two stanchions behind his back was only inches above the catwalk at its centre. Too late Parsons realised what was happening; the giggle changed to a shrill scream and he toppled backwards into the basin where the bombed destroyer shone in the rain like black ice.

Fallows peered wildly around, his mind reeling. He had heard no splash, nor even a cry for help, for unknown to him Parsons had hit the concrete knuckle of the dock as he fell and had probably been dead when he struck the water.

Fallows waited, the rain bouncing off his cap, trying to steady his thoughts, to stop himself running for help. Then after what seemed like an eternity he straightened his back and stared along the basin to the next berth.

He saw Parson's cap, lying where it had fallen on the catwalk. Fallows started to laugh, and for several minutes was unable to stop. Then he kicked the cap carelessly into the basin and continued towards his own ship.

# 18

# Signals

'Flamborough Head bears three-three-zero, seven miles, sir!'

Ransome peered down at the chart on the bridge-table, his head and shoulder beneath the waterproof hood while he studied the pencilled fixes and bearings. He could feel the rain slashing across his buttocks and legs, hammering on his oilskin like pellets.

January in the North Sea again. Three shades of grey, all bleak and hostile. He rubbed his eyes and felt his elbows press on the table as the hull lifted and rolled drunkenly in a steep quarter sea. The North Sea never had the great storms of the Western Ocean, but this sickening, corkscrewing motion was in many ways much worse.

He heard Lieutenant Morgan rebuking the quartermaster in a fierce whisper for straying slightly off course. It was unusual for him to be on edge, but the whole ship had been like it since they had left Devonport without waiting for Christmas. That was almost exactly a month ago. Now as *Rob Roy* lifted and staggered at the head of her diagonal line of consorts, the Mediterranean and the sunshine, the exotic places like Malta and Alex were barely more than a blurred memory.

Even the other events of the war seemed remote, as if they were no longer a part of it. On Boxing Day for instance, when they had been sweeping this same channel, the German battle cruiser *Scharnhorst*, the last of Hitler's major warships, was destroyed by the guns of HMS *Duke of York*. It was a terrible fight in Arctic conditions and in the midst of a snow blizzard. Enemy or not, *Scharnhorst* had always been admired by her enemies; her luck and skill had become part of naval legend. Without her lurking presence, more British warships could be spared for the buildup of an invasion fleet.

Important though that victory was, it barely touched the weary men of the minesweepers.

Ransome often thought of that precious moment beside the *Barracuda*. Her simple gesture when she touched the hull beneath the tarpaulin. Sometimes when he was snatching a few hours in his sea-cabin, the 'coop' as Kellett the P.O. steward called it, he would jerk wide awake, almost pinching himself to make her words become clear in his mind. That the cottage she wanted to call *ours* was not merely part of a taunting dream.

He withdrew his head from the chart-table and crossed to his chair, holding on to it, stamping his scuffed seaboots on the deck to make his circulation come alive. It reminded him of the time he had waited outside the abbey when —

He turned as Sub-Lieutenant Fallows clattered up the ladder and paused to look at the tossing whitecaps, the grey murk, no beginning or end, no horizon either. It was noon, and the watch was changing. That was another reason for the edginess, Ransome knew. There were several new faces in the ship to replace others who had gone to courses ashore, or to other ships where their experience would be vital amongst the stream of new recruits.

Sherwood was still ashore. Cusack had kept close contact with one of his colleagues, whom he telephoned whenever *Rob Roy* was able to take some time in port.

Sherwood would be coming back, but as Bliss had predicted, his work as an R.M.S.O. was over. As an experienced watchkeeper he was badly missed, and as a friend too.

Another face absent from the wardroom was the Gunner (T) Mr Bone. Ransome had seen him in the privacy of his cabin to inform him of the signal. Bone was being sent to a training depot, to instruct raw seamen in the business of minesweeping.

Bone was a hard man. He had shown neither pleasure nor disappointment. After all his years in the service his widowed mother had chosen for her fourteen-year-old son, it was likely he could not be surprised at anything.

'S'pose I'll get used to it. I'll miss the duty-free booze though.' He had not been making a joke. Bone rarely did.

He surprised Ransome by thrusting out his spade-shaped hand and muttering, 'You've been a good captain, sir. I'd not get a better.' He had tried to grin. 'One thing, I'll not 'ave to muster the lads or 'ear that pipe "Out Sweeps" again, not in my lifetime!'

Another missing face was that of Pansy Masefield, the P.O. sick berth attendant. He had never really settled down after Cusack had taken over the ship's health and welfare, and had accepted his draftchit to a big hospital in Portsmouth without argument.

Ransome recalled how they had all tried to make their own Christmas a happy one. It had been a uphill task. *Rob Roy* and half of the flotilla had been sweeping this same channel from the Wash to Flamborough Head to keep open all the vital approaches to the Humber Estuary and the port of Hull.

He remembered the P.O. steward, Kellett, who always wore his hair plastered diagonally across his forehead anyway, donning a small false moustache and doing a lively impersonation of Adolf Hitler at the forecastle's 'Sods' Opera.' Leading Seaman Hoggan had sung *This Old Hat of Mine*, always a popular sailors' ditty, becoming bawdier and drunker by the minute and tossing his clothes aside until he was completely naked but for a lanyard upon which hung a bag of contraceptives.

The youngest, and by far the smallest member of the ship's company, Ordinary Seaman Gold, had stuttered his way through the part of playing the captain for Christmas Day, although one of Ransome's reefer jackets had reached almost to his knees.

It had all been compressed into a few precious hours while the ship was in harbour to refuel. *Rob Roy* had lain at a buoy, not even alongside in any contact with the land.

He heard Mackay speaking with the young signalman who had just come on watch. Mackay still wore the sailor's square-rig, but had the crown and crossed anchors on his sleeve now to show his promotion to petty officer. A yeoman of signals. It was unlikely that *Rob Roy* would be able to hold on to him once his full advancement had been confirmed. He would be greatly missed, as would his expertise.

Morgan was saying, 'Time to make the turn in seven minutes, Sub.'

It was not meant to be condescending. It was what a one-striper was usually called.

But Ransome had sensed the barrier between them, and it did not come from Morgan. He was openly delighted that his promotion had been posted without his having to take up another course.

'I shall be able to stay in *Rob Roy*, see?' He had stared around the wet, dismal bridge. 'I'd not want to go until I was ordered, sir.'

Fallows stood beside him now as they compared notes by the chart-table. He had got terribly drunk at Christmas, and Hargrave had threatened to take him in front of the captain, higher if need be. After that Fallows had improved considerably, and was making a great effort to keep out of the first lieutenant's way. He was more withdrawn than usual, his mouth turned down in a permanent frown.

'Forenoon watch relieved, sir!' Morgan touched the peak of his cap. 'I'll bring the new snotty with me in the dog-watches if I may, sir. He's got to start somewhere.'

Ransome smiled. Davenport's replacement was called Colin Piers. A round-faced eighteen-year-old who looked about twelve. Nobody had really had much time to either make him welcome or get his measure, as he had been horribly seasick almost from the day he had stepped aboard.

Ransome's request for Ordinary Seaman Boyes's C.W. papers to be started again had been granted, and the Mention-in-Despatches had been announced on the same day. Ransome had told him personally, and had been moved by the youngster's thanks and sincerity. He had made the right decision, and in his heart knew that many captains would not have bothered once the first decision had been made.

One thing was certain, Boyes was getting plenty of experience on chartwork and the radar plot machine, for with the new midshipman rolling about the ship with his face as green as grass, he was doing everything himself.

Fallows had walked to the forepart of the bridge, while his assistant Sub-Lieutenant Tritton stood by the voicepipes.

Tritton, young and inexpert as he was, had been forced to take over Bone's duties and part of ship. Thank God for the Buffer, Ransome thought. But what Tritton lacked in experience he more than made up for with his good humour, which kept the men he worked with grinning at some of his schoolboy jokes. He had been able to put the memory of the air attack behind him. It was the first, the most difficult step of all, and they had all been made to face up to it, one way or the other.

Ransome said, 'Tell the first lieutenant to take in the sweep.' He glanced at Fallows. 'Your department all buttoned up, Sub?'

Fallows half-turned, showing his profile, the red hair flapping beneath his cap like a bird's wing. He no longer wore his ridiculous rabbit.

'Yes sir. Able Seaman Norton has settled down quite well as trainer on 'A' Gun. Quite well.'

Ransome glanced at him. It had been a surprise when Able Seaman Parsons had failed to return from shore leave. He had long requested the gunnery course at Whale Island, and it would be stupid to miss the chance because of overstaying his leave.

Ransome had expected a signal explaining that he had been taken ill, or had overslept in some sailors' boarding house. He smiled at the old naval excuse. *Slept at Aggie Weston's and never heard the bell, sir.*

The coxswain had been told that Parsons had gone off to celebrate his transfer with some old friends. Beckett had remarked darkly, '*Friends*, sir? A skate like that one don't 'ave no mates!'

But there had been no signal, so the police and provost department had had to be informed. It was a pity, but his chance of advancement had probably gone forever.

Ransome lifted his binoculars and trained them on the next astern; it was *Firebrand*, showing her bilge one moment, then her open bridge the next as she rolled steeply. The strange light made her bow wave and wash look dirty yellow. He lowered the binoculars slightly and saw Hargrave's wind-reddened face leap into the lens. He was first-rate at his job now, but always kept at a distance from his men. A hard thing to do in such a small ship; but he seemed to manage it.

'Sweep's secure, sir!' The boatswain's mate watched Fallows as he climbed to the gyro repeater. Everyone was busy, but the boatswain's mate, O'Connor, had a moment to relax. He was thinking of Christmas too. How he had been on watch while the ship lay at her buoy, and had listened to the carol singing on the messdecks, his insides protected from the bitter cold by two helpings of roast turkey and several tots of 'neaters'.

Like some of the others O'Connor had good cause to dislike Fallows – he had smelt his breath once, and accused O'Connor of drinking on watch. It had been a rare and unfortunate occasion for O'Connor that Fallows had been stone cold sober.

Fallows had taken him in front of the first lieutenant as a defaulter, with the result that he had lost his only good conduct badge, and had been given extra work as punishment. He had never forgotten.

At the Christmas party, Fallows had taken more than usual and had lurched on deck, without his jacket despite the wind and rain, and fallen dead drunk on a rack of depth-charges.

He had gone to rouse the officer, but as he had gripped his outflung arm he had been horrified to find that he wanted to tip him over the side. He had even levered the unconscious officer against the guardrails before he knew what he was going to do. Nobody would have noticed, and with a stiff tide running past the buoy, everyone would think Fallows had stumbled overboard.

A stoker had appeared through an engine-room hatch and had offered cheerfully, ' 'Ere, Pat, I'll give you a 'and to get the pig down aft again!'

Fallows had known nothing about it. O'Connor watched him balefully. *Would I have done it?* He was afraid of the answer.

Ransome said, 'Take her round, Sub.'

An oilskinned figure clambered into the bridge and handed Ransome a folded signal flimsy.

'Thanks, Sparks.'

He held it below the screen to shield it from the rain and spray and read it before the telegraphist's lettering began to run down the paper.

'They found A.B. Parsons. He was dead. Drowned apparently.'

He heard Tritton exclaim, 'The *turn*, Bunny!'

Ransome snapped, 'Starboard twenty!' He pushed past Fallows and peered across the compass repeater. 'What the hell's the matter? You've taken over the con many times by now, man!'

Fallows opened and closed his mouth. 'I – I'm sorry, sir.'

'Midships.' He heard the quartermaster's response. 'Steady.'

The quartermaster called up the voicepipe. 'Steady, sir! Course zero-seven-zero!' It was exact. They had done this channel so often it was hardly surprising.

Ransome stepped away and raised his glasses to watch the faint splash of colour as a fresh dan buoy was dropped by the trawler *Senja*.

Only then did he looked at Fallows. 'You know the narrow margin, Sub. So in future just *watch it*!'

He was being harsh with someone who could not answer back. But *Rob Roy* and all her company were far more important than some bruised feelings.

He settled in his chair and said, 'Make the signal. *Out sweeps to starboard. Take station on me.*'

And so it went on, in weather so bad that it was hard to hold station on their set courses; and there was the additional fear they might not see a drifter if it came amongst them, its obscene horns hidden by the North Sea's steep waves.

He thought of Eve, of the letters she had written, of the ones which might be waiting when they returned to harbour to refuel and restock their provisions.

Fallows moved away from the chair and trained his glasses abeam. They had found Parsons. He must have been trapped under the bombed destroyer. Fallows had made himself walk back past the basin on the following day. Some men had been working on the damaged ship, but there was no alarm, not even Parson's cap.

He had sweated about it for days. Suppose Parsons had drag-

276

ged himself clear? Maybe a watchman had found him alive?

At Christmas it had become too much for him, and only Hargrave's fury had made him take a grip on his nerves.

Now it was all behind him. Parsons was really dead. They'd say he had fallen in by accident, drunk.

He felt the same insane grin cracking his jaws and had to grate his teeth together to prevent it.

It had all been a mistake, but Parsons was the one who had made it.

It was mid-February, while *Rob Roy* and *Ranger* lay alongside each other in Hull to refuel, that their private worlds were upset once again.

Ransome sat in his cabin reading a letter from Eve, while the ship stood at arm's length beyond the door, and routine flowed around him, leaving him momentarily alone. Heavy rain pattered on the decks and made thick silver bars across the scuttles, with only the occasional creak of tackles or a muffled shout to show that anything was actually happening.

Hull seemed an unhappy place to be, even when they had been at sea with barely a break. It had been bombed so many times that the place was barely recognisable. But the work went on, and it was said that the turnround of ships in the port was quicker than ever.

He put Eve's letter down as Petty Officer Kellett opened the door a few inches.

'Beg pardon, sir, but *Ranger*'s captain 'as come aboard.'

Lieutenant Commander Gregory strode into the cabin, nodding only briefly to Kellett. 'Sorry to barge in, Ian.' He dragged a tin of duty-free cigarettes from his pocket. 'Knew you wouldn't mind.'

Ransome watched him, the quick nervous movements of his hands as he lit another cigarette.

'What is it, Jim?'

Lieutenant Commander James Gregory tried to settle in the other chair and blew a thin stream of smoke to the deckhead.

'I'm leaving, Ian. That's what.'

Ransome waited. They had come through so much together.

Their small, hardworked group of fleet minesweepers, each one a personality. They had watched others go down, those whose luck had run out. *Fawn*, *Dunlin* and *Scythe*, with other names they could scarcely remember. Ships and men torn apart in a war which was without glamour and beyond the headlines, yet one which was as vital today as it had been right from the start.

Gregory shrugged. 'It's all part of the scheme for a bigger support group for the next invasion. I'm to take over a new flotilla of motor minesweepers as senior officer. I shall have a free hand, with Bliss's blessing of course.'

Ransome asked, 'Are you pleased? It shows what they think of you – I agree, you're just the bloke for it. Somebody who knows what it's all about.'

Gregory glanced around the cabin; it was an exact replica of his own.

'I'll miss her, Ian.'

'I know. We'll all miss you too.'

Outside the tannoy bawled, 'D'you hear there! Cooks to the galley! Senior hands of messes muster for rum!'

Ransome grimaced. 'The right idea, I think.' He took out a bottle and two glasses. *Ranger* would not be the same without Gregory. He felt the same about losing her.

He pushed a full glass across the table. 'Cheers!'

Gregory drank some of it and swallowed hard. 'Christ!' Then he studied Ransome and said, 'You really don't know, do you?'

'Know what?'

'*Ranger*'s new skipper is Lieutenant Trevor Hargrave.'

Ransome stared at him with astonishment. 'No, by God, I didn't!'

Gregory smiled. 'I suppose I shouldn't care. I've served under skippers who thought that nobody could ever be good enough to take their places. All the same –'

Ransome refilled the glasses. He was losing Hargrave. A command of his own. He felt suddenly angry. The Old Pals' Act; it had to be. Hargrave's father had pulled strings. On the face of it, Gregory was being promoted, and as *Ranger*'s Number One was fairly new to the job, Hargrave might seem the logical choice. He was experienced, a good ship-handler, and even if he was new to *Ranger*, he was not to the flotilla.

The door opened and Leading Writer Wakeford peered into the cabin.

'Oh, sorry, sir. I'll come back later.'

Ransome saw the thick envelope in his hand and said, 'Bring it in.'

He watched as the Leading Writer laid the various items on the desk. He was as before, self-contained, studious, quiet. It was hard to see him crouched on the field telephone as Bliss had described it to him, speaking to Sherwood, waiting to write it all down, to hear his final words if the mine sprung its fuse.

Wakeford did not look at Gregory as he said, 'This one is about the first lieutenant, sir.'

It was the usual formal wording. 'Upon receipt of these orders you will etc. etc.'

Ransome looked up at his friend. 'Sherwood's coming back tomorrow. As first lieutenant.'

Gregory was still contemplating his own change of direction. 'That's a shaft of light, anyway.'

The big sealed envelope had been signed for by the O.O.D., Tritton. Ransome read it quickly. 'I think another enormous drink is in order.' Then he said quietly, 'We're moving to Falmouth in three days, Jim. Hargrave will assume command there.'

'Falmouth.' Gregory watched him thoughtfully. 'That's where I'm to take over the flotilla of Mickey-Mouses. Does that mean —?'

Ransome poured the drinks and shook the bottle. His stock was almost finished.

He replied, 'I think it does. It will be a work-up for the invasion. The big one.'

Gregory glanced at his watch. 'I'd best get back. I'll tell my lot in the wardroom. They'll all be gathering there for lunch anyway.'

He stood up, momentarily lost. 'I thought I'd end the bloody war in *Ranger*, does that sound potty? I know we have no say in these things, but I'm loathe to leave the old girl.' He met Ransome's questioning glance. 'No, not because of Hargrave. He'll probably do a good job. It's just —'

'I know.' It was like Moncrieff's last moments when he had relieved him. 'I'd be the same.'

When Gregory had gone, he took the bulkhead telephone from its bracket and jabbed one of the buttons.

He heard Kellett's chirpy voice reply, 'Wardroom!'

'Would you ask the first lieutenant to spare me a few minutes, please?'

He replaced the telephone and then straightened Tony's picture. He had written to him twice. That was quite something. Tony had never been a great letter-writer.

He was feeling much better, mainly, Ransome suspected, because he had been appointed to a destroyer which was still on the stocks and only half-built. It would be many months before he got to sea again. Their mother would be pleased about that.

Tony had written, *So I'm all right, big brother. To tell the truth I'd have taken the job running a NAAFI manager's boat rather than be beached!* He had ended by saying, *Eve's a lovely girl. You're so right for each other. I envy you.*

There was a knock on the door. It was Hargrave.

'You wanted me, sir?'

Ransome pushed the orders across the desk. 'You'd better sit down before you read this.'

He saw Hargrave's eyes moving slowly across the curt, unemotional wording. Even when he received his own for taking command they would lack any of the excitement they usually represented.

One thing was obvious, Hargrave did not know either. He was not that good an actor.

'But – but, I don't understand, sir.' Hargrave stared at him. '*Ranger* – she's our sister-ship.' He looked at his hands. Even that one word *our* was a thing of the past.

Ransome smiled grimly. 'I'll not tell you about the birds and the bees. You've learned well, considering it was not all that long since we were facing each other here for the first time. We are going to Falmouth again. Sail in *Ranger* and watch everything Gregory does. *Ranger* may be a twin, but her people are used to him and his ways. If we are going into Europe they'll need all their confidence. It's not time for the new broom syndrome.' He spread his hands in apology. 'Sorry. The birds and the bees win after all!'

Hargrave stood up. 'If I'm any good at it, sir, it will be your doing.' Then he almost lurched from the cabin.

Ransome sat staring at the closed door. *Into Europe.* How easy it was to say.

It was not like losing poor David. He had been a true friend, the closest he had ever had before or since joining the navy. He often saw him still. Those chilling nights on the bridge, booted feet on the ladder. Or a shadowy oilskinned figure hurrying aft when the order to prepare the sweep was piped. The women in black. The schoolgirl who had looked like Eve.

He picked up her letter again and thought of her writing it.

*Dearest of Men – It feels so long since –*

Ransome found that he could lean back and smile. He would telephone her this evening. Just to tell her he was coming. Without breaking the Official Secrets Act, of course.

He heard footsteps moving away and knew that Hargrave had been standing there, putting his thoughts in order, grappling with his change of fortune.

Hargrave was indeed thinking of nothing else. He walked right past the Buffer who was about to offer him a list of names, a rearrangement of the watch bill, his mouth already opened to speak.

As he strode aft the Buffer gaped after him. 'Gawd, Jimmy's like a whore at a christenin' today!'

He saw the new S.B.A., a small, pimply youth, leaning on the guardrail and staring down at the trapped water between the two hulls.

'Stand up straight! Never 'ang on them rails, sonny!'

'I – I thought –'

The Buffer roared, 'Leave thinkin' to 'orses, they've got bigger 'eads than you 'ave!'

He bustled away, the first lieutenant's behaviour forgotten. He usually felt better after he had offered someone a good bollocking.

Hargrave paused by the big winch and the Oropesa float, resting on its chocks like a faceless dolphin.

His mind kept returning to Ross Pearce, what she had said, the cool way she had outlined what she believed he needed. Like moving pawns on a board. Gregory's promotion to all intents and purposes, and a ready opening in *Ranger*. It would probably mean a half-stripe, albeit lost again when the war ended. He stared round and up at the deserted bridge. What was the matter with him? Sherwood was right. The war might go on for years. Even if the invasion was a success it could drag out in stalemate. Then there was the Pacific and Burma. It seemed endless. None of the people he had seen today as requestmen or defaulters, working about the ship, or queueing impatiently for their rum issue, might be alive by then.

He was sure of one thing. He was completely infatuated with Ross Pearce. Without effort she had fenced with him, keeping him at a distance, giving no real hint of promise. He had met nobody like her. The more he had seen of her the less he could imagine his father having any more success than he had.

He looked across at *Ranger*. The sentry and quartermaster were watching him without apparently doing so. The buzz would be all through the ship. *Rob Roy*'s Jimmy was getting the Old Man's chair.

He thought of Ransome's quiet advice. *They'll need all their confidence.*

It was what he had been trained for. This was just the next step on the ladder. He might never know if his first command had been engineered, or influenced by his father. But it seemed likely. Ross's father was a viscount, and had a deep interest in service matters and stood on a House of Lords committee. What was good for Hargrave might easily turn out to be even more advantageous for his father the vice-admiral.

*Shall I miss Rob Roy?*

Only time would answer that.

The girl stood behind her mother and watched her reflection in the dressing-table mirror. She could hear the wind exploring the windows and sighing against the roof, but the rain had gone, and tomorrow was going to be a fine day, according to the postman.

The postman was old for the job, but had come back to work

to help fill the gaps left by the younger men who had gone to war. He had his own special signal as he wheeled his red bicycle up the twisting driveway if he saw Eve waiting for him.

A wave if there was a letter from him. A thumbs-up if there was not. Meaning that there would be soon.

That morning he had given a wave.

He handed over a great pile of mail for Codrington House, all the usual replies to appeals, applications for jobs, offers of homes for the bombed-out and dispossessed. It never stopped. He had given her the letter in its familiar buff envelope.

'I reckon he's telling you he still loves you in this 'un, Miss Eve.' He pulled her leg quite mercilessly. His defence was that he was old enough to be her grandfather.

It was a lovely letter. They all were. She could hear his voice, see his grey eyes, touch his hand in every line.

He had telephoned as well. Another awful connection, but he had been lucky to get through at all.

He was coming south. To her.

Her fingers slipped on the comb as she completed setting her mother's hair, and their eyes met suddenly in the dressing-table mirror.

'What is it, dear?'

Eve smiled although it touched her deeply to see her mother like this. They had always been so close. She had been as much a friend and companion as mother.

'I had a letter this morning.' She watched for some hint of curiosity. 'From Ian.'

'Who, dear?'

Eve picked up a brush and touched up the sides of her mother's hair. She had always had such fine hair. How had they met, she wondered?

'Ian Ransome.'

She paused with her brush in mid-air. It was like a curtain being lifted, a light illuminating a darkened room. Her mother's eyes were as they were before. Clear, questioning, amused.

'You really love him, don't you, Eve?'

Eve nodded, almost afraid to move.

'Then take him, my darling. While you can. Love him. I can see that he worships the ground you walk on.'

Somewhere a loose shutter banged against the wall; the noise, or the interruption, broke the contact.

Eve whispered, 'I do love him so much. I want him to be *safe*!'

But the eyes in the mirror did not reply.

Then her mother said indifferently, 'Fetch my glasses, will you, dear? I left them in the study.' As Eve went to the door she heard her murmur, 'Or was it in —'

The study was much as it had always been since the great house was built, she thought. Shelves from floor to ceiling, now mostly filled with her father's ledgers and personal books. The rest lay empty, a reminder of the house's better days.

She heard the wireless from the outer hall, the night porter's prop for staying awake.

Her heart turned to ice. As it always did.

'The Secretary of the Admiralty regrets to announce the loss of HM Submarine *Skilful*, and of . . .'

*And of . . . and of . . . and of . . .*

'Next of kin have been informed.'

She clutched her hands across her breast and waited for her breathing to steady. It was always the same now. The real meaning of that flat announcement. The sense of gratitude, then of shame, sympathy for the men who had died somewhere, in what conditions she could only guess at.

She looked around the shadowed study. *Ian was coming back.* Then she remembered what her mother had sent her for. But there was no sign of her reading-glasses. Her mother had often come here to work on her various charities before suffering the shock of the bombing.

Eve smiled. She had probably left them in the desk drawer. It would not be the first time.

It was strange that she felt guilty at opening her father's desk. She wanted to laugh, to cry out that she had shared her love with her mother. She pulled out the drawer, careless of the sound. Her father was in the city.

Then she froze. At the back of the drawer was a big envelope, marked with the newspaper's crest and the bold sticker, PHOTOGRAPH – DO NOT FOLD. It was addressed to her. The posting

284

date she did not even need to examine.

With great care she slit open the envelope and removed the stiff cardboard protection.

For several minutes she studied the photograph, to which was pinned the newspaper's compliment slip.

So clear. So vivid. Ian on his bridge, pointing at the sky, his beloved face so tense, so strong.

With the picture clutched to her breast she mounted the stairs and looked into her mother's bedroom. She was wearing her reading-glasses and studying an album of holiday postcards which she had once collected.

Had she forgotten that she had kept her reading-glasses near her? Or was it her way of reaching her daughter, to tell her that her father had intercepted the picture of the man she loved and had tried to keep it from her?

Eve ran to her room and threw herself down.

*How could he?*

Then after a time she left the bed and rested the photograph against her bedside clock, while she took out the white nightdress from her drawer.

# 19

# *Love and Remembrance*

Spring seemed to have come late to the West Country this year. It was true that the skies were often blue and cloudless, and the hedgerows and cottage gardens bright with colour. But the Channel which remained unimpressed and restless along the Cornish coasts often crashed amongst the jagged rocks as if it were reluctant to leave winter behind.

Ransome walked up from the tiny ferry and paused to stare across at the boatyard. Like the rest of the Fowey Estuary it was almost hidden by landing-craft and small warships of every class and use, some of which had probably begun life under old Jack Weese's supervision. You could *feel* it along this coast, Ransome thought. Everywhere you went, in the narrow streets and in crowded harbours, it was more of a sensation than anything spoken. Like the murmur of far-off drums. Something which was stirring, and yet filled with menace.

The war had moved closer again. Perhaps that was it. Along these shores they had seen enough of it, but never before had they been so involved in what was now inevitable.

Here in Polruan, directly opposite the place which even in memory had become his only home, Ransome could sense it. It was no longer the free-and-easy village it had been even during the darkest days of the war. There were troops and armoured vehicles all around, just as the vessels which would soon carry them into battle on the other side of the English Channel filled every creek and river, until invasion seemed to become a secret quite impossible to keep.

In other parts of the world the conflict raged on. In the Pacific and on the Russian front, where millions were said to have perished in that last bitter winter. In Burma, the forgotten Fourteenth Army was no longer in retreat, and even if the Allies in Italy were making only slow progress there were other benefits. The Italians, at least those lucky enough to be on the right side of the lines, had surrendered to the Allies, their fleet secured under the guns of Malta, a great achievement which had once seemed like a pipe-dream.

But the *here* and the *now* were more relevant. The sandbagged gun emplacements, the depressing barriers of barbed wire on tiny Cornish beaches where children had once explored and played. Many of them would now be in uniform, waiting for D-Day.

Ransome wondered what his parents really thought about the cottage in Polruan. Local people would know about it soon enough, but the events to come might put it into perspective.

He had mentioned this again to Eve when he had telephoned her to say that he was free at last to come to her.

She had replied, 'Just come. I'll be waiting. It has to be there, Ian. Don't you see? I want it to be clean, decent. To be able to face anyone and say, *This is how it was.* No matter what.'

Ransome turned and looked at the little pub, The Lugger, where he had taken her on that sunny day. Bare-legged, her eyes sometimes so grave, at other times laughing like another voice. Too young to go inside for a drink, but now he knew that she had loved him even then.

When he had called her from Falmouth to tell her he had secured the cottage she had gasped with disbelief.

'How did you manage it?'

He smiled now. Manage it? Old Isaac Proby who owned three of the little cottages had been more than eager to let him take it. People did not come here for their holidays any more. There were too many restricted areas, warnings of minefields, forbidden walks along the cliffs.

Old Proby had added, 'I'll air the place out. They gets a bit damp, y'know.'

Ransome walked up the little pavement. On one side it was a

wall, to lean on and reflect, with a lower bank of cottages below, and then the water.

He paused to rest his elbows on the worn stones. It was really happening. So it must be as she wanted it. There might be pain enough later. He stared hard at the racing current, the way some moored landing-craft tugged at their cables and nearly dragged their buoys beneath the surface.

It was going to be soon. They had been briefed and briefed until they could digest no more. Ships, commanders, landing instructions, army units, the whole strategy of invasion.

Many would fall that day, whenever it was. Some, like the disfigured airmen he had seen in the abbey, would wish they had.

He must give her no hint, no suggestion of what might smash down their happiness. It was a matter of odds, luck, and fate. He had now been over two years in command of *Rob Roy*, with thousands of miles steamed, and countless mines swept and rendered harmless. At the beginning he had imagined he would survive six months, and no longer. Today he was on borrowed time. The most dangerous of all.

He shook himself and walked more quickly up the sloping pavement.

There were plenty of khaki and blue uniforms about and he was glad to reach the tiny passageway which led to the cottage's entrance. Away from the salutes, the curious stares, an occasional twitch of curtains as he passed.

The rugged stones of the cottage were newly painted, and the tiny garden at the rear was a vivid confusion of rhododendrons and blue and purple lupins. The gardens of these cottages were allowed to grow much as they pleased, but Ransome knew that somebody had made an effort to tidy this one up.

The door flew open and she held out her arms to him.

He held her very tightly, his mouth brushing her long hair, neither of them speaking.

Beyond her he saw more flowers, and some fresh rhododendrons which she must have cut from the bushes and had arranged in a large copper pot.

There was a fire burning in the grate of the living-room and she twisted round in his arms as he took her through the door.

She said, 'I had to light it, May or not. It was so damp!' She was laughing, helping him with his cap and jacket, waiting for him to lose his nervousness. It was something she had not felt for a long while. Since the last time they had been together? Or when she had discovered the hidden photograph? It seemed like something destined. What she had wanted, always wanted. Now, with the door closed, and the sunlight reflecting on a framed print of Polperro, she wanted only for him to be happy, to feel at peace.

Ransome looked at the table, the knives and forks. 'But they're –'

She nodded, her eyes shining. 'Your father sent them across from your house, and some other things too.' A little of her courage faded and she added, 'I didn't bring much. It was a bit difficult.'

She waited for him to sit beside, if not in front of the fire, and watched as he filled his pipe. She looked around the room, remembering all those holidays, but picturing it as it might have been. A dog perhaps, or a cat like Jellicoe drowsing on the wall with one eye on the gulls.

She knelt by his legs and rested her head on his knees so that her hair hung down to the floor.

She said, 'I must ask. How long do we have?'

Ransome tried not to picture the ship, the other minesweepers waiting for the final decisions to be made. Sherwood had suggested that the whole thing might be postponed indefinitely despite all the weight of preparations. The Met reports were unfavourable. But so had they been before Sicily. And all the while the great armada waited. Ships and men. Flesh and steel.

'If I'm not recalled, two days.'

'There's no telephone here.' It was like a cry of protest.

He ruffled her hair. It was like warm silk. 'They always find a way.'

The coastguard knew where he would be. A message would reach him in minutes. After that –

Eve said, 'We *can* have some walks?' She looked up at him, searching his face. 'Please?'

'Of course. Lots.'

She lowered her chin to his knee. 'Your father sent a message too.' Her mouth trembled but she made another effort. 'He wrote that he would look after me when you left. That he would drive me –' She broke off and wrapped her arms around him. 'Not yet, dearest Ian. Please, not yet.'

Ransome reached out to his jacket, which hung on a chair. He had intended to wait, but now she needed him: it was no longer just the other way around.

He took out a small package. 'I meant to get a proper box. Anyway you might not like it, it was just an impulse. I –'

She pulled off the wrapping and held the ring up to the sunlight. It seemed to glow, first red then white, the tiny rubies and diamonds flowing into each other.

In a small voice she asked, 'Where did you *get* it?'

Ransome took it gently from her and looked at it. *Rob Roy* had been in Alexandria and he had been ordered to Cairo, to meet some senior officers who had apparently been involved in supplying weapons to the partisans. Their beliefs and their politics did not matter. If they hated the Germans enough to pull a trigger they would be given arms to use for the job. God alone knew what would happen when the partisans and the vague resistance groups went back to being bandits again.

Without effort he could see the shop, the old jeweller watching intently while he had picked out this ring.

It was neither a wedding nor an engagement ring in the accepted sense. But it had seemed right for Eve.

When he had told her about the strange little shop she said, 'I think it's lovely.' She lifted herself higher and kissed him gently on the mouth. 'You're always full of surprises!' Then she looked at him, her eyes big and very steady. 'Put it on for me.'

She offered her left hand. 'Please.'

He held her wrist and said, 'It may not fit.' It was as if this very moment had also been a part of destiny.

He said, 'I do love you, Eve. One day –'

She raised her finger very slightly. 'Until that day –' Then she withdrew her hand and held it to the sunlight again. 'We're engaged!'

They faced each other and laughed like conspirators. Like children. Then she got to her feet, and when he attempted to hold her she shook her head.

'I was going to be sensible. To make you eat something, or at least have a drink.'

She was backing away very slowly, as if she could not bear to lose sight of him.

'I can't *be* sensible, dearest Ian. I've wanted you for so long. Why be sensible now?'

He stood looking at her, watching the firelight playing in her eyes. So many emotions. Determination and a sweet unsureness, even fear.

She whispered, 'Give me five minutes.' Then she held up her ring and exclaimed, 'I'm so *happy!*'

She ran into the adjoining room and closed the door.

So his father knew all about it, but not, it seemed, her own. The consequences neither of them could guess; but there would be no regrets.

The war and the danger were alien, not even intruders in this place.

He hesitated, then pushed open the door.

He did not know what he had been expecting. That Eve might be in bed, her eyes on the door; nervous perhaps, shy now that the moment had arrived. Wondering if the reality would spoil the dream they had both cherished.

But she was standing by the window, one hand gripping the heavy black-out curtain while she peered towards the darkening estuary. She was wearing a white nightgown, with small delicate patterns of lace around the neckline and hem. Just two thin cords across her shoulders, her hair hanging free and shining faintly in the light from the solitary bedside lamp.

He saw her tense as he walked towards her.

She said, 'I – I wanted to be perfect for you.'

Ransome put his hands on her shoulders and was shocked to discover they were so cold despite the humid air and the fire they had left in the other room.

Very gently he turned her to face him, holding her at arm's length. Her hand released its grip on the curtain and fell to her side; she did not look up, as if she could feel his eyes on her.

He said in a whisper, 'You're so lovely, Eve.' He put one arm around her and pulled her against him. He could feel her supple body through the thin silk, the pressure of her breasts against him, and when she did at last look into his face he saw the warmth, the pleasure of his words shining in her eyes.

She threw her arms around his neck and shook some hair from her face.

'Wanton, and I don't care. I'm not going to spoil anything because I'm inexperienced. I want to be adult —' It would not hold, and she nestled her face against his, her body trembling as she sensed his need of her.

'You may have grown up, Eve. But you're the same girl.' She did not protest as he led her to the bed and sat her down. 'You couldn't spoil anything, as you put it.' He sat beside her and kissed her gently at first, and then with a passion he had never known before. He felt his heart pounding like blood, and gripped her more firmly as her mouth responded to his, her lips parting while she drew him closer.

She lay back on the bed and spread her arms as if crucified. He touched her body, her breasts, caressing them through the silk. Then he leaned over her and kissed her, he did not know how many times. Through the nightdress, across her bare shoulders until she gasped, 'Oh, Ian, I never thought —'

She raised herself as he slipped the nightdress away, watching his eyes while she lay naked, her long hair across the pillows and over the side of the bed.

She whispered, 'Don't turn away.' She did not move as he undressed, and only the beat of her heart below one uplifted breast gave away her emotion, her longing for him, not just for this moment but for all the months, the dreams, the fears.

Then he knelt beside her and ran his fingers over her breast, down still further to the dark triangle he had seen through the nightdress when she had turned from the window.

She reached up and held his shoulders. 'I've never been with any other man. You know that, don't you?'

He nodded. 'I shall be gentle, my darling girl.'

'It's not that. I'm — quite small. You may hurt me.' Her fingers gripped him more tightly. 'But I don't want you to stop.' Her eyes were pleading. 'I can bear the pain . . . it will get better in time.'

She gasped when he touched her, as she felt his body dividing hers. Ransome slipped his arm beneath her shoulders and kissed her very slowly. He wanted to hold his breath, to prevent himself from crying out. He felt her back arch to receive him, then the first precious moment. She drew him down, her hands slipping down his back, pulling him until her nails must surely have broken the skin.

She gasped, 'Now, Ian, please, *now*!'

Ransome felt her body surrendering, then kissed her hard on the mouth as he entered her and was enclosed, received like part of herself.

They lay together for a long time, she on her side with one leg thrown across him, her foot playing with his.

She said, 'It was beautiful.' Her eyes were very near to his, filling her face. 'I knew it would be like that. I just knew. Now nothing can keep us apart.'

Ransome stroked the hair from her cheek. 'And I knew you would be as you are. When I saw you lying here it was all I could do not to take you then and there. You're so lovely, you've no idea.'

She moved closer. 'I want us to make love again as soon as we can.'

He smiled. 'Yes, you *are* wanton.'

They kissed, but this time the embrace did not break.

The next day they went for a long walk along the cliffs, and watched the sea. It looked angry and hostile, with serried rows of jagged breakers and blown spume.

Then far, far out to sea, almost hidden in horizon haze, they saw the ships. Ransome's heart sank: it was something he had hoped to avoid. Like the long arm reaching out, leaving nowhere to hide.

'What are they, Ian?' She clung to his arm, her hair barely contained by a scarf, her face so relaxed and happy he did not want to reply.

Suddenly a thin white waterspout made a flaw in the dull horizon, and seconds later a muffled boom thudded against the cliffs.

She said quietly, 'They're minesweepers, aren't they?'

He nodded. 'Trawlers out of Falmouth, most likely.'

She gripped his arm more tightly. 'They look so small. It's a wonder they hold together with great explosions like that.'

Ransome turned her towards a different path. No escape. The field where he and Tony had once hiked was commanded by a slit-eyed, concrete machine-gun bunker, the lush grass dotted with tall poles to prevent gliders or small planes from landing here.

She whispered, 'You will be careful. Promise!'

'Trust me.' He turned toward her and kissed her, tasted a tear on her cheek. 'I love you. We love each other. We were meant to share.'

They walked down the path, the sound of the sea fading behind them.

'Will you be going back to Codrington House?'

She shook her head. 'Not yet. Your father said I could stay with them for as long as I want. My mother knows. She likes you very much.'

'I'm glad.'

What was wrong? Was it seeing the minesweepers? She was going to stay with his parents. She would not feel so cut off there. His father's hand was in this too, he thought. He would know that the invasion was on the doorstep; he met more Admiralty officials and naval officers than anyone.

The thought touched his mind like a scalpel. They were his next of kin, and would be told first if anything went wrong.

He tightened his grip around her shoulders. She would be there, sharing it.

'It's been wonderful –' They turned into the street, and he saw the coastguard's car parked as close as it could get to the cottages.

*Oh God.* He slowed his pace, trying to find the words. *I am afraid.*

He said, 'He's here to fetch me. It's a recall.'

She turned and stared at him. 'Not yet, Ian! We've only had one night together . . .' She tilted her chin and said in a controlled voice, 'I'm not being very much help, am I?'

They walked down to the car and the coastguard handed Ransome a sealed note.

He said, 'Came just now, zur, must be urgent. They'm sending a car for 'e.'

'I'll not be long.' They entered the cottage and stared around in silent desperation.

She said brokenly, 'I loved it here, darling!'

He watched her roll her nightgown and place it in her bag with great care.

'Just a moment.' He took it from the bag and held it to his face, the memories of their brief time together sweeping over him to torment him further.

'Such a lovely smell. I shall never forget.'

Their eyes met and held like a last embrace.

She said simply, 'It was the sachet. Roses and rosemary.' Then she came to him and whispered against his face. 'Love and remembrance.'

# 20

# *Day of Reckoning*

HM Minesweeper *Rob Roy* completed another slow turn and settled on to the next leg of her prescribed sweep.

Standing in the forepart of the bridge Ransome watched the sweep-wire's float with its little green flag cutting above the waves, then trained his glasses on the other ships taking up station astern.

It was evening, very dull with a hint of drizzle, not at all like the end of a June day.

He heard Beckett's voice from the wheelhouse. 'Steady on two-zero-zero, sir.'

Ransome tugged his cap down over his hair and shifted restlessly. Like any other day and yet so completely different. He could feel it all around him: expectancy, relief, anxiety, and, most of all, the sailor's attitude of resignation. The waiting and the doubts were all behind them, although to the men working aft by the sweep, or at their guns and lookout positions, they could have had the Channel to themselves.

Ransome heard Morgan speaking to the coxswain again, and pictured his small company throughout the ship, on deck and in the engine-room. Commander Bliss had called a conference of all his captains as soon as Ransome had returned to Falmouth. The group was to be at first-degree readiness, no matter what the Met buffs had threatened about the weather. More delays and uncertainties, with some of the old hands already suggesting that the top brass had made another timely cock-up. Forty-eight hours of conflicting signals, more intelligence packs and recognition instructions.

Then Bliss had sent for Ransome and had announced without fuss, 'It's on. Tuesday morning we hit Normandy as planned.'

Now they were here in mid-Channel, heading towards the French coast. It was no longer a plan or a conception of one; it was not even next month. It was dawn tomorrow.

Ransome felt a shiver run through him. It was hard to imagine it. All those vessels, hundreds of them, converging from east and west to the great assembly point south of the Isle of Wight, already aptly nicknamed Piccadilly Circus. From Harwich, Chatham and the Nore. From Portsmouth and Weymouth Bay, from Plymouth and every inlet in the West Country; all those ships. Only a cruising gull would be able to get a complete picture. The forty-eight hour delay might cost them dearly. Too much. For even with air supremacy over the south coast, with the American and British squadrons keeping up unbroken patrols by day and night, the enemy must surely know by now what was coming.

When the minesweepers and other small support vessels of Bliss's group had sailed directly to their prescribed areas from Falmouth, they had only caught a glimpse of the massive build-up. Every type and size of landing-ship, tanks, men, and weapons, while other strange-looking craft followed close behind carrying steel bridges, portable jetties, and the vital supplies of fuel to keep it all moving.

They had been challenged several times by vigilant patrols and escorts, but Ransome had been fired on in the past by over-zealous commanders, and had ordered Mackay to be ready to flick the minesweeping lights on to reveal their intentions, rather than risk unnecessary injury or death.

He heard Fallows' sharp voice from 'A' Gun below the bridge and pondered again over Bliss's last-minute, private comments.

'That subbie of yours, Fallows. I've had a signal about him from the security chaps. A spot of bother about some forgery on a supply docket – pusser's paint going to the black market, would you believe!'

Fallows had certainly been behaving strangely, Ransome

thought, but he had imagined it was over something else.

Bliss had added smoothly, 'It will probably mean a court martial – you know how it is, Ian. He'll certainly be required to face a full inquiry. It's your responsibility, of course, about when you tell him. You don't want any changes or upsets at this stage, with all hell about to break loose, eh?' He had smiled warmly. 'Entirely up to you.'

In other words, if anything misfired, Ransome and not Bliss would carry the can.

Ransome moved across the bridge past a look-out, and the young replacement signalman named Darley. It was all so fresh and new to him that he kept jumping up and down, fetching things for the yeoman, like a puppy with an old dog.

He peered astern, his glasses misting in the drifting drizzle and salt spray.

*Ranger* was on the quarter, dipping and lifting again in the steep swell; her outline was already blurred. It would be dark soon, but the sweep would have to be completed whatever happened.

He wondered briefly how Hargrave was managing with his first command, and what Gregory thought of his gaggle of motor minesweepers, which were somewhere astern with the Rescue M.Ls and *Bedworth*. Someone handed him a mug of cocoa, 'kye', and he felt it sticking to his throat like treacle. There was more than a hint of rum in it. Beckett's work, no doubt.

Ransome rested his elbow on his bridge chair and tried not to let his mind stray from his ship, the wires and voicepipes which connected him with the men who listened and waited; who had only him to rely on.

But he thought of that short stay in Polruan, the room which had been so small and yet barely able to contain their love. He recalled his surprise at seeing his own photograph in a frame by the bed lamp, as if it belonged there, had always been a part of the place. He had mentioned it, but she had said little about it. There was another story there somewhere, he thought.

He touched his coat pocket and felt the outline of his oilskin pouch. This time it held another picture, a small self-portrait she had shyly offered him just before they had set off for that last walk along the cliffs.

It showed her sitting at an easel, her knees drawn up and displaying those familiar paint stains. She had put *Barracuda* in the background — remarkably accurately, considering the boat had been under canvas for so long.

On the reverse of the painting she had written, 'To the dearest of men.'

It had not been the only message she had given him. The last one had been in a sealed envelope; she had handed it to him just before the naval car had driven him away, before he had had time to open it. She had called, 'Read it later on!' Then as the car had gathered speed she had shouted, '*I love you!*' And she had turned away. He had known it was because of her tears.

She must have selected the sonnet with great care. It had reminded him of his schooldays, but she had somehow brought it up to date, to their dangerous world, in her own handwriting. Like a calm pool in a forest.

> *Let me not to the marriage of true minds*
> *Admit impediments. Love is not love*
> *Which alters when it alteration finds,*
> *Or bends with the remover to remove . . .*

There was more, but in those first lines he could hear her speaking to him, reassuring him. As if she were here beside him.

Ransome recrossed the bridge, knowing that Morgan wanted to talk, but had been respecting these remaining moments of privacy.

He peered at the shaded compass repeater and felt his ship rolling heavily in the troughs. With an opposing current, and the heavy sweep trailing astern, *Rob Roy* was barely making seven knots.

He stamped his old leather seaboots on the deck and felt the restless strain thrusting into him again. Was it fear? Or was it fear of failure, of overlooking some small but vital point?

Directly below his feet Ordinary Seaman Boyes heard the thuds and glanced up at the wheelhouse deckhead. Beside him, the new midshipman, Piers, stared at him wide-eyed.

'What was that?'

Beckett lounged easily behind the wheel, his eyes on the gyro tape. 'No sweat. Just the skipper lettin' off steam.' He did not even bother to add *sir*. It didn't seem to matter, he thought, as he watched the ticking lubber's line.

There had been some cheeky comment when he had taken over the wheel. He would be on it until they'd done what they'd come for. Beckett was dressed in his best Number One jacket, with the shining gold-wire badges on each lapel.

He had rasped at the quartermaster, 'An' why not? This is the big 'un. It's got to be done right — look proper, see?'

Nobody argued with the coxswain.

He still felt the scar on his thigh where the red-hot splinter had torn into him; but what the hell. You lose something, and you fetch up gaining something. He had been awarded a bar to his Conspicuous Gallantry Medal, which he had got when the Old Man had got his gong from the King. Made 'em all sit up at home, although his dad had been enjoying His Majesty's pleasure in a different style.

The door opened and closed and the Buffer, carrying a heavy torch, glanced in as he made a final check on damage-control.

Beckett gave a lazy grin. 'I 'ope you've got a tin-'at for yer weddin' tackle, Buffer! Wouldn't like nuffin to get shot off!'

The Buffer snapped back, 'I thought *you'd* be wearin' yer brown trousers this time, Swain!'

Boyes watched the Buffer bustle away. He drew comfort from their casual banter, their warm hostility toward each other.

He tried to push Connie from his thoughts, but she kept returning. He saw her on the bed, then wrapped in his arms; felt his face flush as he recalled what they had done, and how she had guided him to that overwhelming climax.

He had tried to telephone her several times, a difficult and expensive exercise. The battery guardroom had been unable or unwilling to help him, but on the third occasion, with a queue of impatient and fuming sailors outside the only telephone box, her friend Sheila had been brought to speak to him.

'You're a nice bloke, Gerry, but in some ways just a kid. You're not like Connie — you're like chalk and cheese. She's my best friend. I know more about her than most.'

'But I must speak to her!' A sailor had rapped with his coins on the glass.

She had said, 'Connie's fond of you, 'course she is. But it's not the real thing.' She had hesitated, balancing Boyes' despair against her own betrayal. 'She was in love once, with a bloke from this battery. He treated her badly, then he pushed off to North Africa, God rot him! Well, now he's back, and Connie's making a fool of herself all over again. So just forget it. Wouldn't work anyway. You'll be an officer soon. Then what?'

Boyes had left the box as if he was in a trance. He loved her. They would have managed.

On the messdeck it had been the tough A.B. Jardine who had asked, 'Wot the hell's up with you, Gerry? You got a face like a wet Sunday in Liverpool!'

The mess had been deserted at the time and Boyes had found himself spilling it out to Jardine, expecting him to mock him for his juvenile behaviour.

Jardine had regarded him thoughtfully. 'She sounds a right little raver.' Then he had relented. 'See 'ere, Wings, she's not for you. 'Er mate was right. She's not your sort, no more than I am. When you've got a bit o' gold on yer sleeve, you'll remember us, an' wot you've gained – least I 'ope you do.'

Boyes had stared at him. 'You knew?'

Jardine had laughed. '*Course!* The 'ole bloody ship knows. But it's different now, see? Maybe they was right to turn you down for your wavy stripe, but not no more they ain't. Even if you are going to be one o' *them*, you're all right, Wings. So just remember this lass as experience.' Then he had shaken his head. '*Love?* Gawd, Gerry-lad, she'd 'ave you fer breakfast!'

Boyes was still unconvinced.

The midshipman whispered, 'Do you think we'll be going into action?'

Boyes smiled. 'It's hard to tell.' He pointed at the vibrating plot-table. 'Now look at this –'

They all stared up as Sherwood's voice came across the bridge intercom.

'The float's no longer watching, sir!'

Midshipman Piers forgot his authority and seized Boyes' arm.

'What's he talking about?'

Boyes swallowed hard. 'It means that the Oropesa float has disappeared, gone below the surface. We must have snared something.' He looked for understanding, but there was none. He remembered Jardine's words. Maybe they had been right to turn him down for the chance of a commission: but not any longer. In the face of Piers's anxiety, he thought he knew what the tough seaman meant.

Beckett interrupted, 'Stand by, my beauties. Time to earn yer pay!'

Lieutenant Sherwood gripped a davit and watched the sea boiling up beneath the stern from the racing screws. They were making slow progress, but down aft, with the water rising almost level with the deck as Rob Roy pushed into the oncoming crests, they got an impression of speed.

He saw Ranger's murky silhouette riding out on the quarter, the spray bursting above her stem as she held station on the leader. The remainder of the sweepers were already lost in early darkness. Sherwood buttoned the neck of his oilskin. Inside the heavy coat he was sweating badly, but without it he knew he would soon be drenched to the skin and shivering. You couldn't win.

Stoker Petty Officer Nobby Clarke crouched on his little steel seat while he controlled the winch, spray dripping off the peak of his cap as he squinted into the criss-cross of foam from the ship's wake. Sherwood found he was able to accept all that was happening, what he could see around him, and that which he could only imagine from reading the intelligence packs.

They had all known it was coming. Now it was here, or soon would be. To have lived this long was the real bonus.

Had anyone else spoken such thoughts aloud, Sherwood would have torn him apart. Once. How could he have altered so much? He had believed it madness to consider a true friendship, let alone a marriage, in wartime. He could almost hear himself warning others against it. But that moment beside the parachute-mine had changed him.

He glanced around at the other shining figures in his party, the slender barrel of the after four-inch gun overhead.

*Whatever happened to caution? To our disbelief in survival?*

He smiled to himself as he recalled his unusual reserve when he had told Ransome, the day he had returned to the ship to take over Hargrave's work.

'I've asked her to marry me.' He had grinned, surprised at his own shyness, his new faith.

Ransome had shaken his hand warmly and then said, '*Snap!*'

So the skipper had a girl too, although nobody had ever guessed it. The news was another precious secret, like the one he had shared in Sicily.

Stoker Petty Officer Clarke snapped, 'The float, sir!'

The older hands could often sense such things. By the sound or the vibration of a sweep-wire.

Clarke exclaimed, 'There's somethin' there!' His eyes showed white in the gloom. 'Better tell the Old Man, sir.'

Sherwood snatched up the handset. 'The float's no longer "watching", sir.' He saw Guttridge peering down from the four-inch. The leading hand had come back from leave with a pair of black eyes. But he was a hard character, not a man to be laughed at.

'Captain here.' He pictured Ransome on the bridge, assessing it, making a plan, preparing another if it all went sour.

'Recover the sweep.' He hesitated. 'Take it easy, Philip.'

Sherwood nodded to Clarke. 'Bring it in.' He heard the Buffer panting along the side-deck. 'Clear the quarterdeck and take cover!'

He waited, half-expecting his limbs to defy him, to begin shaking.

'Nice and easy, Stokes. It's probably a bit of wreckage.'

Clarke said nothing, but reached out with a gloved hand to let the incoming wire slide over it. He remarked flatly, 'Clean as a whistle.'

Sherwood waited. Even in the poor light he could see the wire, bright and burnished, proof, if any was needed with old sweats like Clarke on the job, that the wire had been running along the bottom.

'Guttridge! Fall out the gun's crew.' Sherwood glanced around. He could barely see beyond the guardrail.

If it was a mine, it was coming in right now towards the counter.

'Pass the word to the bridge, Buffer.'

The Buffer stood his ground and called, 'Gipsy, tell the bridge. It's probably a mine.' To Sherwood he said affably, 'I'll stay with you, if you don't mind, sir.' He folded his arms and could have been grinning at him. 'I 'ear congratulations is in order, sir?'

Sherwood gave a short laugh. Maybe that was it. They were all going quietly round the bend without realising it.

'*Slower*, Stokes!'

Clarke gritted his teeth. He could feel it now, as if he and not the winch was taking the full strain, like a fisherman with a marlin on his line.

Sherwood got down on his knees and winced as a rivet dug into his leg.

'It's there. It must be.' He made up his mind. 'Tell the captain.' He reached up and added, 'Give me that flashlight, Buffer. I'm going to have a look, and to hell with the bloody black-out!'

He switched on the light and saw several things at once. The float trying to rise to the surface as it floundered towards the winch, the otter already shining brightly in the beam while it moved nearer. Directly below his outstretched arm was the mine.

Sherwood heard Clarke give a gasp, and as if from a mile away someone calling to the bridge on the intercom. The deck seemed to tilt right over, and he guessed that one screw had been thrown into full astern to pivot the ship round.

He saw the mine sway towards him, but found he could watch it without fear. Seconds only to live. He shouted into the spray, '*I love you!*'

Then the mine veered away, caught unawares by the violent change of course. It collided with the otter at the end of the sweep and the dark sea lit up to a vivid explosion.

Sherwood felt himself knocked flat by a solid waterfall which swept over the deck without making a sound. But as his hearing returned he caught snatches of cheering, and felt the Buffer thumping his back and yelling, 'We're goin' to need a new float, sir!'

A seaman called, 'All them dead fish! Pity we can't 'ang about to net 'em for the galley!'

Sherwood staggered to his feet. His cap had vanished, as had the Buffer's flashlight. *A bloody close thing.* There was nothing in the manuals about using a torch in enemy waters.

Down in the engine-room Campbell watched the revolution counters moving into unison again, and saw one of his stokers giving him a thumbs-up while the glistening machinery roared round within inches of his hand.

The whole place had boomed like an oil drum beaten by a giant hammer. Campbell looked for his E.R.A. and they exchanged quick grins.

Then he turned back to his dials, his lips moving to the tune of an old hymn.

'Sweeping, sweeping, sweeping,
Always bloody well sweeping,
Sweeping in the morning,
And in the afternoon . . .'

Campbell wiped his streaming face. Alf Bone had been right to get out of it, he thought. Just for a split second back there . . .

He had felt his eyes fixed on the curved side, streaked with oil, each droplet quivering to the beat of the twin propellers as if it was alive.

Just for one agonising moment he had believed that which all of them dreaded had happened.

The telephone shrilled noisily beside his little metal shelf, where he kept his engine-room log.

'Chief here.' He had to press one grimy hand over his other ear.

'This is the captain. All right? Sorry about the noise – don't know what the neighbours will think.'

The Chief grinned and felt the tension draining away like sand from a glass. 'We're okay, sir. Let me know when you intend to do it again!'

On the bridge Ransome gave the handset to the boatswain's mate. To Morgan he said, 'Let's hope that'll be the last of them!'

Morgan removed his cap and allowed the spray to soak into his curly hair.

He had imagined that he actually saw the mine as Ransome had flung the ship hard over. Another moment, and – He felt his legs shaking. *No casualties, no damage.*

305

Then the boatswain's mate turned from a voicepipe and said unsteadily, 'Beg pardon, sir, but the gunnery officer is reportin' the starboard guardrail 'as carried away in the – er – bang!' It was all he could do to prevent himself from bursting into insane laughter.

Ransome climbed into his chair for the first time and nodded gravely.

'Tell Mr Fallows that I shall indent for a new one when we return to harbour!'

Mackay hid a broad grin, and touched his young assistant's arm.

'Like a bunch of kids!' But he did not hide his admiration, or his relief.

Long before dawn it was obvious to everyone that there was no last-minute change of plans. The full force of the attack was under way.

Throughout the night Ransome and the watchkeepers who shared the bridge with him had felt the air trembling to an unbroken procession of bombers flying toward the Normandy coast. There must have been hundreds of them, perhaps thousands.

And now, as dawn made a reluctant grey brushstroke on the clouds, the coastline was outlined by a backcloth of fire. Red and orange, with a wall of smoke rising like the gateway to Hell.

How must it look to the thousands of troops who would be in their landing-craft? Heading towards their next rendezvous, a cross on a map, an aerial photograph at some last briefing?

Very few of these many craft were yet visible from *Rob Roy*'s bridge, but Ransome knew they were stretched across the Channel, the rearguard still leaving the assembly area while the leaders were preparing for their baptism of fire.

Ransome levelled his glasses and watched the ripple of flashes which seemed to dart from the land itself. Seconds later the heavy shells began to fall amongst the invisible armada, while the air quaked to the echo of their explosions.

As at Sicily, the big ships were firing from below the horizon, the glow of each fall of shot giving shape to the land, like a terrible panorama of death.

*Bedworth* cruised through the support craft with an impressive bow wave, her signal light flashing briefly like a solitary blue eye.

'*Proceed as ordered*, sir.' Mackay lowered his father's big telescope.

'Slow ahead together.' Ransome rested his hands on the screen and watched the first low shapes of landing-craft butting into the choppy water abeam. No bagpipes this time. It seemed wrong somehow. They had survived this far. The greatest invasion of all time had begun.

He saw some fast motor launches leading the way as the larger landing-craft turned obediently to follow.

Part of the Canadian Third Division, heading for the beach codenamed Juno.

Ransome thought of the pipe-smoking major he had met on the beach in Sicily. Perhaps he was here too on this bleak, terrible morning.

It prompted him to call, 'Yeoman! Hoist battle ensigns! Let's show 'em!'

Mackay stared at him, then nodded. 'Aye, *aye*, sir!' He jabbed the young signalman. 'Here, Nipper, help me bend them on!' He laughed aloud. 'Something to remember, eh, kid?'

Morgan raised his glasses as the lenses glowed red from a fiery reflection across the water.

'Some poor devil's brewed up, sir.'

Ransome turned away as more waterspouts burst skyward amongst the lines of landing-craft.

He looked above and watched as the first great ensign floated from *Rob Roy*'s starboard yard, then a second one to port. This ship was too small for such a display; but it might give some of the watching soldiers heart while they waited, counting seconds, hoping the ramps would fall and their helplessness would end.

An upended landing-craft floated abeam, with two soldiers standing on the keel, casting off their boots and weapons as the hull began to sink beneath them. One of them waved, or it could have been a mock salute.

Great shells thundered overhead, and once when Ransome trained his glasses on a hardening ridge of land he saw a four-engined bomber fall like a leaf to vanish into the smoke. There was some sort of electrical storm making the clouds shine like silver, and a second plane fell without ever sighting its objective.

Ransome watched, and found himself hoping. Praying. But no tell-tale parachutes drifted clear. Their war had ended, here.

'Port ten. Midships. *Steady*.'

Morgan turned and looked up at him. 'Steady on one-six-zero, sir.'

The minesweepers had achieved what they came to do. Even as the thought crossed his mind, Ransome saw some of the big warships which had doubtless been the last to leave the assembly point surging past, guns high-angled and already shooting far inland.

Sherwood climbed to the bridge. 'Sweep secured, sir.' He watched the tall waterspouts shredding down near the landing-craft, some of which appeared to be swamped, only to emerge as determined as ever.

Ransome said, 'Go and clear the after guns. Stand by scrambling-nets. We'll be needed in support soon.'

He heard cheering and saw some of his men pointing and gesturing astern. *Ranger* and the rest of the flotilla had followed his example, and looked even smaller under their big White Ensigns.

Sub-Lieutenant Fallows stood with his hands on his hips and glared as Leading Seaman Guttridge strolled toward him on the forecastle.

'Buffer said you want some 'elp, sir?' It was as close to being insolent as he could get. Guttridge was still smarting over the hiding he had received when he had gone home to sort out his wife and her boyfriend. He had not expected the latter to be a six-foot tall commando, nor had he anticipated that her two brothers, both squaddies, would be there to fill him in.

She had screamed, 'You talk about bein' faithful, you slag! Wot about all the girls you've put in the club?' They had beaten the hell out of him. His body was still a mass of bruises. He was in no mood to put up with Bunny Fallows, bloody D-Day or not.

Fallows barked, 'This guardrail —' He pointed at the trailing wires. The explosion had snapped a small shackle like a carrot. 'It's a *mess*!'

'Wot d'you expect me to do about it?' Guttridge saw the crew of 'A' Gun rising above the shield to listen to this unexpected diversion.

Someone shouted, ' 'Ere come the Glory Boys!'

A tight arrowhead of motor gunboats roared diagonally towards the port bow, their cannon and machine-guns already tracking round towards the land. With their ensigns streaming from each gaff, and the oilskinned officers wearing their dashing white scarves, they looked every inch the schoolboy's dream of the country's heroes.

Some of the seamen waved as *Rob Roy* plodded on at a steady eight knots.

Fallows yelled, '*I'm speaking to you!* Don't you be so bloody insolent or I'll have that hook off your arm!'

He had to grip the remaining guardrail as the combined wash of the three fast-moving gunboats thundered around the bows and lifted them effortlessly on a small tidal wave.

Guttridge watched the sub-lieutenant and hoped he would lose his balance and pitch over the side. There was not a single matelot who would offer him a line.

But Fallows was clinging to a stanchion, his eyes popping from his head as he stared down past the receding bow wave.

He wanted to cry out, to make himself heard and obeyed. But in those swift seconds he saw only the mine as it spiralled lazily from the depths, where it had probably been lying for years undisturbed.

Guttridge saw his terror and yelled, 'Hit the deck! *Get down!*'

Then the mine rasped against the hull, and the world fell apart.

Lieutenant Trevor Hargrave stared overhead as another great salvo of shells thundered towards the shore. It sounded like a dozen express trains passing at the same time, so loud that you almost expected to see something.

The seaman with the quarterdeck handset reported, 'Sweep secured, sir!'

Hargrave nodded. How long would it take, he wondered? To stop fitting *Rob Roy*'s faces to the men he now commanded?

He glanced around the bridge, at the crouching look-outs, the leading signalman who should have been Mackay as he took a couple of turns on a signal halliard and watched the big, clean ensign streaming out on the wet breeze.

*Ranger* was his command. *Mine.* He felt pride matched only by an unexpected sense of loss.

He saw *Bedworth* tearing through the groups of motor mine-sweepers, and smiled bitterly. In Falmouth he had bumped into an old classmate who was now a lieutenant-commander on the naval staff.

He had asked him about Bliss, and why he did not appear to get on with Vice-Admiral Hargrave.

His friend had grinned and punched his arm. 'By God, Trevor, they must be a close bunch in your family to smother such a juicy secret!'

When Hargrave had pressed him further he had explained, 'Your old man was once Bliss's commanding officer in a fleet destroyer. The *word* went round that he was chasing Bliss's young wife – and with some success to all accounts. No love lost since, it seems.'

Hargrave bit his lip. He found it easy to believe now, when once he would have defended his father's name from any quarter.

He felt the pain and the humiliation returning. The beautiful Ross Pierce had offered him her private telephone number.

'Next time we meet, Trevor, we *may* start a few fires together!' And he had believed it.

He had phoned her at that number, a flat she owned with a Mayfair exchange, two nights before *Rob Roy* had received her final orders for Operation 'Neptune', the navy's equivalent of 'Overlord'. Obviously she liked him quite a lot, but had held him at arm's length, which only made him want her all the more.

His father had answered the call, and Hargrave put down the receiver without speaking. It still hurt him more than he would have thought possible.

Sub-Lieutenant John Dent, whose sister drove staff cars in the WRNS, exclaimed, 'From the W/T office, sir. The first troops are ashore!'

Hargrave looked at the bleak sky, the choppy sea with its mounting litter of upended or burned-out landing vessels.

*They had done it.*

He thought of his father and the Wren officer together and tried to accept what he must do. He would use them both, just as they were using one another.

He heard muffled cheers from the wheelhouse and leaned over the voicepipe.

'Stow the noise down there.' He glanced at the gyro repeater. 'The course is one-six-zero, not two degrees off!'

He knew he was being unfair, that he was taking out his resentment on those who could not retaliate.

He looked round again. New faces. Probably clinging to Gregory's memory, his methods and personality.

Spray dashed over the glass screen and soaked Hargrave's shirt. He saw the sub-lieutenant trying to suppress a smile and said ruefully, 'I was wrong. D-Day or not, collars and ties are *not* suitable.'

There was a livid flash, followed by an explosion that hit *Ranger*'s flanks like something solid. For an instant longer Hargrave thought they had struck a submerged wreck or an unmarked sandbar. Then he stared appalled at the tall column of water which appeared to be rising from the deck of *Rob Roy*, towering higher and higher as if it would never disperse. *Ranger*'s first lieutenant, a young New Zealander, clattered on to the bridge.

'Dead alongside, sir! She's hit a mine, God damn it!' It sounded personal, beyond belief.

Hargrave watched as the white column cascaded down, the way she seemed to rock right over, and stay there.

The leading signalman shouted, 'From *Bedworth*, sir. *Take command of flotilla. Rescue M.Ls will close on Rob Roy.*'

Hargrave stared at their sister ship until his eyes smarted. Pictures stood out like those in an album. Fallows, too drunk to answer his questions. Ransome in his little cabin, like the one he now occupied when *Ranger* was in harbour. Campbell, old Bone and the hostile Sherwood. Beckett and the Buffer, and the midshipman who had been killed.

He said harshly, 'Disregard! Make to *Firebrand. Assume control. We are assisting.*'

He pounded the screen with his fist as he had seen Ransome do.

'Full ahead together!' He was disobeying Bliss's direct order, but suddenly it no longer mattered. All the petty manoeuvring and the plans for his future counted for nothing.

*Rob Roy* was still his ship. She mattered. Men were dying unnoticed against the background of greater events.

He shouted aloud, *'Well, they bloody matter to me!'*

The first lieutenant and the subbie exchanged glances. There was more to their new captain after all.

Ransome leaned on the chart-table with Morgan crowded against him under the canvas screen.

Ransome said, 'We shall remain on the present course until we reach *this* point.' He tapped the pencilled cross with his dividers. 'Six miles offshore.'

Morgan rubbed his chin. It made a rasping sound, as he often had to shave twice a day.

He said, 'After that –'

The explosion seemed to be right beneath their feet. The noise was shattering, and the hull rebounded from it with terrible violence.

Ransome found himself on his knees, Morgan sprawled and coughing beside him. There was smoke everywhere, and when Ransome struggled to his feet he almost fell again, and knew that the deck's angle was increasing.

He reached out to help Morgan from the litter of broken glass and buckled voicepipes but a pain like hot iron lanced through his side.

Morgan clambered up beside him. 'What is it?'

Ransome clawed his way to the chair and held on to it, gritting his teeth against the agony. He gasped, 'Couple of ribs, I think!'

He stared round the tilting bridge, his mind shocked and dazed by the explosion.

*Rob Roy*, his ship, had hit a mine. It was probably fatal. He must think. Accept it. Carry out the drill he had always dreaded.

He shouted, *'Stop engines!'*

The reply came back from the wheelhouse. 'No communications, sir!' He heard Beckett coughing. Then he said, 'Bit of a potmess down 'ere, sir. Steering gone – compass – the lot –'

312

Ransome beckoned to Morgan. 'Take over. Clear the wheelhouse. I must speak with the Chief.' He stared, sickened, at one of the look-outs. He had been flung back from that side by the blast; his head was smashed against the grey steel like an eggshell. There was a smear of blood down to the gratings, and much more of it running in the scuppers. Mackay knelt on an upended flag-locker, mopping his cheek where a piece of glass from the broken screen had slashed his face to the bone. The boatswain's mate sat with hands folded in his lap as if resting. Only the broken handset and his bulging eyes showed that he had been killed instantly by the blast; he was otherwise unmarked.

If he had not been crouching over the chart-table . . . Ransome controlled his thoughts with a terrible effort and pulled himself toward the ladder. In his sea-cabin there was another telephone which was connected directly to the engine-room.

Even as he reached it, he realised that the engines' beat had ceased. The cabin looked as if it had been ransacked by madmen.

He pulled the handset from its bracket, and Campbell answered before he could speak.

He said tersely, 'Taking water fast, starboard side forrard. Losing fuel from the tanks there too.'

Ransome pressed his forehead against the cold steel and nodded, his eyes closed. He had already smelled the stench of fuel. He had been present often enough when other ships had died. Like their blood draining away.

'Get your men out of there, Chief.'

Campbell replied, 'The pumps are holding, sir. I'll stay with them.'

Ransome saw Sherwood watching from the door, noticed how his figure was set at a crooked angle; he knew it was the ship going over. Men were shouting, and he heard metal scraping across the deck, feet running, disorder when moments before –

Sherwood watched his anguish and said, 'All depth-charges are set to safe, sir. The Buffer's standing by with floats and rafts. The whaler's ready for lowering, but the motor boat's had it.'

He helped him to his feet, feeling his pain, and the worse agony for his ship. He did not mention that the motor boat which hung from its starboard davits had taken much of the blast when the mine had exploded.

Sub-Lieutenant Tritton had been smashed to the deck when the 'skimming-dish' had been hurled inboard, and was still pinned under the wreckage. Cusack was with him, and he had seen the frightened S.B.A. handing him his instruments. Sherwood felt sickened by the thought of his cutting away at flesh and then bone while the ship settled down more steeply in the water.

Shells roared from the sky, and a drifting L.S.T. took one below her bridge, where two abandoned tanks were already burning from the last straddle.

Sherwood considered it. They were just a few miles offshore, and those guns would soon shift their sights to *Rob Roy* once the L.S.T. had been put down.

Ransome asked, 'How many casualties?' He moved through the door, his arm around Sherwood's shoulders as they lurched toward the ladder.

'Bunny Fallows bought it, sir. Guttridge too. Some of 'A' Gun's crew are badly shaken up, but only Hoggan was seriously wounded.' He thought of the burly leading hand with the tattoo around his wrist. 'He's been blinded.'

The deck gave another lurch. Ransome pulled himself to the bridge and threw back his head to take several gulps of air. But for Campbell's quick thinking when he had stopped the engines, the next bulkhead would have collapsed under the strain, and *Rob Roy* would be lying on the bottom.

He heard footsteps and saw Cusack striding across the broken glass. Cusack sensed the question in Sherwood's eyes and shrugged. 'Had to take the leg off. No choice.' He helped Ransome into the chair and said, 'Let me take a look.'

Ransome said, 'Too much to do. Shove off and see to the yeoman.'

Mackay was peering over the rear of the bridge, then turned, his eyes red with shock and disbelief.

*'Just a kid!'* He stared around at their faces. 'That's all he was, for Christ's sake! What are we, that we can let this happen to boys like him?'

Sherwood climbed onto a locker, the same one that the young signalman named Darley had been using when he had reached up to free one of the ensigns which had become tangled in the halliards. The blast had flung him from the bridge like a bundle of rags. His slight figure lay on the deck below, his eyes still staring at the clouds as if he could not accept what had happened.

Ransome said, 'Get down there, Number One.'

Sherwood faced him. Was there any point in prolonging it? Then he saw Ransome's despair. 'I'll do what I can.'

Beckett climbed on to the bridge and touched his cap.

Like Boyes and the terrified midshipman who followed him he was speckled with chips of white paint from the deckhead, as if he had been in the snow.

'No casualties in the wheel'ouse, sir.' He stared at the L.S.T., which was now fiercely ablaze from bow to stern. 'A few bleedin' 'eadaches, that's about all.'

He saw Mackay and added roughly, 'Never mind, Yeo. Coulda bin anyone.'

Mackay picked up his father's telescope and wiped it on his sleeve. He did not even look up as another shell exploded in the sea less than a cable away.

Ransome tried again. *Abandon ship*. He had no choice, unless he put the ship before her people, his pride before their survival.

Morgan said hesitantly, 'Some R.M.Ls are heading our way, sir.'

Ransome levered himself to his feet. Thank God, Cusack had gone elsewhere where he was needed. He winced and clapped one hand to his side.

'Muster the wounded. Stand by to lower the Carley floats and rafts.'

He stared at the sloping deck, the corpses lying where they had fallen.

He was leaving her. After all they had done together. All those miles, and all those bloody mines she had swept so that others might be safe.

The hull gave another shudder, and the remains of the topmast, which had been felled by the blast, slithered over the bridge with the remnants of the shattered radar lantern.

*If only they could move.* He would get her home somehow, if he had to go astern on one screw all the way.

The Buffer appeared at the top of the ladder, his face like a mask.

' 'Ands mustered, sir. Eight wounded. Five killed.' He hesitated. 'Two missing.'

Ransome pushed his fingers through his hair. The latter must be Fallows and Guttridge. They would never be found. There would be nothing left.

The Buffer glanced anxiously at his friend. 'Okay, Swain?'

Beckett sighed. 'Not 'appy, Buffer.'

The Buffer looked around, like a man who has been robbed of something precious.

'Me neither.'

Some one said in a dull voice, 'There goes our bloody Senior Officer.'

So Bliss had seen what had happened. *Rob Roy* was already in the past, written off.

Ransome moved to the rear of the bridge and stared at the deck's stark angle. Both screws must be almost out of the water; the forecastle was well down, the anchors awash. If only –

Sherwood came back and reported, 'Bulkhead's holding, sir, though God knows how.' He thought of the gaping hole in the messdeck which had begun deep in the bilges before exploding upwards to the sky. Their private world invaded, soiled. Seaboot stockings hung to dry, floating in the gushing, foul oil. A letter from home, a man's cap with its best shoregoing tally, *HM Minesweeper*, still managing to shine through the filth. Like an epitaph.

Sherwood watched him, feeling it, as if she was his ship; sharing it.

'Shall I give the word, sir? If we stay here, the Jerries –'

'I know.' The two words were torn from his lips.

His hand touched the oilskin pouch in his pocket. Eve would know. Would be reaching out to him.

He nodded abruptly. 'I'll do it.'

He cupped his hands and saw them all staring up at the bridge, unable to accept it. Unwilling to leave.

Mackay stood up and stretched his cramped muscles. Then he trained his long telescope and said brokenly, 'If only you could see this, Nipper!'

Ransome thought he had finally cracked. Nobody could blame him.

Then Mackay said in a stronger voice, 'From *Ranger*, sir. *Intend to take you in tow.*'

Ransome stared at him. The flotilla had gone ahead as ordered; so how could Hargrave be here to offer assistance?

Sherwood looked at him.

'What do you think, sir?'

Ransome faced them. They had never been closer than at this moment.

'Make to *Ranger*. *We shall stick together*.' He heard the clatter of Mackay's lamp and said, 'We'll tow from aft, Number One.' He was surprised at the new strength in his voice. 'We might just do it.'

While Sherwood and the Buffer hurried aft to prepare the towing-hawser, *Ranger* was already turning steeply towards them, her deck angled over as far as *Rob Roy*'s as she came in on a diagonal course. Hargrave had assessed the danger from the coastal battery and was not wasting any time.

Ransome looked down at the great oil slick which was spreading out around his ship, flattening the waves like a greasy blanket. It might just help when the hawser took that first, critical strain.

There were more men on deck now, moving to the shouted commands, but their eyes were on the damage all around them. Most of the extra hands were stokers, sent on deck by the Chief, who with an E.R.A. had remained in the engine-room to nurse the pumps, as they fought to contain the great weight of water trapped between two bulkheads. If one more collapsed *Rob Roy* would sink in minutes.

Ransome heard Able Seaman Jardine exclaim, 'You should see the bloody hole in the side! You could drive a double-decker bus through it!' That was certainly how it felt.

He was relieved to see that the wounded were gathered near one of the big Carley floats, so that they would have a better chance if the worst happened. The dead had been covered with strips of canvas, and the little S.B.A. sat beside Sub-Lieutenant Tritton, oblivious to all that was happening, even when a shell whimpered overhead. He watched Tritton's face, which was the colour of chalk, holding his wrist and listening to his laboured breathing. It was to be hoped that Cusack had made sure he would feel nothing until —

He watched another float being manhandled toward the side. Could anything worse happen? Could he even begin to believe that the worst was behind them?

He thought of the one mine which had found them. After all the miles they had steamed, the risks they had shared, the mines they had destroyed.

It had probably lain there for years after being dropped, very likely by the British, to delay coastal shipping. Its sinker must have jammed when it had first been laid, and it had rested there undisturbed all that time until those jubilant motor gunboats had awakened it with their impressive wash.

He moved around the bridge, his boots slipping on the slanting plates, his eyes seeking and feeling her pain like his own. The blast had buckled the wheelhouse's protective steel like a piece of cheap tin, and swept down the starboard side, missing some, hurling others aside. Like the Oerlikon gunner who had died below the bridge. No wonder sailors hated wearing steel helmets, no matter how many times the order was enforced. The blast had ripped the helmet from his head so that he had been garrotted by the chinstay, as if by human hands.

He saw order emerging from confusion. Wires, ropes and strops filled one side-deck, and it all had to be moved by muscle-power. If they were attacked by an enemy aircraft there would be no point in trying to fight back. They needed every spare hand on the towing-hawser, and the power-operated guns were useless anyway.

He raised his glasses and saw Hargrave staring across at him while *Ranger* straightened up and backed stern first towards him, her screws beating up foam even through the great slick of oil.

A heaving-line snaked across and fell short. Then another, this time with a heavy piece of iron on the end, just to make sure. Hands reached out, and Ransome heard the Buffer give vent to some foul language as one of the seamen got under his feet.

But he studied Hargrave, saw him force a grin, and turn to call an order as his ship's screws stopped, then turned slowly ahead to avoid a collision at the last moment.

Morgan whispered, 'There she goes, see!'

The blazing L.S.T. was turning on her side, the tanks crashing down and through the thin plating while a few small figures ran away from the sea, which with an almost lazy contempt swept them from their final handhold, and swallowed them as the vessel took a last dive.

A shell crashed into the sea near one of the Rescue M.Ls. Then another, so that the launch gathered speed and scuttled into a bank of drifting smoke.

Morgan said nothing, but thought, *Now it's our turn.*

Ransome held his breath as the shining hawser began to nod its way across the gap. From the bridge, the line being hauled inboard by his men was invisible against the murky water, so that the hawser appeared to be moving unaided, like a great serpent.

There was a cheer as the eye of the wire was made fast and the slack taken in. Ransome looked at the faces of his men near the bridge. Cheering, some laughing, others weeping and holding on to each other, their best friends probably. For they had not all survived this time.

He turned away and saw Mackay watching him. The yeoman said quietly, 'She always was a good 'un, sir.'

Beckett had been observing *Ranger*'s agile movements, while she paid out the long hawser until its centre vanished into the drifting oil.

'I 'ave to admit, 'e 'andles her fair enough. Still, *Ranger*'s got a good coxswain, o' course.'

Ransome gripped the oilskin pouch against his aching side.

He said, 'She trained him well. Like the rest of us.'

*Ranger*'s siren gave a banshee screech and very slowly at first, then with more confidence, she took the full strain on the tow.

Ransome gripped the rail beneath the smashed screen and watched the other ship until she appeared to be obscured by mist.

Then he said softly, 'It's over. So let's take her home, shall we?'

Douglas Reeman
**The Iron Pirate** £2.95

*'Surprise will be total. It will show the world what we can do. You will do it for Germany!'*

The crack German heavy cruiser *Prinz Luitpold* had always been lucky in battle. To the beleaguered army on the Baltic coast she was their one remaining symbol of hope. But it is the summer of 1944, and on every front the war is going badly for Germany.

When the order comes to leave the Baltic to attack and destroy enemy shipping in the Atlantic, Kapitan zur See Dieter Hechler knows that once out in this vast killing ground it will only be a matter of time before the hunter becomes the hunted. The *Prinz* will need all of her legendary luck to survive.

As he faces the challenges of his enormous task, Hechler's problems increase when a ruthless, glory-seeking admiral arrives on board with some mysterious boxes, a floatplane and a beautiful girl pilot . . .

## Derek Robinson
**Piece of Cake** £3.99

Their flying was breath-taking, they played God in the sky. They lived as they flew — reckless, flamboyant, no time to lose. For Hornet Squadron even dying was a piece of cake. From the early days of the war in France to the Battle of Britain's 'finest hour' the squadron fights on through terrible losses and triumphant victories.

'Destined for a place in the literary clouds' PRESS AND JOURNAL

## War Story £3.50

'There is going to be the most enormous battle, and the war will be over by Christmas. Which Christmas, God alone knows . . .'

Lieutenant Oliver Paxton was eighteen years old and desperately keen to help win the war, when he was posted to France in June, 1916.

In the war-streaked skies over the Western Front, his education was hurried and painful. The rest of Hornet Squadron thought him a pompous idiot, but a very available lady behind the lines thought him the loveliest killer she'd danced with all night, while he could hardly wait to get a Hun in his sights when the order came for the Big Push.

And the fearsome first day on the Somme waited gaunt in the wings of history . .

## Goshawk Squadron £2.50

Wooley was a professional, in business with death — flying with him is like living with a maniac. Brutal, callous and obscene, without manners or morals, he moulds green young pilots into ruthless killers. By 1918 chivalry had been a long time dead.

'One of the most powerful indictments of war I have ever read . . . savage, funny and heartbreaking' SUNDAY TELEGRAPH

Nicholas Monsarrat
## The Master Mariner: Running Proud £1.50

'He will not die: he will wander the wild waters until all the seas run dry . . .'

The flawed courage of one man imperilled Admiral Drake's masterstroke on the day the English fireships sailed against the Armada in the Calais Roads. That coward was Matthew Lawe, Drake's coxswain, cursed from that day to sail the seas for all time to purge his guilt – through centuries of wind, wave and warfare . . . with the doomed Hudson to the Arctic, to the sunbleached Main with Morgan the pirate, as clerk to Pepys at the Admiralty, with Cook to bloodstained Hawaii and with Nelson at Cape Trafalgar.

'The cruel sea and the valiant men who sailed on it through all the generations' DAILY MAIL

## Three Corvettes £2.50

The Battle of the Atlantic was the one battle Britain had to win if she were to exist at all. But from 1940 until 1943 it was touch and go. The convoys which endlessly plied back and forth across this cruel sea, carrying supplies vital to the war effort, were harried remorselessly by wolf packs of U-Boats and long range bombers. Escorting the merchant ships all the while were the tough little corvettes of the Royal Navy.

Based on the author's own experiences, these three gripping stories of heroism, fear and death at sea, are a tribute to the unflinching courage of the men of the Royal Navy and to the resilience of the remarkable little ships in which they sailed.

J. D. Gilman and John Clive
**KG 200 The Force with No Face** £1.75

They flew Flying Fortresses. They wore American uniforms . . . but they were Germans!

KG 200
– the phantom arm of Hitler's Luftwaffe.

From a secret base in occupied Norway, crack German pilots plan the ultimate mission of KG 200 – Operation Ulysses. The raid that would bring Allied defeat crashing from the exploding skies . . .

Inspired by the best-kept secret of World War Two, KG 200 unfolds one of the most enthralling novels of air warfare, espionage and manhunt ever written.